The Kankakee Kid

Life brought Tyler Tomas from the Grand Kankakee Marsh to the Devil's Tower. Each turn on the trail took a bit of his innocence.

James Oliver Virmala

Edition 1

Cover Photo By James Oliver Virmala

"Devil's Tower, Wyoming"

Copyright © 2023 James Oliver Virmala

ISBN: 978-1-7340021-8-8

Forward

The Grand Kankakee Marsh

In 1843 the Grand Kankakee Marsh covered almost a million acres across Indiana and Illinois. The Kankakee River wound through the marsh for 250 miles. It was called "The Everglades of the North." The growing city of Chicago depended on it for much of its food, such as fowl, bison, and deer.

After 50 years of ditching and draining under the federal Swamp Land Act of 1850, it was a fraction of the original size by the early 1900s. Attempts are now being made to restore some of the wetlands, but the 250-mile winding Kankakee River that fed the marsh will remain a 90-mile ditch carrying most of the water away.

The Punt Gun

The "Punt Gun" in this story is based on one owned by Richard Russell, my friend and hunting partner. It was proofed at the Birmingham Company in England, is 7' 3" long, weighs 45 pounds and has a bore diameter of 1.160, which is a 3 gauge. The gun was made as a flintlock in approximately 1813.

Often the market hunters loaded them with nails, screws, nuts or bolts in place of the more expensive shot. Mounted in a punt boat, the hunters floated near a flock of ducks or geese and when in range fired, killing many birds with one shot. The ducks and geese were taken to market, thus the name "Market Hunters".

In the 1860s most states had banned the use of punt guns and in 1918 market hunting was outlawed, prohibiting the use of punt guns or other methods of harvesting waterfowl. It is still legal to possess a punt gun.

DEDICATION

To Ducks Unlimited and the members who work tirelessly restoring and improving waterfowl habitat, and to Canandaigua Lake Duck Hunters, Inc.

CONTENTS

FORWARD

DEDICATION

BOOKS BY THE AUTHOR

Oli's Gold Book One
Search For Oli's Gold Book Two
Return To Oli's Gold Book Three
To Be A Mountain Man
Trouble On The Kansas Plains
Frontier Justice
Return Of The Mountain Man
The Tall Man
The Prospector
The Green Valley
Twilight Of The Mountain Man
The Mother Lode
Quest Of The Mountain Man
Journey's End
Rufus Pike
Rufus And The Pup
The Winding Trail Home
Rufus The Lost Years
The Kankakee Kid
Bogus Island
Tyler Tomas The Brothers' War
War of 1812 The Choice

CHAPTER ONE

A shock went through the punt boat and the 3-gauge shotgun discharged. 12-year-old Tyler Tomas had his eyes closed and his fingers in his ears as the smoke from the shot blew over him. "Let's pick 'em up, grandson," his grandpa told him.

It was the fall of 1843 and the scene of harvesting ducks had been repeated for the past five years. Tyler scrambled to grab the pole and push the punt boat through the morning fog towards the dead and dying ducks floating on the surface of the Kankakee Marsh. His grandpa Nikolas swung the flintlock punt gun on its pintle and secured the butt to the side of the flat-bottomed boat.

Moving back and forth along the treads on the boat's bottom, Tyler maneuvered the square-ended craft toward the ducks while his grandpa scooped them up and tossed them into the boat. "We got 22 with that shot!" his grandfather exclaimed.

Wiping his hands on a rag, the old man began to load the punt gun for the next shot. Using a thin metal piece, he poked the touch hole to make sure the black powder hadn't plugged it. Then tilting the barrel up by placing the butt on the bottom of the boat, the old man poured a measure of powder into the large bore of the barrel and tamped it down with the ramrod. Then, taking 300 lead pellets wrapped in paper, Nikolas rammed it down the barrel. The old man then pulled the punt gun to half-cock and primed the pan.

While his grandfather readied for the next shot, young Tyler had been watching flocks of birds circling the marsh. He noticed that ducks continued to land just beyond a point about an eighth of a mile up the shoreline. Tyler slowly pushed the punt boat towards them. "Hurry up, Grandpa," the boy said. "Another nice flock just landed."

As the boy pushed the pole into the muck-covered bottom, the boat glided on the water toward the point. Cattails masked the ducks as the boat moved along the shore. Once at the point, grandpa pulled the gun to full-cock.

The fog rose like steam off the swamp, obscuring the ducks toward the back. Less than 50 yards away there was a solid mass of the birds, quacking and feeding on the duckweed. The punt boat was now floating closer due to its own momentum as Nikolas and Tyler crouched motionless, the boy's heart pounding with anticipation of the gun firing.

Using small paddles, Grandpa had the large gun lined up on the flock and placed his finger onto the trigger. Tyler closed his eyes and put his fingers into his ears. The roar of the punt gun propelled the boat back, forcing the young boy to grab hold of the gunwale. The shot echoed across the marsh, lost in the cries of the ducks lifting off the water.

Grabbing the pole, Tyler pushed the boat toward the swathe of downed ducks. The dripping birds were piled up in the center of the boat, the swamp water running off their feathers, filling the bottom just over the two-inch threads. The count for the second shot was 31.

The two hunters sat on the short platform on each end of the boat and floated in the morning mist. Ducks continued to fly in and out of the fog around them as they searched for a place to land. "A few of them landed right back near us," grandpa said. "Most of them flew further up the marsh. I figure 53 is enough for today. Take us home, grandson."

Feeling like an equal partner in the hunt, the young boy poled the boat towards the dock in front of their cabin. His grandpa put a chew in his cheek and rolled it before he spat. "This here marsh gives us all we need to live off," the old man told him. "We get ducks and geese that fly through twice a year. When they finish, we got muskrat, otter, mink and beaver to go after. All year long we got fish."

Tyler watched as his grandpa went silent, the old man's mind elsewhere for the moment. As the dock came into view through the mist, Nikolas readied the line to tie up. "Yes, grandson. The marsh will give a man that's willing to work a good living." As he looped the line around a post, he added. "And then we got buffalo, deer and bear nearby if we get a hankering to hunt them."

Nikolas Tomas had thinned white hair and a tobacco-stained white beard. He was a short, barrel-chested man. The life of hard work had given him a rugged look along with scarred hands and forearms. He had little formal education, but had the ability to fix or build most anything and make money or barter on everything he did.

Tyler Tomas was tall for his age. He had a lanky frame and had a thoughtful way about him. The boy had reddish-brown hair and a face covered with freckles. Tyler stuck close to his grandpa and offered to be of help at whatever needed done.

Tyler's parents had died from cholera in '38. The boy's grandpa had taken him and what few goods they had and left Virginia, heading west. The wagon they had been traveling in broke down near the Grand Kankakee Marsh and the old man considered it a sign sent from above. They had traveled far enough and would now be safe from the killing disease.

When they arrived at the marsh, Nikolas found a site on high ground on the northside of the water and had built a two-room cabin with a loft. There was a large fieldstone fireplace at one end for heat and cooking. They had fished along the shore, or shot grouse and rabbits with a smooth-bore flintlock. They also dug cattail roots for their meals while working on getting a roof over their heads.

Nikolas had worked at a shipyard in England before he'd emigrated to America in '25. He had taken the punt gun and the knowledge of building skiffs with him. The skiffs Nikolas had built in England had flat bottoms and a square bow and stern. They were designed to travel shallow rivers and marshes, and were without seats or structure from the bow to stern to allow carrying cargo or harvesting waterfowl. They used a pole or small paddles to propel or steer the boat.

The old man had immediately seen the Kankakee Marsh as a source of making a living. Before the necessary furniture was built for the cabin, Nikolas began to build a skiff. He wanted the boat for hunting with the punt gun and made it 20 feet long and just over three feet wide. The sides were two feet high and the treads crossing the flat bottom where about a foot apart. The bow and stern were square. Both had a slight slope.

The punt gun that would be mounted was over 7 feet long with a 1.160-inch bore. The gun had a stock similar to regular shotguns, but the recoil would be more than a man could handle, therefore the need for the fixed mount on the front of the skiff.

The two hunters climbed onto the dock and Tyler went ahead to get the poles and line that they would use to string up the ducks. Coming back with the poles, he hung them onto the tall posts on the far side of the dock. The posts were fitted with wooden pegs to hold the poles. The line had loops in it to put the bird's heads through to hang them.

While the boy was doing this, his grandpa was sorting the ducks and stacking them on the edge of the dock. "We got 12 canvasbacks, 31 mallards, six blacks, one merganser, and two green-wing teal."

They hung the ducks, supporting the weight with the poles. The merganser and the teal were left on the dock. The other ducks would be sold to a man named Arnold, and he'd take them to the city markets to the north. Grandpa would cook the merganser and teal for their meal. The fish-eating merganser had a taste that the city folks didn't like and the teal were too small.

There was one more step before the duck would be ready to sell. The two hunters took their knives and made a slit at the bottom of each hanging duck and pulled out the innards, tossing them into a bucket. What missed the bucket was kicked into the water. By tomorrow the fish, raccoons, and other vermin would have all evidence of the gutting cleaned up.

The ducks were hung onto two poles with just over 50 pounds on each. With grandpa leading the way, the two hunters carried the game with a pole over each shoulder and brought them to the hanging rack near the cabin.

Tyler saw a towheaded young boy running along the trail to the cabin. Hanging the game onto posts near the cabin, he went to meet his friend. "We got over 50 ducks!" Tyler called out.

Wil was one of the first children Tyler met when grandpa had sent him to school, two miles north in Cedar Creek. The blond-haired boy was the same age as Tyler but was slighter built. Wil had a quick smile and a wit about him that often got him into trouble with other students. The two quickly became friends after the towhead had gotten into a confrontation in the school yard and Tyler came to his rescue, using his size and a cold stare to ward off the attackers.

The two boys watched as grandpa inspected each of the ducks for shot damage. If too much lead from the punt gun hit a duck, the bird would be too torn up for sale to the market. It would not be wasted, though. It would go into Tyler's and grandpa's soup pot. "They are all good," Nikolas said.

"Let's go into the woods and work on our fort," Wil suggested.

"I got to clean and pluck the three ducks left on the dock, and feed the pigs and the horse," Tyler told his friend. "After that we can go."

Following his friend down to the dock, Wil didn't understand why Tyler didn't just take off to the woods and let his grandpa clean the ducks. There was a fort to finish and imaginary Indians to fight off. The merganser and teal lay on the dock. Picking them up, Tyler sat on the edge with his bare feet in the water. Meanwhile Wil jumped into the skiff and pretended to shoot the punt gun.

Peeling the feathers off the ducks was almost like peeling an orange. The feathers were put into a small wicker basket. They would be dried and used in pillows or mattress tics. Quickly Tyler had the three ducks stripped of their feathers and then, taking his knife from a sheath hanging around his neck, he removed the feet, wings, and heads. The young boy then slit the ducks and removed the entrails, saving the hearts and gizzards. The rest of the guts went into the bucket.

Rinsing the ducks and washing his hands, Tyler headed back to the cabin with Wil following carrying the bucket. He saw his grandpa talking to Arnold. The merchant was looking over the ducks and nodding. "You got some nice ones here," Arnold said. "We got the weekend coming and I could use about 100 the day after tomorrow."

Grandpa smiled. "We'll see what we can do. The flocks get thicker every day and soon we'll be chasing them off with a stick just to pole through them."

The two men laughed as the merchant dug into his bag for coins. Arnold would pay from two bits to four bits per duck, depending on the time of the year. He also supplied grandpa with powder and lead pellets.

Arnold would take the ducks and sell some to local markets in Chicago while others, went to a processor, where the ducks would be stripped of feathers and packed with salt in barrels and shipped to cities as far away as St. Louis.

With the ducks in his wagon, Arnold waved goodbye and continued his route around the marsh, buying birds from market hunters. Grandpa dug through the coins, picking out a few and called Tyler over. He handed 2 cents for each duck to the young boy and said, "Now go feed the hogs and horse, grandson. Then you can work on your fort. I'll cook up the merganser. Be back in about two hours."

Tyler ran into the cabin, and climbed up to the loft and put the money into a tin can under his bed.

Almost leaping down the ladder, he was out of the cabin and grabbed the bucket, taking it around back of the cabin. There was a small structure that was three logs high and had a thatched roof. It had a board fence at the front and it housed two pigs.

Their barn with the horse was on the small side. It had a bay running through the middle, with two stalls on the right and an area where hay was stacked on the left. A buckboard and sleigh sat in the bay for use around the place or going to town for supplies. There was also a corral on the west side for the horse.

The boy dumped the contents of the bucket into the pig trough and then went to the handpump in the pump shed and rinsed out the bucket before refilling it. He could hear the hogs grunting as they chewed on the duck innards. It was fall and soon it would be butchering time.

"Enjoy the meal while you can," Wil called to the pigs as he waited for Tyler.

Placing the bucket into the horse's stall so it could drink, Tyler then got the two-prong wooden fork to pitch hay in for the mare. It had a white coat and a gentle disposition. The only way the boy could ride the horse was bareback and his grandpa would only use it for pulling the buckboard.

Rubbing the side of its neck he said, "We'll be digging some parsnips from the garden soon and I'll bring you a nice big one."

With the chores done, the two boys headed for the woods. There was a carpet of leaves covering the ground that they shuffled through. "You should go to my uncle's trading post with the money," Wil suggested. "He has lots of candy and other good things you could buy."

As the two boys headed along the path into the trees, Tyler replied, "That money is for a squirrel gun. I'm going to get one just like grandpa and then I will shoot rabbits and grouse to sell to Mr. Arnold."

Wil didn't understand his friend. When you got money there were lots of good things that could be bought right away. Shaking his head, Wil followed his friend. The fort was just a crude structure made from windfalls. It had no door and to get in the boys had to climb over the four-foot-high walls. Their plan was to make a roof out of logs and drape a tarp over it to keep the rain out and eventually cut a doorway. The two had great plans of spending nights in the woods.

Soon the two of them were sitting in the six-by-six fort. The logs had been notched some to fit them closer together. Should anyone approach their bastion, they would be able to see them coming through the remaining cracks.

The towhead reached into his pocket and produced two peppermint sticks. "I got us these at my uncle's." Wil's uncle owned the trading post which was at the center of the cluster of homes and businesses that made up the small town of Cedar Creek. It was also where the church that housed the school was located.

Tyler took the piece of candy and stuck one end into his mouth. "It tastes really good," he told his friend.

"I can get all I want," Wil replied. "When my uncle is working in the back, it's there for the taking."

"He gives it to you, don't he?" Tyler asked.

"Sometimes," his friend said, smiling slyly.

Suddenly the peppermint stick didn't taste quite as good. From the time Tyler could remember, he'd been taught that you work for what you get and that it was wrong to take what wasn't yours. He had once come home with a watermelon from a garden along the road from school. His grandpa had asked him who had given it to him.

"It was just sitting there growing halfway out on the road," the young boy had replied. "I figured it wouldn't be missed."

While his grandpa wasn't one to hit a misbehaving child, the look he gave Tyler was crushing. Making the boy carry the watermelon, they walked back up the trail to the melon patch. Tyler was made to bring the fruit to the owner's door and knock.

A kindly lady had opened the door and looked at the boy and the melon. "You didn't pick that from my garden, did you?" she asked.

"I . . . I did," Tyler stammered. "I was wrong not to ask for it grandpa told me. I would like to weed your melons for the rest of the summer."

The lady looked up at grandpa standing by the road. "The patch could use some weeding. I'll keep a hoe near the road for you so you can do it on your way to or from school."

The lady took the melon and went inside. Tyler walked back to the cabin with his grandpa. On the way he learned that the lady, Mrs. Webber, had lost her husband and made her living growing vegetables and melons to sell. He was feeling just awful by the time they got home. Starting the next day, he weeded her garden and it had never looked as good as it did that year.

Right now, Tyler was thinking about the melon drink the woman would bring out to him on the hot days when Wil interrupted his thoughts. "Pa came home drunk again last night. He's been drinking a lot lately."

The boy's pa worked at a sawmill on the Kankakee River. Wil's mother had died when he was only four years-old. Often the boy would stay at his uncle's and occasionally he'd stay at the cabin. When at home, Wil would try really hard to stay out of his father's way.

"Your pa works hard at the mill," Tyler told him. "Maybe that's why he tends to drink."

"Nah," Wil replied. "He's just a drunk. I heard my uncle call him that."

Changing the subject, Tyler suggested, "We should start getting poles for the roof."

CHAPTER TWO

The next day, the two hunters worked until midday bagging just over 100 ducks. They also got four geese that were swimming within one of the rafts. Tyler missed school that day, which grandpa said was okay because they had a big order of ducks to get.

As the boy pushed the skiff toward the dock, he marveled at the load of birds that were heaped in the center of the boat. The geese would be a bonus because they'd get almost a dollar for them. Tyler was excited.

Last spring, he had mentioned to Mr. Arnold that he wanted to buy a squirrel gun. The man had told him that he knew of one that Tyler could get at a good price. This morning the young boy had counted the money in the tin can and it was just over $10. He was going to ask Mr. Arnold what the rifle would cost and he hoped he had enough.

With the ducks and geese gutted and hung, Tyler sat near the front door of the cabin fidgeting and watching the trail. Grandpa came out and looked at the boy. "Looks like you're waiting for something and it can't be the soup I got on."

"Do you think Mr. Arnold already went by while we were out on the marsh?" Tyler asked. "We got back kind of late."

"If we weren't back when he came by, he'll swing around and check on us later," Nikolas told the boy. "You must be thinking about asking him about the gun."

"He didn't give me a price when he told me about it, but I think I got enough in the can," Tyler replied.

"He'll be along soon," the old man told him. "Maybe the soup will be ready and we can have him eat with us."

Tyler thought that was a good idea. It might soften Mr. Arnold up and the price might be better. It was another hour before the rattling of the wagon was heard. The young boy was up like a shot and watching the trail.

Arnold was pleased with the geese and happy that there was the number of ducks. After checking them over, he got out the bag and gave grandpa the coins. Nikolas also got some heavier shot for the geese. He had plans of doing some evening hunting when the geese came in from feeding in the fields.

The two hunters were joined by Mr. Arnold for some soup. Before agreeing to the meal, he had asked if the soup was made with a merganser. He didn't like the fishy taste of the meat. Grandpa assured him that it was made from some tender teal.

With the meal finished, Tyler dawdled at the table while the men talked. Finally, grandpa said, "I think the boy wants to ask you about the squirrel gun."

Scratching his head, Mr. Arnold said, "I guess I did mention I knew of one. Now where was that?"

The boy's heart sank. He was sure the gun had already been sold. "I been saving my money and I think I have enough," Tyler told him.

"Oh, yes," the man said. "I remember now. A fellow on the other side of the river spoke of wanting to sell one."

"Do you think he still has it?" Tyler asked his eyes large.

"He ain't talked of selling it," Arnold said. "He did mention wanting $10 for it."

The boy's heart leapt. He had the money! Grandpa had taught him never to seem too anxious when dickering on a price. Fighting to suppress his joy, Tyler said, "That sounds kind of high for a used squirrel gun."

Smiling Arnold said, "He was coming back from hunting once and I did see the gun. It pretty much looked like new. He also has a mold and shooting bag to go with it for another $2."

They boy could not suppress his joy and replied, "Really!" With the 100 ducks they got today, he'd have the needed money.

Mr. Arnold thanked them for the soup, climbed onto his wagon and drove away from the cabin. Grandpa headed down toward the dock to get the punt gun. He wanted to clean and oil it so it would be ready for the next hunt. Tyler followed the old man to help carry the 45-pound gun.

"When do you think he'll bring the squirrel gun?" Tyler asked.

"It depends when he sees the man that's selling it again," grandpa said. "I got to warn you though. There is always a chance that the gun may have been sold. But I wouldn't worry too much about that. There is always another one that can be bought."

Tyler did not like the thought of it being sold. In his mind he already owned it. By late afternoon the two of them had all their chores done. The gun was cleaned, the skiff had been swamped out, the hogs fed, and their kitchen garden tended to. The young boy was in a daze the whole afternoon thinking about the gun.

About an hour before sunset, Wil came down the trail with a blanket roll under his arm. "It's payday and pa may be drinking until late. I figured I could sleep here tonight."

"Grandpa is warming up the soup," Tyler said. "You're welcome to have some."

"Is it merganser?" the boy asked.

Grinning at hearing the question twice in one day, Tyler replied, "It ain't merganser."

After finishing the meal, the two boys walked in the dark down to their fort. The moon was near full and there was an eerie light filtering through the trees. "What if Indians come? We couldn't see them in the dark," Wil whispered.

"The Pottawatomi moved west with the Treaty of Tippecanoe in 1832," Tyler told him. "We haven't got any Indians that we got to worry about."

"Then why did we build the fort?" Wil asked.

Feeling frustration, Tyler replied, "Not because of . . . Let's call it a shack."

It was late when the two boys got back to the cabin. Grandpa had left a candle burning on the table. After Wil climbed up into the loft, Tyler blew it out and followed him. It was full light when the sounds of grandpa making porridge for breakfast woke the boys. Both had slept fully dressed and after Wil rolled up his blankets, the two of them climbed down from the loft.

"I thought I'd be eating alone this morning," the old man kidded them.

"I got to be going," Wil said. "Pa will be waking soon and I got to be home." The young boy then headed out the door and was gone.

Shaking his head, Tyler said, "His pa will be off to work by now."

"He probably had things he'd like to do today," grandpa replied.

The fog was thick on the marsh, so there was no hunting that morning. By late afternoon the fog lifted and the two hunters readied the boat for an evening hunt. It would be two days before Arnold would be back, but the nights were cold and the days even required a long sleeve shirt, so any ducks or geese they got would hold that long.

The evening hunt was a bust. The wind had picked up and ducks were scattered or hunkered down in nearby fields. Tyler pushed the boat back to the dock. They had flushed a few ducks and went within shooting distance of a few. The squirrel gun would have been useful. They might have gotten a dozen ducks or even a couple of geese.

Tyler wasn't disappointed by the bad day. He had enough money and all he could think of was buying the squirrel gun. Grandpa had a Brown Bess muzzle loader that shot a .75 caliber ball. It weighed around 10 pounds and had an effective range of 100 yards. It could be used for hunting fowl if pellets were loaded instead of a ball, but the cumbersome length and weight made grandpa prefer to leave it in the cabin. It was good for hunting deer and other land-bound game.

That night Tyler had a hard time sleeping. He had hoped Wil would come over so he could discuss the squirrel gun with him, but he must have stayed at his uncle's. The boy reached under his cot and felt the tin can. He shook it, liking the sound of the coins in it. Finally, his mind quit racing enough for sleep to overtake him.

The next morning the two hunters were on the swamp before daylight. It was cold and damp on the marsh. Tyler shivered as he pushed the boat from the dock. There was little fog and they could hear the ducks and geese in the distance. As the sounds got closer, they sat floating on the water, waiting for the sun to come up.

The boy sat at the back, leaning against the stern, arms folded over his chest, trying to keep warm. He was still going barefooted and his feet were cold. Tyler was dozing when he heard his grandpa say, "A nice raft floating to the left."

Begrudging having to move, the boy soundlessly prepared to push the skiff with the pole. Grandpa lay stretched out sighting along the punt gun barrel and using a small paddle to steer the boat, getting the gun lined up on the ducks.

The crash of the punt gun broke the silence of the marsh and the harvest began. Soon Tyler had forgotten about the cold as he maneuvered the skiff to retrieve the ducks, his breath coming out in clouds of steam.

It was late morning when they returned to the dock with over 70 birds. The bright sun made him almost too warm in the wool shirt. Once the ducks were hung and cleaned, they carried the laden poles and hung the catch in front of the cabin.

Quickly the after-hunt chores were completed and grandpa came from the cabin with his fishing pole. "I figured we'd like a change from duck today and thought I would catch us some fish."

"I'll wait here for Mr. Arnold," Tyler told him.

"I bet you will," his grandpa said, smiling.

The boy watched the old man push the skiff out a short distance from the dock. He began to fish using bits of the innards from the ducks. Tyler wheeled around and climbed up into the loft. He took the tin can and poured out the money. Slowly he counted it out. Then he frowned and counted it again. The can was short!

It was missing almost $3. He thought back how he could have lost it. He did tend to take it out and pour it onto the loft floor and play with it, making stacks and dreaming about what it could buy. Could he have made a mistake in his counting? Maybe he had wanted it to be $12 so bad that he'd double counted some of the coins.

Sitting back against the cot with the money lying in front of him, he knew better than that. Some money was missing and he could only think of one person who might have taken it. In the past he'd had thought that he'd miscounted the money and it was just a little less than he'd expected. Tyler hadn't thought too much of it and blamed it on his own math. But this was too much.

Grandpa came back with four nice catfish. "We'll be eating good today," he told his grandson.

Tyler was sitting in front of the cabin with the tin can in his lap. He looked up at his grandpa and tried to smile. "That's good," the boy replied in barely a whisper.

The old man had a look of concern. "Are you having second thoughts about spending your money on the gun, grandson? Given time you'll have more money in that can."

Tears came into Tyler's eyes. He had been

fighting them back since discovering the missing money. "I . . . I," he couldn't trust his voice out of fear of bawling out loud.

Setting the fish down, Nikolas sat next to the boy. "Take a breath and tell me what's wrong."

"I don't have enough money," Tyler said, his voice weak. He was fearful of telling his grandpa what he thought happened to the missing coins.

"You have been counting that money every day, son," his grandpa said. "You knew you had the money he was asking. At least that was the impression I got yesterday."

The boy looked down at his dust-covered feet. "I thought I did." Tears began to run down his freckled cheeks.

Then his grandpa's voice became stern. "What do you think happened to the money?"

Tyler shrugged, unable to speak. His grandpa stood up and walked back and forth for a bit and then asked, "You're trying to protect someone, aren't you?"

Wiping his nose on his sleeve, the boy said, "I can have the money after a couple more hunts. Maybe Mr. Arnold will hold the gun for me."

"How much are you short?" his grandpa asked.

"After today's hunt, almost $2." Tyler replied.

"I got to ask you a question," his grandpa said. "Is there a chance that you might have spent some of the money? Just a little at a time can add up pretty fast."

"This summer I bought the knife," the boy told him. "Maybe a coin or two may have fallen in the cracks of the boards."

"When did you last count it?" his grandpa asked.

Taking a deep breath and brushing the tears away with his hands, Tyler looked at his grandpa. "Yesterday. It was there . . ."

"Are you protecting Wil?" the old man asked.

"He wouldn't need it," Tyler replied. "He takes whatever he wants from the trading post."

"I'm sure he does and from other places," Nikolas said, his voice cold.

Looking up at his grandpa with fear in his heart, Tyler said, "He's got it hard. His father is a drunk and is mean to him. Wil is my friend and helps me a lot with the cleanup. Maybe he felt he earned it."

A look of anger flashed across Nikolas's bearded face and then his eyes became compassionate. "You are a good friend to Wil. A far better friend than he is to you. I will let you deal with your friend. In the meantime, keep your money hidden."

Relief went through the boy. How he would deal with Wil he did not know, but at least his grandpa wasn't going to go after him. Then he heard the sound of the duck wagon coming. He looked at the can and wondered if he could just buy the squirrel gun and then get the mold and shot bag later on.

The boy made an excuse that he had to check

on something behind the cabin as Arnold's wagon rolled up. It would take his grandpa some time to finish his business and Tyler didn't want to be asked about buying the squirrel gun until the end. Being a little short of money to buy it, it would come soon enough.

Working the pump handle, the boy washed his face, removing any signs of the tears. At least he'd have the squirrel gun today. It wouldn't take too long to save for the mold and bag.

Tyler stood behind the cabin, leaning against the wall. He could hear his grandpa and Arnold laughing as the man looked over the ducks. It sounded like they were about to wind things up and Tyler didn't want his grandpa to have to call for him so, taking a deep breath, he went back around the cabin.

His eyes went wide when he saw Arnold showing the squirrel gun to his grandpa. It looked glorious. There on the wagon lay a shiny shot bag with a powder horn. It was one like he'd seen soldiers carrying. Looking up, Arnold saw him.

"I was about to leave," he called out. "I figured you had changed your mind."

Clutching the can of coins, Tyler forced his legs to work as he walked over to the wagon. He felt dread as he said the next words. "I will have to wait on the shot bag and mold. I only got enough for the gun."

"Well, you did ask me to dicker with the man and after some earnest discussions, I managed to get him to come down just a little," Arnold told him. "I pointed out that once he sold the squirrel gun, he'd have no use for the shot bag and the mold."

The boy stared at the duck merchant, fearful of what he'd hear. "How much did he want?"

"Well, after we chewed and spat some, he finally said his best price was $10 for the whole kit and caboodle," Mr. Arnold said.

Excitement soared through the boy, then unsure he asked, "What is kit and caboodle?"

Laughing, Arnold replied, "If you got the $10, you now own the gun, bag, horn, mold, and whatever else is in the bag."

With shaking hands, Tyler began to fish the coins out of the can. Being that they were of small denominations, there were lots of coins to count. After counting out the $10 there were still a couple left in the can to rattle.

"Here's your squirrel gun," Arnold said, handing it to the boy. The weight of the seven-pound gun prevented the men from noticing that Tyler's hands were shaking with anticipation. Then the shot bag was slung over his shoulder.

"Out west they call that bag a possible bag because you can carry things you may possibly need," the duck merchant told him.

Tyler stood with his new gun and bag as Mr. Arnold climbed onto the wagon and drove away. His grandpa headed for the cabin. "You best put those up for now. Later I will show you how to shoot and take care of the gun."

The boy was in a daze as he followed his grandpa. He now had his own squirrel gun. The 32-inch octagonal barrel tilted down in front of him. It was a flintlock and would shoot .32 caliber balls. Tyler wondered if there were any balls in the possible bag.

What the young boy did not know was that his grandpa had talked to Arnold about the money that had disappeared and had given the man $2 to lower the price that Tyler had to pay so he could get the squirrel gun today. Tyler was a good boy and a lot of help, so it was little enough to do for him.

CHAPTER THREE

Two things had happened on the day Tyler got the rifle. One was getting the rifle while the other was he turned 13. Birthdays weren't much of a cause for celebration, but this one Tyler would remember for the rest of his life.

While Tyler was very impatient to shoot, he tried not to show it while his grandpa taught him how to take care of the squirrel gun and how to handle it safely. It was lighter than the muzzle loader that his grandpa had and he wanted to take it out on the marsh in the worst way. This the old man refused to let him do.

The possible bag had a wealth of things he'd need to take care of and shoot the gun. It had lead balls, greased patches, spare flints, the mold, tools for cleaning the gun, and several things that would be needed for camping, including a flint and steel. Many of the things looked new and Tyler suspected that Mr. Arnold had picked them up for him.

Finally, it was time to fire the squirrel gun. "You know you won't be able to shoot with your fingers in your ears," his grandpa told him.

Blushing, Tyler replied, "I know that."

"We'll load it with a little less than a full measure of powder first," his grandpa told him. "I don't want you to develop a flinch when you pull the trigger. I will shoot first, then you."

Pouring a half-measure of powder into the barrel, his grandpa then rammed in a ball and patch. While describing what he was doing Nikolas readied the gun, using the steps he'd learned years ago when he was in the British army.

When he was ready to fire, he told Tyler to watch when he pulled the trigger and to notice when the gun fired. It wasn't much, but there was a delay and the shooter had to keep the sight on the target until the pan flashed and the gun fired.

Tyler didn't see much of a delay, but knew that the flash first would be the challenge. Taking the squirrel gun, the boy poured a half-measure of powder down the octagonal barrel. He then placed the patch over the bore, put a .32 caliber ball onto it and pushed it flush with his thumb. He pushed it in a little with a piece of deer antler. Then taking the wooden ramrod from under the barrel, he placed it into the bore. As he rammed the ball down, he was surprised how hard he had to tamp to get the ball to the bottom. Once he felt additional resistance he stopped, not wanting to over-pack the powder.

After priming the pan, Tyler brought it to his

shoulder and pulled the gun to full-cock. He was aiming at an alder tree. Again, he was surprised at how heavy the barrel was and how hard it was to keep the sights on his target. He lowered the heavy weapon to give his arm a break.

"Unless you have the barrel on a rest," his grandpa told him, "pull the trigger as soon as you get it on target and then hold it there until it fires. Try and keep your eyes open and do not anticipate the recoil."

His first shot was not spectacular. Tyler only nicked the side of the alder, almost missing it completely. For the next hour his patient grandpa worked with Tyler, loading the gun for him. Sometimes there was only powder in the pan and others there was no powder in the pan. Most often the squirrel gun was properly loaded and soon Tyler was putting, center shots into the tree.

With the sun going down, the two headed back to the cabin. Grandpa assured Tyler that he'd have plenty of time to practice after the marsh froze over. For the next few weeks, they'd be kept busy harvesting ducks and geese.

Tyler went to sleep that night with the squirrel gun next to his cot. He laid there with an arm hanging over the edge running his hand over the contours of the weapon. There was only one cloud over the joy of the day. The missing money. Tyler wasn't sure how he was going to handle the problem. It was doubtful that Wil had the money anymore. He would have spent it at his uncle's trading post.

Arnold would come by every other day to

purchase their catch. With the need to be out on the marsh Tyler only got to school a couple of days a week. He was still able to keep up on his learning. The teacher understood the need for boys to help at home, so he'd give them homework to return on the days they came to school.

In the afternoons or evenings Tyler would do his reading, writing, and arithmetic, either out front of the cabin or in the light of the fireplace. Most often when he read, the boy would do it out loud so his grandpa could listen.

It was three days before Tyler got back to school and Wil hadn't been by the cabin. Walking the two miles north to Cedar Creek, he went into the school yard. Tyler saw his friend talking to a young girl named Emma Wilson. Emma was a year younger than he and Wil. She was a pretty, blue-eyed brunette that most of the boys took a shine to.

Tyler avoided the two and went straight into the school room. He noticed the Wil had on a new hat and it was cocked to one side, making him look pretty dapper. Mr. Woods was the teacher and minister of the church.

He looked up and smiled when Tyler walked in. "You got the school work done?"

"Yes sir," the boy replied. "I had a little trouble with the math, but grandpa helped me figure it out."

"That would be on the angles," Mr. Woods replied. "Nikolas is a builder and would know about those things."

Then the pastor looked at the right side of Tyler's face. "You got a pretty good smudge on your cheek."

The boy's eyes lit up. "That's because I've been practicing with the squirrel gun I bought."

The man rubbed his whiskered chin and said, "So you got a squirrel gun. Maybe some time you can shoot a brace of grouse for Bethel and me."

It was time for school and Mr. Woods rang a bell, calling the students in. Wil sat near Tyler and had placed the new hat under his chair. "How was the hunting?" he whispered.

"Okay," Tyler replied, keeping his attention to what the pastor was setting up.

Pastor Woods didn't allow any whispering between students, which made ignoring Wil easier for Tyler. When they were let out at midday, Wil grabbed his hat and was off in pursuit of Emma. Tyler took his time putting his stuff together.

He was the last one to reach the school yard. The first thing he noticed was that Wil was in a confrontation with two bigger boys. Tyler guessed it was probably over the girl. One of the boys knocked the new hat to the ground and then kicked it while the other poked at Wil.

"Serves him right," Tyler muttered. "Maybe a beat'in might do him good."

When the two boys tripped Wil and appeared they were about to kick him, Tyler couldn't stand by any longer. Running across the yard, Tyler slammed into one boy knocking, him into the other. "I come over here to make this fight a little fairer," Tyler snarled.

While the two boys were older, they weren't about to take on the large-boned redhead. Tyler's face was flushed and the veins in his temples were pulsing. He was mad, mad about two picking on one and even madder that he had to help the boy that stole his money.

"Tell him to stay away from the girl," one of the boys threatened.

"I don't think she cares much for either of you," Tyler replied, feeling some of the heat go out of his body. "You two better leave her alone also, unless she asks for your company."

As the two boys moved to the far side of the school yard, Tyler heard them speaking disparagingly about him being a swamp rat. It didn't bother Tyler at all. He liked living on the marsh. Turning, he held a hand out and helped Wil up.

"Good thing you came along," the towhead said. "I was about to get up and show them what for."

"I figured you'd do that right after they kicked the snot out of you," Tyler replied, still feeling an anger towards his friend.

Wil picked up the hat and dusted it off. "I see you got a new hat." Tyler said.

"My uncle gave it to me for helping him," Wil replied.

"It must have been some help," Tyler said. "That looks like a $3 hat."

He noticed his friend turned red and pulled the brim down some. "I don't know what it cost."

The bell range and it was time to go back in. Tyler did not figure the issue of the money was settled yet, but now wasn't the time to confront Wil about it.

His friend stayed away the next couple of days while Tyler and his grandpa hunted the marsh. Each evening, he'd take out the squirrel gun and take a few shots. After each practice Tyler would clean the gun and ready it for the next time.

Grandpa had gotten some smaller shot and gave it to Tyler. "You may want to use this to go after some of the grouse we've been hearing. I figure they're eating thorn apples to the west of the barn."

The thought excited the boy. Several times a week he and his grandpa would hunt the marsh for ducks, but that was just making a living. The thought of going out for the grouse was a whole different thing. He'd be coming back with food for the table.

Wasting no time with the idea, Tyler took the squirrel gun and headed out the next Saturday after the morning hunt and chores were done. It was about a quarter-mile to the patch of thorn apple bushes. Tyler went in slowly as he stalked the birds. He could hear the clucking. Then he saw a nice hen.

The young boy had no idea how close he had to be to kill the bird with the shot in his gun. Fearing that he'd flush it, Tyler brought the butt to his shoulder. Pulling the squirrel gun to full-cock, he sighted on the bird and fired.

The black powder smoke blocked his view of his target and he heard several grouse flush from the thorn apples. His heart was pounding with excitement as the smoke cleared and he saw the bird flapping on the ground. "I got it!" he exclaimed.

As Tyler picked up the grouse, he froze. Within range in a tree was another bird and his gun was empty. Now he wished he had reloaded before going to pick up his kill. In slow motion, Tyler put in the powder and shot, tamping it with the ramrod. He then pulled the gun to half-cock and primed the pan. Noiselessly he brought the squirrel gun to his shoulder.

The next day at church, Tyler proudly presented Pastor Woods with a brace of grouse. His grandpa stood behind him with a great deal of pride on his face. The pastor managed to weave the birds into his sermon that Sunday.

Wil and his father Hugo Lane, were standing outside of the church when Tyler came out with his grandpa. His grandpa stopped to talk with the pastor as Tyler continued into the yard. Wil's father looked at him with his watery eyes and said, "Bringing birds to church ain't going to get you into heaven, but it might help your school grades."

The man had a harsh way of speaking, but more than likely was just making conversation. Tyler could smell the whiskey on him. "I just enjoyed hunting them," Tyler replied, forcing a smile on his face.

"Wil tells me you got yourself a long gun," Hugo said.

"I bought it from Mr. Arnold," the boy said, wishing his grandpa would hurry along.

"Soon you'll be shooting all the birds off the marsh as well as them in the woods," Hugo told him. "That will leave nothing for the rest of us. You should spend your money on a good hat like my boy Wil."

"Maybe I can shoot some birds for Mr. Arnold and do that," Tyler said, moving away when he saw his grandpa coming.

As they walked down the trail towards the cabin, Nikolas asked, "I see you're making friends with Hugo."

"Seeing him makes me feel sorry for Wil," Tyler replied.

* * *

The first snow came in early November and the cold weather was bringing down the diving ducks. Daylight would find the two hunters on the marsh looking for goldeneyes, scaups, ringnecks, buffleheads and redheads. There were still plenty of mallards and blacks, which wouldn't leave until the marsh iced over.

As the two men huddled to keep warm, grandpa said, "This snow won't last, grandson. I have seen some years that we were in shirt sleeves in November."

"Thinking of that won't make me feel any warmer," Tyler complained.

The sky got light in the east and it was time to start shooting. This time of year the marsh water was cold, and it was hand-numbing work retrieving the ducks. By noon they returned with a nice mix of ducks.

Grandpa had talked of butchering the pigs next week. They had a small smoke house in the back and folks would be looking for hams for the coming holidays. In past years they'd wrestled the pigs and hold them while the throat was cut. Tyler did the wrestling and wondered if his grandpa would let him shoot them with the squirrel gun.

The answer came soon enough, when the water got hot in the big metal tub and his grandpa asked, "Are you ready to get in a tussle with them hogs?"

They had set up a small fenced area outside the pig pen to keep things cleaner and one of the pigs was driven into it. Then Tyler got it down, trying to avoid the flailing hooves as his grandpa slit the throat and caught the blood in a small bucket. The racket of the squeals ended quickly after the hog bled out.

Once the animal was killed, they quickly dragged it over to the hot water. Three poles formed a tripod over the metal tub, and it had a block and tackle hanging above it. Tying one end to the back legs, the bled-out hog could be lifted and lowered into the steaming water decreasing the pull Tyler had to put on the rope. Sloshing the hog back and forth, his grandpa would check the looseness of the bristly hair. After a few minutes the old man said, "Pull her up."

Then the scraping and scrubbing began and the loosened hair was removed. A wooden tub was then brought over and the hog was gutted, catching the entrails for processing. While grandpa gutted the pig, Tyler went into the barn and led the mare hitched to the buckboard. The animal was laid onto the wagon and taken to the barn to hang and cool in the bay.

The whole process took just over an hour. As they came out of the barn, a wagon with two ladies came into the yard. They came for the blood and would go through the tub of innards, salvaging most of it for one thing or another. Tyler waved to them and he headed for the pig pen to get the second hog.

By nightfall everything had pretty much been cleaned up and the two hog carcasses were cooling in the barn. Grandpa had some sawhorses and an old door that he'd use to cut the hogs up the next day. Again, the two ladies would be there to collect scraps and parts that grandpa didn't want.

Grandpa would give them the fat to render and they would then bring back some of the lard. He had already given them both heads, the feet, and the neck bones. Again, they'd bring him back some headcheese, pickled pig's feet and some blood sausage.

The next day grandpa and the ladies cut the two hogs up while Tyler hauled and split wood for the smoke house. They would smoke the hams, shoulders, and side meat, as well as other parts that wouldn't be salted down. Only a small amount of the hogs was eaten as fresh roasts or chops. All of the trimmings and some of the meat would be made into sausage and smoked.

The farmyard behind the cabin seemed empty with the noise from the hogs now gone. Come spring, grandpa would purchase two young ones to raise next year and the musical grunts would be back. Tyler sat near the barn remembering what his grandpa had always claimed: "The only thing you can't use on a hog is the squeal."

CHAPTER FOUR

The fire was crackling, as Tyler tossed wood onto the flames to make smoke for the smoke house. Grandpa always said it took a certain mix of woods to make good-tasting smoke, and that the dampers on the stone pit had to be kept closed most of the time to keep the heat down and prevent cooking the meat.

That morning the meat had been taken out of the brine water and hung to drip in mesh bags. They were then brought into the smoke-filled building. The two hogs made lots of tasty side meat and ham. Two-thirds of the meat was pre-sold and would be kept in a pump shed behind the cabin until the buyer came to pick it up. The nights were below freezing now and the days barely above. The marsh had iced over and the skiff had been stored upside down on the dock. Tyler liked the feel of the heat coming off the smoke house fire. He continued to turn to keep himself warm.

Once the cured pork was put into the pump shed, Tyler's work was done, and all that was left was to enjoy the benefit of their work. Word got out quickly that the hams and side meat were ready, and folks would come and pick them up.

Tyler wasted little time hanging around the cabin. When he wasn't in school, he was wandering the woods and fields with his squirrel gun. He managed to keep a fair amount of meat on the table. One evening when he returned Tyler had leaned the gun against the cabin wall and heard footsteps behind him.

As he turned something struck his chest, pinning him against the wall. He was looking into the hate filled-eyes of Hugo. "Where the hell is that kid!" he growled. "Is he hiding in your damn cabin?"

Being slammed into the wall had almost knocked the wind out of Tyler. At the moment he felt helpless and expected the threatening words to be followed by a bruising fist. "Let that boy go!" a loud voice commanded.

Grandpa had come out of the cabin after hearing Tyler hit the wall. If Hugo was angry, Nikolas was livid and had blood in his eyes. "You are only seconds from meeting your maker!" Grandpa threatened.

Letting Tyler go, Hugo turned to face Nikolas. "That damn kid of mine stole money from me. I know he come here to hide."

Nikolas' voice softened. "He isn't here, Hugo. It is freezing out here and if you drove him out of your house the boy could die."

Shaking with anger, the red-faced man turned away and said, "When I find him, he will wish he was dead."

"You don't mean that, Hugo," Nikolas told him. "He may be a kid that has done wrong, but there are other ways to make things right."

With that, the angry man stomped away, leaving Tyler and his grandpa worrying about Wil's safety. "Where do you think he would go?" grandpa asked Tyler.

"Most of the snow melted off the last couple of days," the boy said. "Hugo must have found a couple of tracks coming this way or he wouldn't have been so sure Wil was here."

"I'll get my coat and we can look around for him," grandpa suggested.

"I got an idea," Tyler said. "Wait until I get back."

Taking his gun, the boy headed for the woods. Sure, enough he spotted tracks in the snow under the trees. As he came up to their crude fort he called out, "Wil are you in there?"

The two boys had built a roof with a tarp over the top and had cut out a small opening in the side to get in and out. Again, Tyler called, "Wil, are you there? Your pa came looking for you."

"Tell him to go to hell," a voice from inside the fort said.

"You can't stay in there," Tyler told him. "You'll freeze overnight."

"I got blankets enough," Wil said.

Crawling into the fort, Tyler sat against the wall opposite Wil. He cradled his squirrel gun in his lap. "Is that your gun? I ain't seen it yet."

"That's because you ain't been coming around," Tyler replied.

In a weak voice, his friend said, "I knew you knew I took the money from the can. You wouldn't say anything about it and I figured we weren't friends anymore."

"If you're wondering, I ain't over you taking the money yet," Tyler told him. "I guess I kept hoping you would make it right with me."

"I have no way of making money," Wil told him. "My pa won't give me none"

"Did you ever think about working for your uncle?" Tyler asked him.

"My uncle doesn't trust . . ." the boy didn't finish the sentence.

"I'm cold," Tyler said. "Your pa won't be back tonight. Let's go up to the cabin."

In silence the two boys walked toward the cabin with only the sounds of their feet shuffling leaves or crunching the remaining snow. The theft from the tin can was heavy on Tyler's mind. Though he had never directly challenged Wil on the money, he now knew. It was becoming very apparent that the young boy tended to take whatever he wanted. It was no longer a piece of candy or other insignificant items.

Grandpa was sitting up drinking the last of the coffee from supper. "Everything okay?" he asked.

"I told Wil that his pa wouldn't be back and he is going to sleep here tonight," Tyler explained.

"In the loft?" Nikolas asked.

It may have been an innocent question, but Tyler knew it was a warning. He would be near the tin can. The red-headed boy wasn't worried. He had found a better hiding place that would keep his money safe. Grandpa watched the two boys climb the ladder to the loft. He knew his grandson needed a best friend, but he only wished Wil was someone who could be trusted.

Lying in the dark loft with only the occasional flicker of flame by the fireplace flashing shadows on the ceiling, Tyler could not shut down his mind. He listened to Wil's even breathing. He doubted his friend was sleeping.

"Are you warm enough?" Tyler whispered.

"Yeah," came the single word response.

Finally, Tyler knew he had to purge what he felt inside. He only hoped that Wil wouldn't run. "You were right. I knew you took money from my can and I think it was more than once."

There was silence in the loft. He had expected some kind of response from Wil. Maybe admission or even a denial of the other times. Tyler had opened the door to the fact and felt a need to say more.

"We have been friends a long time and it has added to my enjoyment living near the marsh. We have had countless adventures and have had each other's backs, when necessary," Tyler said, wondering if Wil was even listening.

Deciding to go on, the boy said, "I knew for a long time that the peppermint sticks and other things you would bring with you were taken from your uncle's and not given to you. I was wrong to take them and not say anything. I fear you are now taking bigger things, noticeable things and that you are going to get in trouble. It will be the kind of trouble that I can't have your back with."

Knowing there was more to say, Tyler lay in silence, fearful that he'd already said too much. Then an idea came to him. "You said you couldn't work for your uncle. Come down here and help my grandpa and I will share the money he gives to me. I don't have anything big that I need and wouldn't miss that money."

There was still no response from Wil and Tyler wondered if he had fallen asleep. With nothing more to say, he rolled over and pulled the blankets tight under his chin.

* * *

The next morning the two boys got up and Tyler expected Wil to say something or at least act different, but he did not. After some breakfast and with his usual smile he said, "Be seeing you," and was gone.

"Smells like snow out there," Grandpa said. "If you shot the gun yesterday, you best clean it."

Tyler lingered at the table. As his grandpa was heading for the door to go take care of the horse, the boy said, "I talked to Wil last night, or at least I think I did. He might have gone to sleep and not heard me."

With his hand on the latch of the door, Nikolas told him, "I heard what you said last night. It was a good speech. I doubt if he was sleeping. Maybe it gave him something to think about."

Grandpa was right about that and about the snow. It came down hard, with the wind behind it. For two days the two men hunkered down in the cabin. They only went out to water and feed the horse, use the little house, or haul in wood.

These were what Nikolas called lazy days. Tyler did not mind them. The two of them would play some checkers, do some whittling, and play a couple of hands of cards. To keep it fun, the two made small bets, but each time they played grandpa would give a short lecture on the dangers of gambling.

With the storm over, Tyler had to go to school. He took a few coins from the can to purchase a Christmas present for his grandpa. Like birthdays, Christmas was a modest holiday, with church on the night before and then a ham roasted in the fireplace.

After school he planned to stop at the trading post and try and select something. Tyler was a little early at school and Pastor Woods was shoveling the steps. "Grab the other shovel and then you can help me haul in some wood," the pastor called to him.

The two men took large shovels full of the drifted snow and tossed them clear of the front. "How old are you now?" the pastor asked.

"I turned 13 in August," Tyler replied.

"You're about at the end of the books," Pastor Woods told him, leaning on his shovel. "They got grades up to 12 in the school at Momence. I know the minister there and you could stay with him and come home every weekend. I know he'd let you take time off for hunting."

Momence was 14 miles from the cabin. His grandpa had taken him there once with the buckboard to buy the tub used to dunk the hogs. Tyler had never considered going to more school. There wasn't a lot of benefit in book learning to harvest ducks and raise hogs.

"I'll talk to my grandpa," Tyler promised. While he loved learning, 14 miles was a long way away and after he was out of school grandpa had told him he'd make him a partner.

The snow was shoveled and the wood in the stove had flames snapping, making the room quite comfortable before the other kids came. Emma was the first to arrive and she came over to Tyler. He really didn't know what he was supposed to say when talking to girls. Tyler blushed and answered her questions with one-word replies.

He was thankful when some of the other students came in. While Emma didn't leave and kept talking with him, Wil came in and saved him. He was sporting a bruise on the side of his face, but that didn't prevent him from smiling and saying all kinds of interesting things to Emma.

Tyler found it hard to concentrate on his studies with what the pastor had told him and also trying to decide what to buy at the trading post. Most of the boys had quit school and gone to work at the mill by the time they were 13. Grandpa had insisted that Tyler stay in to finish the 8th grade.

The trading post had been the first building near Cedar Creek and the others grew up around it. Along with homes, there was a tavern that served meals, a livery owned by Edmond, a jail with Sheriff Kent, a lawyer, and a man who did barbering out of his house. The two ladies who came and helped with the hog butchering also did some sewing and laundry.

When Pastor Woods set his glasses onto the small oak desk and announced that school was over, Tyler was quick to go for his coat hanging on a peg on the wall. Emma sat three desks in front of him, and she'd gotten up and was coming towards him. Again, Wil saved the day and cut her off.

He had planned to ask Wil if he wanted to join him at the trading post, but he didn't want to do so in front of Emma, who might even offer to go with him. With a quick wave to his friend, Tyler left the room, pulling his wool coat on. He had a stocking cap that his grandpa called a tuque to keep his ears warm.

The trading post was a long building with household goods and clothing in the front, and hunting, trapping, or farming items toward the back. Wagons could pull up to the two large doors in the back to load or unload items.

Jules Martin was the owner, also Wil's uncle. Kicking the step to get the snow off his feet, Tyler went in out of the cold and was greeted with warmth radiating from the potbelly stove located 20 feet inside the door. Pulling off the tuque and opening his coat, Tyler stomped his feet to warm them.

"Don't be getting the floor all covered," a voice from the back said. "Knock the snow off outside."

"I did sir," the boy said. "I was just trying to get my feet warm."

Once a month grandpa would hitch up the mare to the buckboard and make a trip to the trading post to purchase items that the two of them needed.

Often it was done while Tyler was in school. During the summer the boy would join him.

The smells and shelves loaded with items for purchase made Tyler forget all about the difficult day at school with Emma wanting to talk with him. "Can I help you?" Jules asked.

"I was hoping to find something for my grandpa," Tyler replied.

"We got some nice things right up front," the owner told him, his voice rather direct.

The boy had a particular item in mind. His grandpa liked to smoke a pipe in the evenings and his old corncob was breaking down. Tyler hoped to buy a new one with some of the good smelling tobacco. Thanking the owner, the boy gazed at the items around him.

Tyler liked to look at the farm stuff towards the back and he wandered in that direction. There were axes, shovels, iron forks and all kinds of nails. The harnesses smelled of new leather and he liked to feel how flexible they were. Glancing up, he saw Mr. Martin over his shoulder.

"You going to buy an axe?" the owner asked.

"No," Tyler admitted. "I just like to look at the stuff."

"Well, if you ain't buying back here, go up front and get what you come in for," Mr. Martin told him. "I ain't got time to watch you all day."

Figuring the owner was having a bad day, Tyler didn't want to hang around and bother him. As he walked toward the front the owner said, "You damn upstarts come in here and clean me out and then leave without paying. I watch your kind."

The owners attitude riled the boy and he couldn't understand why he talked like that to him, but the desire to get the pipe for his grandpa was strong enough that Tyler went straight to the counter and pointed at the items.

"I'd like the pipe and that green tin of tobacco," he requested.

"That's the good stuff," Mr. Martin told him. "You got enough money for it? I don't allow young'uns to charge."

Tyler knew his face was red as he fought down the feeling of anger inside. "I got money."

"That's four bits for the pipe and $2 for the tobacco," the owner said.

Reaching inside his coat for the small leather bag, Tyler took out the coins needed and placed them onto the counter. Taking them and handing the items to the boy, the owner put the money in a wooden box under the counter.

"Don't be looking at this money box," Mr. Martin told him. "I keep a close eye on it. Your grandfather best keep an eye on his too."

Shocked at the exchange, Tyler left the trading post clutching the items. The joy of buying the presents for his grandpa was pretty much gone. He had intended to get some lead to cast balls and a peppermint stick for himself, but the encounter with the owner had made the boy buy only what he had to.

It was a long walk home as Tyler tried to figure out what he might have done to anger the owner.

Someone had dragged a log crossway along the road from town that packed down the snow. When the boy turned onto the trail leading to the cabin, he was in snow almost up to his knees and he tried to step in the tracks from this morning.

Tyler went around to the pump shed where they'd hung the hams and hid the pipe and tobacco. It was still a week from Christmas and the boy wanted to surprise his grandpa on Christmas morning. The sun went down early this time of year and it was almost dark when he entered the cabin. Grandpa had a pot of bean soup with a little pork cooking in the fireplace.

"You were running late, so I took care of the horse so you could get right to any school work you might have," his grandpa told him.

"I'm sorry I took so long," Tyler told him. "I should have checked on the mare before coming in."

"I needed to get out for some fresh air," Nikolas told the boy, laughing. "I been cooped up inside all day."

Then the old man noticed that his grandson wasn't joining in on his attempt to be humorous. "Grandson, did something happen in school today?"

"School was good," the boy told his grandpa. "I stopped in the trading post and Mr. Martin treated me kind of bad. I got the feeling that he thought I come in to steal something."

"Jules got a business and I am sure he was just being careful," Nikolas told him. "I wouldn't pay it too much mind."

The boy's mood didn't improve much as they sat to eat. "Do you worry that I might take money from you?"

His grandpa set his spoon into the bowl of soup and sat back. "Why would you ask me that? You taking money is the last thing I'd worry about."

"When I went into the trading post, Mr. Martin followed me around and told me I should just go to what I was going to buy," Tyler told him. "When I paid, he told me not to look at his money box and that he keeps an eye on it and said you should do the same."

Grandpa hand hit the table, startling Tyler. "He told you that did he?"

The boy didn't reply because his throat hurt and he felt like crying. He was now 13 and too old to be crying. Tyler watched as his grandpa got up, leaving his soup to go cold. "Where are the things you bought?" his grandpa asked.

Suddenly Tyler had another problem. The things were a surprise for Christmas. "I put them . . ." The boy looked down at his bowl. "I got you something for Christmas. You weren't supposed to know."

"I think Christmas is close enough," Nikolas said. "Go get the items for me."

Tyler left the table and slipped on his coat. Now both of their soups would get cold. Inside, the boy felt he was being punished as he went around the cabin, in the dark, to the pump shed. Taking the pipe and tobacco, he went back into the cabin. His grandpa was standing by the fireplace leaning against the mantle. He did not look up.

"Set them here near the fireplace," he requested.

Placing them next to his grandpa, Tyler stepped back. "They are for you. Merry Christmas."

This grandpa knelt down and picked up the items. "It's a good pipe and some real fine tobacco. Thank you, grandson."

Suddenly the boy felt better. The feelings left by his experience in the store was gone. "I knew you needed a new pipe and I like the smell of that tobacco."

Smiling at the boy, Nikolas said, "What I am going to do now has nothing to do with these wonderful gifts you got for me. I am going to go and see Jules."

The boy stood with his mouth hanging open as he watched his grandpa put on his coat and walk out of the cabin with the gifts. The crunching sounds of his footsteps disappeared as he went away. Tyler stood near the fireplace for a full two minutes, expecting his grandpa to return.

Still being hungry, he finally went back to the table and his soup. He then looked at the other bowl across from him. Sliding it over, Tyler began to eat both soups, wondering where grandpa had gone.

With the meal eaten and the dishes washed, Tyler moved the soup pot a little farther from the coals. He got his squirrel gun and a rag with some oil, then rubbed the surface until the gun glistened in the light of the coals. He began to feel tired and also to worry about his grandpa. He hoped he'd come back soon.

Climbing up the ladder, Tyler decided that he'd lay down on the blanket while waiting. He had the squirrel gun next to him. His mind wandered and he was soon on an adventure, lying in the wilds with his gun at his side. Then he was asleep.

CHAPTER FIVE

The sound of metal on metal woke the 13-year-old redhead. There was light coming in from the windows. He was still on the cot, but sometime during the night he'd pulled one side of the blanket over himself. The sound of his feet hitting the floor alerted his grandpa.

"I thought you were going to sleep all day," a voice came from below.

"I was waiting for you to come back," the boy called back.

He climbed down the ladder, gripping the rungs with one hand and the gun with the other. Leaning the weapon against the wall, he pulled on his boots and grabbed his coat. "I'll be right back."

The little house was cold and he could see his breath as he took care of business. Then he decided he'd take care of the horse before going back inside. The mare snorted as he entered. Clipping a lead rope to the halter, he led the animal to the marsh and took the axe near the dock. Chopping a hole through the ice, he let the horse drink.

With the horse back in the barn, he pitched some hay into the stall. "I'll be back in a little while to clean your stall," he promised. Tyler smiled when it bobbed its head, like the mare understood.

Grandpa was warming the bean soup for their breakfast. It was nice and thick, almost like a porridge. Tyler glanced around and did not see the tobacco or pipe anywhere. Getting the bowls off the sideboard, he brought them to warm up near the fire.

"After we eat, we'll hitch up the mare to the sleigh," grandpa told him.

"Are we going visiting?" Tyler asked. What he really wanted to ask was what happened at the trading post. No doubt some strong words went back and forth.

"I thought we'd go to Momence," he told Tyler.

The coincidence of mentioning that town was too much and the boy asked, "Did you run into Pastor Woods last night?"

"No, why?" the grandpa asked

"Just something about me going to school there," Tyler replied.

"You're about done at this school," Nikolas said. "Do you want to go to Momence?"

"I don't think so," Tyler told him. "Why are we going?"

"Supplies," grandpa replied. "Now hold the bowls while I fill them."

It was seldom that they took the horse out with the sleigh, and they almost never went to Momence for supplies. Today they were going to do both.

Bits of snow flew off the horse's hooves striking the front of the sleight as they drove toward Momence. Grandpa had a buffalo robe draped over their legs and lap to keep them warm. Tyler loved riding on the sleigh and wondered why they didn't take it out more often.

The trip to Momence was 14 miles and would take just under three hours. The road was packed snow and somewhat rutted, but it made easy travel for the mare. Tyler sat next to his grandpa and wondered if he should ask about the trip to the trading post. It could not have been too bad because grandpa was in a good mood.

The sleigh reached a stream that had water flowing, and Nikolas stopped to give the horse a breather and let it drink. There were trees on both sides of the road with their leafless branches reaching toward the sky. The rich, dark evergreens were nestled within the trees. Chickadees flitted from branch to branch calling out chick-a-dee-dee-dee.

As they took off from the stream, they startled a whitetail deer and it bounded away, flashing the tail it was named for. Squinting from the bright snow and cold breeze as the horse trotted along the winding road, Tyler began to think about all the items he'd be able to look at or touch in the bigger mercantile. He'd heard they had chocolate and he planned to buy some. He had never tasted chocolate before.

Seeing a few scattered homes let the two know that they were approaching the town. Tyler leaned forward in the seat, anxious to catch sight of the mercantile. Walking the mare to let it cool down, they went by the clapboard buildings lining the street. When they passed the school, Tyler felt a chill. Maybe his grandpa wanted him to see it in case he came there.

Tyler had been told they were coming after supplies. The boy was sure that they must be some special kind of supplies because this was a long way to go for the usual ones. Then he saw the long front porch of the mercantile. There were boxes and barrels filled with goods to attract folks in.

Pulling up in front of the building, grandpa pushed the buffalo robe over the front of the sleigh. Tyler hurried out and tied the mare to a ring on the post in front of the store. Walking in was like dying and going to heaven for Tyler. He closed his eyes and took in all the smells. He could only imagine all the places the items had come from.

"I got this back for you," grandpa said, handing him $2.50. "Look around and I wouldn't mind you getting them again."

That's why grandpa had gone last night, Tyler realized. He had gone and got his money back. Gripping the coins in his gloved hand, the boy began to take in the mercantile. While he wandered around, Nikolas went to the counter and gave the merchant a list of things he needed.

Slowly Tyler walked through the store. There were many colored bolts of cloth, stacks of clothing, boots, shelves of tin goods, elixirs that could cure almost everything, spices, bags of beans, corn, coffee, rice, and more.

When he reached the tools, the boy stopped and picked up a hatchet, or short axe. He'd seen men carry them in their belt. It sure could be handy. It was only $2.50. Placing it back down, the boy realized that the money he had was for his grandpa's gift, but it sure was a nice axe.

His thoughts were interrupted when Nikolas said, "It will be about a half-hour for our order. I saw a café next door. Let's have us a store-bought meal."

Breaking into a smile, Tyler said, "Sure thing, grandpa."

While it was just a simple café, the boy felt they were underdressed for the place. The tables had red and white checked cloths on them and fancy curtains on the window. A young woman with a frilly apron was waiting on tables.

Coming over, she placed a menu onto the table and said, "Todays special is hot roast beef sandwiches. While you're deciding, can I get you something to drink?"

Grandpa said, "I'll have coffee and I think the boy here would like a sarsaparilla."

There were two things Tyler had never had. One was a sarsaparilla and the other a hot roast beef sandwich. In fact, with the cabin not having an oven, they rarely had any bread and he'd never had any kind of sandwich. The drinks came and it was time to order food.

"I'll have the hot roast beef sandwich," Nikolas said.

Tyler was feeling pretty hungry and he looked at his grandpa. Whispering, he asked, "Can I have two sandwiches?"

Smiling, his grandpa said, "Two sandwiches for the boy here."

The sarsaparilla was served in a bottle. Picking it up, the boy took a sip and almost spit. The drink had bubbles in it. Sloshing it around his mouth, he swallowed. The flavor was very pleasant. The two of them nursed their beverages while waiting for the meal. Then it came.

The sandwich was served on a large plate with potatoes on the side of the sandwich and gravy over everything. One plate was set in front of grandpa and two were set in front of Tyler. The boy's eyes went large and he realized what he had to eat.

The roast beef was tender, and the gravy tasty, and it wasn't too long before the meal was finished. Tyler was scraping the last of his potatoes from the second plate when grandpa asked, "I suppose you don't have room for pie?"

Blushing, the boy said sheepishly, "I could eat some pie."

When the two left the café, Tyler's stomach had never been fuller and he'd never been so satisfied with a meal. The order was ready at the mercantile. The boy stood at the counter looking at the pipes and tobacco. There were the same ones that he'd gotten at the trading post.

Grandpa had picked up some of the supplies to take to the sleigh and Tyler told the merchant, "I'd like a pipe and a green can of the tobacco."

"You're kind of young to be taking up smoking," the man told him.

"It's for grandpa," Tyler told him in a low voice.

"Oh," the merchant said. "That will be $2."

"I want the pipe too," the boy replied.

"Yep," he said, "and that will be $2."

Realizing it was a present, the merchant put it into a small flour bag. Tyler gave the $2 to the man and put the rest back into the leather bag under his shirt.

With all the items in the sleigh, grandpa kicked the runners to break them loose and climbed on. The buffalo robe was pulled over their laps and they were on their way back home. Tyler had been thinking and said to his grandpa. "The stuff I bought cost less here than at the trading post. Do you think Mr. Martin cheated me?"

"I wouldn't say that," Nikolas said. "Cedar Creek is farther than Momence from the supply houses. It is quite possible that Jules gets some supplies from Momence. He can't sell them for the same amount as he buys them and make a living."

Thinking about what grandpa said, Tyler asked, "Does Mr. Arnold get more for our ducks than he pays us?"

"He does grandson. Maybe twice as much," Nikolas replied.

"It doesn't sound fair," the boy said.

"It costs us $3 to shoot 50 ducks. Do you think we should charge Arnold that amount for the birds?" his grandpa asked.

"We got to have a boat and gun," Tyler told him.

"And they got to have wagons, teams, and their time. Time is worth money," the redhead was told.

As the two of them traveled along, the boy had just got his first lesson in business. It made sense to Tyler. Then he said, "You bought our supplies in Momence. Mr. Martin won't be able to make money on what we got."

"Next month he will, but this month I am still a little disappointed in the way he treated you," his grandpa told him. "But it wasn't all his fault."

The boy looked at his grandpa. "But he was mean to me."

"It was because of who you associate with," Nikolas told the boy, trying to choose his words carefully. "You are a good and honest boy. You hang out with Wil that . . . that is not. He had often taken things from the trading post that Mr. Martin didn't give him or tell him he could have. Jules made the mistake of thinking if Wil took things then so would his friends."

"So, I shouldn't hang around with Wil?" Tyler asked.

"I didn't say that, but if you do and someone questions your honesty, you got to understand why," grandpa told him. "A time will come when Wil will go one way and you'll go another. In the meantime, you can be a good example for him. If he offers you something that you know he couldn't have bought, don't take it. If you do, it only encourages him to take more to share with you, his friend."

By this time, Tyler was totally confused, but some of what his grandpa said made sense. All those peppermint sticks came to mind. Then another thing came to mind. "Can I go into the trading post?"

"I think Jules and I got to a good understanding on that," grandpa told him. "I don't think Mr. Martin will be worrying about you, but if you do go in you should know what you want, ask for it and then leave. People wandering through a business always worries an owner."

The last suggestion did bother the boy. One of the joys when in town was looking at all the wonderful things on the shelves. He now had to decide if Wil friendship was worth more than looking around the trading post.

With a full belly and all this talking, Tyler leaned back to think. Within moments he was sleeping, only to wake up when the sleigh pulled up to the cabin. Once the supplies were put into the cabin and only the sacks of grain left in the sleigh, the boy led the mare to the barn.

After unhooking the horse, he watered it and gave it some grain and hay. Then Tyler dragged the sleigh into its place next to the buckboard. He stopped by the wood pile, split an armload and carried it into the cabin. Grandpa had put everything away except the flour sack with the tobacco and pipe.

"Do you want to wait for your gift?" he asked grandpa.

"I think I should," the old man told his grandson.

The two walked to the church on Christmas Eve, listened to the sermon on the birth of Jesus and sang familiar Christmas songs. After the service was over, the pastor's wife Bethel served cake and a flavored drink or coffee. The drink wasn't nearly as good as the sarsaparilla, but it was still good.

It was late when the two got back to the cabin. The fire had burned down to just a few coals and it was cool in the cabin. Grandpa added a few pieces of wood to the fireplace with a few chips to help start the fire. "We should get some sleep," he told the boy.

Climbing into the loft, it felt a bit warmer as he pulled off his clothes. He kind of wished grandpa had taken out the pipe and tobacco and smoked a bowl. It was still in the flour bag near the fireplace and grandpa knew what it was. Tomorrow was Christmas and he'd just have to wait to smell the sweet tobacco.

Tyler woke and lay under his blankets. There were no sounds below. The cabin was cold. The boy wondered what time it was. It was still dark in the cabin. Closing his eyes, the boy waited to hear sounds from below. He thought about the mercantile in Momence, about the café and the special drink. Then a frown came to his face as he thought about what his grandpa had said on the trip home.

Finally, he could wait no more. He got up and grabbed his clothes before climbing down from the loft. The plank floor was cold on his bare feet. A feeble light was coming through the windows, so Tyler could make things out in the cabin. Approaching the fireplace, he felt around with his hand and there was no warmth.

Using a piece of wood, he pushed the ashes to one side. He then took some tinder out of the bin near the fireplace, put a small pile in the center and placed some wood chips around them. Tyler went to the corner of the room where his squirrel gun and possible bag were kept. Reaching into the bag he got his flint and steel.

Back at the fireplace he showered the tinder with sparks and soon had it smoldering. Then, with a little blowing it broke into flames. As the chips caught fire, the boy then carefully put pieces of wood around it.

The coffee pot had been filled the night before and now had a layer of ice in it, so Tyler placed it near the flames to heat. He smiled at the thought that he'd have coffee ready for grandpa when he got up.

Sitting near the fire to keep warm, Tyler looked around the cabin. It had a lonely feel. It wasn't home until grandpa was up. He thought about calling to him but decided against it. It was almost an hour and the boy was dozing on and off near the fireplace when the sounds of his grandpa getting up came to his attention.

Turning, he realized that the coffee water was hot, but he hadn't put any grounds into it. They had a tin with some ground beans on a shelf above the sideboard. Tiptoeing, he went over and got the tin and dumped some into the pot. Then bringing it back to the shelf, he began to put on his clothes. He could smell the coffee. That would be perfect when grandpa came out of his room.

Pushing back the curtain, the old man came out and took a deep breath. "Is that coffee I smell?"

"Yes, it is," Tyler replied. "All it needs is a stir and it will be ready."

"That was good cake last night," grandpa said, making conversation.

"It was," Tyler agreed. "Do you want to look what I got in the bag?"

"Let me have some coffee first," the old man said. Getting a cup, he poured it full. Then dragging a chair near the fireplace, he sat down. Taking a sip, he cleared his throat. "Did you measure the amount you put in the pot?"

"Sort of," the boy replied.

"It is good, but kind a strong," his grandpa told him.

The water bucket also had ice in it and it was placed near the fireplace to melt. "Now, bring me that bag."

Scampering to pick it up, Tyler handed it to his grandpa. The old man took the items out of the bag and the look of pleasure was just as much as when he saw them the first time. "I thank you for these, grandson."

Sitting next to the fire and hugging his knees, Tyler said, "Your welcome, grandpa."

With the first cup of coffee finished, the old man threw the dregs into the fireplace. He then went to his room and came out with something wrapped in a grain sack. He set it down near the boy. Tyler picked it up. It was heavy. He then unrolled the bag and took the item out. It was a brand-new hatchet!

"Thanks grandpa!" he exclaimed. "This is the one I was looking at in Momence!"

"Merry Christmas," he told the boy. "Now I am going to add a little more water to the coffee and have another cup."

* * *

The winter months of January and February dragged on and it wasn't until the second week of March that the first signs of the winter ending came. Using snowshoes that grandpa had taught him to make, Tyler had spent several days hunting rabbits and grouse. They also ice fished when the wind wasn't too cutting, and caught pike and catfish. Some they sold to the trading post and many where broiled or went into their soup pot.

He managed to shoot a fox one day and his grandpa showed him how to skin it and told him he'd be able to get some money for the fur. He had gotten within range of a deer one day but chose not to shoot. They had plenty of meat to last until spring and the deer had been living off cedars and would have had that taste in the meat.

When they got up to the sound of water dripping from the icicles, both were in a hurry to get outside. It was another two weeks before most of the snow was melted and water was beginning to show around the marsh.

A couple of the boards on the flat bottom of the skiff needed replacing, and wood had been gotten from the mill last fall and dried in the barn. The two were able to get the skiff from the dock to the bay in the barn. Grandpa had Tyler help him remove and replace the boards, fit each so there was almost no space left between them. They then caulked them with cord and pine tar.

Bringing the boat back to the marsh, it was put into the water to swell the boards and create a watertight seal. Most of the ice was gone from around the shores and the sound of the occasional duck could be heard. Soon the migrating birds would be on the marsh.

Mr. Martin gave Tyler $1 for the fox fur. The boy had also trapped a few minks and several weasels during the winter. These the trading post owner also purchased. The boy came home with almost $4.50 for his year's trapping.

"This money should go into your can," Tyler told his grandpa.

"Put it in yours, grandson," the old man told the boy. "We are still in good shape."

After putting the money away, Tyler went out to the barn and dug out sacks of number one traps used for muskrat. Laying them out in front of the cabin, he checked the tripping mechanisms to make sure they were working. Then in a ring of rocks in front of the cabin he built a fire and hung a caldron from a metal tripod. Filling it with water and some oil, he waited for it to heat.

Grandpa came out and had his pipe lit. The pleasant-smelling smoke drifted past the boy. "I thought you had used all the tobacco by now."

"I save some back for special occasions," the old man said.

"This is special?" Tyler asked.

"Come tomorrow we'll be roasting muskrat," Nikolas replied. "It is a sweet meat."

While grandpa pushed the skiff, Tyler would make a dent in the muskrat mound and set the trap. The muskrats liked to carry their food out of the water and eat it on the mounds. While doing so they'd trip the trap, then try and escape into the water and drown. Those that didn't drown would be dispatched with a short club, or maybe now with the squirrel gun.

By evening they had forty traps set. The traps were about a mile along the edge of the marsh. It was getting cool by the time they reached the dock. The skiff was watertight and with the new boards they'd get years of service.

Wil was waiting at the dock and had been waving and calling as he'd watched their slow progress. Tyler noticed that he was wearing the hat. He knew he'd have to shake it off. "How many traps did you set?" Wil asked.

"Thirty-five, maybe forty," Tyler said, smiling.

Grandpa tossed the line to Wil and soon they had the boat tied up. "How's your pa?" Nikolas asked the boy.

"He's been sick much of the winter," Wil replied. "He doesn't seem to be getting much better."

"We got a couple of nice catfish on a stringer at the end of the dock," grandpa told him. "Take them back to your pa when you go."

"Thank you, Mr. Tomas," the boy replied. "He'll like that."

The two boys hung around the front of the cabin and talked. They had a plank leaning against a tree and they would practice throwing their knives and the hatchet. They had outgrown the fort. Tyler was into hunting and Wil was chasing girls.

"Come by in the morning and you can help me check the traps," Tyler suggested.

"I could do that," Wil replied.

"We can split the catch three ways," he offered his friend.

"Do I have to skin mine?" the towhead asked.

"You and me will skin them all," Tyler told his friend. "We should get the planks out."

Leading the way, Tyler headed for the barn. He had over 100 planks to stretch the muskrat furs on. He had cut some cedar blocks and planned to split some more in the next day or so.

Wil stopped near the mare. "You should ride her to school every day."

"The horse is getting up in years and then it would be standing in the sun all day," Tyler told his friend.

"It's just an old horse," Wil replied. "It wouldn't know no better."

Ignoring the comment, Tyler dragged out the sacks of boards. Looking them over in the barn, he found that most were still in good shape. He would use the plank door and the sawhorses to skin the muskrat. He had Wil help set them up in front of the barn.

It was getting near supper when Wil took the fish and headed for home. Tyler watched him, wondering if he'd show in the morning. Often, he would say yes and then not come. Wil always had some kind of excuse. Now that his pa was sick it was easier to find one.

That night supper was side meat and parsnips cooked over the fire in the yard. As soon as it got comfortable, he and grandpa would cook outside on the firepit to keep the heat out of the cabin. They took their meals inside and sat at the table.

"I kind of had a hankering for the catfish, but the boy's pa is sick," grandpa said.

"Nate said he was getting kind of yellow and figured it was his liver," Tyler told his pa. Nate or Nathan did most of the doctoring in Cedar Creek. He'd gotten his training in the army or from books had no real medical school.

The next morning, Tyler sat outside the cabin poking a stick into the dying breakfast fire. The sun had been up almost two hours and it didn't look like Wil was coming. Grandpa came from the barn and looked out at the marsh.

"We best go and fetch the muskrats," he told the boy. "Wil may not want to leave his pa."

"His pa hell," Tyler muttered. "He is just lazy. I even offered him a split."

Tyler sat at the front of the skiff while grandpa pushed it with the pole. The first traps were just a couple of hundred feet from the dock. The boy felt an excitement that came with the beginning of each hunting season. He stood to see the first trap. It was empty.

"You had better kneel down," Nikolas told him. "You're rocking the boat and we'll both end up in the water."

While he'd felt disappointment at the first trap, the next one had been pulled into the water and had a muskrat on it. Pulling the rodent up using the chain, Tyler took the rat from the trap and rubbed his hand down the body, squeezing out some of the water before tossing it into the skiff. The trap was then reset and they moved on.

Three more were found drowned before he had a live one. The rat squeaked angrily as it tried to bite at the boy. A quick rap with the short club took care of it and soon it was lying in the bottom of the boat. As they collected more muskrats the odor of their sweet, musky glands drifted across the skiff.

The muskrats hadn't gotten trap-wise yet and the catch was good. They had 39 rats in the bottom of the boat at the end of the trapline. "We got a good population of the rats and should put another line on the east shore," grandpa suggested.

"I'll get more traps out and we can do that tomorrow," Tyler told him.

Arriving back at the dock, the boy had half expected to find Wil waiting. He was not. Using the metal tub, they carried the muskrats to the barn. The same poles and strings that they used for the duck were hung between posts.

The rats had to be dried before skinning. Fastening the string around one of the front legs, Tyler and grandpa quickly had the muskrats hung for drying. Later today they would give them a quick brush to remove any debris from the fur, then they'd skin, scrape, and stretch the muskrats.

Grandpa stopped for a moment and looked and listened for duck activity in the marsh. "Another week, maybe two we'll have ducks."

While grandpa went into the barn, Tyler went to the pump shed and got a single bit axe, a wooden mallet, and a fore. There was a stump near the smokehouse where the boy placed a block of straight-grained cedar. Using the single bit axe and the mallet, he split the block in half. He then cut each side, leaving the amount needed for stretching the muskrat.

Then, taking the fore, which was a straight piece of iron sharpened on one edge and a with a grip on one end, he placed it onto the cut end of the block. With a few raps onto the fore with the mallet, a slab popped off. Normally the fore is used for making shingles, but grandpa found that it worked well for making stretcher boards for the muskrat.

Grandpa came from the barn carrying the shaving horse and draw knife. This he would sit on and by pushing the treadle with his foot, the lever would clamp the rough shingle in front of him and he would shape it into a stretching board for the muskrat furs. Then he'd use a bung auger and put a hole in one end to hang the fur to dry.

Working together, the two made another 100 boards. It took three days to dry a muskrat pelt, so it they continued to get around 50 rats a day, they would need what they already had and these new ones. Grandpa carried the bench back to the barn and Tyler collected the shavings to use for tinder. He then brought the tools back to the pump shed.

The old man came from the barn with a chew in his cheek. He spat and then said, "I checked the rats and they are ready to skin. We can roast some for our supper."

"I'll get the stone for my knife and be right back," Tyler said, hurrying to the cabin. It would be his job to skin the muskrats while grandpa scraped the fat off, put them onto a board and hung them to dry.

It was the same process they'd used since Tyler was old enough to help. Grandpa would give a quick brushing to the hanging muskrat. He'd then toss it onto the table for Tyler. Tyler would make a slit along the back legs to the tail on each side. Then pushing his thumb through the fur on top of the tail, he'd make a cut. The end of the fur would now be loose. He'd then pull the fur off each of the back legs, ripping it rather than cutting it.

Tyler then put one hand on the head, held the skin flap on the back and pushed the head through, turning the pelt inside out. He would continue to work the pelt off the body and, ripping them off the front legs, he'd pull it to the head. After quick cuts at the ears, eyes, jaw, whiskers and nose, the pelt was off. The process would take just over a minute once the boy got the rhythm going.

Grandpa would take the pelt and slide it over a tapered board leaning against the table, then using a scraper he'd remove the fat without taking the red membrane off the skin. Leaving it inside out, he'd slip it onto a stretching board. It was then stacked at the end of the table to be stretched and hung after all the muskrats were skinned.

Not much was said during the process. Once in a while Tyler would mention, "This one was in a fight." The damage could be seen on the inside of the fur and would decrease the value. After an hour of steady work, the rats were ready to stretch and hang.

Choosing some nice ones for their supper, the rest of the carcasses and the scrapings were hauled away from the cabin. Coyotes, fox, and other scavengers would make short work of them. Tyler was walking to the marsh to wash his hands when he saw Wil coming down the trail.

"You're too late," he called to his tardy friend. "We got the rats skinned and hung."

Tyler was squatting near the water scrubbing the blood and fat off when his 13-year-old friend came up behind him. He had some more words for Wil, but he'd wait unit his hands were clean.

"Pa died today," the towheaded friend told him.

Stopping the washing and letting the water drip off his hands, Tyler slowly got up and turned to his friend. Wil was too young to have lost both his mother and his father. He wished there was a way to take back the words he'd just said. "I'm sorry, Wil."

The towhead shrugged. "They said it was the drinking that killed him. I guess he won't be hitting me anymore." The words were not angry, just sort of matter-of-fact. Tyler saw moistness in his friend's eyes.

"Is there anything I can do?" Tyler asked, fully aware that he had no idea what to do in this situation.

"Kin I stay here tonight?" Wil asked. "I don't want to stay in pa's house."

"Sure. You can stay as long as you'd like," he told his friend, then was ashamed when a thought that he'd have to hide his money can went through his mind.

"I wish we had done a better job on the fort," the boy said, half smiling. "I could stay there."

Grandpa came down to the marsh. He had heard enough to know Hugo had died. "Do you need me to go talk to anyone about making arrangements?" he asked the boy.

"Nate Jones and Pastor Woods are taking care of things," Wil told him, his eyes on the ground.

"Is there money for the burial?" Nikolas asked.

A look of concern flashed across the boy's face and then he said, "Pa drank everything he made at the mill." Then he looked up at grandpa. "He liked the fish you sent to him."

Then Tyler saw a look on his grandpa's face that he'd never saw before. It was a look like he was about to cry. Hell, they were all about to start bawling any minute.

Needing to get away, Tyler said, "I'll go grab a couple more of the rats before anything gets into them." Making a hasty retreat, he headed for the carcasses. Tears filled his eyes and the boy didn't understand why. He had never even liked Hugo. But someone had died and a friend of his was involved.

When he returned with two more rats, grandpa told Ty, "You can roast the muskrats. I'll be back in about an hour." Then grandpa headed into Cedar Creek.

Tyler went into the cabin, gutted the muskrats and added them to the others in the dishpan. He heard Wil come in. "Can we shoot your squirrel gun?"

"Sure," he told his friend. "I just got to put a little salt on our supper." Rubbing some salt onto the muskrats, he shook the extra off and wiped his hands on his pants.

They went just inside the woods and set up a target. Tyler reached into the possible bag and got what he needed to load the gun. The two boys took turns shooting. The familiar smile came back onto Wil's face. It was like he'd been able to forget about his father for a moment.

After several shots, Tyler said, "I best get back and get the fire going. Grandpa will be back soon."

"Can I carry the squirrel gun?" Wil asked.

"Sure," he told his friend. He had never offered to let the boy carry the gun, but today was different.

Six muskrats were roasting over the firepit when grandpa got back. Wil was sitting cradling the squirrel gun in his arms and Tyler was digging some lead out of a block of wood that they'd used for a target.

"The funeral is tomorrow at the church," he told the boys. Then to Wil he said, "You may want to run to your house and get something better to wear."

"These are as good as I got," the boy said.

The muskrats were tasty and the three of them sat around the fire and ate their meal. Grandpa had put on a pot of coffee and they all had some. The boys put in a little sugar.

CHAPTER SIX

Tyler had only been to his folks funeral before, and remembered little of it. Hugo's was a closed coffin affair. The 13-year-old thought that he must have looked pretty bad. There were few tears. It gave the pastor a chance to remind everyone the importance of going to church because you never knew when your time would come. It was unlikely that Hugo had ever gone to church much.

After putting him into the grave next to the church, a meal was served by the ladies. It was very good and even included pie. Tyler figured that that was the only upside of a funeral. The rest was kind of sad.

Wil went to stay with Mr. Martin and his wife. He didn't look too happy about it, but they were family. Tyler waved goodbye and followed his grandpa home. "Where did the money come for the food and everything?" he asked.

"Folks pitch in helping those that haven't got it for themselves," grandpa said.

"Did we pitch in?" Tyler asked. "We didn't even like Hugo."

"It is not a matter of like," he told the boy. "It is the right thing to do. Also, Wil is a friend of yours."

The morning catch of muskrats were hanging in the barn waiting for them when they got home. There were also flocks of ducks landing on the marsh. It would be the busy time of the year. While at the funeral grandpa had made arrangement on two pigs. They would be there tomorrow so Tyler would have to get the pen ready.

It was a week before Wil came by. Tyler was at the pig pen teasing the piglets. He looked up and noticed his friend was better dressed than usual. "Are you going to church?" he asked Wil.

"Uncle Jules gave me some new clothes to wear," Wil replied. "I can't hardly do anything. I might get them dirty."

Tyler thought about the baggy pants with suspenders that he was wearing. "They look good on you," he said, feeling a bit shabby about his clothes.

"There is a dance in town tonight," Wil told him. "I'm meeting Emma there. I wondered if you were going?"

"Maybe I will," Tyler replied. "Grandpa and I got lots to do tomorrow, but it can't hurt to enjoy an evening."

"See you there," Wil said and he headed back up the trail. Surprised that he hadn't stayed longer, the young man went back to teasing the piglets.

As they sat at the fire drinking coffee after their supper, Tyler told his grandpa, "There's a dance in town and I figured I might go."

"You should," grandpa said. "You need to get out with friends."

Tossing the last of his coffee out, Tyler said, "I best get changed."

Climbing up to the loft, the boy went through his clothes. He had two other pair of pants and they both had rips in them. He had been meaning to sew them. Sitting on the cot, he realized that he wasn't going into town. He had nothing to wear.

Climbing slowly down from the loft, he heard grandpa come into the cabin. Seeing the boy in his baggy pants and suspenders, he asked, "Aren't you going to the dance?"

"I changed my mind," Tyler told him. "I decided not to go."

Walking out to the dock, the boy stood there listening to the ducks come in. He realized that his friend's father had died and he went from having nothing to living with an uncle and aunt that had everything. If his grandpa died, nothing would change for him, except he'd be alone and missing his grandpa.

Tyler didn't envy his friend. Wil had lived a difficult life with his pa. When Hugo drank, he could be abusive and Wil would come to the cabin to avoid his pa. He didn't come around as much anymore and the redhead missed seeing his skinny friend coming down the trail. Turning to go take care of the horse and the hogs, the boy realized that maybe, just maybe, he was a little envious of Wil.

The ducks were coming in and Tyler was kept busy with his grandpa. Between trapping muskrat and harvesting ducks, the days were full and profitable. Mr. Arnold would come by every couple of days and always asked him about the squirrel gun. The truth was that during busy times the boy had no time to use it.

By June the flocks had flown through and it was time to give the muskrats a break so they could breed and multiply. Grandpa was weeding the garden when he saw the boy come back from hunting, carrying a rabbit.

"When I finish with the weeding, we should go into Cedar Creek," he told Tyler.

"I do need to get some flint for the squirrel gun," the boy replied.

Hanging the rabbit in the pump shed, Tyler figured to skin and clean it when they got back. Grandpa would probably put it into a soup.

The two of them walked up the trail to Cedar Creek just after midday. Grandpa would always comment on things as they walked, be it a bird, berry bush, or even the grass. "It sure is green right now," the old man told the boy. "Come another couple of weeks they go to seed and then they start to lose color. Before you know it, you got brown grass. I sure do like this time of year."

There were a few wagons parked along the main road and near the tavern. A couple of horses dozed in the afternoon sun. Wil was sweeping the porch of the trading post. Tyler waved to him and called, "It's nice to see you keeping busy."

Wil tossed the broom onto a pile of wood and ran to meet them. "How were the ducks this spring?"

Suddenly Tyler realized that it had been over a month since the two had seen each other. "It was a good spring," he told his friend. "We also got 381 muskrats."

As they stepped up onto the porch Wil said, "You didn't come to the dance. Emma had a friend she wanted you to dance with."

"I got busy," Tyler lied. "Maybe I'll come to the 4th of July dance," he promised.

As they went into the trading post, Jules told Wil to go unpack some boxes. "Helping his uncle and aunt out has been good for Wil," grandpa noted. "Maybe it will keep him out of trouble."

Grandpa had a list of goods they needed and gave it to the merchant. "Put some flint for the squirrel gun on it too," he said.

"I could buy the flint," the grandson told him.

"You been fetching most of our meals with that gun," grandpa replied, "so I figure it should come out of our money."

Then grandpa stopped in front of the clothing. "We ain't got anything that don't have patches in them, so it's time we got some new church clothes. They'll work well for dances also."

New clothes were generally bought at the end of the summer. Tyler mostly needed them because he'd outgrown his. Each got a pair of pants and two shirts. One other thing Tyler got was a belt. Up until now he'd always used suspenders to hold up his britches.

Carrying the items up to the counter, Nikolas settled up with Jules Martin. The redhead walked toward the back where Wil was working. "It is good that you can earn some money working for your uncle."

"It ain't like I got a choice," Wil complained. "He told me that someday I might want to take over the business. As far as I am concerned, someday I will be far from this town."

"On your day off, you should come down to the marsh," Tyler suggested. "We could do some shooting."

"Sunday after church," Wil said, smiling. "It's the only day I get off."

The rest of the week went by quickly for Tyler. Along with the normal chores that kept him and grandpa busy, the fur buyer came to the cabin. For an hour he went through the furs, sorting them based on size and damage. The largest pile, which were the best, got them five cents each. The others went for three or four cents. The man was feeling generous and rounded the catch up to $24.

Grandpa handed $12 to Tyler. "This should go into your can," the boy objected.

"Duck money and hog money goes into the household can," his grandpa told him. "You're of age when you will be needing some money for dances, or whatever."

While grandpa said "whatever," he was probably thinking he should buy a little something for a girl. Confused by the sudden windfall, the boy climbed into the loft, got the can and dropped the coins in. *Maybe I'll look for a hat*, he thought.

Tyler showed up for church wearing his new store-bought clothes and the belt. The pants and shirt were almost too new and the boy was tempted to rub just a little dust on them. Wil noticed the belt and smiled. "Don't you look all grown up," he chided.

After church, the two of them hurried down the trail ahead of grandpa. "I got to change out of these new clothes before we shoot," he told Wil and then he climbed into the loft.

"Can I help you find anything?" he heard his grandpa ask.

"No, I'm just waiting for Tyler," the towhead told him.

Dressed in his old clothes, Tyler climbed down the ladder. He felt frustrated that Wil might have been poking around in their stuff and grandpa caught him. Trying to shake it off, he said, "I'll grab the gun and we can go into the woods. Maybe we'll see a rabbit or squirrel."

The day wasn't ruined by the incident. The two boys managed to shoot two rabbits and one squirrel. They also did a fair amount of target shooting. When they got back to the cabin, Wil asked if he could keep the rabbits.

Grandpa had a soup going at the fire pit and watched as Wil headed up the road, whistling. "That is one happy boy," he said.

"I think he wanted to be able to brag about getting the rabbits for his aunt and uncle's supper," Tyler told the old man.

"Did he shoot them?" grandpa asked.

"He shot one," the boy replied. "I got the other and the squirrel."

"Well, get the squirrel cleaned and we can add it to the soup," Nikolas told him.

* * *

Tyler was up early on July 4th. While Cedar Creek was a small town, it did attract vendors and folks from around the area to its celebration. Red, white and blue bunting hung from the businesses and some of the houses. The town folks cleaned up an area near the creek so games could be played.

The 13-year-old was looking forward to the vendors. One in particular was Roy's Guns, because he not only had guns but he also had a variety of things that were often sought by mountain men: Knives, axes, knife sheaths, moccasins, playing cards, and any number of other items. Right now, Tyler was most interested in a knife sheath that could be carried on a belt.

"We should take the mare with us," grandpa suggested.

"It's not that far to town and one of us would have to walk anyway unless we took the wagon," the boy replied.

"I got the saddle in the barn," Nikolas replied. "We can put it onto the horse and you could ride it in the parade."

Not wanting to hurt his grandpa's feelings, it made no sense to the redhead. The mare was an old horse and his lanky body on the animal would not be very striking. Plus, he didn't want to be in a parade.

His grandpa wasn't dissuaded and soon they were walking towards town leading the saddled horse. At the old man's request, Tyler was carrying his squirrel gun and wearing his new clothes and a belt.

It was near noon when they got to Cedar Creek and the street of the small town was already crowded. "I'm going for a drink at the tavern," grandpa told him. "Tie the horse up at the church."

Tyler felt a bit foolish leading the old mare through the celebrants. He was glad once they got to the church and he could ditch the horse. The boy still had his squirrel gun and feared leaving it in case someone took it.

"That's all right," he muttered after tying the horse. "I'm going to see Roy's and I can say I wanted him to look it over."

"Who you talking to?" a sweet voice asked him.

He turned, blushing, and saw Emma. "I was telling the horse to stay put and I'd be back," he lied.

"It sounded like you were going to see Roy," she said innocently.

"Yes," he said. "I told it I was going to see Roy. I want him to look at my gun."

"Is that the squirrel gun that Wil shot the rabbits with?" she asked. "My mother made a rabbit pie with them and invited Wil to eat with us."

Wil shot the rabbits? he thought, but then said, "Yes, it is. It's a straight-shooting gun."

"Why do you need to have Roy look at it?" she asked.

84

The boy racked his brain for a minute and then replied, "I was thinking of having it converted to shooting with caps."

"You look good with that belt," Emma told him.

"Thanks," Tyler told her, "I got to go now."

Hurrying away, he glanced back and saw her petting the side of the horse. When Tyler arrived at Roy's wagon, the man was showing a customer a powder horn. Much of what was in the wagon could be found or ordered at the trading post, but for some reason it felt special getting it out of a wagon.

A couple of other customers were poking around the wagon, but noticing the squirrel gun Roy turned to Tyler. "You look like a man that wants to talk rifles."

"I got a knife with a 6-inch blade and I need a sheath that will go onto my belt," the boy replied.

"Let me see that squirrel gun," the man said.

"Do you have any sheaths?" Tyler asked.

"All sizes," Roy replied. "Did you ever think about converting this to percussion caps?"

"Ain't caps expensive?" the boy asked.

"Not so very much with the flint and powder you save," the man replied, going into his sales pitch. "I got the parts and could have the gun back to you tomorrow afternoon."

The boy heard himself ask, "How much?" even though he had no intention of having it done.

"Let see now," Roy said, crinkling up his face as he figured. "I'll be in town a week. If I can keep the gun and show the conversion to others, I can save you a couple dollars."

Again, Tyler heard himself say, "I could leave it a week."

"I like you kid," the man said. "How does $7 sound?"

Giving the gun dealer a pensive look, Tyler asked, "Would that include the knife sheath?"

In his hardy voice Roy replied, "I like you. You've got a head for dickering. How does a dollar more for the sheath sound?"

"Okay," Tyler said. "I might need the squirrel gun sometime this afternoon."

"It'll be right here, any time you need it," Roy said, placing it into his wagon.

The boy walked away in a bit of a daze. "What the hell did you just do?" he asked himself. "$8 is a lot of money and the gun shot just fine with the flint."

"Hey, Tyler!" he heard Wil call. "I heard you were going to be in the parade."

"Who told you that?" the boy said, challenging the statement.

"Your grandpa was talking to my uncle," Wil told him, taken aback. "You don't have to bite my head off."

"I ain't been in town 10 minutes and ain't one thing went right yet," Tyler told his friend.

"Well, this will," Wil promised. "There's a guy out of Chicago that come here and he is making ice cream."

Feeling the money bag under his shirt, he asked, "How much is this here ice cream?"

"He'll let you taste it for a penny, but for five cents he fills a mug and lets you keep the mug."

Following his friend to this ice cream place, Tyler saw a man cranking away on something sitting on the tailgate of a wagon. The wagon was painted in colorful designs. Tin mugs hung on the side of the wagon, and by the looks of them they weren't nearly as big as a coffee mug.

"If you boys are after ice cream, it will be done in just a bit," the man told them, sweating as he cranked.

Tyler had never eaten ice cream and wasn't sure what the five cents would get him. Trusting his friend that it would be good, he dug the money out of his leather sack. They were in front of the line that quickly grew as people heard that the ice cream was almost done.

As he finished the man looked out at the crowd. "This here ice cream is a meal in itself. Some folks will pick wild berries and put in it. I hope to have some later this afternoon, and for just a penny more you will have a treat that will last you a lifetime."

Lifting the cover off, Tyler saw the creamy white concoction. It kind of reminded him of butter in the churn and figured he was about to spend a lot of money for a little butter. Following his friend, the two of them got tin mugs filled with a slight heap.

"Bring the mug back and I'll give you a penny," the man told them.

The first lick of the frozen ice cream would never be forgotten by Tyler. The stuff was great! The two boys walked through the crowds to a grove of trees and sat down. "I told you it would be good," Wil said.

"I never had ice cream before," the redhead told his friend.

"I paid a penny for a taste earlier," the boy said. "It was then I knew I had to have some."

Grandpa came and saw Tyler scraping the bottom of the tin cup with his finger to get the last of the goodness. "The parade starts in half an hour," he told the boy. "You need to come with me to the trading post."

Then he looked around. "Where did you leave the squirrel gun?"

"Roy's going to do something to it," he replied.

"You'll need the gun," grandpa said. "Let's go get it."

His hands were sticky from the ice cream and he had hoped to run down to the creek and wash them, but grandpa was insistent. "I'll get the squirrel gun and meet you at the trading post."

Tossing the cup to Wil he said, "You get our penny back."

Tyler ran toward Roy's wagon by way of the church. He noticed that the horse was gone. His mind was racing as he worked the handle of the pump, he rinsed his hands. *It can't be too hard to find a white horse,* he thought. Wiping them onto his pants, Tyler went to get his gun. Roy saw him coming and smiled. "You forgot to get the knife sheath."

"I thought I had to wait until I paid for the gun," the boy told him.

"Normally I would want the money up front, but I trust you," he said.

"Grandpa said I needed the gun for a little bit,"

"No problem," Roy said, reaching into the wagon. "I'll keep the sheath here for you until you get back."

Taking the squirrel gun, the boy trotted towards the trading post. Evidently Roy didn't trust him that much. Relief flooded over Tyler when he saw the horse at the trading post. They had put a bunting over its rump and had some colorful ribbons tied to the halter.

Grandpa was smiling and talking with Jules when the boy reached them. "We got some things for you to put on before you ride in the parade."

Looking at his grandpa, Tyler asked, "What things?" He expected them to bring out another piece of bunting and hang it on him.

"You are going to be the Kankakee Kid in the parade," Jules told him. "We got a buckskin jacket, a proper hat, and a belt for a knife, and a pistol. The boots and pants you got on will work just fine."

All the boy could remember was "pistol." He had never touched a pistol before. They heard someone holler that it was time for the parade. Tyler checked the cinch on the horse and then put on the leather jacket. It was heavy and warm.

He then took the belt they had and put it around the jacket to keep it closed. He stuck an eight-inch knife into the belt, and then he took the pistol.

"Careful with that. It's loaded. At the end of the parade you fire it into the air," Mr. Martin told him.

Carefully he put it into the belt. The leather, flat-brimmed hat fit nicely on his head. Grandpa was holding the squirrel gun. "I'll carry this to the starting area for you," he said, beaming as he looked at his grandson.

Climbing onto the mare, he rode slowly behind Mr. Martin and his grandpa. Tyler steadied himself using the saddle horn. He had ridden a fair amount bareback on the horse, but very little in a saddle. With all the stuff he had on, he was unsure if he'd stay in the saddle. Then another thought came to him. When he shot the pistol, the horse might be spooked.

Resigned to his fate, the redhead decided if it happened he'd just hang on and let the horse take him all the way to the barn. Then there was no way he was going to come back to the celebration and Roy would be glad he didn't give Tyler the sheath.

Grandpa handed him the squirrel gun and Tyler arranged things so he could carry it in front across the saddle. With the reins in one hand and the squirrel gun in the other, the boy had no idea how he'd be able to shoot the pistol. He was starting to get a slow burn at his dilemma.

The parade started and he was going to be the finale. He sat waiting for the others to string out. Tyler began to try and figure out how he was going to shoot the pistol and, in his mind, doing that was the only thing that made the parade worth it.

After he got the horse going, he let the reins hang over the saddle. The horse seemed content to just follow others in the parade. The boy felt some relief. Then he realized that the squirrel gun was cradled in his right arm. He was right-handed and he'd have to shoot the pistol with the left. He moved the pistol around, to make sure he didn't shoot his own personal areas off when he grabbed it. Now he was ready.

Those in front of him were waving to the onlookers, so the redhead did the same, waving and touching his hat. He liked the hat and wondered what it would cost. The crowd cheered as he went by and the boy began to feel kind of proud, representing Kankakee.

Feeling a bit cocky by the end, Tyler turned the white mare around and waved to the crowd. He then pulled the pistol and raised it into the air. He cocked it and squeezed the trigger. He felt the recoil in his hand and the mare tense. "Oh, damn," he said, then he tucked the pistol under the arm cradling the squirrel gun and grabbed the reins. As the horse danced around he spoke softly, expecting it to bolt and leave him lying in a heap on the ground.

The mare settled down as the crowd cheered, "Kankakee Kid!" Tyler's heart was in his throat and he was thanking the lord that the horse didn't run. Dropping the reins onto the saddle, he waved some more at the crowd.

Riding back to the trading post, Tyler handed the squirrel gun to his grandpa and climbed off the horse. His shirt was wet with sweat under the leather jacket. Wil was there and held the horse's reins as the redhead handed Jules the items he had on.

Lastly, he took off the hat and was going to hand it to Mr. Martin. "That's yours, grandson," grandpa told him. "Jules and I had a bet on whether you would ride in the parade. If you did, I got the hat for half price."

Tyler placed it back onto his head. "How about the pistol?" he asked.

Laughing, grandpa handed him the squirrel gun. "Now you're pushing it. A man named Roy came by and mentioned he was going to do some work on the gun for you. You best get it to him."

The horse remained at the trading post and Wil followed as he went to bring the squirrel gun back to Roy's. "What was it like shooting a pistol?" the towhead asked.

"I'm not sure," Tyler said. "After pulling the trigger I was busy trying not to fall off the horse."

Roy saw the two boys coming and stood by the wagon with his hands on his hips. "So, you're the Kankakee Kid," he told the boy. "It will be an honor converting your squirrel gun."

CHAPTER SEVEN

The week was up and 13-year-old redhead went to Cedar Creek to get the squirrel gun. In his pouch he had the $8. Roy's wagon was parked near the creek and he had a troop tent erected behind it. He was poking at his fire and had a pot of coffee brewing.

"Mister, I got the money for the conversion and sheath," Tyler called to him.

"The coffee is almost done if you care for a cup," the man replied.

"I got to get back home," the boy told him. "We got hay to take in for the horse."

Pulling the tarp open at the end of the wagon, Roy reached in and brought out the squirrel gun. Tyler was surprised. While there was no doubt that it was the same gun, but without the pan and frizzen, it looked different, sleeker.

The redhead reached into his shirt for the pouch and fished out some coins. Roy leaned the squirrel gun against the side of the wagon. "What do you shoot with this gun?" the man asked.

"Rabbits, grouse, squirrels, and maybe some ducks or muskrat," Tyler told him.

"Ever want to shoot anything bigger?" Roy asked. "You got bison, bear, and some nice deer around here."

"If I got close, I'd take down a deer," the boy replied.

"I like you son," Roy said. "The way you rode the horse in the parade and controlled it after shooting the pistol showed something most folks don't have."

"What's that?" Tyler asked.

Ignoring the question, the man asked, "Do you have a minute more?"

Turning, he reached into the wagon and brought out a Hawken rifle. "This here rifle was owned by a real live mountain man. With the price of beaver being down, he was on hard times."

Getting the gist of where the man was going, Tyler told him, "I ain't got the kind of money that rifle would cost. I best pay you for mine and be off."

"Just hold it for a moment," Roy told him, handing the rifle over.

The boy took it and noticed that it weighed no more than his, and the barrel looked shorter. He did like the feel of the rifle. It was also converted to caps. "Why do you call it a rifle?" he asked.

"That's because the bore has spiral cuts in it called rifling. It spins the ball, making it go straighter," Roy replied. "That rifle will put a .53 caliber ball into a deer at 400 paces."

"Must not be much of a hunter that can't get closer to a deer than that," Tyler told him.

The man burst out laughing. "You are right there, but say an Indian or a man wanting to steal that white horse of yours was coming across the plain. With the squirrel gun, you'd have to wait till he was 100 paces away before you could shoot. With the Hawken you're shooting four times as far and have time to load twice, maybe three times before he gets to you."

Holding the rifle out for the man to take, Tyler told him, "You best take this and the money I owe you. I ain't got near enough money to buy that long shooting rifle."

The man put his hands on his hips instead of taking the rifle. "Did you ever trade something you had for something a friend had?"

Holding the rifle out made Tyler's arms tired. Putting the butt on the ground, he held the barrel. "Everybody has done that," he told the man.

"Was what you gave in trade worth nothing while your friends was worth money?" Roy asked.

"They were both worth something," the boy replied.

"You got a squirrel gun right there leaning on the wagon that is worth quite a bit," the man said. "Even more now that it uses caps. I am talking about us trading."

"My gun isn't worth as much as this rifle," the boy told him.

"No, it is not," Roy admitted as he went into his close. "But for a few more dollars, we could have a deal."

"I already owe you $8," Tyler said. "I don't have but a few dollars left."

"Well, I can't hardly charge you for the conversion if you buy the Hawken," Roy told him. "Before I done anything to the squirrel gun it would cost, eight, maybe $10."

"It was . . . I was told it was $10," the boy said.

"Let's see," the man said, rubbing his chin. "The Hawken would sell for $20 and I'd have to make some money on your gun, so . . ."

"I thought we were trading not making money on the trade," Tyler said as he realized the possibility of buying the Hawken was within his grasp.

"The coffee is done," Roy said. "Let's have a cup and think on this."

Tyler felt he was trapped. Right now, he wanted the Hawken, but grandpa's talk about not wasting money was strong in the boy. He already had the squirrel gun. More money for the rifle would still leave him with something to shoot vermin and rabbits.

"Coffee sure tastes good this time of day," the man said.

The coffee did taste good to Tyler, but he knew he had to be going. "I'll give you $10 and my gun for the Hawken."

"You got a .53 caliber mold to make balls?" Roy asked.

"I got a .32 caliber mold I will trade, even," the boy told him.

Again, the reply got a hardy laugh out of the man. "Have you shot much?"

"I have," Tyler told him.

"Do you hit what you shoot at?" Roy prodded.

"I do, and in a minute, I am going to give you the $8 and take my squirrel gun home," the boy told him. "I got hay to make."

"I need your squirrel gun and just $13 and we got a deal," the gun seller said.

If the boy spent everything he had in the pouch, he would have the $13, but he knew that his grandpa would never accept him spending that much on something he didn't need. Tyler saw the Hawken slipping away. All he could do was shake his head no.

He finished the coffee and set the cup down. "I appreciate the offer, but I best give you the $8 and head home with my gun."

"You say you can shoot," Roy replied. "I'll make you a deal that you cannot refuse. We'll set up a target and 200 paces. You shoot the Hawken, and if you hit it the price is $10 and your squirrel gun. If you miss . . . hell, I'll knock another dollar off and it will be $12 and your gun."

At 200 paces he had hit a target two, sometimes three time out of five shots. The Hawken shot straighter. Tyler did want the rifle, so with the chance of meeting his price, he said "Yes."

Roy took a board and paced off two hundred steps. Tyler noticed that the steps were a little long and the board was only about 5 inches wide. The boy watched as the man loaded the Hawken. He then put a cap onto the nipple.

"The Hawken has two triggers," Roy told him. "You pull the back one first to set the rifle. Then you pull the front one to shoot."

Knowing he had already tilted the scales in his favor, the man then said. "It takes a real light touch on the front trigger to fire."

Taking the Hawken from Roy, Tyler brought it to his shoulder. The rifle fit him well. He then brought it down again and pulled the rifle to full cock. He was feeling the pressure of the wager. He reminded himself it was just $3 he was risking. Just 60 muskrats.

Then Tyler brought the Hawken to his shoulder again. He set the back trigger. Then drawing down to the target, he touched off the front trigger and felt the rifle recoil against his shoulder and smoke belched from the barrel, but none from a pan. This fact had the boy's full attention and he wasn't even looking to see if he'd hit the target.

"Well, that's that," Roy said.

Tyler looked and the board was still leaning against the tree. His heart sank. He'd have to explain why he spent the extra money on the rifle and his grandpa wouldn't like the fact that he had lost it wagering.

"Your squirrel gun and $10," the man said.

As the words sunk in, he realized that he must have hit the board. "Can I go down and look at it?" Tyler asked.

"You want to rub it in, hey," Roy said, and the two of them walked to the target.

The boy didn't think about the chance he was taking. It was possible that the ball had struck the tree and deflected bark that made the board move. Wanting to see the target could cost him another $3.

He needn't worry. The .53 caliber ball had struck the board near center. As the man looked at the results he said, "It serves me right, assuming that a youngster like you couldn't shoot that well. Go get the mold and we'll settle up."

Hearing those words, the boy smiled and said, "You don't mess with the Kankakee Kid," and was off like a shot, running the full distance to the cabin. Panting for air, he went and got the mold. Coming back out of the cabin, the boy saw his grandpa in the field with the scythe, cutting swaths of the prairie grass. Guilt went through him that made him hurry back to get the rifle.

As he trotted back, he realized that Roy had both weapons and could very well have pulled his tent down and left Cedar Creek with both. He needn't have had the thought, because the wagon was waiting right by the creek when he got back.

Gasping for breath, the money and molds were exchanged and Tyler left with the Hawken, calling "Thank you," as he headed down the trail.

"The Kankakee Kid," Roy said, shaking his head.

* * *

Grandpa didn't seem to be displeased with the new rifle. After looking it over while they waited for supper to cook, he said, "You'll use more powder and lead when you shoot the next rabbit. If you hit the body, there be less left to eat."

The boy sat near the fire, keeping quiet. So far, grandpa didn't sound too disappointed. "Come fall you can shoot me a buffalo. I could use another robe." Hearing this made him feel kind of good.

What Tyler couldn't know was that Roy was very happy with the deal. He had a customer wanting a squirrel gun and had offered to pay $15 for a converted gun, plus the man would need a mold.

Soon the excitement of the celebration was in the past. Hay was made, the garden harvested, another birthday came and went, and as soon as it got cold enough it would be pig butchering time. The fall days found Tyler and his grandpa out on the marsh, after ducks. Traps were set on the muskrat mound and they were checked after the ducks were cleaned.

As the two hunters came back from the evening harvest, they heard crashing in the woods. "I'm betting they were buffalo," grandpa told the boy.

"They tend to graze in the meadow to the west," the 14-year-old redhead replied.

"We've been having fog on the marsh in the mornings," the old man said. "Maybe you should go and knock one down tomorrow."

With the hunting and butchering of a buffalo, a whole day of going after ducks would be lost, but they'd have meat for the winter and the buffalo hide. They had had frost most every night, so the meat would hold in the pump shed.

With the ducks ready for Arnold and the punt gun cleaned for the next hunt, Tyler got the Hawken ready. Sitting at the fireplace, he melted lead and poured a dozen balls. As they cooled, he worked on the blade of his knife with a whetstone.

Grandpa came out of his room with an 8-inch Green River knife. "You may want to sharpen this also."

The next morning, Tyler was up before daylight. There had been a little snow, which made the area look untouched. With luck he'd find the buffalo less than a mile from the cabin, and if grandpa heard the shot, he'd come with the mare to drag the buffalo home. Using the block and tackle mounted in the barn they'd be able to use to raise the animal for skinning. Tyler would gut it where it dropped.

The hairs in his nose froze as the boy walked away from the cabin, the Hawken in his gloved hands. The cold air turned his breath into a cloud. His stomach had butterflies, anticipating shooting the biggest animal of his life.

The meadow he was heading for was over 20 acres and surrounded halfway around by marsh water. As he came out of the trees, he stopped. In the meadow there were over a dozen buffalo. Some were in range of the Hawken, but not within range of Tyler's confidence.

Moving back into the trees, the boy moved as quietly as possible along the edge of the meadow, which would bring him closer to the buffalo. Finally, he felt he was close enough. Grandpa had told him to aim just behind the front shoulder, which would hit the lungs and drop the animal.

Pulling the gloves off, he stuffed them inside his coat. The buffalo were grazing away from him, offering only a view of their hindquarters. For a half-hour Tyler watched the animals. They were heading west toward the far end of the meadow and would soon be out of range even if they turned broadside.

Continuing around the meadow, he maneuvered around branches and trees that littered the forest floor. Tyler reached an area were the marsh extended into the meadow. He had to either go through the water in the woods, or circle back around the meadow and come at them from the other side.

To circle back would take about an hour, and in that time if the buffalo grazed back this way they'd once again be out of range, or offer no side shots. Or even worse, they could decide to leave the meadow.

Tyler wore low-heeled boots that came just below the calf. Deciding to cut through the water, the boy removed his boots and wool socks. He then rolled his pants up over his knees. His long johns would get wet, but he would experience a minimum of discomfort.

With the laces tied together he looped the boots around his neck. The dusting of snow was cold on his feet. Wading into the marsh, he moved along the edge of the trees, trying to keep an eye on the buffalo while not tripping on something under the water.

The bottom was muck-covered and his feet sank in, bringing the water just about to his rolled-up pants. The buffalo had swung back in his direction. He'd made the right decision. One cow stood broadside to him and would have been within range. Standing in the marsh, he was not ready to shoot.

Then there was the splash of a beaver! "Don't you stampede the damn buffalo!" he hissed.

Reaching the far side of the water, Tyler stood, his feet aching with cold as he watched the buffalo. They had moved away again and there was no shot. Running his hands down his legs to squeeze the water out of the long johns, he continued to watch.

Sitting onto a windfall, he pulled on the socks and boots. Tyler wiggled his toes, trying to warm them up. Where he sat was a good place to wait for the buffalo. It was unlikely that they would go into the marsh away from him and should continue around the meadow. That would bring them back to him.

For an hour he sat and watched the wooly animal's graze. Grandpa had recommended he shoot a cow if possible. The meat would be better because the bulls had just come out of rutting and would have used much of their fat reserves up.

Suddenly something disturbed the herd. A few ran, and others turned, snorting. Two coyotes had come into the meadow. At this time of the year, they wouldn't be a danger to the buffalo, but they would still rile them up.

Tyler watched and waited as the standoff went on. The dampness of the long johns was making his legs cold. Soon he'd have to get up and walk to prevent shivering. Three buffalo ran from the herd and then stopped, turning broadside to the boy as they watched the coyotes.

Here we go, Tyler thought as he pulled the Hawken to half-cock and dug out a cap from his possible bag. His fingers were cold and it was difficult to hang onto the cap. Finally, he forced it onto the nipple. Bringing the rifle to full-cock, he brought it to his shoulder.

Pulling the set trigger, he then sighted on the bigger of the cows. With a touch of the hair trigger the rifle fired, sending the .53 caliber ball across the meadow and striking the buffalo. Tyler anticipated the stampede as the shot echoed in the trees. The buffalo that he'd shot took two steps and fell over onto its side. The rest just kept watching the coyotes that were beating a hasty retreat from the meadow.

Remembering that his grandpa had told him to reload the rifle before checking on the downed animal, Tyler poured a measure of powder down the barrel and then pressed a ball wrapped in a patch of oiled cloth into the end of the barrel. Using a piece of antler, the boy pushed the ball a couple of inches in then took the ramrod and tamped it down.

He saw that the other buffalo had come and stood around the downed animal. Tyler removed the spent cap and pushed on a fresh one as he stood and watched the buffalo. He stepped out of the trees, anticipating the herd running away. They did not.

He raised the Hawken and waved it yelling at the buffalo. They turned towards him and snorted, but did not leave. Not wanting to cause them to charge him, Tyler stood helplessly looking at the wooly beasts.

His thoughts went to shooting another, or maybe just firing the rifle. Shaking his head, he muttered, "If the first shot didn't scare them another wouldn't." Then he laughed remembering his first thought. "That would be a hell of a lot of meat!" he shouted at the stubborn animals.

After what seemed like forever, the herd finished grazing, heading back toward the west. Walking out to the downed buffalo, Tyler tapped it with the octagonal cast iron barrel. It was like thumping a mound of dirt. The buffalo had been dead moments after being shot.

The plan had been to gut the animal where it was shot and then drag it to the barn. Removing his coat, Tyler placed it and the Hawken onto the ground. He then took the Green River knife his grandpa had loaned him, deciding how to start. Grabbing one of the back legs, he attempted to roll the buffalo onto its back.

The 1,000-pound beast didn't budge. Trotting back to the trees, the boy grabbed a sturdy branch. Returning to the buffalo, he raised the leg as much as he could and then propped it up with the branch. Stepping back, he said, "Now I am ready."

He could feel the cold through his shirt and thought about putting on the jacket again. Deciding against it, the boy gripped the knife. First, he cut around the butt end and the udder of the animal. He then began to cut from the rear towards the front or sternum. The thick, hair-covered hide was a lot harder to cut than smaller animals or even hogs. He also had to be careful not to puncture the stomach or intestines.

Tyler had planned to cut through the sternum, but after cutting into the cartilage for a short way, he gave up. He then removed the hide near the throat, cut the windpipe and attempted to pulled out the tongue. That did not work out and the boy decided to wait until they got the animal to the barn.

The guts created steam in the cold air. Tyler was no longer chilled and was beginning to sweat. Grabbing the intestines from the back, the boy began to pull them out, making small slits as necessary. He then reached into the carcass and attempted to cut the diaphragm out to get at the heart and lungs. The boy then pulled out whatever would come.

After much effort the blood-covered boy stood looking at the innards of the buffalo scattered around the meadow grass. Set to one side were the liver, heart, and kidneys. By this time, Tyler had hoped that his grandpa would show up with the mare. He began to wonder if he'd heard the shot?

He began to feel a chill from sweating while gutting the animal. Not wanting to get the fat and blood onto this coat, Tyler went to the marsh and washed as much as he could off his hands and shirt sleeves. By the time he was finished, he was beginning to feel very cold.

Leaning the Hawken against the buffalo, he put the coat on. His hands were shaking and he found it hard to work the buttons. Then cradling the rifle in the crook of his arm, Tyler took one more look at the buffalo and began walking back to the cabin. "I hope the hell the coyotes don't come back," he said.

The boy had walked a short distance from the meadow when he caught sight of his grandpa coming with the mare. Having the coat on and walking had done a lot to help warm him up. Tyler knew that if he stopped for a while the cold would again affect him.

"I heard the shot," his grandpa called to him. "I assume you got a buffalo."

By this time, he was close enough to see the results of the boy's efforts. Smiling, he added, "By the looks of you, you have either been in a war or you did some gutting."

"It was a damn big animal," Tyler replied. "I tried to roll it on its back and it was too heavy."

While grandpa didn't like hearing the boy use profanity, he overlooked it. Shooting the buffalo was no small thing. When they got to the meadow, the coyotes hadn't been back and the buffalo was just like he'd left it.

Shaking his head as he saw the scattered entrails, grandpa put the heart, liver, and kidneys into a bag. The branch was still propping up the back leg. Pointing at it, the old man said, "That was a good idea. It helps cool the meat."

Tyler agreed, but that thought had never crossed his mind. Grandpa also noticed that he hadn't gotten the tongue out and told him they'd get it at the barn. It took only a moment to secure the buffalo to the trace straps and then they were on their way to the barn, leaving the carnage of the gutting behind.

Once back it took only a short while before they had the buffalo skinned and quartered, ready to hang for cooling in the barn. Grandpa's quick cuts seemed effortless, removing the hide. With a saw, they'd split the animal down the back. The boy had never seen such a large animal prepared for butchering and marveled at how quickly the buffalo was cut into manageable pieces. The head was set in front of the barn, staring with sightless eyes towards the marsh.

Once back in the cabin, Tyler stood in front of the crackling fireplace, shivering as he stripped down. A cauldron full of water hung on the simple fireplace crane, heating so the boy could wash up. He also had his clothes to scrub.

The two men enjoyed the liver that night while Tyler regaled in the story of shooting the buffalo. Grandpa planned to pickle the heart and tongue. The kidneys were given to one of the ladies in town. She would make a pie out of them for her family.

Fortunately, the boy had no ill effects from the chills he'd endured the day before. When he got up, grandpa was already out of the cabin. Waiting on the table was some more of the fried liver and potatoes.

Eating quickly, and washing it down with a drink of water, the boy headed for the barn. He passed his clothing hanging on the line and felt them. They were frozen stiff. The buffalo head was gone from the front of the barn. The boy found it in the barn, split open with the brain removed. Grandpa was busy scraping the hide.

"What are you doing?" he asked, even though what Nikolas was doing was obvious.

"Getting the hide ready for tanning," the old man told him.

"You took the brain out of the buffalo head," Tyler pointed out.

"It's used for the tanning. The Potawatomi and other tribes have used brain tanning for years." Nikolas told him.

Tyler seldom questioned his grandpa's knowledge and accepted what he said. He walked through the barn, looking at the hanging meat. He had no idea how they could eat it all. That afternoon the question was answered. Two wagons came into the yard. One of them held the two ladies and the other held Jules and Wil. They had come to purchase some of the meat.

Wil came over to his friend, very excited. "You shot the buffalo?" he said. "I didn't think a squirrel gun could kill an animal that big."

It made Tyler realize that his friend hadn't been to the cabin since before July 4th and didn't even know about the Hawken. "I got a bigger rifle now," he told Wil.

"Let me see it," the towhead said. "You never told me you had a rifle!"

The two boys went into the cabin and he handed his friend the Hawken. "Damn, that's a nice rifle!" Wil exclaimed. "Can I shoot it?"

"Not today," Tyler told him. "But come by in a day or so and we'll take it out and shoot."

"Can I shoot a buffalo?" Wil asked.

"I don't think grandpa would want all that meat, but rabbits or maybe a deer would be okay," he told his friend.

Plans were made to do some shooting after church on Sunday. Wil would have that day off from work. The two boys went back to the barn and Tyler saw that only a front quarter was still hanging in the barn. The ladies had taken half of the buffalo and Mr. Martin had taken a hind quarter.

Soon the two wagons drove up the trail towards Cedar Creek. Grandpa went back into the barn to work on the buffalo hide. "I saw the ladies took a whole half of the buffalo," he told the old man.

"They'll be canning a good portion of the meat and be bringing some of it back to us," he told the boy. "Jules was impressed that you shot the animal."

Feeling good about the compliment, the boy said, "Thanks."

"Now go and split some wood and stack it near the cabin," his grandpa told him. "I feel we got some cold weather coming. This afternoon we'll cut up the front quarter."

Life at the cabin was mostly work. Sunday was always a day off to do other things. Tyler headed for the wood pile without question. Using a stone, he touched up the axe and began to split wood. He liked their life on the marsh and never minded work. He had eaten the lady's canned venison before and looked forward to the canned buffalo. This was on his mind as he swung the axe in a fluid motion, sending the wood flying.

CHAPTER EIGHT

Time went by on the marsh and not much changed from year to year. The two of them hunted, trapped, and raised hogs. Tyler had finished school, and every 4th of July he'd compete in Roy's target shoot and won at fifteen. The young man had turned sixteen the past August and Grandpa's health had declined some. Tyler was shooting the punt gun this year.

While he and Wil remained friends, they saw less and less of each other. Their interests had gone in different directions. Wil was talking about marrying Emma, and Tyler's head was still into hunting. Each year since word got out about him shooting the buffalo, he had received several requests to provide meat for local families.

The young man was nearly full-grown at 6 feet, and had added muscle through hard work. As grandpa's age caught up with him, he'd become more dependent on Tyler to keep up the business of trapping muskrat and harvesting ducks.

They had gotten a 10-plate stove for heat and cooking, and had blocked off the opening of the fireplace. Grandpa had cut an opening into the fireplace chimney to accept the stove pipe from the 10-plate. The cold weather would cause the old man's rheumatism to flare up, so he had Tyler bring the shaving horse into the cabin so he could shape some replacement spokes for the buckboard.

Tyler now slept in the back room. It had gotten too cold for grandpa's joints, so he now slept on the cot brought down from the loft. It was set up near the inside wall. At first the young man felt odd sleeping in grandpa's room, but with time it became his.

The mare was also showing its age, and they only used it to pull the buckboard or sled to Cedar Creek. There were no more trips such as to Momence. Tyler had been talking with the hostler at the livery about another horse. Horse flesh was scarce due to the Mexican-American war and the prices were high.

After feeding and watering the horse, Tyler spent a little extra time in the barn to give the animal some company. The buffalo hide that Nikolas had tanned was draped over the sled. The hay had been good the past summer, and the young man figured they'd have some extra left this year. He might even sell it to the livery.

Money meant very little to Tyler. He and grandpa had always had enough and it bought the things they needed. Over the years, the old man had shown his grandson the many ways to earn money around the Kankakee Marsh.

Rubbing the side of the horse's head, he told it, "We got church tomorrow and I plan to use the sled. Grandpa has a hard time walking that far in the cold."

He had been giving the animal extra grain, hoping that it would keep up the mare's strength. Walking back to the cabin with an arm load of wood, Tyler ducked under the header as he went inside. The old man was sitting on the shaving horse. "I would have built the door higher had I known you were going to get so tall," he kidded the grandson.

"As long as I remember to duck, I save getting a knot on my head," the young man replied as he dumped his load into the wood box.

Checking on the soup bubbling on the stove, Tyler gave it a stir. "I figured we'd take the sleigh to church in the morning. The mare needs some exercise."

"You know I can still walk to church," grandpa told him, drawing a thin shaving off the spoke.

"That won't exercise the mare," Tyler told him. "It smells like spring outside"

"Is it the end of March, or is April here already?" grandpa asked.

"It is the last of March," the young man told him.

Grandpa's memory tended to slip a little. Often, he would ask Tyler the same question over and over. Th grandson figured it just gave them more to talk about. "Ducks should be back in a few weeks," the young man told him.

Overnight they'd gotten a little snow, so when the two men rode to church the next morning, they were surrounded by glistening white fields. Even though the winter had been long, it had its moments. The two pulled up at the church and parked with the other wagons or sleighs.

Pastor Woods was near the door, welcoming parishioners. Seeing Tyler, he said, "I have some more books for you to read. See me before you go."

The redhead looked around and didn't see Wil. His friend tended to have a few drinks while playing cards some Saturday nights and often missed church. Jules Martin and his wife were there and nodded to him and grandpa when they came in.

After a sermon on the evils of drinking and being idle, the pastor's wife Bethel served coffee and a yellow cake. This was something Tyler enjoyed, because they didn't do any baking at the cabin. Their meals consisted mainly of soup or something burned in the frying pan.

Jules got Tyler aside and asked, "Is there a way you could have a talk with Wil? I worry about his drinking and card playing."

"Does he still work for you?" the young man asked.

"He does, but everything I pay him he wastes at that damn tavern." Realizing what he'd said, Jules put his hand to his mouth and said, "Those kinds of words don't belong in church."

"I don't see much of Wil," Tyler admitted. "Maybe I can come into town this week and catch him in the store."

"There is a dance at the hall this next Friday," the man replied. "Maybe you could talk to him there."

"I will try," the young man promised.

The community hall had been built last year. The men around town, including Tyler, had spent their spare time working on it. It was a place for town meetings and other gatherings. Before they left to go back to the cabin, the pastor gave Tyler the books. They were on government and the law. While they weren't gripping reading, the young man did enjoy them.

Mr. Martin's request weighed heavily on Tyler. While he and Wil were friends, the young man didn't have much influence on him. Wil hung around with a tough crowd at the tavern and now sported a moustache. His blond hair had darkened some, and he had a lean frame and was a few inches shorter than Tyler.

Spending the week getting things ready for trapping, he thought about the many ways he could approach the uncle's concerns. Tyler knew all of them were lame and would do little to change Wil's ways. While boiling the traps, he had an idea. Maybe Emma could convince him to give up the cards or drinking.

Friday came around and Tyler put on his good clothes. Grandpa saw him and asked, "Is it Sunday already?"

"No, it isn't grandpa," the young man told him. "I'm going to a dance at the hall. I won't be gone late."

"Hall. Where they hell is the hall?" the old man muttered.

Walking in the brisk night air, the redhead had the flat brimmed-hat pulled low in the front to cut the wind. The tuque would have made more sense, but he didn't want to wear something that practical to a dance.

As he reached town the snow crunched under his boots and he had to watch out for the wagon ruts in the frozen slush of the street.

He could hear the sound of music coming from the hall and the windows glowed in the night. Walking in, he felt the welcoming warm air. Removing his coat and hat, he hung them on one of the pegs affixed to the wall. Tyler recognized most folks in the hall, but only knew a handful well. Couples were dancing to the lively music and one of them was Wil and Emma.

Going to the side with a table that had things to eat and some kind of drink, Tyler helped himself to a fried dough and a fruit-flavored drink. Standing near the side, sipping, the drink and enjoying the sugar-covered dough, Tyler waited for the dancers to come off the floor.

When they did, Wil went over to some of the crowd that hung out at the tavern. Emma saw him and came over, giving Tyler a sweet smile and a shake of her brown hair. "I was wondering if you planned to come to the dance," she said.

"I heard you'd be here and wouldn't miss it," he told her. Over the past few years, he'd gotten to know her better and found it easy to talk and kid with her.

"Is the drink good?" she asked.

"Yes, it is," he told her. Then he asked, "Can I get you some?"

"I'd like that," she said.

Tyler noticed that his hand was shaking as he dipped the drink. Bringing her a glass he, figured it was just being worried about what he had to ask her to do. Handing her the drink, Tyler began to formulate what he was going to say.

"I need you to talk to Wil for me," Emma said.

He was thinking so hard of what he was going to say that Tyler almost didn't hear her request. The young man's heart sank. He had no idea what to say that would get through to his friend. Hell, he hadn't even seen Wil much. Maybe he wasn't even a friend anymore.

"What do you mean?" Tyler asked.

"He's hanging around with the wrong crowd and they just steal his money playing cards," she whispered to him. "I was told they play with marked cards."

"Marked cards?" he replied. The young man had no idea what marked cards were. He and grandpa played cards, but he didn't think they played marked cards.

"Yes, and he thinks they are his friends," she told him. "You're a real friend. I want you to talk with him and tell him they are cheating him."

The fiddler started again, and before he could ask her to dance, Emma said, "He's coming. Remember, talk to him." He watched them meet on the floor and start dancing.

His plan hadn't worked and Tyler was feeling pretty blue. Then a voice near him said, "Do you dance, Tyler?"

It was Mary. She had been a grade behind him in school and had been skinny, with teeth too big. She was no longer skinny and her teeth fit her mouth just fine. "Yes, I do," he told her. Taking her hand, the redhead led her to the floor.

The music was moderately fast and the two of them moved around, flowing with the other dancers. Mary's shoulder-length auburn hair swayed back and forth as they turned. Her green eyes sparkled with her smile. They passed Wil and Emma, and his friend noticed them dancing. A quick smile came to his lips as he recognized Tyler.

When the song stopped, Tyler felt invigorated from the lively dance. He and Mary went back to the drink. "I haven't danced like that in a long time," she said, a little breathless.

"Would you like a drink?" he asked.

"Get one for us also, Tyler," he heard and there was Wil and Emma.

The four of them stood making small talk as the fiddler played another song. Emma kept looking at Tyler. He was sure she didn't want him to talk to Wil right now, so he tried to avoid her eyes.

"How's your grandpa?" Wil asked.

"He is getting stiffer all the time and forgets things, but all in all he's doing fine," Tyler told him. "You should come out to the cabin and see him. Maybe we can do some shooting."

"I get Sundays off," his friend said. "Maybe I will."

Tyler noticed that the conversation pleased Emma. He feared whatever he said to Wil would do no good. Then a slower song began. Wil took Emma's hand and headed for the dance floor.

Mary looked at Tyler with expectant eyes, and he held his hand out for her. The dance went okay. The two of them danced closely, but without their bodies touching. The girl came up to his chest and she tilted her head up slightly as they moved across the floor.

The evening was pleasant, and it appeared to Tyler that Mary had decided to stay near him. Several townspeople walked past them smiling, and the young man nodded back to them. One time coming off from dancing, he guided her holding her hand. Reaching a clear area to stand, she continued to hold his hand and he would have had to pull his away to end the contact. Finally, he offered to get her another drink and was free.

There was no doubt that Tyler was enjoying the night. Several times Wil and Emma had joined them between dances. The crowd that Wil had been hanging around had left to go to the tavern. Then the lanterns were lowered for the last dance. It was a slow one, and the fiddle player said, "Take your sweetheart onto the dance floor."

Mary looked up expectantly. Tyler held out his hand. As they glided over the dance floor, he looked over her head at Wil. If he came to shoot this Sunday, he'd have to figure out what to tell him. These thoughts were heavy on his mind, and then suddenly they weren't.

She lay her head on his chest as they danced. He felt the warmth of her body as they moved as one. The feelings going through Tyler were confusing as the barriers he'd lived with all of his life were breaking down. His world was a man's world and women had never figured into it.

The song seemed to go on forever, and while he wished it would end it wasn't so bad dancing like this. When the song finished several of the couples kissed while he just stood, still holding Mary.

Mayor Weems joined the fiddler and said a few words, thanking the musician and those who provided the refreshment. When he asked if the crowd would like to do this again, there was loud applause and some shouts of agreement.

Excusing himself, Tyler went to get his coat and hat. He turned and Mary was still near him, holding her coat. "Would you like to walk me home?" she asked.

"Are your folks still here?" he asked looking around.

"They left some time ago," she said. "I told them you'd walk me."

Surprised, Tyler said, "It will be my pleasure," as he helped her with her coat.

His pleasure or not, the young man knew that he had to escort Mary home. She lived a half-mile in the other direction from the cabin and would have to walk past the tavern on her way. It wouldn't be right to leave a lady alone at night.

Adjusting his hat and saying goodbyes to those they knew, Tyler guided her out of the hall. The night was crisp, and the sky clear with a full moon. Mary was having trouble walking on the rutted street, so Tyler gave her his arm to prevent her from falling.

The moonlight cast shadows onto the remaining snow. From the woods came the sounds of coyotes howling. Just ahead they heard the piano playing in the tavern. A few men stood outside and made comments as they walked by.

"Ignore them," Tyler told her. "It's the whiskey talking."

Mary's folks lived in a small clapboard house with a shed and barn in the back. Her father worked in the mill and her mother did sewing. Tyler expected her to step away as they reached the house, but she did not. Together they stepped onto the front porch.

She turned and looked up at him. "I enjoyed dancing with you tonight."

Tyler knew he had to say something in return. "It was a very nice evening."

Then she said something that the young man was not prepared for. "You can kiss me if you want."

The last thing he wanted to have to do was kiss her goodnight. He had never kissed anyone. He might do it all wrong! Then she tilted her head up and closed her eyes, her lips slightly parted. The moonlight on her face made her look like an angel.

Damn! he thought. Tilting his head down, he gave her a quick kiss. Her lips and nose felt cold and he wasn't even sure if he'd managed to find both of her lips. But it was done. Stepping back, he said, "Thank you. I best be going."

Stepping from the porch, he headed away. Not hearing her door, he glanced back. She was still standing on the porch and she waved. Returning a half wave, he picked up the pace. "I best stay clear from her," he muttered.

Grandpa was in his cot when Tyler got back to the cabin. The redhead's ears, hands, and feet were feeling the cold. Opening the fire box of the stove, he put more wood in, leaving it open for a little light. "With you clanging the stove, how can a man sleep?" a voice came from the cot.

"Sorry grandpa," Tyler said. "I got a chill walking back from the dance."

"Dance? Where was the dance?" he asked, swinging his legs out of the cot.

"It was in town," the young man told him.

"Did you dance?" grandpa asked.

"Yes, I did," Tyler told him. "I danced several dances."

"You best watch them pretty gals," he warned. "That Emma's got eyes for you."

Tyler took a candle and lit it before closing the stove. He then set it onto the table. "It's Wil that Emma's got eyes for," he replied.

The old man in his long johns got the coffee pot from the sideboard and placed it onto the stove. "Some left from supper. We may as well drink it if we're going to stay up and jaw."

Even though Tyler's mind was racing with thoughts of the evening, he hadn't planned to stay up. Then he remembered something. "What are marked cards?"

"You been gambling?" grandpa asked.

"No, but Wil has," he told the old man. "Emma says the men he plays with are cheating him and use marked cards."

Snorting, Nikolas replied, "More than likely they are."

Then his grandpa got up and limped to the back room. Tyler could hear him rummaging in his trunk. It was a place where Tyler was told never to get into. Out of respect for his grandpa he never did. Soon the old man returned with a pack of cards.

"I took these off a man that used them to make a living," grandpa told him. "I figured the man didn't need them anymore."

There was a message there, but the young man chose not to ask. Sitting across the table from him, grandpa shuffled the deck. He then dealt five cards to each. Without picking his up, the old man looked across the table and said, "You got a queen and two jacks. The rest are small."

"How did you know?" Tyler asked, showing the cards.

Without answering, grandpa said, "I got two aces. Odds are I win."

"You haven't picked up your cards," the young man told him. "Maybe I win."

"Maybe so," grandpa said, "but I wouldn't recommend you bet too much money on that hand."

Clearing his throat, the old man said, "This here is a marked deck. On the backs there are marks. They are small but I know what to look for and I can pretty much figure out your hand."

Tyler turned the card over and looked at the backs. Then grandpa pointed at the marks. "I read them when I deal them. That way if you shield your cards, it's too late."

The coffee was warm, and the young man got two cups and poured the strong, stale brew. Taking a sip, the old man said, "That's only one way to cheat. I could also have a confederate that helps raise up the bid. He and I will have signals to know when to raise the bid and get more of your money. You may think its three players, but it is actually two against one."

Then Tyler frowned. "Where did you learn all this stuff?"

"On the waterfront before I met your grandma," he replied. "I did a little drinking back then and a lot of card playing. I pretty much stayed broke. Your grandma saved me."

Leaning back, Tyler looked at the old man sitting across from him. He couldn't remember what he did yesterday, yet his mind was clear from years ago. And then he shook his head. Grandpa a gambler.

The next morning, Tyler woke up thinking about Mary. He thought about the kiss. He wished that he had kissed her better. There had been very little kissing in his life. He didn't ever remember his mother and father kissing, and grandma died before he was born.

Suddenly there was swearing from the front room. Getting out of bed, Tyler hurried out of his room. There was grandpa holding the coffee pot, and he banged it down on the stove. "What's the matter?" Tyler asked.

"Some lowlife come in here last night and drank the rest of our coffee," he snapped.

A look of worry crossed the young man's face. "I drank it grandpa. Last night when I got in late, I had some."

Satisfied with the answer, Nikolas put the pot onto the sideboard. "You should have woken me. We could have drunk it together."

"I'll get the stove going and put on another pot," Tyler offered.

"You get dressed and I will do it," the old man said.

As the young man went back into his room, he heard muttering behind him. "Where the hell did he have to go last night?"

Hurrying to get into his clothes, Tyler found his grandpa sitting at the table. Water was heating on the stove for the coffee. The old man's brow was furled. "Have you been into my trunk?"

"You told me never to open it and I never have," Tyler said.

"These cards are from the trunk," the old man replied.

"You got them out yesterday and were going to tell me about marked cards," the young man told him.

"I must have forgotten," grandpa said, smiling. "The old memory ain't what it once was."

Then for the next half-hour his grandpa taught him about cheating at cards. The story was about the same, but it made Tyler wonder even more about the prior owner's health.

There was still much to do getting things ready for the ducks and muskrat. As soon as the marsh melted along the shore, Tyler would put out the muskrat traps. Then it would only be a few weeks and the ducks would start coming in.

With the help of grandpa, Tyler dragged the skiff near the cabin to fix whatever was needed on it. While he was old and forgetful, the old man still had a good eye on what the boat needed. He pointed out several things, with the main one being sealing the bottom boards. Two side knees also had to be fixed. The old man took over the responsibility of fixing the skiff while Tyler worked on stretching boards and lines for hanging the ducks and furs and setting up the table. He had also taken on all the barn chores.

This year they decided that they would not raise the hogs. While Tyler had to remind grandpa of this several times, with shooting buffalo in the fall there was little time to butcher the pigs. Others would bring pork over for them to smoke, so in exchange he and grandpa would still have ham and side meat hanging in the shed.

Duck hunting was different with grandpa on the pole. Tyler lay alongside the punt gun, and using the paddles would line up on the rafts of ducks. Without warning, the old man would start pushing again and once flushed the whole flock.

Tyler learned quickly to line the boat up and fire the gun. Then there was retrieving the ducks. Standing on his unsteady feet, grandpa would want to get up front to grab the ducks from the water. While these things were a problem, the young man learned to anticipate them and prevent most from happening.

When Arnold came Tyler would be waiting for him. Grandpa would come out and see the man looking over the ducks. "I already checked them over. Just make a count and give me the money."

The first time it happened, the duck buyer was taken aback, but after the young man explained things to him, he would make up some reason he had to check them again. Grandpa still took the money and gave Tyler two cents a duck. He would then go into the back room and put it somewhere. The young man only hoped it was into the trunk.

As far as the muskrats, Tyler would just go after them alone. If grandpa asked where he was going, the young man would tell him "Fishing." The old man seldom asked him if he caught anything when he got back.

CHAPTER NINE

That summer two things happened. The first was that the mare quit eating and quickly got weak. One day while grandpa was napping, Tyler took a pistol that he'd borrowed from Mr. Martin and led the horse out into the woods.

He had thought about digging a hole, but the root-covered ground was hard to dig in, and once you got a foot down, you had water. On the back part of the forty, Tyler spent time with the animal, remembering better times. Then lining the pistol up on its forehead with the white horse's dark eyes looking at him, the young man sent it to the other side.

With tears in his eyes, he piled branches and sticks onto the carcass. The stack got quite large and before leaving Tyler said, "When they come to chew on you, they will have to work at it."

The young man wished that the walk back had been longer. His eyes still stung with tears as he saw the cabin come into sight. Tyler went straight into the pump shed and flushed his eyes and face several times.

He decided he'd not tell grandpa. He could always make an excuse for why the horse wasn't around.

The second thing happened on the 4th of July. Tyler had gone and rented a horse from the livery so he could bring grandpa in on the buckboard. That morning the spirits were high in the cabin as they got ready to go. Tyler was taking the Hawken because they always had a shooting competition.

Tyler suggested his grandpa wait in front of the cabin while he got the buckboard. Rounding the end of the cabin with the buckboard pulled by a bay, the old man seemed confused.

"Where is the mare?" he asked.

"I figured it needed a rest, so I borrowed this one for today," the young man replied.

Climbing onto the buckboard, the old man said, "We got a perfectly good horse to pull the buckboard. It doesn't make any sense to borrow one."

Other than that, it didn't seem that grandpa had a problem with the bay. The town was busy with people. Some had ridden from Momence and Lowell to enjoy the festivities. The redhead parked near the church and put a blanket over the Hawken in the back of the buckboard.

Tyler left his grandpa near the trading post. They had a fine bench to sit on and he'd have folks he knew going by. Then he went into the building and gave the pistol back to Mr. Martin. Looking around, the young man saw Wil in the store. Smiling, he went over. "I figured you'd be spending time with Emma," the young man told him.

Wil gave him a look that said that he didn't appreciate the friendly kidding. Then he seemed to shake it off and the quick smile was back. "I got to work today. We got some fireworks in if you want to see them."

This was the first time Tyler had seen his friend since the dance. Wil had never come down to shoot. The young man told him he'd like to see the fireworks, and wondered how to start a conversation about him being cheated at cards.

The colorful, paper-wrapped rockets were toward the back of the trading post. "We got to keep these away from any type of fire. Even a cigar could blow the whole works," he told Tyler.

"If you're going to be working, what is Emma doing?" the young man asked.

In a weak voice, Wil said, "We're married."

"Married!" Tyler exclaimed. "When was the wedding?"

"Weren't no real wedding," his friend said. "Just us, the pastor, and her folks. She's having a baby. I'm going to be a father."

"Baby?" Tyler asked. "Where are you living?"

"We're at her folks," he replied. "We hope to get a place of our own soon."

Suddenly the full impact of what his friend had said hit Tyler. "You're married and going to have a child! Congratulations," he said, slapping his friend on the back.

A wry grin came to Wil's face. "Thanks. By the way, Mary has been asking about you. She ain't seen you since the dance this spring."

"I been meaning to go see her," Tyler lied.

While keeping busy at the cabin took all his time, when he did have to come into Cedar Creek he'd watch for her, ready to duck out of sight if he saw her. Tyler did like the girl, but what scared him was that she seemed to like him a whole lot more than he did her. That kiss still haunted him.

Leaving the trading post, Tyler went over to the man making ice cream and got some for himself and grandpa. The man had some kind of small paper bowl covered with wax that he served it in. Tyler just licked his, while he got a spoon from Miles for grandpa.

The parade was still two hours away, so Tyler headed for the creek to find Roy's Guns. He stopped when he heard his name. Turning, he came face to face with Mary. "I thought you might have joined the army," she said. "You just disappeared."

"It's our busy time," he tried to explain. "Grandpa and I make most of our money during the past few months."

While not sounding angry, she asked, "Don't you have to come into town for supplies or maybe some more powder?"

"We do have to do that, but they had to be quick trips," he told her. Then a thought came to mind that he wasn't too proud of saying. "I also spent time with our horse. It was sick and I couldn't leave it. I finally had to . . . put it down." Saying it hurt all over but he had to use everything he had.

It worked. He saw tears come to her eyes. "I understand how hard that can be. Last year pa had to put our dog down. I cried for a week."

Mary was dressed in a pretty pink dress and had a pink bow in her hair. She walked up to Tyler and put her arm around him. "I wish you had told me. I could have been there for you."

Been there hell, he thought. *If I could, I'd run the other way right now.*

It was obvious that she planned to stay close and console him. "I have to go and see this guy, Roy. It's kind of man stuff," he told her.

"I'll stay out of your way while you're talking to him," she promised.

Giving her a weak smile, the two of them headed for Roy's, his hand away from his side so she couldn't take it. As they walked, she told him about her summer so far. Her voice was gentle and he did like talking with her, but he had to find a way to tell her he didn't have time for a girl right now.

Roy saw him and called over, "Hey, Kankakee Kid, I was wondering if you'd show. I got to get some of my money back this year."

"You took his money?" she whispered. "And why did he call you the Kankakee Kid?"

"I didn't take his money," Tyler replied. "I just out-dickered him a few years ago. I don't know why he calls me the Kankakee Kid, but he just does." He didn't want to tell her about him dressing up for the parade.

Then, as she promised, she gave his arm a little squeeze and moved away so he could do business.

"Who's the young lady?" Roy asked.

"I sort of ran into her earlier," he said, looking at some stuff in the wagon.

"You best be careful there," the gun salesman replied. "She has her sights on you."

Tyler blushed at the thought. "The Hawken is still in good shape. I made more money shooting buffalo last fall."

"You should join up with some hide hunters. In a month you'd make more money than most men make all year," Roy told him.

"I got my grandpa to take care of," he replied.

"I got a contest going this year for a Colt Paterson revolver," the man told him.

"What's the contest?" the young man asked.

"Anyone that puts three shots in a three-inch circle at 30 yards gets it for half price." Roy said.

"That's no contest," Tyler replied. "A person shouldn't have to pay something to win something."

Reaching into the wagon, Roy brought out the Colt. "Hold this for a minute."

Taking the revolver, the young man looked it over. "It looks nice," he said. Then he noticed that it didn't have a trigger. He was sure Roy was kidding with him.

"It'll shoot five times before you have to load it," the man told him.

"It does all that without a trigger," Tyler said, looking at Roy out of the corner of his eyes.

Laughing, Roy told him, "Pull back the hammer." When the young man seemed confused, the man pointed. "That thing there."

Pulling back the hammer, the trigger appeared. "Seems they could have let the trigger remain out." Tyler noted.

"It has no trigger guard to get caught on your clothes," Roy told him. "The revolver has nice, clean lines that way."

Looking at the barrel, the young man asked, "Kind of small caliber, and there ain't any ramrod. Do you carry that in your possible bag?"

Realizing that Tyler had started dickering, Roy smiled. He'd have a sale before this was all over. "What if I told you that you didn't need a ramrod. The lever under the barrel is all you need."

"How much do they cost?" Tyler asked.

"You interested in a contest?" the man asked.

The young man looked up towards Mary. She was looking on and frowning. It was not lost on Roy. Whispering, he said, "Come back when the little lady isn't with you."

Agreeing, the young man said he'd be back. Getting rid of Mary was more of a problem than Tyler expected. They went for a walk. He bought her ice cream. They visited with her folks, who seemed to like him just fine, and they invited him and grandpa to have a picnic in the park with them.

Finally, they ran into Emma, who wasn't showing yet, and she wanted Mary to come and see something Wil was going to buy her.

Tyler told her he had something he had to do and left her with Emma. The picnic wouldn't be until after the parade and other festivities. The young man hurried back to see Roy. When he got there, he stopped in shock. There was a big sign that read, "Beat The Kankakee Kid in a shootout and get 25% off any gun."

Roy came over with a big smile on his face. "I got a half-dozen men lined up to compete. If you beat them all, I will give you a Colt Paterson revolver. If you beat half of them, you will get half off the revolver."

"What if I don't beat any of them?" Tyler asked.

"Well, then I couldn't hardly give you something off the Colt, but don't be thinking that way," the man told him. "You're a fine shot and shouldn't have any problem beating them."

"And what's The Kankakee Kid thing?" the young man asked. "I was that in one parade years ago."

Shaking his head, Roy said, "You don't understand. Ain't nobody going to want to shoot against Tyler Tomas. But the chance to beat the Kankakee Kid, now that is something they could brag about to their friends."

Tyler just had his first lesson in marketing and he didn't like it. But the carrot that Roy was hanging out was too big. A chance to get a revolver without spending any money. "I ain't going to wear any funny outfit while shooting," Tyler said.

"I do have a shirt that I'd like you to wear," Roy said. "If you think it will hamper your shooting you let me know and you don't have to wear it."

The man went to get the shirt and the young man waited, muttering, "Ain't no way in hell I am going to put on anything he brings back."

Roy came back with a package. Opening it, he took out a white, collarless, linen shirt with some needle work designs on it. There was a red bandana for his neck and a white-crowned hat with a curved brim. Tyler looked at them and had to admit they did look good.

Then Roy dropped the other shoe. "You wouldn't mind if I gave you a little trim of your hair and a shave?" the man asked.

They didn't have a mirror in the cabin, but when Tyler was at the trading post he'd see himself and notice that he was starting to grow a beard. His reddish-brown hair had a wave in it but was to his shoulders. Usually, grandpa cut his hair in the spring, but with rheumatism in his hands he hadn't done so yet.

"Will you leave a moustache?" he asked.

Smiling broadly, Roy said, "Of course I will."

Quickly, Tyler realized that more than a little pre-planning had gone into this contest. Roy had printed posters that he sent some young boys to spread around town. They all touted the shootout with the Kankakee Kid.

The young man was seated behind the wagon when a man carrying everything needed for a haircut and shave showed up. His scissors flashed in the sunlight as he snipped long chunks of the hair. Roy stood a short distance away and said, "Remember, don't make it look like he just got a haircut."

The man mumbled yes and kept cutting. Then there was the shave. This was the first shave Tyler had ever had. The feel of the whiskers being cut by the straight razor was a little unsettling. Before he knew it, the man was done. He sprinkled some good-smelling stuff onto Tyler's hair and rubbed some on his face.

Then the man held up a mirror for the young man to look at. Tyler did not know the man in the mirror. The hair was cut to the bottom of the ear and had the look like it had always been that way. The clean-shaven face with the reddish-brown moustache looked like a picture you'd see on a store package.

Thanking the man, Roy handed him the shirt. "Hurry and get this on. I'd like to have you in the parade and after that I want you to shoot the Hawken."

"Not the parade," Tyler said.

"I'll let you wear the Colt and I got a real nice horse for you to ride," Roy said, smiling. Then a man came in leading a chestnut gelding. It was a handsome horse and had been groomed for the parade.

"At the end of the parade, you turn the horse and fire four shots from the Colt," the man told him.

"I'll have the rifle and what do I do, carry the reins in my teeth?" Tyler said, remembering the problems he'd had in the last parade.

"Why no," Roy said. "You'll keep it in the scabbard, and it won't be your Hawken. I got a new one sighted in and so accurate that you could shoot the wings off a fly at 100 paces."

By this time, the young man was all in and could see no way out. He was shooting a strange rifle, wearing a fancy outfit, and riding in a damn parade. The young man knew he'd never be able to show his face again in Cedar Creek.

With only a little time left before the parade, Roy showed Tyler the shooting range. "I want you to fire this new rifle and make sure that you're comfortable hitting the targets the way you are dressed."

Then another man came over with the Hawken. "This here is Chet. He will be loading the Hawken for you."

"I don't do my own loading?" the young man asked.

"I want you to just concentrate on shooting," Roy told him.

After a couple of shots, the man was satisfied that Tyler wouldn't have a problem hitting the targets. There were shouts that the parade would start in 30 minutes. Chet took the Hawken and put it into the scabbard on the chestnut.

After brushing some hair off his pants Tyler looked up in surprise. Mary had come back down to the wagon and stood looking at him in amazement. If the young man had ever hoped to dissuade her from liking him, he had just eliminated that possibility.

"I hear you are going to be in the parade as the Kankakee Kid," she told him, her eyes large and a light blush on her cheeks.

"That's what I heard also," he said. "Things got kind of strange when I got back down here."

"I guess so," Mary agreed.

"Could you make sure grandpa gets to the parade?" Tyler asked. "I don't think he would even know me if I walked up to him."

"Okay," she said. "You smell really nice."

The young man turned red and thanked her.

What Tyler didn't know was that Roy set up a similar contest in various towns that he traveled to each year. He had spotted the young man's ability with a rifle and had started planning the contest right after. This was the year he decided to do it, and if for some reason Tyler had left the area and he couldn't find another Kankakee Kid, he would have been out the money for the posters and would have tried to come up with another contest.

Swinging onto the chestnut, Tyler felt like a king. The expensive rig was well-polished and adorned with silver. He wore the white collarless shirt with a red bandana. A new Hawken protruded from the saddle scabbard and the loaded Colt was in a holster on his hip.

Roy had him ride around the back of the buildings to the starting point of the parade. Waiting to go, Tyler rubbed the neck of the finest horse he'd ever sat on. He watched as the parade began. It involved Mayor Weems going first riding in a buggy, school children carrying flags, six men playing horns, and all the local businesses carrying, leading, or waving something to bring attention to what they sold. Sheriff Kent stood near the jail, looking on.

As soon as Tyler started, a group of boys ran alongside hollering, "Kankakee Kid! Kankakee Kid!" Cheers went up on both sides of the street. The young man took the hat off and waved to the crowd, smiling from ear to ear. He was truly enjoying the attention.

When he passed grandpa, the old man smiled and saluted him. Mary was standing near him and blew him a kiss. While he could have done without that, he was riding on a cloud. Emma waved vigorously at him as she stood with Wil.

As he reached the end of the slow-moving parade, he turned the chestnut and drew the Colt Paterson. He fired the four shots, into the air receiving a cheer after each one. Anticipating a reaction from the chestnut, none came.

As to prior instructions, he rode to the wagon, followed by a large group looking forward to the competition. Roy stopped the crowd and began his sales pitch. Tyler dismounted and Chet said, "I am supposed to reload the Colt and then you try to hit that target."

Tyler looked up and saw a 10-inch diameter target out at 65 feet. He watched as the man loaded the Colt. Everything Chet needed was in a cupboard near the wagon. While the young man listened to Roy on the other side of the wagon, he waited to shoot.

Standing at the line that Chet pointed to, Tyler pulled the Colt from the holster and took aim. There was a front blade and a notch on the hammer for sighting the Colt. He fired three times, taking a moment to line up each time. He then pulled the revolver and held it out as thought he was pointing with his finger. The young man fired and saw the edge of the target move. He saw a frown on Chet's face.

To the crowd, Tyler heard Roy say, "It sounds like the Kankakee Kid is anxious to start. Line up on the right and put your name or mark on the paper. Let's do some shooting!"

Each contestant would get two shots at the 100-pace target. If they were close to matching the Kankakee Kid, they would get a third shot at 150 paces.

Another helper named Hal would stand down range and checked the targets.

Just before walking out, Chet told him, "Don't be talking with the shooters too much. Just smile and beat them and your job is done."

The young man had never had handlers before, and when he came around the wagon cradling the Hawken, Chet was right by his side. "The Kankakee Kid!" Roy shouted, and the crowd cheered.

The first man who came up was familiar to Tyler. He had seen the shooter at the trading post and in church several times but had never talked to him. The man had the first shot and said, "Don't be taking this personal, young man, when I beat the pants off you."

As the Kankakee Kid, Tyler just smiled. He suddenly realized that he'd be seeing many of them around Cedar Creek after the competition. *So be it*, he thought.

The man loaded his muzzle loader and took aim. Smoke belched from the barrel and the young man saw the target move. Smiling, the man watched as Hal pointed to the hit. While the man started to reload his gun, Tyler took the Hawken from Chet. Pulling it to full-cock, the young man brought the rifle to his shoulder and fired. When the smoke cleared Hal pointed to the hit and the young man's was closer to the center. Handing the Hawken back to Chet to load, Tyler waited for the man to shoot his second time.

For the next few hours, the young man watched and shot with each contestant. Some never hit the target, others would get two shots into the target but the spread was more than the young man's. One lone contestant required shooting at the longer target, and while it was close, Tyler's was closer to the center.

The young man was tired and his ears were ringing by the end of the contest. He had held up his part of the bargain and now he stood by the wagon, waiting for Roy to finish closing deals on the guns.

Several of those he'd shot against came over and complimented his ability. Two who hung out at the tavern sneered, "You wouldn't be that good if another man was shooting back."

With the crowd dispersing, Tyler went behind the wagon and changed into his own clothes. As he came back around, Roy looked up. "You didn't have to change. I was hoping you walked around town a bit."

"I figured it was time for Tyler Tomas to come back," he told the man. "I would like to see what I spent the afternoon working for."

"I got it right here," Roy said. "He reached into the wagon and brought out a revolver equipped with a loading lever. "This came to me from a man in Chicago that only shot it a few times. He traded it for a shotgun that didn't need the steady hand of a Colt."

Tyler took the Colt and looked it over. It was a .36 caliber with a loading lever. It would take the same cap as the Hawken. Then he asked, "Does it come with a mold and a holster?"

"We only talked about the revolver. I do have both of those in my wagon, but they would cost extra."

"How about tools to maintain the Colt?" Tyler asked.

"Those too will cost . . ." then Roy paused. "Hell, you did some fine shooting today so I will throw the tools in with the deal."

It did cost the young man $2 for the mold. The tools were wrapped in a leather piece that had pouches for each tool. It fit nicely into the possible bag with the mold. He stuck the Colt into his waist band, then changed his mind and got it to fit into the possible bag. Tyler left Roy's wagon to find grandpa and there was a picnic to go to.

As he walked away, the young man overheard Chet tell Roy, "We ain't never had anyone that shot that good with the Hawken. He even hit the target four times with the Colt. We should take him along."

The young man was too far away to hear Roy's response but it made him feel pretty good inside. Figuring he'd have to walk around until he found the picnickers was solved when he saw Mary coming to find him.

"I heard the shooting stop and figured you'd be along soon," she called to him.

Grandpa was already seated and enjoying fried chicken when the two of them got to the creek. Mary had taken his hand as they walked together and after his day Tyler didn't mind at all. The two of them filled their plates from the wicker basket and looked for a spot to sit down.

Tyler sat next to his grandpa and took a bite of the chicken. While him and grandpa ate plenty of fowl in their diet, chicken wasn't one of them. The tender, juicy meat covered in the fried crust was delicious.

Swallowing a savory bite, Tyler asked his grandpa. "Did you like the parade?"

Smiling and wiping some food from his moustache and beard, the old man replied, "Yes, I did. Especially the fellow on the chestnut. I forget what they called him, but he was something to look at." Then he asked Tyler, "Did you see him."

Feeling true disappointment, the young man replied, "Yes, I did."

Mary was sitting across by her mother and had heard the conversation. She gave Tyler a weak smile and shrugged her shoulders. After the chicken and cornbread, there was a huckleberry pie for dessert and the meal was washed down with a sweet drink poured into mugs from quart jars.

While Tyler didn't join into the conversations much at the picnic, he enjoyed the family gathering. The young man had wondered if his grandpa would notice the haircut or shave, but the old man never mentioned it.

Wil and Emma came over and sat with them after the meal. Then Mary suggested they take a walk. Her mother said, "Don't be gone too long. You can help pick up and carry the basket home."

Speaking for Mary, Tyler said, "We'll be back to help."

The two couples walked along the creek, tossing a stick or a stone in every so often. Even though the young man knew that Emma was with child, his mind hadn't fully accepted it. She didn't look pregnant. Other ladies in the town who had been with child had had large, protruding stomachs.

The young man thought about marriage. He wondered what it would be like to have a woman waiting for him when he got back to the cabin. Supper would be ready and some of his chores would have been done. Then came the thoughts of how lonely it would be for a wife, stuck in the cabin two miles from anyone. He knew it wouldn't be right.

Then he thought about grandpa. He'd be there some of the time. Then sadness swept through him. He probably wouldn't know who Mary was most of the time. He hadn't recognized him in the parade.

"You're being very quiet," Mary told him.

"I was just . . . just thinking of how nice it is today," he lied to her. "It was a perfect day for the celebration."

"I agree," she said. "I only wish you hadn't had to spend so much time with Roy."

"I'm not," Wil said. "I won a week's pay betting on Tyler."

"They were betting?" the young man asked him.

"Roy was taking bets on you," his friend said, "and so was I. I knew you could beat them other guys."

The couples got back to the picnic and Mary's mother had everything ready to haul. To Tyler's surprise, Wil grabbed the basket and said, "I'll carry this."

Her father and mother picked up the few other items, so there was nothing for the redhead to carry. Grandpa was acting confused with everyone moving around. Turning to Mary, he said, "I best get grandpa home."

There was disappointment on her face. "I understand," she said. Then to her mother, Mary said, "I'm going to walk with Tyler to his wagon."

"I guess it's okay," the woman told her daughter. "Don't take too long. We'll wait for you at the trading post. I promised to bring Mrs. Martin some of the cornbread."

Slinging the heavy possible bag over his shoulder, Tyler took her extended hand and they walked slowly towards the church. Grandpa lagged behind just a little, and took notice of interesting things and pointed them out.

As they reached the church, the bay stood waiting, hitched to the buckboard. Tyler placed his possible bag into the back and grandpa stood back a little. "That ain't our rig, grandson," he said. "We got the white mare. Someone may have moved it or maybe we parked near the trading post."

"No grandpa," the young man said. "The mare has a bad hoof and I borrowed the bay here to bring us to town."

"Well, I could have walked," the old man replied. But Tyler was looking at the confusion on Mary's face. He had just told her that he'd put the horse down.

"I've got to go," the girl said. "My folks are waiting."

"Okay . . ." he said, his voice trailing off. He was about to run after her to explain, when grandpa started to try and climb onto the buckboard and his foot slipped.

"Damn shoes," the old man complained. "I need new soles put on them."

Assisting his grandpa, they were soon heading out of Cedar Creek. The emotional high that Tyler had been feeling was gone, and while he didn't have plans to pursue Mary, he did not want her thinking he'd lied about why he hadn't seen her sooner. Then he accepted that he had lied about why he hadn't been to see her, but about putting down the horse was the truth. Why wasn't life simpler, he wondered.

"Who were those folks that give us the chicken?" grandpa asked. "They seemed nice but I felt funny eating their food."

"I forgot to tell you that they wanted us to join them," the young man told his grandpa. "I went to school with the young girl, Mary."

"She's a nice one," the old man said. "I think she likes you."

CHAPTER TEN

For the next week, Tyler was busy cutting hay. He owed three loads to the livery for the use of the horse. The rest of the hay, he'd need the horse to haul it into the barn. The celebration had left his mind all twisted up, and the methodical swings of the scythe were calming. It relaxed him and gave him other things to think about, like the Colt he had just acquired.

After cutting in the morning, the young man would bunch yesterday's cutting into piles. He'd borrowed a wagon from the livery to load and haul the hay. Glancing back at the cabin from the field, he could see grandpa weeding the garden.

Tired and sweat-covered, Tyler headed toward the cabin in the late afternoon. Grandpa was sitting in front of the cabin, cussing. "What's wrong?" the redhead asked.

"The damn carrots," he said. "It must have been poor soil, because they didn't get any size at all. With the frost coming soon, I picked them. I should have dug them after the first frost."

It was still July, a full month too early to pick carrots. Tyler told him, "Let's wash the dirt off them. We can put them into our soup tonight. At least we'll get something out of them."

"I'll give the tops to the mare," the old man said.

"It's at the livery," the young man told him. "Give them to the bay. I got a load of hay left to pick up and it'll give it more strength."

"Carrots are beautifiers," grandpa said. "Without them this winter we will look awful come spring." Then the old man laughed at his own joke.

One morning, Tyler was getting ready to do some fishing when he heard a wagon coming. Setting the pole on the dock, he walked out to see who was coming along the trail. He saw the bright colors and wording of "Roy's Guns" on the side.

The man pulled up in the yard and climbed off the wagon, "I'm headed to a fair in Ohio," he said with a broad smile. "I wish you were coming with me."

"Is that so you can bet on me like a race horse?" Tyler asked.

"Don't get me wrong," Roy said. "I only do the betting because folks want it."

"You must have done quite well," the redhead said. "I know my friend did."

Smiling, the man said, "You sure could shoot. I ain't never run into anyone with your steady hand. We could take that Kankakee Kid thing across the states."

"I hate to tell you but the Kankakee Kit has retired," Tyler told him. "I got an $18 revolver while

149

you made serious money. My friend bet much less than you and made a week's pay."

"After you left, I dressed Chet up as the kid," Roy told him. "Folks come in and shot, but he could only beat three out of five. I can tell you, with him I made a lot less."

Tyler realized that he wasn't getting his point across and was getting more and more angry at the man. "You should have told me about the betting."

"If I had, it would have only put more pressure on you," Roy told him. "While the revolver was our deal, remember I did give you the tools."

The gun dealer went to his wagon and dug around for a bit. "I don't want you feeling bad about things," he said. Then Roy came back with a black holster and belt. "This here is worth maybe 10 to $12. I want you to have it as a thank you. And if you change your mind about traveling with me, just find out where the fairs are and you'll find me."

The young man stood with the holster in his hand as Roy climbed up into his wagon. "With your skill, we could make some good money." With that he was off. The redhead looked at the holster and felt a little better.

Tyler went into the cabin and got the Colt. Slipping it into the holster, he was pleased at how nicely it fit. The holster had a flap over the revolver. He'd have to think about whether he wanted to remove it or not. Strapping it on, he liked the way it felt. He decided that he'd put the knife sheath on the other side.

Feeling better and better about the deal, he loaded the revolver and walked to the marsh. Picking various things out for targets he shot four times, hitting or narrowly missing each one. Satisfied, he headed back for the cabin. He had work to do.

That afternoon, Tyler brought the last load of hay to the livery. The hostler's name was Edmond. He was dark-haired, with a little white in his beard showing his age. He had a wiry build and a grip of steel.

Together, he and the redhead pitched the load into the haymow. Then brushing the dust off their clothes, they went to the pump to have a drink. "Are you ready to buy the bay?" Edmond asked.

"I'll need a horse come spring," Tyler said, "but if I got one now, I'd just end up feeding it through the winter."

"Your grandpa needs a way to get to town," the hostler reminded him.

"You want too much for the bay," the redhead told him. "I ain't got $75."

"It is good for pulling a wagon or riding. It is 16 hands, or maybe a little more, and you are a tall man."

"I'm not ready yet," Tyler told him. "Maybe we'll have a good season hunting ducks and trapping muskrat and then we'll talk."

"You mean dicker, don't you," Edmond said, smiling. "You best make up your mind, because this horse won't be around long."

Pulling the wagon out of the back doors of the livery bay, Tyler headed back to the cabin. He still had three day's use of the horse and wagon and had hay lying in the field. Driving up near the barn, the young man unhitched the bay and put it into the barn. He did not put it into the mare's stall. It just wouldn't feel right.

There was the sound of grunting and a man chasing something down the trail. *For being out from town, there sure was a lot of traffic coming to the cabin,* Tyler thought.

This traffic he had been expecting. While at the celebration, a man had asked him if he would finish raising two hogs. A grass fire had burnt down his pen and he had been keeping them in a shed, but as they got bigger it was a problem. He offered one to Tyler for raising them and he'd come out and help with the butchering. Then the meat would be smoked in the smokehouse.

Driving them with a small switch, the man brought them up the trail. Tyler went and opened the fence to the pigpen and then helped to guide the hogs in.

"I appreciate you doing this for me, Tyler," the man said. "Jules had told me you had a pen you weren't using."

"Come November we can butcher these pigs, and in the end, you'll have plenty of smoked hams and bacon," Tyler promised.

"I enjoyed seeing you in the parade. You looked good as the Kankakee Kid," the man told him. "I heard you shot quite well too."

Thanking the man, Tyler watched him leave, whistling as he walked back toward Cedar Creek. He had heard that a lot when he made trips to town. The young man headed for the cabin to tell grandpa about the hogs and was pleased to hear the familiar grunting coming from the pen.

With the midsummer work done, it was time to start thinking about trapping muskrat. Grandpa's memory had continued to slide, but so far Tyler had been able to work with it. One of the ladies in town had a husband with memory problems and she had learned to agree and change the subject. It had seemed to work most of the time.

Tyler was boiling traps at the fire pit when grandpa came from behind the cabin. "I was planning to pick a couple carrots for the mare but the damn hogs must have gotten into them. There wasn't one left."

"The carrots will probably make the meat taste better, and the mare is getting kind of fat and doesn't need them," the redhead replied. "Do you want to help me boil these traps? I figured we could cook our supper out here tonight."

The skiff required very little attention before trapping. Tyler had plenty of boards to stretch the furs. As he worked at the fire, he was doing the math in his mind and hoped to purchase the bay. With luck the animal would be in their barn by the end of October.

The heat of the summer was gone and it was mid-August. The redhead pushed the skiff as he checked the traps. He had 70 traps out and would catch 40 to 60 rats a day. It kept Tyler busy skinning and scraping, but he was like a man possessed. Each muskrat got him a bit closer to the bay.

After a successful day, the young man pushed the skiff to the dock. There in front of the cabin talking to grandpa sat Mary and Emma. He noticed that Emma had gotten bigger. Tyler felt some frustration seeing them because he had rats to take care of. He was also wearing baggy britches held up by suspenders and a worn, stained shirt.

When the girls waved, he waved back. Tying the boat up, he saw them say something to grandpa and head down to the water. "We wanted to see the fish you caught," Emma said.

"I got muskrat, not fish," the redhead told them, trying to hide the feelings of embarrassment he felt.

"Your grandpa told us you went fishing," Mary replied.

"There is a lot of that with grandpa," Tyler said.

"Just tell us what to do and we'll help you," Emma offered.

Accepting the fact that they'd seen him and they weren't going away, the young man tried to smile and said, "Sure."

Tyler had made a sledge for moving the muskrats from the skiff to the barn. It dragged a little hard, but saved several trips. It was waiting near the dock. "First I got to toss these muskrats into the sledge, and then I pull it to the skinning table," he told them.

Normally he would toss them from the skiff to the sledge, or have grandpa help, but Emma told him to hand them up and they would toss them into the sledge. Neither girl was squeamish as they took the rats from Tyler and tossed them. Soon the sledge was heaped with muskrats.

"They have a smell to them," Mary said and she rinsed her hands in the water.

"Yes, it is a sweet, musky smell," Emma said.

Then the two of them laughed and said, "Muskrats!" at the same time.

Grandpa stood watching and smiling. "They're taking my job, grandson."

The two girls and grandpa followed as Tyler pulled the 150 pounds of muskrat on the sledge. Reaching the barn, the redhead gasped for breath and took a moment.

Mary walked into the barn and stopped in front of the stall. She looked back at Tyler and asked, "Which stall was the mare in?"

Grandpa answered quickly, "The last stall," he said. "Do you have it picketed out on the grass?" the old man asked Tyler.

"Yes," the young man said, avoiding his grandpa's eyes. "Farther up the field."

For just a moment there was an awkward silence, and Emma gave Mary a stern look. Then she broke the moment and asked, "What do you do next?"

"I've got to hang them to dry for a couple hours before skinning," Tyler explained.

"We'll help you," Mary said, realizing she shouldn't have asked about the horse. Then as fast as he and grandpa hung the muskrats the girls were there with another.

They all went back to the pump shed and washed their hands. "The fur was really soft," Mary told Tyler.

"They're used for collars and other trim as well as coats," he told her.

As they walked around to the front of the cabin, the redhead told Emma, "Wil and I built a fort in the woods when we were young. He used to come up here quite a bit."

"Is that the one that Wil ran away to?" she asked.

"Yes, it's the one," he replied.

"I want to see it," Emma said, and Mary agreed.

"Let me get the Colt," the young man said. "Grandpa's rule is to never go out into the woods without a gun. You never know when supper's going to wander by."

Hurrying back into the cabin, Tyler took the Colt which was hanging in the holster on a peg. He had been too busy since getting the Colt and holster to do much shooting, but he was happy to show them to the girls.

He came back out with the holster around his waist and realized that the pants didn't seem as baggy anymore. He also had the possible bag slung over his shoulder. "I have to load the Colt before we go."

Both girls seemed very interested as they watched him pour measures of powder and work the lever to press in the .36 caliber balls. Emma noticed that he loaded only four chambers. "That's because the hammer rests on the fifth chamber and if I bumped it, the Colt might fire and put a hole through my holster."

You would have thought that Tyler was the funniest comedian in the world the way the two girls laughed. He then took percussion caps from a small, fleece-lined cap box on the belt and used a small tool to put them onto the nipples. Lastly, he put a dab of fat to seal the ball in each chamber.

"There," he said, wiping his fingers on his pants. "We are ready to go into the woods."

"Why did you put on the grease?" Mary asked.

"So sparks from the shot don't set off the chamber next to it," he explained.

"I take it that wouldn't be good," Emma agreed.

With Tyler feeling more comfortable around Emma, he was always closer to her while they were handling the muskrats. As the three of them headed for the woods, Mary made sure she was closer to Tyler.

As they started out, she whispered to Tyler, "The horse is gone, right?"

"Yes," he said softly, "but grandpa doesn't know."

The trail into the woods hadn't been used as much, and several branches had fallen across it, so the three of them had to take care not to trip. Whether they made noise or not was not important. In fact, the two girls kept up a constant chatter as they went.

The fort was the worse for wear, having been neglected for several years. The tarp had been taken off the roof and some of the roof logs had broken and fallen in. Weeds and saplings had grown up around and within the structure.

"That was our fort," Tyler announced. "Wil and I had great plans for it but, I guess we outgrew fighting imaginary Indians and bad guys."

Emma walked up to the wall and looked in. Her face looked sad. "He sat right in here in the cold, afraid to go home."

Mary had moved close to him, and Tyler was tempted to step away, but did not. "I found him after his pa came to the cabin looking for him." The young man almost blurted out the reason his pa was looking for him, but instead said, "I found him and talked him into sleeping in the cabin."

Then Emma gave him a look of compassion. "You were a good friend to Wil. I think he knew it," then added, "I know I did."

Touched by what they were saying, Mary took Tyler's arm and leaned closer to him. Emma wanted to walk a little further into the woods and led the way. They went along the edge of the marsh, weaving in and around the brush. Mary seemed to need help, so the redhead kept ahold of her arm.

Suddenly, Emma stopped. "Look," she whispered. There was a bobcat drinking from the marsh only 50 feet ahead of them.

Letting go of Mary's arm, Tyler pulled the Colt. Emma looked back at him and shook her head no. Slowly the young man slipped the Colt back into the holster. That was a $3 bobcat sitting well within the range of his revolver.

Suddenly it noticed them, and with a hiss it was off, bounding through the trees. "Wasn't that great?" Emma said.

As they started back, Mary whispered to Tyler, "I would have let you shoot the cat."

When passing the fort again, Emma said, "When Wil got home the next day, his father beat him bad. I think that is why he had no tears for his pa when he died."

Tyler remembered seeing the bruise on his friend's face at school. Evidently, he'd talk to Emma about these things, and the redhead was glad Wil had someone to listen. It was apparent his friend had never told Emma why his pa was angry.

When the girls got back to the cabin, they told him they'd better head back for town. While he didn't really have the time, Tyler told them, "I would be happy to walk with you."

While Mary seemed interested, Emma was quick to say, "We know you have work to do with the muskrats. We'll come and visit again sometime."

Mary gave his arm a little squeeze and then followed her friend. Just before the trail turned, they looked back. Tyler was still watching them and they waved to him. Giving a big wave in return, the young man headed for the barn to start skinning. He found grandpa in the barn with a fork full of hay.

"I was going to give some feed to the mare, but it ain't there," he said.

"I brought it to the smithy to have it shoes fixed," Tyler replied. "Would you like to help with the skinning?"

"When did you get the muskrats?" the old man asked.

"This morning," Tyler told him.

"Good," grandpa said, "we can have some for supper."

While Nikolas' memory had slipped, his ability to scrape and stretch the hide hadn't. The young man knew his grandpa would complain about his hands aching tonight, but it was nice working together.

Everything that Tyler did that fall had the goal of purchasing the bay. While grandpa was still taking the money, the young man was sure he could talk him into purchasing the bay. He'd have to tell him about the mare. It would hurt his grandpa, but Tyler knew the pain would be short-lived.

They had large flocks of egrets and other white birds coming in and some hunters shot them for the feathers, but grandpa never let Tyler shoot them. Even now when the young man was kind of in charge, he still left them alone.

Again, in the fall Tyler had to rent the bay for making wood. Each morning after hunting ducks, he took the animal into the woods to drag logs to the pile. First he would drag in the windfalls, and fell those standing dead on the stump. A few live trees had to be dropped to clear a trail for the horse when skidding.

Then with the buck saw, he cut blocks whenever he had time. By the first snow, he had enough wood stacked for the winter. The only time the young man had off was Sunday for church. Mary and Emma were there each week and they would spend time after the service to visit.

Emma was large and the baby would come in the next couple of months. She got her share of odd looks from some of the parishioners who knew she had had to get married. It did not seem to bother her. Emma was excited about having a baby.

As much as he had fought it, Tyler and Mary were getting closer. They were now considered a couple and whenever a function happened, he would walk to her house and escort her. He had become very good at kissing when they said goodnight on her porch. There was a swing, and on nice nights they would sit and talk. Tyler always avoided conversations about marriage.

One afternoon he got back from church. Grandpa hadn't gone because of gout in his left foot. When Tyler came into the cabin he could hear swearing in the backroom and there were sounds of stuff hitting the floor.

The young man ran across the floor and burst through the curtain between the rooms. There he saw grandpa kneeling in front of the trunk with stuff scattered all about. "What are you looking for?" Tyler asked.

"Someone took the damn mare and I got papers on it in this trunk. I don't know where the hell they went!" he said exasperated.

"If someone took it, what good would the papers do?" the young man asked.

"Load your damn squirrel gun for me," grandpa said. "I am going to kill someone."

Tyler sat onto the bed. "Nobody stole the mare, grandpa."

The old man looked at him. "It's gone. I went to feed it and it is gone."

"I had to put it down," Tyler said. "The mare's stomach turned or something. It couldn't eat anymore. I took it to the back of our forty and shot it." His throat ached and the young man didn't know if it was thought of the horse or that the news would hurt his grandpa.

The old man remained on the floor and stared into the trunk. "Oh. I'm sorry you had to do that. We had the horse for a long time." There was a pause for what seemed like an eternity and then grandpa spoke again. "I wish you had told me. I wouldn't have pulled all this stuff out." Then looking around he said, "What a damn mess."

"I'll help you clean it up," Tyler offered.

"No, I'll do it," grandpa said. "I have been meaning to clean it out anyway. I'd like to go and see where the horse is after we eat."

Tyler had the soup warming when grandpa came out. "Half the stuff in the trunk I should throw out," he complained.

"Soup's almost hot," Tyler told him. "After we eat, I'll take you to see where the mare is."

The old man sat at the table, misty-eyed, and said, "You shouldn't have had to put the animal down. I should have done that for you."

The young man was happy to hear these words. They meant a lot to him. He also knew that come tomorrow, grandpa probably wouldn't remember the mare was gone.

The leaves were falling as the two men walked through the woods. "Be snow soon," grandpa said. "I can smell it coming. We'll need to butcher the hogs soon."

Looking at the old man Tyler wondered if he had heard the hogs this morning or if in his mind, they had always had hogs to butcher so they must have them now. Then they got to the pile of branches covering the mare.

Some had been pulled out and an animal had gotten to the horse. Hair and bones showed. "Let's put a few more on it," grandpa said.

After adding some more brush, the two men walked back to the cabin. This trip had been good for Tyler. It sort of gave him closure on the mare. What happen tomorrow would be tomorrow, but today he was at peace.

The air was cool, and the young man put some wood into the stove. He opened the oven door and had thoughts of making biscuits. All they had ever done was warm things, make a ham or bake potatoes. Most of their meals were made in a soup pot.

He looked up when grandpa came out of the back room. He carried a leather bag in his hand. It was obvious that it was filled with coins when the old man placed it on the table. "We got to get another horse," he said. "What do you think one would cost?"

"A horse, maybe $75 and the old harness is pretty dried out, so we should get that also." Tyler said.

"You're of the age that you might need a saddle. Do you think $20 would buy one?" Nikolas asked.

Thought of the rig the chestnut had went through the young man's mind. He could not spend that kind of money. "A saddle would be $40 to $50. And then I'd need a scabbard for the Hawken."

"I think Jules has harnesses," grandpa said. "Of course, a ride to Momence would save you some."

"Mr. Martin had been treating us okay lately," Tyler told him. "We should give him the business."

"Do you think $200 would do it?" the old man asked.

"I think so," the young man replied.

He watched as his grandpa dipped his hand into the bag and brought out coin after coin. Suddenly he asked, "Do we have hay for a horse?"

"I made enough to last two winters," Tyler told him.

"Maybe we should sell some to cover some of these costs," Nikolas suggested.

"Maybe we should," the young man replied, smiling. He wished in the strongest way that his grandpa could be this clear from day to day. Needless to say, Tyler was enjoying this day. It was not getting the money for a horse, it was having his grandpa back for a day.

With the money counted out, Nikolas jotted something down on a scrap of paper and put it into the bag. "I know my memory goes sometimes," he told his grandson, "so I put a note in here about what we done today. If I ask you about the money, just tell me to read the note."

Then Tyler had a thought. That afternoon he dug out a couple posters that he'd taken from Roy about the Kankakee Kid, and on the back he wrote a note. It said: The mare got sick and had to be put down. We bought this horse to replace it. Tyler

Just maybe if grandpa saw the note, he wouldn't be looking for the mare and would understand why the bay was in the stall.

The next morning Tyler was up before daylight and sitting on the dock with the skiff ready. He could hear ducks on the marsh. Using the pole, he pushed the boat in the directions of the sounds. As they grew louder, he stopped and loaded the punt gun.

Three hours later, they young man was back at the dock with 62 ducks piled in the boat. He saw grandpa sitting in front of the cabin. The old man limped down to the dock and said, "I saw that the skiff was gone and thought someone might have taken it. Then I heard you shoot," he said. "You should have woken me."

Tyler began to sort the ducks on the dock before he answered. "I thought of waking you, but we were up late last night and I figured you might like a little more sleep."

"I can sleep when I'm dead," the old man said. "Now let's look at what you got there."

Some time ago, Tyler had discovered he could maneuver the boat and shoot faster alone than with his grandpa. Today he was anxious to purchase the horse before Edmond sold it to someone else.

It was late morning when the ducks were hanging on the rack near the cabin, ready for Arnold to look over. They had another 44 from Saturday night. In the cool weather, the ducks could last three to four days when kept in the shade.

"I have to go into town," Tyler told him.

"I'll put your share onto the table," his grandpa said.

Tyler went in and got the $200 and headed for town. There was no way that grandpa would remember giving it to him, so he said nothing as he left. Edmond was cleaning the stalls when he got to the livery.

"I've had a man come by every day trying to buy the bay," the hostler said. "He even went up to $100."

"I'm here to buy it and will pay that price if you want," Tyler said. He figured that he could wait on the saddle.

Edmond threw the last shovel full of manure into the wheelbarrow and pushed it out of the side door. Returning he said, "I got some coffee on. Let's have a cup."

As they drank the hot brew, the hostler said, "It's a good horse and I gave you a special price because we do things for each other."

"I won't begrudge you asking for the higher price," Tyler told him. "I took all summer coming back to you and you had to feed and care for the animal."

"I appreciate that," Edmond replied. "But I gave you a price and feel I should stick to it."

"Well, I can't argue with that," the young man said, relief flooding through him.

"I need a new harness and a saddle," Tyler told him. "Do you have either that you are selling?"

"Can I get you some more coffee?" the man asked.

Handing him the mug, the redhead waited for his return. As the hostler came back, he said, "Now I got a saddle that I could sell, but it was my brother's. He went east and asked me to hold it for him."

"That's too bad," Tyler replied.

"Well, that was three years ago when he went," Edmond told him. "I ain't heard from him since."

"I imagine it is pretty dried out just sitting in the tack room," the young man said.

"It would have been, but I have been keeping it in top shape for him," he said. "My time alone polishing the leather is worth more than the saddle."

"Are you thinking of selling it?" the young man asked.

"I hadn't until you mentioned needing one," the hostler replied.

"I might be interested in buying it, Tyler said.

"Might?" Edmond questioned him. "Either you are or you are not interested. Hell, it even had a scabbard for that Hawken you own."

The young man looked down at his empty cup. "I am interested and I could give you $40 for the saddle."

"Hell, you ain't even seen it yet," the man replied. "Once you do, you might want to change your offer."

Knowing that the hostler was just toying with him, Tyler made his final offer. "How about $50."

"Well, that is a good price," Edmond said. "I thought you were better than that at dickering. The price I had in mind was $25."

Getting up, the hostler went to the tack room and came back carrying the saddle. It was a fine-looking saddle. The color of the leather showed some age, but it was well taken care off. Tyler blushed when he realized that he'd offered twice what the man would have sold it for.

Setting the saddle in front of the young man, the hostler took their mugs and got more coffee. Returning he said, "Now I got a set of saddle bags that come to me with the saddle. You wouldn't be needing them, would you?"

Wrapping his hand around the hot mug, Tyler said, "I've already spent a good amount of the money grandpa gave me. I still have to find a harness."

"Well, I ain't got much use for the saddle bags," Edmond told him. "How about $50."

There was a look of surprise on the young man's face. "You said $50? That's as much as I'm paying for a whole saddle."

"You misunderstand me," the man replied. "I'm figuring $50 for the saddle and the bags."

As the two sat finishing their coffee there were a few other items like a bridle and bit to haggle about. Once finished, Tyler gave the hostler the money and headed to saddle the bay. Tyler had never owned a riding horse before and was finding it difficult to contain his excitement.

The young man's world up until now had been as far as he could walk to and from in a day, with a rare trip to Momence with the mare. Now he could go for miles in any direction and still make it home before dark.

Thanking Edmond, Tyler climbed into the saddle and rode to the trading post. Mary and her folks were just coming out as he swung down and tied the horse to the rail. She came over and asked, "Did you rent the horse for the day?"

Smiling at her, he said, "Grandpa and I own this horse. I just bought it."

Her father Len came over and started looking it over. "It's a sound animal," he said. "Four, maybe five years old?"

"According to the papers Edmond gave me, it's five years old," the young man told him.

"I've seen it on a buggy before," the man said, "so it should be a good all-around horse."

"I would love to go for a buggy ride," Mary told him.

Smiling at her, Tyler promised, "We'll do that before it gets too cold."

The family headed down the dusty street and the young man went into the trading post to discuss harnesses.

CHAPTER ELEVEN

When winter of 1848 came, the town buzzed with the talk of gold being found in California. Earlier that year, on January 24, a man named James W. Marshall picked up a nugget at Sutter's Mill in Coloma, California. Rumors of the find spread across the country throughout the year and thousands of men were making plans to go west come spring.

All Wil could talk about was going west and getting rich. When Emma had the baby boy, two weeks before Christmas, Tyler and Mary went over to see her. Wil kept the redhead on the front porch talking gold and he had to finally insist that he was going in to see the child.

The labor had been for several hours and Emma looked exhausted as she cuddled the newborn. "What are you going to name him?" Tyler asked.

"The Kankakee Kid," Wil said, laughing. Emma gave him a stern look and said, "I like Adam. He was the first man and this here is my first man child. Adam Tyler Lane"

The young man felt a start hearing his name. "You should make the middle name your father's or . . . maybe a grandpa's."

"Nope," Emma said. "We both agreed on the name. You have been Wil's best friend and I have always considered you a friend. And we want you and Mary to be godparents."

The first thought that came to Tyler was that he and Mary weren't married. Godparents should be married. No doubt Emma was sure it would happen in the near future.

Tyler felt a strong attraction to the scene of the mother and child. He had been seven when his mother and father died. His memories of a family setting were few and he envied Wil having them. As he and Wil left the room, the talk went back to California.

"I plan to go in the spring and I would like you to go with me," his friend said.

Tyler replied, "I've got grandpa to look after and I've been seeing Mary. If I went to California and if I even found gold, it would be two years, maybe more, before I got back."

"Yes, it would be a couple years," Wil replied, "but you would be able to live like a king on the gold you bring back. I read in the paper that gold just lies in the stream bed for the picking."

"I can't go," Tyler repeated. "Grandpa doesn't have many years, and I don't want him to wonder what happened to me when he's on his deathbed."

Such a weak reason made no sense to Wil. The thought of being rich would solve every problem a person could have to face. He continued to pitch the idea of California until it was time for Tyler to leave.

The bay was outside the house, hitched to the sleigh. When Tyler and Mary came out, the young man held out his hand to help her in. They had planned a ride in the country. Tyler had put bells onto the harness and they jingled as the two glided over the snow. Mary sat close to him under the buffalo robe to keep warm.

Emma's baby was the first one that Tyler had seen up close. Others in Cedar Creek had had babies and they had been baptized in the church, but it had been a distant thing to the young man. This one was a child of someone who was close to him, even closer than the girl sitting next to him.

That evening, when Tyler was putting the horse and sleigh up, he felt bad about the thoughts he'd had during the ride. Mary was sweet and had put up with him ignoring her for weeks at a time when they had first met. The young man knew better and that she should be the only one on his mind.

Walking into the cabin, he found grandpa at the table eating soup. "Did you finish the chores?" he asked. "I warmed the soup for you."

"Thank you, grandpa," Tyler replied. He had put the soup to cook when he'd left just before noon. Grandpa had helped him harness the horse to the sleigh. Sometimes a memory would hold for most of a day, other times it was short.

They were invited to the Price's for a Christmas meal after church. Tyler had been told to have something for Mary by Emma, so he gave her a silver cross to wear around her neck. The look on her face when he handed her the small package changed just a little when she saw that it was a cross. Then she kissed him on the cheek and thanked him.

Grandpa would join Tyler on the ice to fish. Most anything they caught they could sell this time of year. They would lay them out onto the ice and freeze the fish. On nicer days, the young man would take the horse out, and wearing the Colt, he'd ride around the edges of the marsh and river watching for rabbits or grouse. He'd become pretty skillful with the revolver, and unless the horse didn't hear him cock the Colt, it wouldn't react much to the noise.

One morning he shot five rabbits, and after dropping two off at the cabin for grandpa to skin, he rode to Mary's. She seemed upset, and when asked what was wrong, Tyler learned that Wil had signed up to go to California with some of the rough crowd at the tavern.

"When I saw her, Emma was crying," Mary told him. "It is like he's forgotten that he has a wife and baby. All he talks about is finding gold in California."

"She has her friends here in Cedar Creek," Tyler told her. "The two years will go by faster than she thinks."

"You wouldn't leave me to go to California, would you?" she asked.

"No, I wouldn't," the young man replied. "Plus, I have grandpa to worry about."

"Is it grandpa that is holding you back?" Mary asked.

Now Tyler knew a trick question when he heard one, and there weren't many ways to answer hers without hurting her feelings. He had never even mentioned marriage to Mary. While he was sure it was implied over time, the young man wasn't ready to take on a wife.

"I have never had a desire to get rich quick," he told her. "Grandpa has taught me many ways to make money enough to be comfortable."

Tyler was sure she was hoping for a yes or no and wanted a no, but his goal was not to hurt Mary. Maybe he'd gotten in too close with her and in time they would marry, but he was only 18 and her 17. There was time.

* * *

On a frigid February morning, Tyler got up and hurried across the cold plank floor and coaxed the ash covered coals to light the tinder. He then put several small pieces of wood onto the fire box along with one bigger one. Shutting the stove door, he checked the coffee pot on top. It had a layer of ice, but should quickly be hot enough to add the coffee.

Hurrying back to his room he pulled on his boots and grabbed his coat. He had urgent business in the little house. He glanced at grandpa's chamber pot and it didn't need emptying. As he relieved himself in the frosty, small building, he suddenly realized the grandpa hadn't complained about him making noise starting the fire.

Walking back around the cabin, the snow crunching under his boots, Tyler went back in. The stove was already offering some warmth. In the dim light he was able to see grandpa curled up on the cot.

"Grandpa. It's time to get up," the young man called. Many a morning they'd gone back to bed after getting the fire going. "Grandpa," he said, walking toward the cot. Then Tyler hesitated. Reaching out, he placed a hand on the old man's shoulder and tried to shake him. Grandpa was cold and stiff. During the night he had gone to be with grandma.

The young man sunk to the floor near the cot. With tearless eyes he stared at the floor in disbelief. The death of the man had been expected for the past couple of years, but he'd always believed that they still had time.

Just the other day they had been talking of taking the sleigh out as soon as the cold spell broke. Maybe they would go to Momence. Tyler had told him he'd like to go to that café again and have two hot roast beef sandwiches. Grandpa might not have remembered the time, but he laughed.

Feeling numb inside, Tyler finally got up and added coffee to the boiling water. Pouring a cup, he sat at the table and stared at the cot. "I hope you found grandma," he said. "Let ma and pa know that I'm doing well."

He continued to talk about things and how he appreciated the old man taking care of him and teaching him so much. Then he added wood to the stove and noticed that grandpa's blanket was back off his shoulder. Going over to the cot, he picked it up and covered the man. Then the tears came.

Tyler sat on the edge of the cot for the longest time, unable to stop crying. Crying helped the ache in his throat but the pain in his heart was almost overwhelming. Throughout the morning Tyler wandered around the cabin. He tried to eat something, but had no appetite. He tried to think what he should do first but his mind was clouded.

Then he thought about the horse. It needed water and to be fed. Putting his coat and tuque on, he headed for the barn. He'd forgotten his gloves, so he stuck his hands into the coat pockets. The horse stood in the stall with a blanket over it to keep off the frigid air.

It felt good to be out of the cabin. For a moment the scene of his grandpa's lifeless body was not in front of him. He led the horse to the marsh and chopped a hole so it could drink. As he led it back to the barn, the animal nuzzled him playfully. Tyler thought, *The world of the horse hasn't changed.*

After giving the animal some grain and hay, the young man spent a long time with the horse. He told it that grandpa had died. He told it about the mare that had been in the barn before. Finally, his feet began to get cold and he had to return to the warmth of the cabin.

As he stepped in, there was the familiar warmth that hit him and the sound of the wood snapping as the fire lapped around it. The smells were the same, but to Tyler, everything had changed. The young man knew what he had to do. The body had to be taken to Nate Jones. He acted as the undertaker as well as offering medical help. Then he needed to go see the pastor.

This routine was the same for anyone who wanted to be buried in the small church cemetery. If it was summer, Tyler could have dug a grave near the cabin and buried grandpa, but during the winter things weren't that easy.

Carefully the young man removed the blankets from grandpa. Tyler noticed that he'd wet himself during death, but that wouldn't matter now. He rolled the body onto its back and straightened the legs. Tyler had feared that grandpa had frozen during the night and he wouldn't be able to straighten him, but it hadn't happened.

After the January thaw the snow had melted down to about a foot and had remained there, so Tyler was sure he'd be able to use the buckboard to haul the body. In the sleigh, he'd have to sit grandpa up next to him and wasn't sure he'd be able to handle that.

Again, he was out of the cabin to hitch the horse to the buckboard and the reality of the death was hidden. The young man led the animal and wagon to the front of the cabin. The horse snorted great clouds of fog into the brisk air.

Entering the cabin, Tyler looked at the long john-clad body of his grandpa. He'd need some clothes for the burial. Getting a shirt and pants, he went out and put them in the buckboard. He then went back in, leaving the door open, and stood near the cot.

"Let me get your coat," he said and reached for it on the peg. Again, the tears came. He sat on the cot with uncontrollable sobs. There beside him was the last link to anything Tyler knew as family. He now had none.

Finally, gathering himself, he picked up the body and was surprised how light the man was. Since he had been a young boy, his grandpa had always appeared big to him. This vision had not changed in Tyler's mind over the years. Moving carefully so as not to bump grandpa's head, Tyler got him into the buckboard.

He then went in and got the coat to put over the body. Carefully he closed the cabin door. As he drove towards town, the young man looked back and it looked like grandpa was peacefully sleeping. It gave Tyler a small amount of comfort.

Nate Jones' house was a short distance beyond the trading post. Tyler pulled up in front and hoped the man was there. Before he got to the door Nate came out and asked, "Your grandpa?"

"Yes," Tyler replied.

"Pull the buckboard around to the back," Nate told him.

There was a large shed in the back that the man used for preparing and storing bodies. On occasion, if folks wanted, funerals could be held there. Nate had a canvas stretcher with the side poles separated by two short poles. He placed it into the buckboard next to grandpa, and with Tyler's help they got him on.

They then carried him into the building and placed the stretcher and body onto a table. Nate covered it with a sheet and the two of them went back outside. "I have some coffee on. Let's go in and get warm," Nate suggested.

Sitting in the kitchen, the man served Tyler some type of sweet bread and the coffee sweetened with sugar. The young man hadn't eaten and realized that he was hungry. "I will take care of things from here," Nate told him. "With the ground frozen we will have to wait until spring to bury your grandpa."

Then there was a knock on the door and the pastor came in. Evidently, he'd seen Tyler come in with the body in the back of the buckboard. "I will prepare your grandfather and we can have a viewing for friends if you'd like. Then he will be kept here until a spring thaw."

"At that time," Pastor Woods said, "We will have a gravesite service."

In just over an hour, things were settled. In two days, there would be a viewing and service at the church, and then come spring another service at the burial. Tyler got the shirt and pants from the buckboard for Nate. He'd have to come by tomorrow with grandpa's frock coat.

The young man didn't want to go back to the cabin and drove the buckboard to the livery. Edmond gave his condolences upon learning that grandpa had died. For a good part of the afternoon, they visited. Tyler, was going to leave the horse and buckboard at the livery and was given the offer to stay at Edmonds. He declined the offer, but did feel some comfort that the man had asked.

Not wanting to go back to the cabin yet and realizing that Edmond had work to do, Tyler left and went to let Wil and Emma know. The two-month-old baby was squalling and Wil was staying as far away from the bedroom as possible.

Wil said he was sorry and then asked, "Does that change your thoughts about California?"

"No, I'll stay right here," he told his friend.

Emma cried for Tyler and held him. It was almost as bad to see her hurt as it was to lose grandpa. While she meant to comfort him, he ended up comforting her.

"Have you told Mary?" she asked.

"Not yet," the young man told her. "I came straight here after dropping the horse at the livery."

"You'll have to let Mary know," Emma told him. "She will be hurt if you wait too long."

This Tyler didn't understand. It was his grandpa who had died. But he trusted Emma and left the house to tell her.

Mary didn't cry. Her eyes and face told him how sorry she was for him. "Come and sit," she said. They sat on the settee and she put her arms around him and said, "I am so sorry. I wish there was something I could do to take away the pain you must be feeling."

She was warm and comforting. Tyler felt like he was in a very weak position with her. He knew what she wanted to hear and he was not going to say it. Instead, he said, "Wil wants me to go to California, but I am not going."

"You saw Wil?" she asked. "Was Emma there?"

"Yes, and the baby," he told her. "It was fussing."

Mary sat up and said, "I am glad you're not going to California."

He felt something wasn't right and asked, "Did I do something wrong?"

"Oh no," she said. "I was just surprised you didn't come here first."

"Their house was on the way from the livery," Tyler explained.

"Of course," Mary told him as she took his hand. "I am glad you let them know."

"There is a viewing the day after tomorrow," he told her.

"Will you be coming for me?" she asked.

"It will be at 11, and I will be here at 10:30," he said. "Is it okay if we walk?"

Holding him close, she said softly, her warm breath caressing his ear, "Yes, it is."

He remained at Mary's until late afternoon and then left so he could be back at the cabin before it was too dark. He declined the offer to spend the night and headed on the two and a half mile walk home.

It felt good to be away from everyone with just his own thoughts. People act differently when they receive sad news. That doesn't make anyone wrong, but Tyler guessed that there must have been a proper way that he should have done things and even as he trudged through the foot-deep snow, he wasn't sure what it was.

The cabin was cold and dark when he got back and had the stillness of death. The stove was cold, so he had to use tinder and a flint to get it burning. He then lit a candle and placed it onto the table. All this time while lighting the stove, his eyes had avoided the cot.

There were dirty dishes on the table and sideboard, and the cot or his bed hadn't been made. The young man was thankful that he'd left the horse at the livery. That was one less thing to think about.

Tomorrow, he had a full day alone at the cabin. He could walk into town, but he didn't want to see all the sad faces.

Grandpa had always told him that it wasn't good to dwell on things. Tyler remembered when his folks had died, they had picked up and left only days after the burial. If you were always looking back, the old man would tell him, you will never see what's coming ahead.

The young man looked around the cabin. The inside began to warm and he removed his coat. Hanging it onto the peg near grandpa's made him pause, but did not bring tears. Then Tyler realized other than a bite or two of the sweet bread, he hadn't eaten all day.

Breaking the ice on the water bucket, the redhead, scooped enough into a pot to boil rice. It would be simple and satisfying for his meal. While the water was heating, he looked at the cot. Only hours ago, his grandpa had lain there as he slipped away. On a small stand near the cot was his grandpa's pocket watch and the green tin containing tobacco. On top of the can sat the pipe.

Fighting down the emotions he felt, Tyler broke the cot down and put it into the loft. The hay tick, he carried outside in the dark and dumped the contents onto the garden spot. There was a cold wind that cut through his wool shirt and he hurried back into the cabin.

After eating the sweetened rice, Tyler sat at the table, knowing it was late and he should try and get some sleep. There was too much going through his head and he knew he wouldn't be able to. The first worry was paying for the funeral. The young man assumed that there was enough money in the trunk, but they had spent a lot on the horse and gear at the end of last year.

Feeling that he'd better check before bringing the coat and things to Nate, Tyler went to the back room. He made his bed, which had been neglected. Then he opened the steamer trunk. He knew it would reveal all the secrets of his grandpa's life.

There was a stack of books. On the cover were two dates, except for the top book. It had only one, which was the date grandpa started using it. Inside the books were blank pages that Nikolas had made entries of sales and expenses. With each dated transaction there was a note of what it was and the remaining total.

Tyler smiled when he saw the entry for the horse and other items. After that expense they still had $853.42. The entries after the horse purchase had become random, with several sales missing and some of the expenses.

One thing he did notice was that grandpa included every payment that went to the young man, no matter how small. Paging back, the young man stopped at the one that had squirrel gun on it. He stared at an entry and his eyes smarted. It read: $2 to Arnold for squirrel gun.

Wiping his eyes with his sleeve, the young man now realize that Arnold had not reduced the price, but rather his grandpa had wanted Tyler to have the gun and bag. If he had taken the time to go through all the books, much of his and grandpa's lives would have unfolded. A quick glance at the cover dates showed that they even went further back to England.

There were decks of cards, including the marked deck in one corner. They brought a smile to his face. Tyler took out other keepsakes in the trunk which must have had meaning to the old man, including a tea tin he'd gotten while still in England. So far there had been no money. With everything out of the trunk, Tyler saw that the inside bottom was two sections.

Removing one half, he saw legal papers such as the property deed, certificates of birth and papers needed when he'd come to America. There were also three paintings, which Tyler assumed were of grandpa's parents and Nikolas as a small boy. Another he recognized as his ma and pa. She was holding a baby that must have been the redhead. Another was of a cottage with a barn and a horse, which must have been grandpa's home in England.

The young man understood why they had been kept in the trunk for safe keeping. If they had been displayed on the wall, the sunlight, temperature swings and fly specks would have taken their toll on the irreplaceable items.

Lifting the other half of the trunk exposed the money. Several small leather bags containing coins were neatly stack and labeled with the amount. One bag had "England" on it without any amount. Looking into the bag, Tyler saw that they were English coins. No doubt there were memories tied to them, now gone with grandpa.

Wave after wave of emotions went through Tyler as he looked through the trunk. Worries over money for the funeral were gone. The young man took $50 in coins out of the trunk and then put all the items back in carefully. Closing the lid, he buckled the leather straps.

Carrying the candle, Tyler went back into the front room. After putting some more wood into the stove, he looked at grandpa's watch on the small stand. It was after four in the morning. It would be light in three hours.

His eye lids had become heavy and the young man finally felt he could sleep. Opening the curtain between the two rooms, he blew out the candle and felt his way to his bed. Kicking off his boots, he lay on top of the covers and was quickly sleeping.

Tyler's dreams were not peaceful. He was looking for something and couldn't find it. He was walking in the forest and something was following him. He couldn't find the squirrel gun. Maybe Wil had it. Unsure of where he was, he looked around. Which way was the fort? His friend would be there. Grandpa had told him to never loan the gun to anyone. Wil must have it.

Then he woke. Light was coming in through the window in the front room. He was cold so he grabbed for the blanket and pulled it over himself. For just a moment, he listened for grandpa to start the stove. Then the memories of yesterday flooded back. For a long time, the young man stared at the roof poles above him. As long as he stayed in bed, he wouldn't have to face the reality that grandpa and the cot were gone.

Finally, the chill of the cabin forced him to get out of bed. "Ain't nobody else to light the fire," he muttered. Then he felt bad for saying it. He was sure that grandpa would have rather been here to light the fire than lying in Nate's shed.

Once he had the fire going, Tyler put the last of the rice with a little water onto the stove along with water in the coffee pot. He kind of wished that the horse was in the barn so he'd have something to do. The pocket watch said it was just after 8 a.m. He didn't plan to make the trek to town until near noon.

The young man took the tin of tobacco and the pipe to the table. He put the stem into his mouth and blew the bits of tobacco out of the stem and bowl. He then tapped it on his palm like he'd seen his grandpa do a number of times. Taking some of the tobacco out of the can, he smelled it. It smelled almost good enough to eat.

He stuffed it into the pipe and held it up, looking at the pipe from the light of the window. Grandpa liked to sit outside in front of the cabin and have his pipe in the evenings. In the winter he would smoke in front of the fire place, and when the stove had come, he'd move to the table. He had often talked of making a rocking chair so he could sit in it near the stove and smoke.

Taking a splinter from the kindling, Tyler lit it and then put the pipe into his mouth. Holding the flame over the tobacco-filled bowl, he drew on the pipe. His mouth filled with smoke and he took a breath, preparing to draw again.

The acrid smoke burned his throat and lungs as Tyler began to cough violently. With tears in his eyes, an awful taste in his mouth, his throat torn by the smoke and coughing, the young man gasped for breath.

How his grandpa could enjoy smoking a pipe was a mystery to Tyler. At this moment the smoke didn't even smell good. Feeling a bit-light headed, the young man figured he needed some fresh air. Placing the pipe onto the table, he grabbed his coat and tuque and headed for the wood pile.

The fresh cold air of winter brought relief to Tyler as he swung the axe and split enough wood for the day. He had about three armfuls to carry in and he headed for the cabin with the first. Pushing open the door, the smell of the pipe smoke hit him.

Tossing the wood down near the stove, he grabbed the sideboard as emotions went through his body. He fought back the tears. The smell of the tobacco had brought back the pain of the loss of grandpa. The smell was his smell that had greeted Tyler every time he came in on winter evenings.

Collecting himself, the young man went out and brought in the next two armloads of wood. He decided that he'd light a bowl now and then, but had to remember not to inhale. The smell of the pipe, would bring back good memories.

Nate was waiting for Tyler when he arrived early afternoon. The young man apologized for being late, but the truth was he had put off going into town as long as he dared. He knew he'd meet people and have to endure their condolences.

"What will everything cost?" Tyler asked.

"Your grandfather was a good friend of mine and he even paid part of Hugo's funeral," the man said. "If you help me get the coat on and lift your grandfather into the coffin, I think $30 would be fair."

Tyler would have liked to shout out, *I'll give you $50 if I don't have to help,* but instead, he thanked Nate and followed him to the shed.

There was a small fire going in the shed stove. It was enough to keep grandpa from freezing, but not enough to keep his body warm. Tyler tried to avoid looking at the body. He could still feel the weight of his grandpa against his arms when he'd carried him out.

The shirt and pants were already on the body, as well as some boots. The two of them got the coat onto the lifeless body and after a little fussing with the coat, hair and beard, Nate was satisfied. The two of them then lifted grandpa into the coffin. Tyler had his feet and wondered where the boots came from.

Nate saw him looking at them. "They are a pair of mine," he said. "After the funeral I'll take them back off before closing the coffin. If you would like him to be buried with boots, bring a pair when you come in next."

"Grandpa liked to kick off his boots and warm his feet near the fire in the evenings," Tyler told him. "I think he'd be happier without boots."

"I've arranged for men to carry the coffin into the church and then help me get him back here after the service," Nate told him. "After that I will prepare him for his winter stay."

Tyler knew that the preparation was to cover him with lime to prevent the smell. It had to be done and the young man just nodded. With this finished, it was time to go. The man invited Tyler to come in and have something to eat. The young man nodded and hoped there was some more sweet bread.

The funeral was well-attended considering that the day was cold, with blowing snow. He had arrived at 10:30 to pick up Mary. Her folks joined them as they walked to the church. Emma and Wil were already there, and when she saw Nikolas lying in the coffin she broke into tears.

After a half-hour of giving those attending time to pass by the coffin, Pastor Woods gave what Tyler considered a very comforting service. He knew what songs grandpa liked, and some of those were sung. At the back of the church Bethel had cakes and such for folks to eat with some type of drink or coffee.

Some of the attendees went back to the coffin before leaving and everyone had something to say to Tyler. Their faces were long and there was sadness throughout the church. It would take a long time before Sunday service would be had without Tyler's memories of this day.

Mary's parents had something waiting for supper after the service. Wil, Emma, her parents, and the Martins came. Someone had a bottle of whiskey and the men sat near the fireplace and had a drink. Tyler had tasted whiskey before and accepted a glass, even though it was not a favorite. In time that would change.

There were a few tears from Emma during the evening, but soon the conversation was lively, with stories of funny things many had done with grandpa. The sound of laugher cleansed the sadness out of the house.

Tyler woke the next morning, sleeping in a strange room. He had been feeling kind of tipsy after a couple of drinks and had accepted the invitation to spend the night. Mary had sat with him for a while after everyone had left, and she had asked him if the silver cross meant they were engaged. He remembered that he had nodded.

A hardy breakfast of pancakes and fried ham was served. There was maple syrup and freshly churned butter to slather over the cakes. They sat at the dining room table and the conversation was kept quite general, with only one reference to the day before, at how well-attended the funeral had been.

It was nearly noon when Tyler was able to get away from the house. Len had asked the young man help him cut ice to store in his ice house on the coming weekend. Tyler promised he would. Each winter many of the residents of Cedar Creek cut ice off the marsh to keep things cool in the coming summer.

Mary followed him out and stood in the cold on the porch, and kissed him several times. Now that they were engaged, the kisses were more intense. As he walked away, Tyler waved and felt a great deal of relief knowing that finally he could just be himself and not act in the way others would expect.

Edmond was happy to see him and was kind enough to talk about anything but the funeral. He didn't want anything for boarding the horse. Tyler insisted that he finally took a dollar. The bay was hitched to the buckboard and stood restlessly, ready to go.

After Tyler climbed onto the wagon, the hostler said, "Like you, your grandpa was a good man."

Smiling at Edmond, the young man replied, "He was."

During the trip back to the cabin he had mixed

emotions. For the past couple of days, he'd been around folks and had not been given much time to think about his loss. Now he would be alone and had to face this fact. Getting married would solve that, but Tyler wasn't ready for that. It was enough that he was engaged.

CHAPTER TWELVE

March was a cold month and kept everything shut down. One snowy day, Wil showed up at the cabin as restless as ever. "This damn snow is putting us behind," he complained. "Me and the boys should already be in St. Louis, joining up with others going to the gold fields."

"St. Louis?" Tyler asked him. "I heard that most folk start out at Independence, Missouri. That's again as far as St. Louis, Sheriff Kent told me."

"We heard that too," the frustrated Wil replied. "By horse it will take over a week to get to St. Louis and then another week to Independence. Our horses will be all worn out just going to get started."

"Pastor Woods gave me a book written by a man that went west to a place called Willamette Valley. In there it said that they had to wait until the grass grew enough so their animals would have something to graze on," Tyler told his friend. "When the snow melts, you got another month before there is any amount of grass."

His friend did not want to hear this kind of talk. "Hell," he said, "all it takes is some places on the sunny side of a hill and you got grass right quick."

"I heard most folks are taking wagons so they can carry supplies for the trip and other needed things that they'd want when they get to California," Tyler told him.

"For a man that ain't even going, you sure do know a lot about what's needed," Wil snapped.

Realizing he'd pushed his friend far enough with his comments, the redhead asked, "Have you put together the things you will need?"

"Most things," Wil replied. "My uncle will let me take one of his horses, but I still need a pack horse."

"They are getting hard to find," Tyler replied.

"I did find a good mule over in Lowell," his friend told him. "Only I am a little short on money to buy it."

Wil hesitated for a moment and added, "You know, with the baby and all, I got to have some for Emma."

"You're still working for your uncle," Tyler replied. "You could earn enough for a mule in two weeks."

"Well, I got to get it really quick before someone else does," Wil told him. "I was hoping you could give me the money. You know, with what your grandpa left you. It would only be a loan and when I come back with the gold, I'll pay you . . . double even."

It had surprised Tyler when Wil had come through the storm to visit, and now the purpose had been stated. The redhead had never talked about the money grandpa had, but they had always lived frugally and most folk assumed there was a passel of money squirreled away somewhere in the cabin. He also noticed that his friend was still wearing the $3 hat.

"Grandpa and I didn't spend much, because we didn't have much money," Tyler told him. "We had to buy the bay when the mare had to be put down. To do that we had to save a bit here and there for years. He didn't leave me much more than the cabin and the marsh out front."

Whether or not what Tyler said was the truth, he knew that his friend was still wasting what he earned at the tavern. Just maybe if Wil didn't have the money to go, he'd have to stay back, and that would be good for Emma and the boy.

"Have you looked everywhere?" Wil asked. "I could help you try and find where he hid it."

"I have cleaned this cabin from top to bottom and been through everything in here," Tyler told him. "While I wasn't looking for money, I didn't find any, either."

"Damn, I was hoping . . ." Then, without finishing the sentence, Wil put on his coat. "I better be heading back to the trading post."

Tyler sat at the table and watched his friend leave. In his heart, he knew that Wil would be going to California, by hook or by crook if necessary. The young man only hoped that he didn't hurt too many people in the process, especially Emma.

With the wind howling outside, Tyler lay in bed thinking about the visit and about the money in the trunk. Suddenly, he realized that he had to do something with the bags of coins. He thought about places he could hide it. If there had been a bank in Cedar Creek, he'd put it there, but the closest bank was in Crown Point.

He woke in the morning with an idea. In the back room there was a trapdoor that opened to a root cellar. Tyler planned to bury most of it under the potato bin. A stone had come loose near the base of the fireplace and the mortar had come out behind it.

Grandpa had always planned to fix it, but time had gotten away on him. It would have enough room to hide coins from one sack with only a bit more digging. By the end of the day, the trunk was empty of sacks of coins and they were all in safe places.

With his money safely hidden, Tyler put on his coat and tuque. There was more ice to cut from the marsh. Several men were supposed to come down and the young man was hoping that the snow wouldn't keep them home. There was good ice now and warmer weather around the corner.

As Tyler walked out onto the ice, he could see several horse-drawn sledges waiting to be loaded with the blocks of frozen water. They had iron tongs to handle the blocks. The young man got there and was glad the men hadn't started cutting.

A coarse toothed saw with a handle on one side was used to cut the blocks. The tricky part was not slipping into the water when retrieving the floating ice. This was Tyler's job. Gripping the blocks, he'd drag them away from the hole and then other men would bring them to the sledges.

The young man enjoyed the work and the camaraderie with the townsmen. Some said this was their last winter cutting ice and they were going to

California come spring. Many were good men and would be missed in Cedar Creek.

Once the ice was cut, it would be put into well-caulked log buildings, or ice houses with the walls insulated with sawdust. The blocks would be packed in clean sawdust from the mill. If done right, the family would have ice throughout the summer months. At midday some town ladies came out with hot coffee and some meat pies to eat.

It was early April when the warm breezes came and the ice on the march began to thaw. Tyler rode the bay into Cedar Creek to purchase some lard to boil his muskrat traps. Jules Martin was in the back putting away a shipment of goods.

"Where's your help?" the redhead called to him.

"The damn kid up and left with the riffraff from the tavern yesterday," Jules replied. "I don't think Emma even knew until he walked out the door."

As the owner came up to the front, Tyler said, "I imagine they were in a hurry to go and get the gold."

"Hell, gold," Jules snorted. "They had to get out of town before folks that had things taken noticed them missing. I dread to think about what I'll find gone."

"Did Wil ever get the mule?" the young man asked.

With a look of disgust on his face, the man said, "I probably won't know until someone comes here looking for one that was stolen."

"It could be that Wil figures to pay everyone he hurt when he comes back with all that gold," Tyler said, sarcastically.

"I told Emma that if her ma would watch the baby, I could give her some hours in here," Jules told him. "You know she's with child again, and he left without leaving her two bits."

"Another child?" Tyler asked.

"About two months I think," the man said.

The young man was floored. Wil came to borrow money and never mentioned that Emma was pregnant. Had he claimed it was for her, Tyler would have given him money. Probably enough to have bought the mule.

"I need some lard to boil my traps," he told Jules.

"I got just the stuff you want. It's a bit rancid, but the traps won't care," the man said, chuckling.

With the discounted lard in hand, Tyler left the trading post. He knew he had to go and see Emma. Stuffing the package of lard into the saddle bag, he climbed onto the bay. Then he hesitated before riding to Emma's. *I best go and see Mary first,* he thought, having learned after his grandpa had died.

Mary was working on the garden with her mother. She looked up and shaded her eyes from the sun as he rode up. "This is a nice surprise," she told him. And then to her mother she said, "Tyler and I are going to have a cool drink."

This was not going to be a quick visit, Tyler realized. Swinging off the bay, he said, "A cool drink would be nice."

He waited for her on the porch. In the distance, he could see Emma's house. Nobody was stirring around it. Mary came out with two glasses. It appeared she had spent a moment tidying up. She handed the young man a glass and sat close to him.

"You must have been coming to the trading post," she observed. "You have your work clothes on."

"I came to get something to boil my traps when I was told Wil had left for California," he told her.

"So that's why you came to see me?" she asked.

"I was in town and wanted to see you," he said, tasting the drink.

Mary seemed satisfied with his answer. "Have you heard that Emma is going to have another baby?"

That question just might be a trap, Tyler figured. She had probably seen him looking at her house. "Mr. Martin mentioned that and about Wil leaving. Have you seen her since he left?"

"I have been meaning to, but mama wanted to get started on the garden," Mary told him.

"After we drink these, we should walk over and make sure she is okay," Tyler suggested.

Looking over at her mother first, she replied, "I think we could, but it will have to be for just a minute. I don't want to leave mama working alone in this sun."

Leaving the bay tied to the porch rail, the two of them walked over after Mary promised her mother that she'd be right back. There was the smell of baking bread as they walked up to the house. The door was partly open to let the heat from the stove escape.

"Mrs. Wilson," Tyler called. "It's Mary and I. We come to see Emma."

The lady came to the door, her gray-streaked hair tied in a tight bun. "Emma is down sick today," she said.

"Could we see her for just a minute?" he asked.

Mary whispered beside him, "Maybe we should let her rest."

"Okay," her mother replied, opening the door all the way to let them in. "She and the baby are in her room."

Tyler noticed that the woman's eyes were red, like she had been crying. No doubt the sadness of Wil leaving. It would have been little difference than when a man went off to war. One never knows if they will make it back.

Moving ahead of Tyler, Mary knocked lightly on the bedroom door. "Tyler and I have come to see you," she said.

"Come in," a weak voice beckoned them.

Emma and the room were a mess. The only thing that showed a sign that it had been taken care of was the baby in its bed. Her bed was disheveled and there were clothes scattered about. A broken flower vase lay shattered in the corner.

The girl's eyes and nose were red from crying and her brown hair hung uncombed. She had on some kind of nightgown and a robe on her lap. "I'm sorry but I am a mess," she said in a hushed voice and pointing at the baby.

Mary knelt near the bed and put her arm around the stricken girl. "You need help," she said, and then to Tyler, "You go out and wait. I'll take care of this."

Banned from the room, Tyler stood in the parlor. "Come have a seat in the kitchen if you can stand the heat," Mrs. Wilson told him.

Sitting at the table, the young man did not mind the heat. He was surrounded by the wonderful smells of baking. "I understand Wil left yesterday," Tyler said, making conversation.

"Left, hell," the woman replied. "Oh, I am sorry. I shouldn't talk like that, but he makes me so mad."

"Wil does have that ability to do things that upset people," the young man replied.

"He took her money, food from the cupboards, and some of Hank's clothes," Ruth told him. "Who knows what else he took from the barn. Hank will have to check when he gets back from the mill."

Speaking guardedly, Tyler said, "I was told that Emma is with child again."

"Yes," she snapped. "He did manage to do that before he left."

Then, like a switch was thrown, Ruth said, "I got some warm bread and butter. Would you like some?"

"I would," Tyler said, breaking into a smile. "I would like that very much."

As he was finishing his second piece of bread, the young man heard the bedroom door open. Emma came out dressed and cleaned up. Not much could be done with the red eyes and nose, but they were even a bit better.

The two girls sat at the table with Tyler. "It is very warm in here," Emma said. "We should sit on the porch."

"With this tasty bread, I hadn't even noticed the heat," Tyler said. Then to Ruth, who was leaning against the dry sink, he said, "Thank you for the bread, Mrs. Wilson."

"You come in anytime you smell it baking," she told him.

Mary sat next to Emma on the porch swing while Tyler took a chair to the side. "You look some better," he told her.

"She has had a very hard day," Mary said in a scolding voice. "Not only did Wil leave, but she has been having sickness in the morning."

"Thank you," Emma told him. "I am glad you both stopped by today. I couldn't even get out of bed this morning."

The visit on the porch didn't last too long before Mary said, "We best let you go and have some of that good smelling bread your mama made. I'll be back later."

With that, they got up and left. Tyler managed to touch Emma's hand and mouth the words, "We'll talk," as they left.

Getting back to Mary's, Tyler stayed near his horse. "I best be going. I want to get the traps set this evening and still have lot to do."

The girl came close and tilted her head back for a kiss. As he kissed her, they heard her mother Helen said, "That's enough, you two. You just came from seeing what that kind of activity can do."

Mary giggled at her comment. It appeared she enjoyed being caught kissing a man by her mother. "We know how to behave," she assured her.

Tyler was glad to be riding back to the cabin. Wil had left and there was sadness at the Wilson home. He appreciated that Mary was a good friend to Emma, but he had hoped to spend some time with the abandoned girl.

Trapping and hunting ducks kept the young man busy for most of April and May. He would clean up for church on Sundays and visit with Mary. Emma missed two Sundays before she came back to church. Lots of folks in Cedar Creek were angry at Wil and the others who had left for California. They had stolen what they couldn't afford to buy. Mostly small things, but they were noticed.

Arnold came to purchase the ducks and geese regularly and would bring news about the gold strike. Thousands of men had picked up and left their families with hopes of getting rich. Some had promised to send for the wives and children once they had enough gold. The truth was, many would not be heard from again, due to illness, accidents, and murder, not to mention the distance.

Tyler hoped for the best for his friend. Wil had his problems, but the redhead believed much of it was due to his father's drinking. Tyler wasn't against drinking. He often would be offered a drink when invited to supper at Mary's. On cool nights drinks would be had in front of crackling fire in the parlor.

On warm nights it was on the front porch, catching the evening breezes blowing toward the marsh.

Another thing the young man had picked up was smoking the pipe. He had learned after the first try not to inhale. The act of filling and lighting the pipe, and then the sweet smell of the smoke, brought back comforting memories of his grandpa.

Having a girlfriend, rather a fiancé, created a new shaving discipline. After a few missed cuts, Tyler got the knack of trimming around the moustache. Instead of getting a haircut twice a year, he now went every other month to a man in town who had a small shop in the front of his house.

Saturday night was bath night, and if he had business in town other than church, there would be washing up before going. A walk or ride into town always meant a visit to Mary's. The mistake of not doing so only happened once.

Laundry became a regular thing, rather than when the clothes got too stiff to wear, and with some things like a work coat, it was worn until it came apart. It seemed to the young man that he was always heating water to wash something, whether it was himself or his clothes.

Tyler was cleaning the horse stall when he heard voices. There was no doubt it was Mary and Emma. Tossing the last shovel full onto the wheelbarrow, he pushed it out the rear bay door to the pile. Not seeing him in the barn yard, they went to the cabin, calling his name.

Parking the wheelbarrow and hanging the shovel onto its pegs, the young man headed for the cabin. "I'll be right there," he called to them.

His freshly washed long johns and some other clothes were hanging on the line behind the pump shed. Quickly he grabbed the damp clothing and took them into the shed. He noticed that his dirty hands had left prints on the washed clothing.

A quick cleanup at the pump, followed with running his fingers through his hair were all he could do to prepare for the visit. The two ladies were looking toward the marsh when he came around front. "I was just doing some chores in the barn," he explained.

"Emma and I would like to take a boat ride on the marsh," Mary announced.

"It will take me a bit to get it ready," Tyler told her. "Why don't you sit in the shade near the cabin."

Mary reached out her hand to be guided to the cabin. Taking her hand, Tyler walked to the bench. Thanking him, she sat and the redhead headed back to the pump shed. He had two boards that fit onto supports in the boat for them to sit.

As Tyler went down to the skiff, he could hear them talking and laughing, anticipating being on the water. Putting the boards into place, he climbed onto the dock. The young man had planned to go fishing after his chores, and had the pole and a tin of worms near the boat. Smiling, he placed then into the skiff.

"It's ready," he called to the ladies.

Standing by, he handed each of them into the boat. Emma was already showing slightly under her dress. She sat on the small platform at the bow. Mary took one of the seats near the back to be near Tyler.

With the help of the ladies, they cast off, and using the pole Tyler guided the skiff onto the water.

"You put a rod into the boat," Mary said. "Are we going fishing or are we going for a slow ride on the marsh?"

"Both, I hope," the young man said.

"I love fishing," Emma blurted out. "When I was young, my papa had a boat and we would go fishing after church."

There was just enough breeze to keep the party comfortable, and yet the water was calm. They saw blue and white herons, ibis, and egrets. Swimming in the water were muskrats, beaver, and otters. Emma squealed when she saw a muskrat. "We helped you with them!"

For an hour they slowly went through the marsh, enjoying the inhabitants and the numerous plants and flowers. To keep their attention on the water a fish would jump ever so often in quest of an insect or attempting to avoid another predator.

Circling around, Tyler finally reached one of his favorite fishing spots. Letting the skiff float, he got the fishing pole baited and offered it to Mary. "Let Emma fish first."

Sitting back on the stern, Tyler kept the boat from drifting and enjoyed watching the two ladies as they impatiently waited for the cork bobber to go down. It finally dipped and Emma shouted, "I got one!"

Fishing in the shallow marsh, the pole just had a line tied to the end and the hook and bait were dropped into the water. When something was caught it was just lifted into the boat. Emma had a plump catfish, and as it landed onto the bottom of the skiff,

Tyler warned them, "It has barbs that can sting you, so let me take it off."

It was a good fishing spot, and soon the worms were gone and the ladies had caught a total of nine fish. They had one bass, two northern pike, and six catfish. Tyler had made a stringer out of some sticks and a piece of line. The fine catch hung in the water behind the skiff as the young man pushed the boat back to the dock.

Both Mary and Emma claimed that they had caught the biggest one, and both were so excited that Tyler feared that the narrow skiff might overturn. Once back at the dock Mary said, "We should fry some of the fish right now."

"Yes, lets," Emma said clapping.

"I have a better idea," Tyler told them. "I will get a fire going in the pit and clean the fish. Then we can broil them outside and make a fine meal."

"Just fish?" Mary asked.

"I have some potatoes in the root cellar," he said. "We can bake them in the fire."

"Won't they burn?" she asked.

"Not the way I do it," Tyler told her. Pulling up the stringer, he said, "Pick out the fish you want to eat and then you two can bring the rest home for your folks."

Tyler got the fire going and went to pick out three potatoes. He then went near the edge of the marsh and dug out some clay and put a thick coat on them. These were then place within the coals and fire.

Meanwhile, Mary and Emma had started cleaning the fish on the bench. "We need some water," Mary called to him.

Getting a bucket in the pump shed, Tyler filled it with cool water and brought it to the ladies. He also brought a dipper in case they were thirsty. All three of them took a long drink. Once the fish were cleaned, they were put into the bucket to wash and hold until the potatoes were done.

Retrieving another bucket, Tyler washed the bench and then took the entrails to the garden. "They make things grow faster," he told Mary and Emma.

Once the young man was sure that the potatoes were about done, he put the three fish onto green sticks, stuck one end into the ground and let them hang over the fire. "How long before they are done?" Emma asked. "I am hungry. You know I am eating for two."

Tyler spread a blanket on the ground near the fire and got plates and eating utensils from the cabin. Taking the blackened potatoes out of the fire, he placed them onto a block of wood. "While I'm getting the potatoes ready, turn the fish one more time," he instructed the ladies.

Using his Green River knife, the young man carefully removed the clay from the potatoes, exposing the steaming tubers. He offered the ladies some bacon grease to put onto the potatoes if they wanted. Both decline and just requested salt.

Soon the three of them sat eating the succulent fish and the nicely baked potatoes. After eating, mostly with their fingers, they went to the pump shed and washed their hands. Then, using the dipper, enjoyed the refreshing water.

It was late afternoon and the ladies had to head back to town. Tyler offered to walk with them but they assured him that they would be okay and he had the mess they'd made to clean up. Emma excused herself and went to use the little house. "It comes with the baby," she said, laughing.

Mary put an arm around Tyler. "I want to thank you for today," she said. "Emma hasn't been doing well since Wil left and being with child doesn't help. She needed a day of just having fun and you did that for her, and also for me."

She then held him tight and they kissed a long and warm kiss. "Hey, you two. I leave for a minute an what do I find?" Emma kidded them.

The three of them laughed and then, carrying the extra fish, the two ladies headed up the trail, turning back several times to wave. Tyler sat on a block near the fire. *Mary is a good friend to Emma*, he thought. He wished . . .

CHAPTER THIRTEEN

Tyler woke early, looking forward to the day. It was 4th of July and he was going to town. He and grandpa had always talked about what they were going to do, and looked forward to some things like ice cream that were only available on that day.

Checking his possible bag, the young man counted out the money he was carrying. Debating a moment whether it would be enough, he finally removed the stone from the fireplace and took out two gold eagles. "That should do it," he said.

With the Colt on his hip and the Hawken in his hand, Tyler left the cabin and headed for the barn. It was a bright, sunny day with just enough breeze to keep one comfortable. He had already fed, watered and groomed the horse earlier after cleaning the stall. Now it stomped in the stall, ready to go.

"You just be patient," Tyler said, leaning the rifle against the buckboard wheel. Opening the stall, he led the horse to the front of the barn and tied it to a post with metal rings. Taking his time, Tyler put the blanket onto its back, letting it slide back a bit to smooth down the hair.

Swinging the saddle onto the bay, he let it settle onto the horse's back. As he talked to the animal about the day's events, he straightened all the straps and strings, making sure none remained under the saddle. Placing the stirrup onto the saddle, Tyler reached under the horse for the cinch strap. He then put the latigo through the D rings on the cinch and saddle to secure it.

Once he had the bridle on, and the Hawken in the scabbard, he checked the cinch once more and climbed into the saddle. The bay started out at a trot and Tyler let it go. The two miles to Cedar Creek went by quickly. In the past two years, three new houses had been built. One of his new neighbors waved as he rode by.

With so many men gone to the gold fields, the town lacked some of the holiday bustle. Tyler was just fine with it. He never was one to like crowds. The young man saw Roy's wagon down by the creek.

The man looked up as Tyler rode up. "You come to take my money again this year?"

"I figured you'd be taking your wagon over the mountains to sell guns to gold miners," Tyler replied.

Roy shook his head. "Not many men get rich at a gold strike, and if they do, not many are able to hold onto the gold."

"I've heard that before," the young man said. "Everything gets expensive, and there are hucksters with ways to take a man's money."

"Are you going to shoot this year?" the man asked.

"Why, hell yes," Tyler told him. "You got anything good to win?"

Smiling, Roy replied, "You already got my good stuff around your waist and in your scabbard."

"I've got someone to go and see," the redhead said, "but I'll be back to shoot."

"Are you still with that pretty, green-eyed gal?" Roy asked.

"We got engaged," Tyler told him. "I was on my way to see her when I spotted your wagon."

"We start shooting right after the parade," the man told him. "Come by and help me make some money."

Promising to return, the young man rode through the town toward Mary's. Her father was sitting on the porch when he rode up. "Come on down and have a drink with me," Len said.

"No whiskey today," Tyler replied, swinging off the bay. "I got to shoot this afternoon." He hung the Colt and holster onto the saddle horn.

"I'll have Mary bring you something then," he said.

The ladies heard them talking and Mary hurried out of the house and gave Tyler a kiss on the cheek. "I've been waiting for you," she said. "We are planning a picnic this afternoon."

"I have to shoot after the parade," he told her. "I hope that's okay."

She didn't look happy. "Why do you have to shoot?" she asked. "Now we'll have to put the picnic off till so late."

The young man stood with his Hawken in the scabbard and the Colt hanging on the saddle, facing a woman who didn't want him to compete in something he always did every year. "I kind a have to Mary," he said. "I am the defending champion."

"You win that thing every year," Mary said, stomping off to the kitchen yelling, "Mama, we have to eat later!"

Len gave him a weak smile. "Are you ready for that drink now?"

Tyler stripped the saddle off the bay and put his gear over the porch rail. Then he led the horse under a spreading oak to keep it out of the sun. With the horse taken care of, he headed back for the porch.

Her father liked a corn liquor made by a friend of his. He poured a little from the jug for Tyler and invited him to sit. "Did you hear about Sheriff Kent?"

Tasting the harsh brew, Tyler asked, "I haven't heard anything. Should I?"

"He was chasing a man who took a horse and fell off his own," Mary's father replied.

"Is he okay?" the young man inquired.

"Hell, he's got plenty of fat and just bounced a few times," Len told him. "I believe he's complaining about his back, no doubt looking for a reason not to work while getting paid."

Hearing footsteps from the kitchen, Tyler looked over. Mary came out with a plate. "We're going to have these at the picnic. I want you to try them."

She handed him the plate and it contained a piece of corn bread and some kind of salad. Taking the fork from her, he tasted each of the two small portions. "I like the corn bread," he replied, "and the salad is very good, but I've never had something like it before."

"It's got potato, some egg, and onion," she said. "Mama makes the dressing out of oil, yokes, and a bit of vinegar."

"It is very good," the young man said, smiling.

"It won't hold in the heat, so we'll have to get more ice," Mary told him. "Or we can eat what she already made before we go to the parade."

"It is good enough to eat twice," Tyler assured her. It appeared she didn't think she'd made her point and, turning quickly, Mary went back to the kitchen.

"I think she's mad at me," the young man told Len.

"It's hard to know what's the right thing to do some time," her father replied, and he offered Tyler some more corn liquor, which the young man declined.

At noon the two men were called into the kitchen and there was a small bowl of the salad in the middle of the table. There was also some ham and a piece of cornbread for each. Mary's mother Helen was all smiles when they came in.

"I hadn't planned a meal before the parade," she said, "but you men would have starved, having to wait until after the shooting."

Mary served Tyler, putting salad and ham onto his plate. "Mama didn't have anything else, so you'll have to have the salad both times," the girl pointed out.

The young man didn't care. He liked it and would enjoy eating it twice. The girl's mood seemed to improve as they ate the meal. She talked of wanting to see the show with the juggler and tumblers. Again, she made it a point that there was one show in the afternoon, but they'd have to wait for the one in the evening.

Her mother asked him about the shooting after the parade. "It'll be down by the creek," he told her. "I'll be using both the rifle and the revolver this year."

"He's good at it," Len told his wife. "Tyler here has won the thing every year."

Feeling uncomfortable with the compliment, the young man continued to eat the salad in front of him. "Can we go for ice cream before the parade?" Mary asked him.

Swallowing the mouthful, Tyler cleared his throat. "I'd like that. I heard that he's got some berries to mix in it this year."

"You best eat it slow," Len warned them. "It's hot out there and cold things can make your head hurt. I heard it crippled a man that ate it too fast."

With the meal finished, Len and Tyler got up with cool glasses of lemon drink and headed for the porch. "Mama wants you to go get more ice for the salad," she told her father, handing him a metal can.

"I'll get it," Tyler offered.

Taking the can, he went around to the ice house. It had clapboard siding like the house. Opening the double plank door, the young man felt the coolness of the interior. Brushing away the sawdust from a block of ice, he used an ice pick to break off some chunks. Then pushing the sawdust back over the exposed block, he carefully closed the door and headed for the kitchen.

With the meal finished, it was time to go into town. Walking hand-in-hand, Tyler and Mary left the house. "I think it is time for ice cream," the young man said.

They met Emma carrying her boy. She was six months along with the next child and her stomach seemed bigger than with the first baby. Releasing Mary's hand, Tyler offered to carry the boy. "He can walk okay," Emma told them, "but outside he tends to run and trip a lot."

As a mother, she had put on a little weight, but the young man still thought she looked good. "We are going for ice cream," Mary told her. "You should come with us."

"No, I can't," Emma replied. "Anyway, I just got little Adam cleaned up and he'd make a mess of himself with the stuff."

Tyler was sure it was the money that was her problem, so he said, "Children should have fun and get messy. I want to buy you and my godson some ice cream."

The ice cream man had a helper cranking a second churn this year. The helper was churning vanilla and the owner had strawberries mixed in. The owner was ready and the line only had a few people in it, so they joined the back, looking forward to the sweet concoction.

They had small, flat wooden spoons to eat the ice cream from the wax-coated dishes. As the man pulled the paddles or dasher from the churn, he noticed Adam in Tyler's arms. Smiling, he took a spoon, scraped a bit off the paddles and gave it to Tyler for the boy. Adam squealed with delight, looking forward to a taste.

After getting their dishes, Tyler paid for the ice cream and they found a grassy spot in the shade to enjoy it. Adam ran from one to another, getting tastes and entertaining the adults. "I wonder if Wil has found any gold yet," Mary asked.

The sound of her husband's name made a cloud pass across Emma's face. It was only for an instant, but the young man saw it. "He would only be at Independence Rock by now," Tyler replied. "It is near 2,000 miles from here to the gold fields."

Neither of the ladies knew where Independence Rock lay along the route, so it gave them no reference to his current possible location. They also did not ask Tyler how he would know that. It made it clear to them that Wil wasn't at the gold fields yet.

As warned, Adam's face and hands were covered with strawberry ice cream by the time they were finished. "I bought the ice cream, so I should clean up the sticky youngster," Tyler said as he scooped the boy up and headed for the pump near the church.

The young man was asked by Mayor Weems to ride in the parade as the champion marksman of Cedar Creek, so after the ice cream treat was over, he left the ladies to visit until parade time and headed back to get the bay.

Tyler liked riding in the parade. While he didn't normally want attention, this was one time he enjoyed it. He always rode at the end and always fired off four shots from the Colt. He only wished his grandpa was there to see him.

Despite so many being gone in quest of gold, it was still a fine parade. It included a bit of a preview of the juggler and tumblers, as well as the mayor and the horn players. Following the various merchants who walked along advertising their businesses, the young man remembered how proud he'd been years back, dressed as The Kankakee Kid, riding Roy's horse. Now he had a fine bay and was outfitted nearly as good.

As the parade slowly progressed, he rode waving to the crowd. A few would shout out "Hey, Kankakee Kid." They hadn't forgotten the past parade. As he rode by Mary and Emma, he waved his hat to them. Little Adam stood clapping making as much noise as he could. Whether he truly knew why his mother and Mary were waving and shouting, it was hard to tell, but he wanted to be part of it.

At the end, he turned the bay and pulled the Colt. Taking his time, he fired as the crowd counted them off. Putting the Colt back into its holster, he rode to the church and tied the horse. He saw Mary and Emma headed his way, the boy running in front.

Adam held his arms up to Tyler. "I think he wants to sit on the horse," his mother said. Picking the boy up, the young man placed him onto the saddle.

"That should keep him happy for a little while," he told the ladies.

It was a half-hour before the shooting would start, so Tyler laughed and talked with Mary and Emma. Mary stayed close the him and kept rubbing his back or giving him hugs. The young man liked the attention and enjoyed the company. He must have put the boy on and off the horse a dozen times while they visited. It had become a game with the lad.

Pulling grandpa's pocket watch, Tyler saw that the shooting would be starting soon. Reaching into the possible bag, he took out one of the eagles. Handing it to Mary, he said, "I want you two to buy Adam something special today and the two of you can take him to the afternoon show. Then tonight Mary you can go again with me."

The suggestion got another hug from the green-eyed girl. Climbing onto the bay, Tyler slowly rode with Adam sitting in front of him as Mary and Emma walked toward the festivities. When they reached them, the young man handed the boy to his mother. There was a moment of clamoring as Adam wanted to get back onto the horse.

With a smile and a wave, Tyler guided the bay through the crowd and headed for the creek. There would come a day when someone would beat him shooting, but the young man felt good and was ready for the challenge. He was glad he'd only had a sip of the corn liquor.

Roy had bunting and other decorations around the wagon as he stood on a small platform entertaining the crowd. When he saw Tyler riding up, he announced, "Here is our champion shooter, The Kankakee Kid!"

Never let a good phrase go to waste, the young man thought. He nodded at the crowd and swung off the bay. Unlike the first time, he did not shoot against every entry, but rather waited his turn to shoot like everyone else.

There were prizes of a Green River knife, a fine leather belt, and a powder horn. On display were rifles and revolvers. The top prize was a white beaver hat with a domed top and curved brim. It was much like the one Tyler had worn years ago.

A fee of $1 was required to compete, and each man would fire twice at the target that had a three-inch black dot in the middle and was 50 paces out. When finished the shooter's name was put onto it. After everyone had shot, Roy and the mayor would choose the winners.

Then there was a second contest for those with pistols or revolvers. The target was closer, but the same format was used. While waiting his turn to shoot, Tyler reloaded the Colt. Then putting it into the holster, he watched the others shoot.

His Hawken was clean and loaded. One of the contestants offered Tyler a drink from a bottle being passed around and he declined. Some of the shooters had been drinking most of the day and could barely score a hit on the outer edge of the target.

Roy was a true professional and never pointed this out, but rather spoke of another fine shot. Those who did poorly, he would meet with and offer to do work on their rifles, or even upgrade them to a better one that would help them put two into the center.

Then it was Tyler's turn. The crowd cheered as he walked up to the line. He nodded to them and waited for the noise to go down. The young man noticed that not everyone was cheering. He took aim at the target. He had already pulled the set trigger. As the sight was on the black dot, he touched off the hair trigger.

The smoke was carried off by a breeze as Tyler reloaded the Hawken. Again, the actions were repeated and fire belched out of the rifle, sending a .53 caliber ball at the target. He felt good about both shots.

Moving out of the way of the next shooter, the young man leaned against the wagon. As Roy looked at the target, he whispered, "Good shooting."

Tyler knew that the man had made bets with others who were shooting that they couldn't match or beat his Kankakee Kid. He always had plenty of takers. When the shooting was finished, there was a short comparison by Roy and the mayor.

"By God, we got one tie," Roy announced. "We'll have a one round shoot off at 100 paces."

Each year, the man would manage to find at least one that would require a shoot off. He'd take all bets against Tyler before the shooting began. The young man had already loaded the Hawken and was ready to shoot. A coin was tossed to see who would shoot first. The man who matched him was to shoot first.

His rival, named Doo, had all the earmarks of an old mountain man. It was said that his scarred Hawken had hit many an enemy at 400 yards. The young man had never seen him before and realized that he might have some tough competition. Tyler looked at the old, bearded man and decided that if he was beat by him, that would be okay. Roy wouldn't like it, but that would be his problem.

The breeze had stopped which would help the shooters. The man spat, and then brought up his rifle. Without hesitation he fired. With a grunt and a nod, he left the firing line. "I believe I left you a little room to get into the center," he said as he passed Tyler.

"That's mighty kind of you," the young man said, walking up to the line. The crowd was hushed. Tyler cocked the Hawken and then brought it to his shoulder and pulled the set trigger. As he brought it down onto the target a group of men started shouting.

Bringing the rifle back up, the young man waited until the caterwauling was finished. He heard Roy say something to them. Then bringing the rifle to his shoulder and putting the sight onto the target, he touched off the hair trigger. The rifle recoiled against him and the spent gunpowder smoke remained between him and the target in the still air.

Roy's helper collected Tyler's target and came running to the wagon. The young man looked in the direction where the shouting had come. It was the crowd from the tavern. Standing by the old mountain man, Tyler waited until Roy and the mayor made their decision. Then they called the two men up.

The two targets lay side-by-side with the shooters' names on the back. "We have chosen the one on the left," the mayor said. "Do you agree with our choice?"

It was damn close, but Tyler had to agree with them. The old mountain man took a quick look and said, "It's the winner."

"We have a winner!" Roy said. The crowd waited in anticipation. Slowly the mayor turned the target around. Relief spread across the gun seller's face. "It is Tyler Tomas, our own Kankakee Kid!"

If there were hoots from the tavern crowd, they weren't heard. The others cheered loudly. When it quieted down, Tyler turned to Doo. "Thank you for leaving me room."

The two targets were posted for the crowds to come by and see. There was a fair amount of debating if the judgement was correct. Lots of men had lost their bets to Roy. Overall, they had to agree on the outcome.

The revolver and pistol shooting were forgotten due to the climatic ending of the rifle shoot. Roy didn't want to break the mood of the crowd. He wanted men talking and staying around and buying things.

Doo spat and leaned on his Hawken. "I didn't want the damn hat anyway. It wouldn't do me no good in the mountains."

"I see you chose the knife," Tyler told him.

"It'll be useful out west," Doo replied. "I just come east to see my family one more time before I die, and was heading back to the mountains when I come across this here celebration."

"You aren't sick, are you?" the young man asked.

"You don't have to be sick to die in the mountains," the old mountain man said. "One misstep, an angry Blackfoot or grizzly that you don't see in time, is all it takes."

The two men visited for a while and Roy gave the hat to Tyler before looking for customers in the crowd. Not many had left because the helper was giving out drinks of whiskey. The two competitors drank to each other and then went their separate ways.

Leading the bay, Tyler walked back into town and had several people congratulate him on winning. He caught up with the two ladies just as they came out of the show. "Did you enjoy it?" he asked them.

"We did," Emma told him and then she asked, "Did you win?"

"Yes, I did," Tyler replied, looking at Mary. She just rolled her eyes.

Mary left for a moment to see if she could find her parents. Seizing the opportunity, the young man dug into his possible bag and fished out some coins. He took Emma's hand and pressed them into her palm. "I want you to have this for you and the boy. I know Wil needed all your money when he left."

"No, I can't . . ." She was cut off by Mary's return. "I leave for a minute and here you are holding hands," she said, kiddingly.

Emma withdrew her hand with the coins. She blinked away the tears that had come to her eyes, and turned to pick up the boy. Then turning back to Mary, she said, "I've got to go and change the baby."

"You will be back to join us for the picnic?" Mary asked. "We will be in the park in about an hour."

Smiling, Emma replied. "I'll be there."

As she walked away, Mary said to Tyler, "She looked sad when I got back."

"She got to thinking about Wil," he lied.

"That's why you were holding her hand," Mary replied. "We'll go back to the house so you can put the horse up. I like that hat you're carrying."

When they went to the picnic, she insisted that Tyler wear it. He liked the feel on his head, but a white hat wouldn't make much sense when he was working around the cabin. He decided he could wear it when going to church or to town.

The meal in the park was enjoyed, and having Adam running around entertained everyone. Not a word was said about Wil due to Mary's warning about it upsetting Emma. Len drank rarely, but on a holiday or special occasions he liked to have a drink. With the shooting over he got Tyler to have a couple of the harsh corn liquor drinks, and soon the young man was feeling it.

The sun was getting low in the western sky when they left the park. After hugs all around, Emma and the boy went into her parents' house. Len was feeling no pain and went straight to bed. He had to be up early to go to the mill.

Mary and Tyler sat close on the porch swing. She nuzzled him, inviting a kiss. Her lips were soft and sweet. Feeling the corn liquor just a bit, he held her tight and continued to kiss her. There were dangerous feelings going through his body.

She pulled back and said, "Oh, my. You are an amorous one."

Tyler blushed at the thoughts he'd been having. "I didn't mean . . ."

"No, it's okay," she said, moving away just a little.

Giving the swing a little nudge, Mary leaned back and said, "I watched you with Adam today."

Controlling his breathing, the young man replied, "He's a good boy."

"I could tell you liked playing with him. I think Emma appreciated having you watch him so she could relax and visit," she said.

Then she moved close again, the swing swaying softly. "I could give you a baby to play with. We have been seeing each other for so long. It's time we got married."

All of a sudden, Tyler was afraid to breathe for fear of what would come out of his mouth. The two sat in silence. "Did you hear me?" Mary asked.

"I did," Tyler replied, unsure of what to say.

"We could live in your cabin while we build a house in town," she said in a purring voice. He could feel her warm breath on his cheek. "Mama has been asking me when we were going to get married. I know she wants grandchildren."

The young man sat rigidly on the swing. The spell that he'd been in was gone. The hot desire had abated. All he could manage to say was, "I'm sorry."

Mary quickly got up. "Sorry! Sorry about what? Sorry I want to get married?"

Her demands came so quickly that he couldn't respond. It mattered little because what he was thinking she did not want to hear, *I am not ready.*

"Mary . . ." It was all he got out as she went into the house crying.

Tyler heard her mother say something and then there was the slamming of another door. There were footsteps coming to the porch. "Is there something wrong?" Helen asked. "Did you do something?"

"No, Mrs. Price," the young man said. "I didn't do anything. I've got to be going now."

His horse was under the tree with the cinch loose. Tyler pulled it tight and climbed into the saddle. The bay started out without any urging. It knew it was heading for home and all the young man had to do is sit and think.

There was something he needed to say. All these years as a couple hadn't changed the way he felt. It was nice to have someone to go to dances and other things with. Her home had been a place to go each time he went to town. Most often she was warm and loving. He did like her, but . . . he had never loved her.

As he rode by the juggler's tent, he realized that they had not gone to the show this evening. It made little difference. As he rode out of town, Tyler began to feel sad. He began to think about his grandpa. He needed another drink. He almost turned the horse around, but it tugged back on the reins and continued towards the barn.

CHAPTER FOURTEEN

Tyler woke the next morning in a sullen mood. He had slept in and sunlight was coming in the front room window. He still had his clothes on as he swung his feet to the floor. He had a headache, but was sure it wasn't just because of the corn liquor.

Walking out to the front room, he saw the white beaver hat on the table. He picked it up for a moment and then dropped it back onto the table. He was the champion. The champion of what? The stove stood open. Last night when he'd gotten in, Tyler had thought about making some coffee. He had decided to lay down for a minute before doing so and now it was morning.

After getting the fire going and putting a pot of water to heat, the young man went to check on the horse. It whinnied as he went into the barn. Leading it out, he took it down to the marsh to drink. While it did so, he relieved himself against some brush on the side.

Letting the horse wander, he walked out onto the dock and leaned against one of the poles used to hang the ducks. "Why didn't you just say yes?" he asked himself. "You think you don't love her because you don't think of her like you do of Emma. Maybe you just feel that way about Emma because she is Wil's and you can't have her."

For a long time, he stood on the dock arguing with himself, with nobody but the horse to hear. Tyler knew what he'd felt last night was something. Maybe that was what love felt like. He wished the hell grandpa was still alive so he could ask him.

After letting the horse graze for a while, Tyler led it back and put it into the corral. He tossed it some hay before heading for the cabin. Stopping at the pump shed, he washed his face and wet down his wild hair.

Breakfast was porridge, and he sat at the table eating a bowl and sipping the coffee. He picked up the hat and looked it over carefully. The young man knew that he would never spend the kind of money on head gear that this hat cost. It was quite the prize. Tyler was happy that Doo had been competing. He respected the old man's ability with a rifle. He was sure that given a few tries, Doo would win some of them.

The young man heard someone call his name. Placing his bowl and cup on the sideboard, Tyler went outside and there stood, Emma all flushed. She had pushed Adam in a baby carriage, two miles from town to see him.

Concerned, he asked, "What are you doing here? You shouldn't be pushing the boy all this way in your condition."

"My condition?" she asked. "My condition doesn't matter. What did you do to Mary last night?"

"She wanted us to get married right away and I . . . I guess I didn't say anything," Tyler said.

"She was at my house at sunup this morning crying her eyes out," Emma told him. "She said you came on to her and then just left."

"Well, you were there. I had a couple drinks and when we got back to her house, we were on the swing and I guess my kisses were more than usual, but that was all," he said, defending himself.

"I need some water," she said. Picking the boy out of the carriage, she let him run and she sat on the bench.

Tyler came back with a dipper of water. He watched Adam running around the yard, investigating everything. Taking the dipper back from Emma, he said, "She wants to get married and I didn't know what to say," he admitted.

Her voice lowered as she said, "Mary wished she had just let you go so she could get pregnant and then you would marry her. She said it worked for Wil."

For a moment the young man stood with his mouth open, unable to speak. He couldn't believe what she had just told him. He decided that he'd best avoid the subject of babies.

"Wil loved you and you loved him," Tyler told her. "I like Mary. She is my friend, but I don't think I love her." The young man couldn't believe he was spilling his heart to Emma. He was saying things that you didn't tell anyone.

"What do you think love is?" she asked.

"I do not know, but what I feel for her can't be love," Tyler said while wanting to shout out that he didn't feel about Mary the way he felt about her, but those words could never be said.

"Mary has loved you since she first saw you," Emma replied. "She told me back in school."

Unable to avoid the earlier statement any longer, Tyler said, "So, she was willing to get pregnant so I would marry her." He then asked, "Is that what love is?"

"I shouldn't have told you that," Emma replied. "Don't ever tell her I told you that."

Tyler had become uncomfortable with the direction the conversation had taken and wanted to get away from it. He asked, "Did you get something to eat this morning? I have some porridge left."

"I did eat, and now I had better go catch that boy before he gets into the water," she said.

"I'll get him," Tyler offered, and he ran down and swooped up the lad.

Emma remained at the cabin for three hours talking to Tyler. She was trying to understand his thinking in the relationship between him and Mary. After a time, she began to think that Mary knew what she wanted and Tyler just didn't know how to say no. Even when she pushed him on marriage, he had just clammed up.

When she said she had to get back, Tyler told her he'd get the buckboard and take her. They rolled up the trail with Adam bouncing on the seat between them. The trail was rough and the young man couldn't believe Emma had pushed that carriage all the way from town.

Roy was still parked by the river, but the rest of the town was mostly back to normal. Tyler pulled up in front of Emma's house and helped her down from the wagon. He then took Adam and set him next to her. Picking up the carriage from the back, he carried it to her porch.

"I have to get some grain from the livery," he told her.

"Don't leave town without seeing Mary," she told him. "Don't leave her hanging on what you didn't say."

Mayor Weems saw him and called him over. Leaving the buckboard in front of Emma's, he walked over. "Come into my office," he said. "I have something to talk to you about."

Following the man into the building, Tyler took the chair that was offered. "First," the mayor said, "I want to congratulate you on your shooting yesterday."

"Thank you, Mayor," Tyler said. "The winds were light and luck was with me."

"The hell luck was with you," the man said. "You are one damn good shot. Now I have an opportunity to talk to you about."

Kind of anxious to get out of the office, the young man asked, "What would that be?"

"You know the sheriff will be stowed up for a while," the mayor said. "With his back and all he can't be riding around doing business."

Tyler nodded and the mayor continued. "I would like to make you a deputy to kind of help him out. You know, if he had a need to ride out to a ranch to check on something or other. You could do the riding out."

"I got hay to make and a garden to tend to," Tyler told him. "Come fall I have hunting and trapping to do. That's how I make my living."

"I don't believe it would take much of your time," the mayor assured him. "And there would be a salary in it for you."

Curious, Tyler asked, "How much?"

"$30 a month and as much as $50 if you chose to put in more time," the man told him.

The young man was surprised. $30 was almost what a man made at the mill working six days a week and he would be working part-time. "I will think about it and get back to you," Tyler promised.

"Don't be thinking about it too long," the mayor said. "I got to get someone soon."

Walking out of the mayor's office, Tyler's head was spinning. The last thing he had ever thought about was being a deputy. He had always thought if he had to do something else it would be to work at the mill.

Taking the reins, the young man led the horse and buckboard toward Mary's. Since last seeing her, he had come up with various reasons for his actions. He hoped she had gotten over being mad at him. If not, he feared that there would be a scene on the porch and her mother and half the town would be privy to it.

Tyler climbed up onto the porch feeling like a misbehaving child on the way to the woodshed. He removed his flat-brimmed hat and held it in front of him as he knocked on the front door. At first, he heard nothing and wondered if the family was gone. In his heart he didn't think that would be a bad thing. He'd have more time to figure out what to say.

Then he heard the footsteps. The door opened and it was Mary's mother. "Come in," she said, more in a commanding voice than an inviting one.

Stepping into the kitchen, she motioned him to sit at the table. Then to his surprise she asked, "Would you like some coffee? I just made a pot."

Worried about what was coming, the young man's throat was dry, and in a weak voice he said, "Yes."

Each of them had a cup of coffee and Mrs. Price sat facing him. "How many years have you been going with my daughter?"

"I guess . . . a little over two years," Tyler replied.

"She was 15 when you walked her home from that dance and now, she's 17 years-old," Helen told him. "Do you realize that they are the years a woman meets a man and gets married?" she asked.

"We are both still young," he said.

"Young? Young you say!" Her face got red. "If you had no intention of marrying her, you just stole the most important years of her life. Do you understand that?"

"It was not my intention to do that," Tyler told her. "Mary and I enjoyed each other's company. We got engaged."

"Yes, she told me about it and that she had to ask you," Mrs. Price replied. "If you did not plan to marry her, you should have said no to the engagement and given her a chance to find somebody else."

"Mama, is that Tyler?" Mary asked, coming from her room.

"He come to see you," her mother told her. Getting up, she added, "I got things to do."

The young man had to get out of that kitchen. At any moment Mrs. Price might come back for round two. "We need to talk," he told Mary. "Would you like to go for a ride?"

"Yes," she said. "I just need to get a wrap."

The young man stood near the door, waiting. He could see redness in her eyes and it appeared she had just woken. It took her a few minutes and Tyler could hear her mother in the parlor. It was a small house and he wanted to be outside.

Tyler was thankful that she came back from her room before Mrs. Price needed to come into the kitchen. As they stepped off the porch, Mary said, "Oh, you've got the buckboard."

After helping her up to the seat, he took the horse's reins and climbed up beside her. Neither spoke as they pulled away from the house. They both sat upright, looking straight ahead. Once out of town, Tyler turned the bay onto a road running along the marsh.

Finally, Mary spoke, "It sounded like mama was angry. Did you say something to her?"

Other than being more formal, the girl acted like nothing had happened last night. The young man knew that he had to open the subject of marriage. "Your mother thinks that I have wasted your past two years."

"We have been good together," she said. "Don't you think so?"

"I think so, but your mother thinks we should . . ."

"Should what?" she asked.

"Mary," he said, his voice softened. "I am not ready to get married."

He heard her breath catch. "Is it marriage that you don't want, or is it marrying me?" she asked. "I saw your buckboard at Emma's for quite some time today. Is it Emma you want?"

"Emma is just a friend that is married to my best friend," Tyler told her. "She is also a good friend to you."

"A good friend wouldn't steal a fiancé," Mary replied.

"Your good friend walked all the way to the cabin this morning, pushing her baby to tell me that I'd better come and see you. She was worried about you," he told her. "I brought them back in the buckboard and then went to see the mayor. I did not even go into the house."

He could hear her quietly weeping next to him. For several minutes they rode in silence. Finally, she asked, "What . . . what did the mayor want?"

"He offered me a part-time job as deputy," he told her.

"Are you going to take it?" Mary asked.

"I don't know," Tyler told her. The subject had changed, but the young man didn't want to leave it without something being solved.

"You seem to worry about Emma," he said. "I have known her since I started school here. She and Wil have been together almost as long as that. She is still my friend, and I try and help her where I can, but she is my friend's wife and I respect that. Other than a friendship, there is nothing else between Emma Lane and me."

"You light up when you see her," Mary told him. "I have never seen that when you see me."

"I'm sorry if that's what you see. With Emma there are no expectation of me, when you and I are together I am always afraid I won't do the right thing or be dressed properly," he said.

He had expected a reply or even an angry response, but Mary remained quiet. He saw a shady spot that they could water and rest the horse. Pulling over, he climbed down and held his hand out to help her down.

They sat in the shade and Tyler saw the dried tears on her cheeks. He really did not want to hurt her, but he didn't know how to fix things. Tyler tried to think as he stared at the bay cropping grass within reach.

Suddenly she spoke. "When I met you, we were only 15 and 16. You had no idea what was expected when you were with a girl. You did alright at the dance the first time we met. I asked my folks to let me walk home with you. On the porch you looked like you were about to flee. I asked you to kiss me so you wouldn't."

He tried to speak, but she hushed him and put her finger to his lips. "You were the first boy I ever kissed and I liked it," she continued. "After that I tried to help guide you to do things a girl expects when we would meet. I will admit I often felt I was competing with Emma. Slowly you came around and I didn't always have to take the first step, but heaven help me you were not very quick to do so."

"I did things," Tyler said. He thought of all the scrubbing and cleaning up he had done. The many things he had changed after once making her angry.

"My mother told me it was probably because you had lost your mother and had lived a bachelor life. She liked you and told me to be patient. There were times that I lost my patience and got angry. I was in love and I wanted to always be first in your life." Then after a pause she added, "I know you did things."

"As grandpa got older, he needed more and more attention," Tyler said. "Things that he had done around the cabin now became my responsibility."

"There were weeks, sometime months that I wouldn't see you," Mary reminded him. "We lived just two miles away and it was like you had disappeared. Then you would show up like nothing had happened. Often after having stopped other places first."

"When I'm harvesting ducks and trapping muskrat, I get pretty gamy and have no time to clean up so I can come to town," Tyler told her. "Some months grandpa and I didn't even go to church. It is different when a man has a job at the mill. Days are long, but you have a certain time that you come home every night."

"If we were married, you would have me to come home to," she said. "I would have your meal ready, your house clean, and washed clothes for you each day."

"You wouldn't be happy living down on the marsh," he told her. "Think of yourself with two or three kids running around and a husband that leaves before daylight and is gone until after dark hunting to make a living. I love the life on the marsh, but you live in town and I don't think you would be happy."

"I would be with you," she said. "Knowing you were coming home would make me happy."

"I am not ready to get married," he told her again. "I don't know if I ever will be. Your mother says I stole the past two years from you. It would be unfair for me to take any more."

There was a pause as the two sat in the shade. Tyler had nothing more to add and feared he had said too much. Then she spoke. "I will wait," she said. "Don't worry about my mother. She would have had me married at 13 if she could have. If it doesn't happen, I will not blame you for stealing my years. I want you to still consider me you girlfriend, maybe fiancé, and when you come to town, you'll come and see me."

Unexpectedly, he felt relief at what she said. "I'd like that," Tyler replied.

"Now you can kiss me," she said.

Tyler couldn't be sure what had changed but he felt different. A gnawing fear that he was misleading her was gone. He held her close and they kissed, feeling the warmth of her body against his while they sat under the shade tree.

After they'd embraced for several minutes, Mary gently pushed him away. "Oh my," she said. "It is getting warm." She discarded her wrap, got up and rinsed her flushed face in the water. As she bent, her simple dress clung to her body, exposing her soft curves.

Averting his eyes, Tyler had to agree that things had gotten heated. Now he had a new worry. Could he control himself and would she decide that he needn't to?

Emma's words about her being willing to get pregnant came back to him. Today Mary had pushed him away in time. The young man realized it would be as much his responsibility to know when to stop as hers.

On the ride back to town, they sat close to each other. He liked the feeling of Mary beside him. He had also decided. He would take the deputy job. It would bring him into town more often.

CHAPTER FIFTEEN

The next morning, while Tyler was making his breakfast, he was thinking about the cool reception he'd received from Mary's mother when they'd gotten back. By the time Len had gotten home from the mill, their supper was ready.

The young man had been sitting on the porch when her father walked up. "Mary and Helen are just finishing the meal," he had told him.

The man nodded. "I hope you and my little one have sorted things out. I lost most of a night sleep," he had told Tyler.

By the end of the meal everyone had been smiling and Tyler figured that Mary had talked to her mother about the ride.

Once Tyler had the breakfast things put away, the young man planned his day. The sun was bright and he needed to cut some hay. After that, Tyler planned to ride into town and talk with the mayor. His scythe was hanging on the pump shed wall. The young man took it down and spent time honing the edge.

That morning as he swung the scythe, cutting swathes of hay, he had time to think about the past couple of days. The 4th of July did not end up as he had hoped but the next day had solved many of the issues between him and Mary.

By noon he had two acres of hay down. Tyler still hadn't developed the broad swing that his grandpa had, but he was pleased with what he had cut. Tonight, he'd come and flip the hay, and by tomorrow noon it should be dry enough to haul in.

Grandpa had peeled spruce poles and had made sides for the buckboard so they could carry larger loads from the field. Out of the two acres, Tyler figured he'd have three, maybe four loads. The hay was good this year.

Stopping at the pump shed, the young man washed up and rinsed his sweat soaked shirt. After draping it over the clothes line, he headed into the cabin. Tyler had made cornmeal mush for his breakfast and there was a small amount left in the cook pot. The young man ate it cold and thought about what he'd say to the mayor.

Looking at grandpa's pocket watch, he saw that it was 2 pm when he arrived in town. Tyler was wearing a gray cotton shirt, dark wool britches, low-heeled boots and his flat-brimmed hat. He only wore the white beaver skin hat to church and special occasions.

On his right hip he had the Colt Paterson, the Green River knife on the left, and his possible bag with extra balls, caps, and a powder flask, hung to the left. The mayor's office was across from the jail, and the front door was open to allow the afternoon breeze to blow in. Tyler felt nervous. He had never applied for a job before. Grandpa had taken him hunting before he was old enough to be of much help. As time went by the young man had become more and more helpful. He guided the bay to the rail and dismounted.

Mayor Weems was sitting behind his desk, inspecting something on his hand. Looking up, the man said, "I got a damn sliver that I just can't get hold of."

Drawing his knife, Tyler said, "Let me try."

"You ain't going to cut the hand, are you?" the mayor asked.

"Nope," the young man said. Using the edge of the knife, he caught the end of the sliver and pinching it with his finger, he pulled the tiny piece of wood out.

Putting the knife back into his sheath, Tyler said, "I've come to take the job."

A smile broke out on the man's face. "Good. I am glad you are," the mayor replied. "By the hardware you are wearing, you look like you're ready to start right now."

"I got some hay down and have to bring it in tomorrow, but after that I can start." Tyler told him.

"Come with me," the mayor said. He led the young man over to the jail next. Inside they found Sheriff Kent lying on a cot in the back corner.

The sheriff struggled to get up and then limped over to his desk. Leaning on it for support, he asked, "What do I owe this pleasure?"

"Tyler Tomas is going to be your new deputy," the mayor announced.

The young man stood a half-head above the stocky sheriff, and the man looked up at him. "You got yourself a place down near the marsh," Sheriff Kent said.

"I do," Tyler told him.

"You still raising hogs or do you have any chickens?" the man asked.

"No, I haven't," the young man said. "We quit raising hogs before my grandpa died."

"He was a good man," the sheriff said. "I was sorry to hear when he passed."

For just a moment, there was some awkwardness in the room and then Sheriff Kent said, "I know you can shoot and hit what you aim at. Most often what we do doesn't call for any shooting. We serve papers, collect fines, and once in a while have to arrest someone."

Having never thought about what the sheriff did, Tyler commented, "The job pays quite a bit for just doing things like serving papers and collecting fines."

"It is the presence of the law that we provide," the sheriff replied, taking a little offense to what Tyler had said. "Without it, the town would be run by ruffians and swindlers."

Realizing that the sheriff didn't like his assessment of the job's requirements, Tyler told him, "I understand and then if one of the ruffians or swindlers come into town, you have to run them out."

Then the sheriff asked, "If you met a man that was breaking the law and wearing a gun, what would you do about it?"

Unsure what the sheriff was getting at and what answer he was looking for, the young man replied, "I guess I would make him aware that he was breaking the law and let his know that we don't let that happen in this town."

"And if he told you to go to hell?" Sheriff Kent asked.

"I would do what's necessary," Tyler replied, "because he can tell me to go to hell, but I don't have to go."

Both of the men laughed at that statement. It wasn't original, because the young man had heard it someplace else, but it seemed to satisfy the sheriff.

Sheriff Kent took a badge out of his desk and asked Tyler to raise his right hand. A few words later, the young man was sworn in as a deputy. "When on duty, you can put you horse up at the livery," the mayor told him. "Just let Edmond know that it is town business and the town will take care of the billing."

"Another thing," the sheriff said, "You get an allowance of powder and lead each month. We expect you to keep your revolver in good shape and practice in case it is needed."

"It'll be hard to keep the powder separate when using my Hawken," Tyler told him.

"You can use it for the Hawken, because you might need it when putting down rabid animals or other vermin," Sheriff Kent replied. "Just don't be using it in that punt gun. For that you buy your own."

The rules seemed simple enough. For each notice that was delivered, the town would pay four bits.

Half would go to Sheriff Kent, the other to Tyler. A similar system was used in fines and apprehensions.

It was decided that Tyler would work Monday, Wednesday, and Saturday. The Saturday would be changed to accommodate a holiday, which he would have to work. "Now that you are sworn in, I do have something I need done," the sheriff said.

"I got hay down in the field," Tyler told him.

"It shouldn't take too long," the man told him. "It's a matter of a horse that was taken. I don't know if it was stolen or just borrowed. I need you to go and get it back and the young lad that took it."

"Is that the one you were after when you fell?" the young man asked.

Before the sheriff could answer, the mayor laughed and said, "It's the one that he was chasing when he fell off his horse."

"I nearly got killed," Sheriff Kent replied, a little edgy.

"Next time you might want to tighten your cinch," the mayor said, still laughing as he left the jail.

New to the job, Tyler ignored the banter that had just happened. "Do you know who took the animal?"

"The Jakobs kid," the sheriff replied. "I was going to go and see him myself in the next day or so, but you might as well earn your keep starting today."

Leaving the jail, Tyler wondered what he might have gotten himself into. He could be going to bring a boy in who could end up in prison. Worse yet, he could be hung, depending on the circumstances that he took the horse.

The boy's name was Alvin and his father was Burt Jakobs. The mother had died some years back during childbirth. They had a small farm raising hogs about seven miles north of town. The round trip would be nearly five hours, which meant that the hay would not be flipped today.

Tyler rode by Mary's house on his way out. She was weeding the garden and quickly got up, brushing herself off as she walked toward him. "I got a little more weeding before I can sit with you."

Swinging off the bay, he gave her a quick kiss. "I had planned to visit today, but now I got the deputy job."

"I see that," she said. "You got a badge and everything."

"I got to ride north of town and bring back a boy and a horse," he told her.

"Is that the one Sheriff Kent was chasing?" Mary asked.

"It was," Tyler told her

"We'll keep some supper warm for you so you can eat before you go back to the cabin," she told him. Then another kiss and he was on the bay riding north.

The young man could already see the benefits of having a fiancé. Once they both understood that marriage wasn't out of the question, but wasn't the question either, they could both be relaxed with each other.

As Tyler rode north his mind was busy on the what-ifs of his visit to the farm. Burt Jakobs was a little ornery and might not take well to having his son taken back to Cedar Creek. He did most of his business in Lowell. He may not trust having his son taken south.

He could hear the sound of the mill ripping logs as he rode by. A steam engine hissed as it powered the saw, sending dark smoke into the air. Without the mill, the town of Cedar Creek would shrink to almost nothing.

In just under two hours, Tyler rode up to the farm. The smell of the hogs met him about a half mile away. By the time he was in the yard it almost stung his eyes in the heat of the day. Burt was feeding the animals and paused when he saw the deputy.

"You lost?" he asked.

"I am here on Cedar Creek business," Tyler told him.

"Is that a badge your wearing?" Burt asked, with a sneer.

"I have business with your son, Alvin," the young man told him. "It has to do with a horse he took."

"That old nag," the man spat. "You come all the way here about that?"

"It was taken without permission from the owner," the deputy told him. "I am tasked with bringing the horse and your son back to Cedar Creek."

Burt picked up a stout pole and began to walk towards Tyler. The young man swung off the bay, not wanting to continue talking down at the man or have him swing and hit the horse. Stepping away from the horse he asked, "What is your intention?"

"I am going to beat you senseless," Burt told him.

With his hand resting on the Colt, Tyler replied, "Then I am going to have to kill you. Now how do you think that will help your son?"

The man stopped. "If you take him back to Cedar Creek, he'll end up in prison or hung. How do you think that will help me?"

"That depends whether he borrowed or stole the horse," Tyler told him. "A borrowed animal that was taken without permission but returned unharmed might get you son 30 days or a $10 fine. If stolen he will get five or less years in prison. It is unlikely he'll be hung if the horse was recovered."

"What the hell kind of talk is that?" Burt growled. "Are you some kind of lawyer too?"

Truth was, Tyler had read about this in the books that Pastor Woods had given him. "It's the law, Mr. Jakobs. It protects the both of us and your son."

"Did he borrow the horse?" the deputy asked.

"The owner wasn't feeding it enough and the boy felt sorry for the horse," the man told him. "Alvin's been feeding it our good grain to bring it back to health."

"That is well and good," Tyler said, "but he didn't have permission to take it."

The man threw the pole down. "Every one of my damn pigs get fed twice a day. They never go thirsty and live well right up to butchering time."

"Can you get Alvin and the horse for me?" Tyler asked.

"If anything happens to the boy, I am coming for you!" Burt threatened.

"If I am not in town, I'll be down on the marsh at my cabin hunting or fishing," the young man replied. "It's the place that was owned by Nikolas Tomas."

Burt stopped. "I knew Nikolas. He bought some of my young hogs. I was sorry to hear he died. He was a good man."

Tyler stood silent beside the bay. He wondered if folks would say the same about Tyler Tomas when he died. So far, he wasn't much liking the deputy job. After a short wait, the boy came out leading the horse. It was an older mare and somewhat run down. It was easy to see that it hadn't been eating well.

Alvin stopped in front of him. "Was there a saddle on the horse?" he asked the boy.

"No, just the lead rope," the boy replied.

"How old are you?" Tyler asked.

"Twelve," Alvin answered.

"You know it was wrong to borrow the horse," the young man told him.

"They weren't feeding it," the boy said. "I took it to give it grain."

"Did it eat the grain?" Tyler asked.

"Not much," Alvin replied. "Pa said its teeth are bad."

Then to Burt, Tyler said, "I am going to take the boy and horse with me. He will be charged with taking the horse without permission so he could feed it. I will assure the court that he intended to bring it back, healthier than when he got it."

"I wasn't ever going to take it back to them," the boy said.

"How old will you be in five years?" Tyler asked.

"I'm not good in math," Alvin replied.

"You will be 17, and that's how old you will be when you get out of prison if you tell that story back in Cedar Creek. Do you understand me?" Tyler asked.

The boy remained silent. "It is your choice, but I believe you did intend to bring it back," Tyler said, sternly.

"I did," Alvin mumbled.

Late afternoon, Tyler rode into Cedar Creek with Alvin sitting behind him on the bay and the mare in tow. They rode up to the jail and climbed down. Bringing the boy into the jail, Tyler had him sit near the door. Sheriff Kent sat at his desk.

"Is this the Jakobs boy?" the sheriff asked.

"It is, and he was about to return the horse after feeding it for the past few days." Tyler replied.

The sheriff looked at the boy. "Why did you take the horse? Did you plan to sell it or keep it?"

Staring at his dirty feet, Alvin replied, "I wanted to feed it. The people that had it weren't feeding it enough."

"After you fed it, what then?" Sheriff Kent asked.

The boy hesitated and looked at Tyler. "I was going to bring it back. I guess I should have asked them if I could take it."

"Put him in the cell," the sheriff said. "I'll deal with this tomorrow."

"How about I take care of him until tomorrow?" Tyler suggested. "We can put the horse at the livery."

"Son, you go wait outside," Sheriff Kent told the boy.

After he left, the sheriff looked at Tyler. "When you go hunting and fire the punt gun into a raft of ducks just enjoying the morning on the water, do you feel sorry for them?"

"No," the young man said. "I sell them to make my living."

"This ain't no different," Sheriff Kent snapped. "He broke the law and lawbreakers sit in jail. The law decides what the punishment is regardless of how old or how good their intentions were. Do you understand?"

"I do," Tyler replied, "and I have read the law on this kind of crime. The boy should get 30 days for borrowing a horse without permission. What happened to you should have no bearing on the sentence."

The sheriff's face was red and he glared at his new deputy. After taking a deep breath, he said, "Have him back here first thing in the morning."

After dropping the mare off at the livery, Tyler took the boy to Mary's. Before knocking he took him to the pump to wash his feet, hands, and face. "I believe we got a meal waiting for us."

Two things surprised Mary when Tyler came into the house. One was the young man having the boy with him and two, the smell the boy brought into the kitchen. The waiting meal, was split with the larger portion going to the hungry boy.

After the meal, it was suggested by Helen that they visit out on the porch. "Why do you have the boy?" Mary asked.

Tyler explained the situation and told her he'd be bringing Alvin back to Sheriff Kent in the morning. "Are you planning on taking care of every prisoner you arrest?" she asked. "If you are, we are going to need a bigger house."

They laughed over the statement, and it was time for Tyler to leave. In the morning he'd have to bring the boy back into town and he had hay down in the field. This deputy thing might make taking care of chores difficult. Then, maybe by the look on Sheriff Kent's face, his job might be over tomorrow.

After a quick stop at the church to talk to Pastor Woods, Tyler rode the two miles back to the cabin with the boy. The bay was put up after watering. Hay was tossed into the stall. Then Tyler got a fire going in the firepit and put the cauldron on to heat water.

"You are going into town tomorrow, scrubbed and in clean clothes. Pastor Woods has a boy about your age and he had some things he'd outgrown that might fit you," Tyler told Alvin.

It was dark when the two of them were finally asleep. The next morning, dressed in clean clothes, hair combed, and clean feet, Alvin walked into the jail. Bill Harvey, the local barber, was waiting, sitting at the sheriff's desk. He was also the town's justice and took care of things that didn't have to involve the county judge, who traveled, holding court in towns as needed.

Bill looked at the boy. "You could use a trim, but I am glad to see you have combed your hair. I was told to expect a strong odor from you but see you have managed to clean up."

The boy stood silent, staring down. Sheriff Kent sat to one side looking on. Tyler stood just behind the boy. He wished that he knew what Bill and the sheriff had talked about before they'd gotten there.

"Do you know why you are here?" the justice asked.

"Yes sir. I took . . . borrowed a horse and didn't get permission," Alvin replied.

"What were your intentions with the horse? Did you plan to sell it?" Bill asked.

"I just wanted to feed it," the boy said.

"Would you like your father to be here for this hearing?" the justice asked. "We could send word for him to come."

"He's got work to do with the hogs," the boy said.

"Do you help him with the hogs?" Bill asked.

"I feed them, and help with butchering," Alvin said.

"Do you know what could happen to you for borrowing the horse?" the justice asked.

"I could go to jail," the boy said. Then he asked, "Is someone going to feed the horse?"

"You're concerned with the horse?" the justice asked. "You should be concerned with yourself. When did you first see this horse?"

"We brought in some hogs for folks that wanted to roast them for the 4th. I saw it then," Alvin replied.

Bill Harvey looked over at the sheriff. "I figure this a first offence and the boy meant no harm to the horse or its owner. $5 or 15 days."

Tyler reached into his possible bag and took out a gold eagle. "I would like to pay the fine for this boy. I'll let him work it off making my hay."

"Is that okay with you, Sheriff Kent?" the justice asked.

"It's his money and he can spend it any way he wants," the sheriff replied.

Bill Harvey then offered to clip the boy's hair and took him over to this shop. Tyler stayed with the sheriff in the jail. "You'll go broke paying people's fines," Sheriff Kent told him.

"The kid saw a starving horse and tried to help it," the deputy replied. "There are worse things like the man that wasn't taking care of his animal."

"Maybe so, but that isn't against the law," the sheriff pointed out.

With a fresh haircut on the boy, Tyler took him back to the cabin and fed the bay some grain in the corral. Then he and the youngster bunched up the hay in the field. After some water and biscuits sent home by Mary, they hitched the bay to the buckboard and hauled the hay into the barn.

With the work done, Tyler took the pole sides off the buckboard and saddled up the bay. The two of them, riding double, headed for the Jakob's place to bring Alvin home. Little was said at the farm except that Tyler hoped he wouldn't find Alvin again in the same circumstances.

It was dark when Tyler got back to Cedar Creek and the lights were on in the Price house. The bay had drunk in the stream a couple of miles back so the young man pulled up and tied the horse. Mary was delighted to see him. She had been sitting up with her mother and her father until they had gone to bed.

An offer was made for him to spend the night, but Tyler declined. He had deputy duties the next day. It was almost midnight and the two of them were still sitting in the swing. He told Mary all about the Jakobs boy. The girl told him that Alvin would have had it easier if he'd have spent the 15 days in jail. He'd have gotten fed regularly and wouldn't have had to feed the hogs every day.

The moon offered enough light for the ride to the cabin. The warmth and sweetness of Mary lingered with him as he rode. *I wonder if I am falling in love?* he thought.

* * *

Somehow Mary found out about his birthday in August. Tyler had worked that day. He'd ridden out of town to deliver some papers to a farm. It was late when he'd gotten back, and he went straight to Mary's house to see her for a few minutes before heading for the cabin.

Swinging off the bay, he felt stiff and tired. Tyler tied the bay to a ring on the post. Brushing the dust from his clothes, he went and knocked on the door.

He still knocked every time he visited. While he was hardly company anymore, it was the proper thing to do. Folks had been known to take a bath in the kitchen. Mary came to the door.

"I was afraid you wouldn't be stopping by tonight," she said.

"I had some work outside of town," he told her. "I'll only be staying a few minutes."

"Then," she said, "you best eat your cake, really fast."

She swung the door open, and there in the small house was most everyone he knew: Emma with Adam, the pastor and his wife, Jules and his, the sheriff, the mayor, and, well everybody. They all shouted, "Happy Birthday."

It was the first birthday party Tyler had had since leaving Virginia. He'd turned 19 today. The party began with a toast using some good whiskey, which was followed with cake and coffee. The fatigue of the long ride was gone and the young man stood among friends, blushing and thanking everyone.

After those attending the party left, Mary gave Tyler his present. It as a silver fob for his grandpa's pocket watch. "That way every time you look at the time you will think of two important people, your grandpa and me."

With a smile on his face, the deputy rode home, fingering the silver fob. He had never received such a nice present before. Suddenly he realized the he didn't know when Mary's birthday was. They had been going out all these years and birthdays had never been talked about.

Being a deputy didn't offer a lot of excitement or glamor with the job. Most days it was just hanging around town and walking the street, which wasn't a very long street. Sheriff Kent still complained about his back and was happy to stay in the office and take the laudanum that Nate provided.

Part of his rounds included the tavern owned by Lee Jackson. Jackson ran a rough and tumble place, with whiskey, gambling and ladies of the night. Most townsmen steered clear of the tavern on the weekends, which brought in plains hunters, trappers, and bachelors from the mill. Tyler's job was to prevent the rough behavior from spilling into the town.

It was September and the ducks would be in soon. Tyler planned to pick up some supplies he'd need from the trading post before heading back for the cabin. The day had been slow and he was glad it was over. He headed for the livery to get the bay when he heard an argument between the new blacksmith, Charlie, who had set up shop near the livery, and one of his customers.

As the young deputy walked up, he heard the unhappy customer shout, "Them damn hinges squeal and creak every time the door is opened. They are driving my wife mad with the noise. I want my money back!"

"Put a little fat on them and they'll quiet down just fine," the smithy said.

"I didn't have to put no fat on the ones that wore out and they were quiet as the grave!" the man snapped.

Now the smithy was twice as big as the scrawny customer and he was trying to reason with the man. The scrawny man's name was Curly. He had lost most of his hair and took offense if it was mentioned. He also had a habit of getting into it with opponents who were bigger than him.

The smithy's patience was worn down and Tyler knew it was going south when the big man said, "No fat on them is why the old ones wore out, you bald-headed bastard."

That was it. Curly went to swinging, striking the big man several times in the body. The smithy was holding him back with one hand and was winding up for a finishing blow with the other. "Charlie! Don't hit him," the young deputy cried out. Tyler feared that one blow would put the scrappy man into the grave.

Pulling the angry customer off the smithy, Tyler threatened, "Settle down Curly, or I'll have to put a knot on your head."

Pulling loose from the deputy, the man said, "He made me hinges that won't work."

"I suggest we go and take a look at the hinges," Tyler said.

Charlie wasn't too happy about going, because his forge was hot and he had been working on some horseshoes. "You go and look. I got stuff to finish here."

The deputy agreed and he and Curly walked a half-mile to the man's house. With a lot of dramatics, the man opened and closed the door. It did make noise. Tyler could see one of the problems. One of the hinges was installed slightly off square.

"You didn't put the bottom one on straight," the young deputy told him.

"I had to put it on that way so I could use two of the old holes," Curly said.

"Did you tell Charlie that you wanted to use the old holes?" Tyler asked.

Getting a little steamed, Curly replied, "I shouldn't have to tell him. He knew I was replacing the old ones."

"Did you bring him the old hinges?" the deputy asked.

"Of course not," the man replied, "they were holding up the door."

The young deputy knew that a little grease or fat on the hinges would have quieted even the crooked one, but he also knew that Curly could be very unreasonable. "Do you have the old hinge?" Tyler asked.

"I do," Curly replied, "but I plan to use them on the shed in the back. It doesn't matter if they are worn and loose."

"I want you to take the new one off and get the old hinge," the young deputy told him.

"How do you suggest I keep the door on?" the feisty man snapped.

"We'll just lean something against it so it won't fall," Tyler said.

"Then ma will have to use the back door," Curly complained. "What if she forgets and tries to use this one?"

Begrudgingly, the man finally did what the deputy asked. When they got back to the blacksmith shop, Charlie was just finishing the last horseshoe and plunged it into a bucket of water, creating a plume of steam from the red-hot metal.

He looked up at the two men. "I ain't giving back your money for them hinges so you can just take the things back home."

Tyler explained the hole problem and he could see the veins standing out on the smithy's forehead. "Is it possible to move the holes just a little?" the young deputy asked.

Curly and Tyler stood outside the shop as Charlie worked the bellows on the forge and heated the hinge. Then there was lots of hammering and the sound of the hot hinge hitting the water. The man came out with the two hinges.

"I worked the old one too, so it wouldn't be so loose," the smithy said.

"You did?" Curly asked. "Then I wouldn't have needed new hinges at all."

The young deputy grabbed the scrawny man's arm and snarled, "The hell you didn't," as he dragged him away from the fuming smithy.

The next morning, Tyler decided to walk back to town for the supplies. He had an old knapsack of grandpa's that was brought from England. It had been patched several times and was still very functional.

The young man stopped at the front of the trading post. There was a poster saying that there was a harvest dance at the hall this coming Friday. Smiling, he said, "That will work out just fine."

"You talking to me?" Jules asked.

"No, Mr. Martin," he replied. "I was happy to see that the dance is on Friday. It's my day off."

After picking up the few things he needed, Tyler placed them onto the counter. "I just got some red ribbon in that would look really nice in Mary's auburn hair," Jules told him.

"I'll take some then," the young man said.

Whistling as he walked, Tyler headed for Mary's to visit before heading back to the cabin. He was carrying a small package with the ribbon for her. She and her mother were busy baking. The windows and kitchen door were open, letting the warm air and the smells of the good things out.

When he stepped onto the porch, the girl noticed him. With a bit of flour on her nose and apron, she stepped out and gave him a quick kiss. "Stick around and you can test the cakes mama is making for the dance."

"I'd like that," the young man said. "If you don't mind, I'll wait on the porch. It will be cooler."

Seeing the small package, she asked, "What's that?"

"Something I got for you," he said. "When you finish, I'll give it to you."

"Oh," she said, pretending to pout. "What if I don't want to wait?"

There was the sound of metal on metal from the kitchen. "I think your mother could use some help," he said.

Smiling, she turned to go in and then called back, "Get some ice. We have lemon drink."

The can they used to get ice was just inside the kitchen door so Tyler got it and headed for the ice house, his knapsack and the package lying next to the swing.

The sound that Tyler had heard from the kitchen was Helen taking the cakes out of the oven. The small cakes were baked in small bowls called ramekins. She could bake ten at a time, and as they cooled the cakes, which were similar to cupcakes, were removed and a glaze was put on the top. If they worked out, she'd make more for the dance.

The young man placed the ice inside the kitchen door and sat back onto the swing. He noticed that the package had been moved. He did not have long to wait and Mary came out with a cool drink and a cake for him. Taking a bite, he chewed the sweet treat. "Well?" the girl asked, looking at him.

Swallowing, Tyler said, "It is so good, it leaves me speechless."

Satisfied, she said, "I'll be right back," and then was off to the kitchen.

During the visit, plans were made for the night of the dance and the present was opened, which thrilled the young girl. She promised to wear it in her hair on Friday. With his knapsack on his back and the taste of the sweet cake still on his tongue, Tyler headed back for the cabin.

By the day of the dance, the young man had everything ready for duck hunting. He had decided not to trap muskrat this year. The job in town gave him plenty of money to replace the furs. Dressed in his Sunday clothes and the white beaver hat, he saddled the bay and put on the saddle bags. He put the Colt and holster in one and his possible bag in the other.

As a deputy, he had to be ready at all times should a problem arise. Sheriff Kent took care of paperwork and spent his days on the cot or sitting in front of the jail. The September night was comfortable, so he just wore the cotton shirt.

Tyler had purchased a pair of medium-heel riding boots. They made his six-foot frame seem even taller. He planned to leave the horse in their barn for the evening and they'd walk from the house to the hall.

Knocking on the door, the young man felt a little nervous. He was kind of duded up and hoped she liked it. When the door opened Mary had her hair up with the ribbon weaved into it. She had on a stunning dress and almost left him tongue-tied.

"I . . . I hope you don't," then, taking a deep breath, he said, "I hope it's okay if we walk."

"I'd like that," she said, her eyes shining. "It is a beautiful night."

Arm in arm, they headed for the hall, giving the tavern plenty of leeway. The music had already started and they could hear the fiddle a good distance from the hall. As they entered, Tyler looked around and noticed that a few men kept their hats on. He had been debating, but then he realized with his height and the medium-heeled boots, he'd tower above everyone if he left the hat on.

Mary gave him her wrap and he hung it along with the hat on a peg. Almost immediately they were on the floor dancing. Years ago, Pastor Woods had taught his students the proper way to dance, and it was still paying off for the young man.

When they went off the floor to catch their breath, Mary saw Emma. She was due anytime, and unable to dance, so she helped with serving the drinks and goodies. "Let's go over and say hi," Mary told Tyler.

Emma's cheeks were flushed as she hurried serving people. "I'd like one of those small cakes," Tyler told her.

"Let me do that," Mary said. "You rest a bit and I'll serve the folks. Tyler, find her a place to sit."

A short distance away there was a bench and one of the occupants got up to make room for Emma. "Thank you," she said, smiling, and then sat. "I am getting tired much easier now. It seemed with the first one, I never had a problem."

"You're lucky that you have your mama to help take care of Adam," he told her.

"I think she enjoys it," she said.

Tyler reached into a pocket and took out two gold eagles. He put them into her hand and said, "The boy's birthday is coming soon. Take this and buy him something for me."

"I don't want you giving me your money," Emma said. "You may need it yourself soon enough."

"It is for the boy," the young man said. "He has things he needs and I want to make sure he can get them."

"I haven't heard from Wil," she said, her eyes filling with tears.

"Placing his hand on her shoulder, Tyler replied, "I don't imagine much mail makes it east from California. He just left this spring." He didn't finish the rest of his thought, which was that it would be a couple of more years at the soonest for him to return.

Mary came to be with them and told Emma. "I found someone else to help serving. I told them you couldn't stay on your feet anymore."

The pregnant girl seemed happy to remain seated. A slow song came and Tyler and Mary went back to the dance floor. He heard her whisper, "That's him."

"What?" the young man asked.

"The man with the feather in his hat came to the table and was asking me to dance with him," Mary said.

Tyler saw the man. He had a grouse feather in his hatband. He recognized him from the tavern. His name was Rex and he'd been one of the men who had made comments when he and Mary had walked by the tavern after the dance where they'd met.

"I've seen him when making my rounds," the young man said. "He shouldn't be any problem once he knows you're with me."

They danced several dances and soon the crude man was forgotten. Emma's father came and she left early. Tyler wondered if she would have danced a slow one had he asked. "It must be tough for her with Wil being gone."

Mary thought for a moment and said, "I am lucky. Emma is married and has a baby and one on the way, but she doesn't have her husband here. I have you and you are happy in Cedar Creek."

Her comment made Tyler feel good. Then came the last dance and the lamps were turned down.

They danced close, while keeping things proper. What one might do on the porch swing would not be acceptable in public.

With the dance ending, Tyler went to get his hat and her wrap. A couple of people talked to him while getting them. When he turned to go back to Mary, he saw Rex holding her arms and trying to get her to go with him.

In three long steps he was near her side and he planted his hand in the middle of Rex's chest and shoved him away. "The lady doesn't want you near her," he said with a threatening voice.

Rex had tripped and fallen. He got up slowly and said, "How the hell would you know? You've had your time and now she needs a man."

Once up, he leaped at Tyler, knocking him backwards, and the two of them went out the door. Rolling in the dirt kicking and punching, they broke apart and the two men stood. Rex came at Tyler again, and with the advantage of reach the young man planted a fist squarely in the middle of the aggressor's face. Tyler felt the man's nose flatten.

The young man followed the first punch with an uppercut to the solar plexus that knocked the wind out of Rex. The man went down, his nose spraying blood, gasping for air. Tyler was seeing red and went back after the downed man. He felt a hand on his shoulder holding him back.

"He's down, Tyler." It was Jules who had stopped him.

Coughing, and dazed, Rex got up. He wiped his nose with his shirt sleeve. Then in a raspy voice he said, "The next time we meet, you best have your Colt. It will be you and me, and I am going to kill you."

A couple of his friends tried to help the man back to the tavern, but Rex just shoved them away. "I will kill him," he repeated. Tyler watched the man leave. He wondered if Rex had the nerve to face someone with a gun, or was he the type to backshoot his enemy?

Mary was at Tyler's side. "He hurt you. You're bleeding," she said.

The young man looked down and could see blood dripping down the front of his cotton shirt. Then he looked around. "My hat?"

"I got it," the merchant told him. "You dropped it when you went after Rex." He saw that Mary had her wrap. He must have dropped that too.

Tyler felt conspicuous with all the attention around him after the fight. "I should walk you home," he told the girl, wanting to get away from the crowd.

"Let me go and get the pistol for you to carry," Jules offered. "That bastard might find a gun and be waiting for you."

"That's not necessary," Tyler said, giving him a half-smile. "Rex should be licking his wounds and getting drunk by now."

Three men walked up. The young man recognized them from the mill. One of them said, "We work with Mary's pa. We'll walk with you to her place."

Again, Tyler wanted to tell them no, but before he could Mary thanked them. As they started for her house, the young man looked at the group around him.

He figured that there would be enough witnesses if Rex came at him with a gun.

After they reached the house, Tyler thanked them and the three escorts headed for the tavern to have a drink after the dance. Mary took his hand and led him onto the porch. "Take the shirt off," she told him. "Mama can rinse the blood out while I patch you up."

Tyler was still wearing his summer underwear and felt awkward taking the shirt off. It was one thing to be bare-chested cutting hay or fishing on a hot summer day, but right here on the porch wasn't right. "I can wash it when I get home," he told her.

Ignoring what he said, she unbuttoned the shirt and moved to the back, removing the garment. "My," she said.

"What?" he asked.

"I never realized how muscular you were," she said, running her hand across his back. "You always wore a baggy shirt that hid them. And I see you must keep the shirt off sometime. You are well-tanned. My papa just has a tan on his arms and neck. They rest is just as white as can be."

The feel of her hand on him sent chills and tingles through his body. He wanted to jump away, but the truth was he didn't want her to stop. "Well," she said, letting out a long breath. "I best get this shirt to mama and find something for that cut near your eye."

Tyler took a seat on the swing as she left, with his arms folded across his stomach. He felt absolutely naked sitting there. It made no sense, though. He had swum many times with his shirt off around others. Then he realized that that had been before leaving

Virginia. Since he had haired over, he'd never been in the presences of a girl without his shirt on.

Mary came back with a wet cloth and some salve. She sat next to him and began to gently clean the cuts on his face. "Mama said I should have had you go into another room and take the shirt off. I told her it didn't matter. I said someday we would be married and scrubbing each other all over on bath nights."

"I imagine she didn't like hearing that," Tyler said, fighting to control the feelings he was having inside.

"She liked the being married part, but I got an angry look when I said scrubbing," Mary told him.

Then she said, "He scratched and bit you when you two were rolling around on the ground. You got toothmarks on your ear. He didn't tear it, though."

As the girl worked on him her comments were very matter-of-fact. The salve had something in it that stung on the cuts. When she finished Mary told him, "The one near your eye will leave a scar. The rest will scab up and disappear."

The two of them sat back on the swing. Without thinking, Tyler put his arm around her. She snuggled against his naked upper torso. "If mama comes out, don't be surprised when I move away quickly," she warned him. In the meantime, she traced his muscles with her gentle fingers.

Tyler fought the urge to shout out, *We will get married tomorrow!* If he had had to stand up at that very moment, the young man knew he could not have. Thankfully the two of them sat and swung, looking at the harvest moon slowly moving across the sky.

Then they heard her mother call, "Mary. I have one of your father's shirts for Tyler. We'll wash his tomorrow."

"I'll get the shirt," she whispered. "You just sit here and relax."

The young man was standing when she came back out. Handing him the shirt, Mary told him, "Mama has coffee and wants us to join her for a cup."

As they walked into the kitchen, the lamp light fell on Mary's arms. Tyler saw the bruises caused by Rex gripping them. Anger flashed through him, "He hurt you."

"It didn't hurt so much," the girl assured him. "He was just holding tight so I couldn't get away."

Tyler sat with them, drinking the coffee and eating another small cake, acting like he hadn't a worry in the world, but inside he was boiling. Rex would pay for putting a bruise on his girl.

CHAPTER SIXTEEN

Rex had left the very next day with some hide hunters, and the earliest he'd be back would be six weeks. This he found out from Sheriff Kent when he went to work the next day. "That Rex is a troublemaker," the sheriff told him. "If you fight him, it won't be a fair one. You'll be fighting with fists, and he will have a knife hidden that he'll slip between your ribs."

By October Tyler was two months into shooting ducks. He was coming back to the dock when he saw someone sitting on the bench in front of the cabin. Then he realized it was Alvin Jakobs. While he was tying the boat, the young boy came trotting down to the water.

"I been waiting for you," he said. "I heard the big gun shoot."

Alvin watched as Tyler sorted the ducks on the dock. He then helped hang them onto the poles. "You got a knife?" the young man asked.

"I do," Alvin said.

"Let me show you how I gut these birds," Tyler told him.

When the ducks were cleaned, he told the boy that he used to feed the entrails to the hogs, but now he dumped them beyond the garden and let the wild animals eat them.

"I brought you a hog," Alvin said. "Pa figured we owed you and he don't like owing nobody."

"A hog?" Tyler asked.

"Yep," the boy said. "It is in the pen. I had to fix the fence some, but it'll hold it now."

The two of them walked behind the cabin carrying the bucket. There in the pigpen was a nice sow rooting around at the weeds that had grown up. "It wasn't necessary to do this," Tyler told the boy.

"Pa also made a deal for the horse," Alvin said. "He gave two nice hams for the animal."

"Your pa got took on that deal," he told the boy. "It'll cost you more than it will ever give back."

"Pa said it was mine to take care of," the youngster replied. "I ain't ever had a horse before."

Tyler just hoped that the animal would last long enough for Alvin to enjoy it. He remembered having to put down the white mare. The thought still made him feel sad.

"Do you have to be anyplace soon?" he asked the boy.

"Pa said to be back waiting at the trading post by six. He gave me his pocket watch so I'd know the time," Alvin told him, proudly showing the watch.

"We got time to go for some afternoon ducks," Tyler told him. "Do you want to go with me?"

Off the two of them went on an afternoon shoot. It took the young boy only a few minutes to learn how to pole the boat. The redhead lay in front with the punt gun. Suddenly Tyler was filled with emotion. He had hunted with grandpa when he was Alvin's age. Now here was the young boy pushing the boat and he was lying ready to aim the punt gun, just like grandpa used to.

With a few minutes to spare, Tyler had the boy at the trading post. He lowered Alvin from the bay and then swung off himself. Burt was already there. He had a wagon pulled by a matched team of chestnuts. On the back was the old horse for Alvin.

"I see he got the hog over to your place," Burt told Tyler.

"Yes, he did," the young man replied. "I appreciated it very much."

"We owed you as much," the man said.

"We went duck hunting," Alvin told his pa.

"Don't be thinking hunting ducks is better than raising hogs, son," Burt told him.

"He gave me two to cook for our supper," the boy said proudly.

"Mergansers?" the man asked.

Smiling, Alvin replied, "No. Mr. Tomas kept them for himself."

Then Tyler saw the man smile for the first time. "I thank you for what you did for Alvin. The duck hunting too."

The boy climbed into the wagon with his pa and waved as the two of them drove away. The rundown horse following behind. The way the boy looked at the horse, you'd have thought he was looking at a thoroughbred.

* * *

That year Tyler's and Mary's Christmas was ruined by a shooting. Evidently the two Basset brothers who worked at the mill were celebrating the holiday and had too much to drink. An argument ensued and then a shot was fired. The elder brother lay mortally wounded and the younger one, Bobby, took the family horse and rode out of town.

Their mother came to the Price residence where Tyler was celebrating Christmas and through her tears told about the shooting. A half-hour later, Tyler was saddled up and on the trail. Mary had given him a sad look and a kiss. "I know you have to go, but be careful. If something happened to you, I would never enjoy another Christmas."

Riding away, Tyler figured it would be a quick capture. Despite his hopes he had a blanket roll in a ground tarp, enough food for a week and a pan to cook it, a coffee pot, some grain for the horse and warm clothing in case the weather turned colder.

The shooter's tracks in the new snow were plain. It appeared he was heading for Lowell. When they turned into the mill, the young deputy figured the chase would be over soon. Bobby Basset had ridden away without extra food and no weapon. He had left the single-shot pistol at the scene of the crime.

The mill was eerily quiet on Christmas day. There was only the sound of the steam engine running at idle. A tender would work the holiday, keeping it running to prevent the boiler from freezing.

Then Tyler pulled the bay up. There was a man lying in the snow outside the mess area. Climbing down, the deputy pulled his Colt. Watching and listening, his revolver ready, Tyler led the bay toward the mess. Stooping down, he checked the man. He wasn't dead, but he had a gash on the side of his head. His hair was frozen to the icy snow.

When the deputy lifted him and pulled the hair loose, the man groaned. Other than the man, Tyler saw no movement or heard no sound. He got the man sitting up and his head rolled back. His eyes opened and again he groaned. "It was the younger Basset boy," he said.

"Is he still around?" Tyler asked.

"I heard him riding away before I passed out," the man said.

That gave the deputy some relief. At least he could help the man without having to worry about an attack coming his way at any time. While getting him into the mess, Tyler learned that Bobby had come here to get supplies and blankets. He had also gotten a revolver from the tender.

"I carry the old .28 caliber Colt to shoot rats. It helps me stay awake at night," the man said.

"Did he get extra balls or powder?" Tyler asked.

"Nope. All he got is the four shots I had loaded," the man said, holding his head. "No, that's not right. He only had three. I shot at a rat this morning. Got the thing, plum center."

When Bobby got to any small town, it would be easy enough to get more powder and lead. "Did he tell you he shot his brother?"

"He shot his brother?" the tender asked. "I ain't surprised. Bobby wanted to go to California after gold and his brother wouldn't go with him and told him he couldn't take the family horse. They would go at it all shift."

That was important information. Now Tyler could be sure he was heading for St. Louis, or Independence. No doubt he planned to hide out there and then hook up with a train going west in the spring. The tender asked him to put some wood into the boiler before he left, and to stop by his place and let the family know so someone could come up and help him the rest of the shift.

After checking the gash, which wasn't too deep and had stopped bleeding, Tyler loaded the boiler and then headed to the man's home. He wasn't sure, but he thought he might have picked up Bobby's tracks past the mill. Finally, the young deputy was back after the shooter.

It was unlikely he'd head for Lowell, because it was less than ten miles from Cedar Creek and most of the businesses would be closed. It was also out of his way if heading west. He was riding a piebald that would stand out anywhere he stopped. Betting that he was heading for Independence, Tyler struck out for Decatur, about four days southwest. From there the shooter would go west.

Due to drifting snow, the fresh tracks of a horse stood out along the road. Tyler just hoped he hadn't guessed wrong. He rode well after dark on the well-defined road with the help of the moonlight. After midnight, he camped near a pond. Using the hatchet his grandpa had bought him years ago, he broke through the ice and watered the horse. After filling the coffee pot, he put together a small fire and put it on to heat. He ate some of the fruit-filled desserts that Mary had sent with him.

Spreading the ground tarp and his blankets under an evergreen, Tyler laid down. "I wonder if Basset is living as well," he mumbled.

The sun was coming up when he was putting the saddle onto the bay. It had finished eating some grain and he'd already watered it. The sun was on his back when Tyler rode away. He had the tuque on to keep his ears warm.

Two hours later he spotted a black spot in the snow alongside the road. Turning the horse towards it, he saw that it was a campsite. He could see where the person had rolled out their blankets on top of the snow. There were also a couple of empty cans that had made the person's meal.

Continuing, Tyler felt that his hunch had been confirmed. Nobody except someone who was running, or someone chasing the runner, would spend the night sleeping in the snow on Christmas day. He figured that he was no more than two hours behind Bobby Basset.

Near noon, Tyler came to a small, no-name town comprised of a couple of dwellings and a small trading post. Stopping at the trading post, the young deputy pushed open the door and stepped into the dim interior.

"Move and you are dead, mister," a man snarled.

"I am a deputy from Cedar Creek. I am after a man that killed his brother," Tyler said, his hands raised slightly.

"Show me your badge," the man demanded.

Taking it out from under his coat, Tyler held it up. "I take it someone visited you looking for supplies and maybe needed .28 caliber balls for his revolver?" he asked.

"He took money and a rifle," the man said. "My name's Kelly, I own this place."

"Did you notice what kind of horse the man was riding?" Tyler asked.

"I sure as hell didn't," Kelly said. "I gave him what he wanted and then the bastard took a shot at me as he left. Hit the damn wall right next to my head."

The young man got a cold feeling inside. The man he was chasing had no regard for life. "How long ago was he here?"

"Not much over an hour, maybe two," the man told him.

Tyler was stiff and his feet were cold from the continuous travel. He would have liked to have stayed and warmed up, but he was too close to catching Bobby. He purchased some jerky and gulped down a cup of lukewarm coffee that Kelly had. He also got a small bag of grain for the bay.

As he was leaving, Kelly said, "When you catch the bastard, let me know. I'll attend his hanging and cheer the hangman."

The young deputy continued out of town. The afternoon travel was against a cold west wind. His only consolation was that the man he was chasing faced the same miserable weather.

After another cold night sleeping on the ground, Tyler woke to a bright morning. The cutting wind had died down. He started off leading the horse, trying to warm up. He should make Urbana before dark. After walking a mile, Tyler climbed onto the horse. The saddle felt stiff and cold.

Urbana had been settled in 1822 and originally called Big Grove. The name had been changed only 10 years ago. Mills manufacturing various items had been built, bringing in additional other businesses. With that came a church for Sundays, and the taverns for Friday nights.

As Tyler rode down the main street, his eyes were on the taverns. A few had horses tied out front, but none were the piebald. The young deputy saw a large building with "Livery" painted on the front. The large bay doors were closed to keep the cold out.

Riding up to the livery, Tyler swung down from the bay. His feet were numb from cold and his muscles were stiff. Built into the left-side big door, was a smaller one with a latch. Tying the bay to a nearby corral, the young deputy went in.

It may have been only 50 degrees in the livery, but it felt like heaven to the chilled rider. "Come over to the stove," the hostler called to him. "I got some coffee just about done."

"I'd like to bring in my horse," Tyler told the man.

The hostler opened one of the big doors and the young man led the bay in. "This horse has carried me a long way and I best take care of it first. Then I will take you up on that coffee."

The hostler stayed close as Tyler stripped the gear off the bay. The winter hair was long and had several bits of twigs and such. The young man knew he had to groom the animal before going any farther.

"My name's Lem," the hostler told him. "It's two bits a night for the horse and another two for grain."

"How much for brushing the burrs and sticks out?" Tyler asked.

Looking the animal over, Lem said, "Six bits gets you the whole shootin' match."

When putting the horse into a stall, the young deputy felt a jolt. Two stalls down was a piebald. "How long has the piebald been here?"

"It come in just after noon," the man said, rubbing his whiskered chin. "The young man that was riding it was nearly froze."

Tyler decided not to tell the hostler about his interest in the piebald, and Lem didn't seem to want to know why he had asked. Once the grain and some hay had been given to the bay, the two men went over to the potbelly stove. The young man's feet were starting to warm up and it was hard to walk with the pins and needles he felt every step.

The hot coffee warmed Tyler's insides and he made small talk with the hostler. While he told the man, that he had come from Cedar Creek, again he did not tell him his purpose. It was starting to get dark and the young deputy made arrangement to sleep in the livery that night.

Leaving the warmth of the building, Tyler headed up the street. He had seen the jail on his way in, but he'd been too cold to stop. Reaching the building, he tried the door. The latch gave and he stepped in.

A burly sheriff sat at a desk to one side. He swiveled on his chair and asked, "What can I do for you?" His eye was on the holster protruding from the bottom of the coat.

"I'm a deputy from Cedar Creek. There was a killing in our town and I believe the shooter is here in Urbana," Tyler said.

"You'll need a U.S. marshal to arrest him," the man told him. "I don't have any warrants for him here in Urbana."

The young deputy opened his coat, exposing the badge. "I am a sworn officer and he killed a man in my town. I am going to take him back."

"I won't stand in your way," the sheriff replied. "Just don't get any of Urbana citizens killed taking him."

"A way back, he robbed a trading post," Tyler said. "After getting what he wanted, he took a shot at the owner. This man's going to shoot and I can't promise that his wild lead won't hit a bystander."

"I run a quiet town here and if you create trouble for the folks," the sheriff said, "I will hold you responsible."

Frustrated, the young deputy realized that he'd have to take Bobby prisoner while outside where *folks* weren't around. Thanking the sheriff, and thinking *for nothing*, Tyler walked out of his office into the coming dusk. There was a café on main street that would give him a good view of anyone coming or going.

The smells of the café reminded the young man of going with his grandpa to Momence. He took a seat near the window. The edges were frost-covered, but he still had plenty of clear glass to see the street. A pretty waitress came over. "We have mulligan stew on special."

Soon there was a bowl of stew, some bread and butter, and a steaming cup of coffee in front of him. Living out of his saddle bags for the past three days had left the young man hungry. While chewing the tasty stew, Tyler saw the sheriff come out of his office and head down the street.

"The bastard could have been more helpful," the young deputy muttered.

He was halfway through the bowl of stew when he heard the shots! Tossing some coins onto the table, Tyler nearly spilt everything as he headed out the door carrying his coat. Again, there was a shot. It was coming from the tavern a few buildings down.

Tucking the coat under his left arm, the young deputy drew his Colt. He hesitated at the tavern door and then went in low, looking for Basset. Lying in the sawdust of the smoky room was the sheriff. Two men were trying to help him. Other than those three and the bartender, the place was empty.

Kneeling next to the sheriff, he saw they'd opened his coat and there was blood coming from two places on his chest. The sheriff had a shocked look on his face. "I should have let you come after him. He saw my badge and started shooting."

"He went out the back door!" the bartender said.

Dropping his coat onto the dirty floor, Tyler went out the front into the dark street. Bobby had to be heading for the livery. He'd probably kill Lem and leave with a fresh horse. As he ran, the young deputy tried to remember how many shots he'd heard. The shooter would have one, maybe two shots left.

In his haste to reach the livery first, he couldn't stop on the icy ground and Tyler slid into the bay door of the building. There was a shot and wood chips flew from the door jamb. Crouching, the young deputy turned and saw the outline of Bobby taking aim. He swung the Colt up and took a snap shot at the man.

Tyler shoved himself away from the door and slid onto his chest with the Colt up and ready. Again, he squeezed the trigger and sent a .36 caliber ball at Bobby's center.

As if in slow motion, Basset dropped the revolver and fell backwards. Tyler heard a whump sound as he hit the ground. Getting to his feet, the young deputy kept the Colt leveled on the still man. He heard running footsteps and he saw someone with a rifle who had come from the tavern.

"You got him!" the man shouted. As he came over carrying a rifle, Tyler saw him wipe his eyes. "He shot the sheriff."

"Stay back," Tyler told him. "He might not be dead."

The man raised the rifle and snapped, "I'll finish the bastard then!"

"Don't!" the young deputy commanded. "I'll take it from here."

Walking up to Bobby with the Colt leveled, he shoved him with his boot. Someone with a lantern came. Tyler saw that blood had spread in the left center of his chest. The young man knew he had hit the heart. The man was now facing his brother on the other side.

Suddenly his legs went weak and the young deputy leaned against the wall. He realized that he had just killed a man. Others had gathered around, commenting on the killing shot. All Tyler kept wishing was that the killing had just been a bad dream. Feeling the cold and looking at the body, he knew it wasn't.

Lem was holding the lantern and came up alongside Tyler and said, "Let me get you into the livery. You're covered with snow and about to freeze."

Almost numb, the young man followed the hostler into the building. Others grabbed Bobby and dragged him in. By lantern light, a half-dozen townspeople stood around Basset, most saying he was lucky he'd been killed and what they'd have done to him for shooting the sheriff.

The young deputy sat near the potbelly stove with a hot mug of coffee, warming his hands. Suddenly he wondered about Bobby's Colt. "I want to see the gun," he called to the gathering. Nobody responded.

"The Colt!" Tyler shouted. "I want to see the damn Colt!"

One of the men said, "I think it's still outside."

Lem nodded to one of the men. "Tiny, go look for the gun and bring it here."

A short slim, man headed out the door. A minute later he came in announcing that he'd found it. Tyler knocked the snow off the Colt. He looked. All the chambers had been fired. "It may have been empty when I shot."

"You were in a firefight," Lem told him. "Nobody has time to count shots at a time like that. I heard his ball hit the building, and then you shot," the hostler said.

"Did you hear two shots when I fired?" Tyler asked.

"I wasn't counting shots," Lem replied. "When the shooting stopped, I come out to look and you were getting up from the ground. The other man wasn't."

Then the men pulled the coat off Bobby. "Hey!" one of the men said, "You hit him twice. You got the right shoulder and one plumb in the middle."

The debate went on around the body. One man said that maybe the sheriff hit the shoulder, and another said that the sheriff had only shot once and, that was when he was going down and that shot went into the ceiling.

More townspeople came to gawk at what had happened. One of the men said that the sheriff was at the doc's and he was working on him. They didn't know anymore. Tyler's coat showed up beside him, brought by someone in the tavern.

An hour later, a wagon came to haul the body away. Tyler still sat with a mug of cold coffee in one hand and the empty Colt in the other. He had no answers whether the gun was empty when he'd shot Bobby, but he did manage to gather his head around the fact that it was a firefight and there hadn't been time to do any second guessing. You just eliminate the danger.

That night Tyler climbed into the loft. He was sure he wouldn't be able to sleep, but it did come, along with bad dreams. He was having trouble seeing and someone was chasing him. Then he was running after somebody and people were cheering him on. He could never see that someone. He woke covered with sweat in the cold loft.

"I got porridge for you," Lem called up. "They brought it from the café. I guess you overpaid for your stew."

Climbing down, Tyler said, "I ain't hungry."

"You best eat something," the hostler told him. "They put cream and sugar into it for you."

The young man was able to eat some after a cup of coffee. A man wearing a frock coat came in just as Tyler was finishing his meal. "Are you the man that was involved in the shooting?"

"I was," he replied. "I am Deputy Tomas from Cedar Creek."

"There will be an inquest in two hours at the courthouse," the man told him. As he turned to leave, he added, "The sheriff survived the night. He's sitting up and talking."

Tyler had read about inquests in the books the pastor had given him. He knew it would establish guilt or innocence. He remembered the sheriff's warning to him. Could it be that they would hold him responsible?

The court house was just up from the jail. Tyler walked there in the bright sunshine of the frigid morning. He wished that he'd have been able to clean up more than just washing his face in the water bucket. There were two buggies in front of the courthouse and another that looked like a hearse.

Over a dozen people had come to observe the inquest. A balding, white-haired man sat behind a desk at the front. Two empty rows of chairs were on the right side that would normally have a jury. There were open chairs at the front for the young deputy to sit in.

Tyler had brought Bobby's revolver and placed it onto the table for the judge to see. "What's this?" the man asked.

"It's the Colt Bobby Basset was carrying," the young deputy replied.

The judge picked it up, looked at it for a moment and then said, "Sit over there."

Then the judge opened the inquest. "This here gathering is to determine if the shooting of," he looked at Tyler and asked, "Bobby Basset?"

"Yes," the young deputy replied.

"Yes, your honor," the judge corrected him. "To determine if the shooting of Bobby Basset was a justified killing."

One of the onlookers jumped up and said, "Hell yes, it was. I saw him shoot the sheriff in cold blood and then he tried to shoot this here deputy."

"Arlo, sit down," the judge said. "We ain't to that part yet."

While the inquest had an air of formality, in reality there was a lot of back and forth between the onlookers and the judge. Tyler had only a brief time and said, "I heard shots and went to the tavern. The sheriff had been wounded and Bobby had gone out the back door. I tried to cut him off at the livery and he shot at me, then I shot at him. Twice."

The young deputy was about to expand on the shooting at the livery, about his fear that Bobby would kill Lem, and others down the road, but the judge was ready to make his decision.

"Justifiable!" he said, emphasizing it with a bang of a gavel.

The inquest was over and those in the courthouse quickly headed for the site of the shooting to have a drink. The judge was at the table collecting his things. Tyler walked up to him. "When can I get the body?"

"The body?" the judge asked, a look of surprise on his face. "We got plans for the body. It will be displayed for a while and then dumped into an unmarked grave."

"Bobby killed his brother and that's why I came after him," the young deputy explained. "Now he's dead, and back in Cedar Creek there is a mother that lost two sons since Christmas. I don't know how much it will help her, but I think she'd like to have the two boys buried in Cedar Creek. She'll have one to cry over and the other to scold."

"Folks won't like it," the judge said. "With the cold weather we could have left him on display for a couple weeks or more."

"You'd be doing me a favor if you let me take him and it would save you the cost of burying him," Tyler said.

The judge asked that they get two days to display Bobby. He said, "After all, with you killing him, you cheated the town out of a hanging."

It was a week before Tyler rode back into Cedar Creek, the frozen body of Bobby Basset slung over the piebald. He had made a quick stop to return the rifle to the trading post owner. The young deputy rode straight to Nate's and dropped off Bobby. The sheriff was summoned and Tyler gave him a copy of the inquest.

"I know the sheriff of Urbana," Kent said. "A kind of big fellow."

Then to Tyler, he said, "You did a good job of tracking this Basset kid down and bringing him back. There ain't no money to pay you for the extra days, but what you did won't be forgotten."

"Well, tomorrow is Saturday and I won't be working," Tyler told him. "I don't expect to be docked for the day."

Leaving Nate's, the tired young man brought the bay to the livery and then walked to Mary's. He still had the rest of Christmas to celebrate, not to mention the New Year he'd missed.

As the winter wore on, Tyler had fewer and fewer bad dreams caused by the shooting. The pastor had been very helpful explaining that in battle a soldier has no choice but to fire at the men charging him. God wouldn't hold it against him, because it was his job to bring Bobby Basset back dead or alive.

Had he brought him back alive, the county would have sentenced him to hang soon after. The young man had to admit that, the mother would have had a lot harder time knowing that her friends and neighbors knew, her son was being hung in nearby Crown Point.

The birth of Wil and Emma's second child, Eve, went a long way to pull Tyler out of the gloom of the shooting and the doldrums of winter. There were two babies born in Cedar Creek on that day. It kept Nate busy, running back and forth, trying to determine which would come first.

CHAPTER SEVENTEEN

The redhead and Mary would often go to visit Emma. The baby was growing fast and little Adam adored Tyler. It had been a year since Wil had left. So far there had been no letters from California. It was the same with the families of the others he'd gone with. It was like Wil had dropped off the end of the world.

Tyler continued to give money to Emma when he could. He always assured her that it was for the children. They were blessed with a warm April and the three of them walked to church with the little ones. The little ones were to be baptized. Emma had put it off for Adam, hoping that Wil would get back to be here for his son.

It felt good for Tyler to be sitting in a pew with the two ladies and the children. He got the feeling that he was surrounded by family. There was a little talk around town that Tyler was awfully close to Emma, but Mary did a good job in public to make sure everyone knew who his lady was.

The baptism went well except for a little fussing of the baby girl, Eve. Afterword there was coffee and sweet breads for the parishioners and a sweet drink for the youngsters. Tyler heard talk of the burial service for the two Basset boys. They'd been buried in a private cemetery.

The ducks and geese were coming in, and on his days off Tyler was in the marsh with the punt gun, harvesting the birds. He had a visit from Alvin, who offered to spend a week helping him hunt. The boy had ridden the old horse and had it in fair shape for its age. Tyler did the same as his grandpa, giving Alvin a few pennies for each duck they sold to Arnold.

It was time for the youngster to leave and Tyler rode to Cedar Creek with him. They parted at the livery, with the old horse plodding along, bringing its young rider home. As usual the young deputy headed to see Mary before starting to make his rounds. He passed the tavern and heard someone call his name.

Turning, he saw that it was Rex. "I am leaving for California tomorrow," the trouble maker said. "We ain't settled our score yet."

"That was a long time back," the young deputy replied. "I figured it had been forgotten."

"Well, I've been gone, making money for my trip to California," Rex told him. "I come back to say goodbye to family and settle old scores."

"Have you said goodbye to your family?" Tyler asked.

"As a matter of fact, I have. Now you're the last thing I have to take care of," the cocky man replied.

"I will give you something to think about," the young deputy told him. "Hold your hat up away from your body."

"Why?" the troublemaker asked.

"Just do it," the deputy replied.

The two men were all of 75 feet apart. Rex took off his hat and held it out. "Now don't be thinking that I am going to shoot you," Tyler assured him, "but I do want to show you something."

Drawing his Colt, Tyler aimed and fired. The ball hit the hat, causing Rex to drop it. "You could have hit my hand!" Rex snapped.

"I could have," the young deputy replied, putting the Colt back into his holster, "but I wasn't aiming at it. I don't think you can kill me at this range, but I sure as hell can kill you."

"We can get closer," Rex said.

"We can, but you will be just as dead when it's over," Tyler told him.

Flustered, the troublemaker felt he had to say something and blurted out, "You can have Cedar Creek, but don't you ever come to California. If I see you there, I will shoot you on sight."

"You've got a deal," Tyler told him. "Now drop your gun there, and it will be at the jail for you when you leave."

Rex hesitated, unsure what to do. "If you don't, I'll arrest you for threatening me, and that will get you 30 days in jail and you'll miss going to California."

A couple of his friends had come out of the tavern and one called to him, "Give him the gun, Rex. We ain't going to wait for you."

After collecting the weapon, Tyler looked at the angry man. "Thank you. I already got one death weighing on me. I didn't want another."

When he got to Mary's she asked, "Was that a shot we heard?"

"Yes," he replied. "Just someone showing off."

The next year went well for the young man. His adversary had left for California, the duck harvests were good, and the town remained quiet. Tyler had cut logs to build onto the cabin and he began to plan another room on the east side. Mary wasn't quite sure why he was doing it, because she had always seen them living in town someday.

He had already laid rocks for the foundation and was using a broad ax to flatten two sides of the logs. He would notch them the same way his grandpa had, making square corners. Mary and Emma would bring the youngsters and pick strawberries or raspberries when in season. Adam's face would be covered with berry juice when he left. Tyler had the promise that there would be jams or pies with the meals.

He had the walls up and the rafter poles before the snow. He had boards for the roof ordered from the mill. Then Sheriff Kent's back got worse, and with the amount of laudanum he was taking he was no longer able to work. While he remained sheriff in name only, Tyler had to decide about going full-time.

That would end his duck harvesting and slow the building to a crawl.

His pay would go from $30 to $50, and he would not have to split the fines and other duties that brought in fees. The deputy would still have Sundays off as long as there were no problems in town. Tyler could spend most nights sleeping on the cot in the jail.

Unable to pass up the extra money, it became necessary to hire two builders to put the roof onto the addition to keep the weather out. His plans to install them himself and make the shingles were gone. The first heavy snow came down in November and the three-room cabin was secure.

Just before Christmas, Tyler went to the trading post and ordered a kitchen stove. It was the latest thing. The cast iron stove had an oven that would roast a full-size turkey, and had two openings on the top for faster cooking and a tank on the side for hot water. When not cooking it would warm the cabin. It would be delivered in March or April.

Tyler ate his meals with Mary and her family each evening, which worked out well. At the jail he had a potbelly stove for heat and making a soup or coffee. Whenever the deputy had the time, he'd go to the cabin and work on the inside, cutting through the wall into the new room and putting in a window that looked out on the marsh. He also had plans to putting a porch along the front, but that would come next year.

Spring came and the deputy would be making his rounds and hear the ducks coming in. While he liked the security of the job, he missed hunting on the marsh. He'd see Arnold regularly in town and was kept updated on the hunting.

Emma still had no word from Wil, and while she didn't admit it, she feared she'd never see him again. Her children filled her days, and when at a dance Tyler would take her out onto the floor at Mary's request.

The cast iron stove came with some assembly required. It was all the buckboard could do to carry it. Jules accompanied him to the cabin to carry the pieces in. The merchant was impressed at how much bigger the cabin looked with the addition.

"Wait until I finish the porch," Tyler said, "you'll be able to watch the ducks come in and see the sky darkened with flocks of passenger pigeons."

* * *

In early August, a rider came into town leading a horse with a man bound with piggin strings. He rode up to the jail and swung off his sorrel. The man was slim and had an olive complexion. His dark, wavy hair was cut to the middle ear and he had brown eyes. One his hip was a Colt Paterson in the saddle scabbard was a Hawken rifle.

The deputy was sitting in front of the jail and got up to welcome the stranger. "I see you got a possible customer for us," he said.

"My name's Tom Lefevre," the slim man said. "I have a U.S. marshal coming for my guest and was told you have a good, secure jail in Cedar Creek."

"We do at that," Tyler said. "Bring him in and we can show him his new quarters."

Tom explained to the deputy that the prisoner was one of a gang that was wanted. "I make it my job to catch them for the reward."

As he locked the door on the cell, the deputy said, "So you hunt men. That's got to be kind of dangerous."

"It's up to the man I'm chasing," Tom replied. "Some I bring in tied to the saddle like this one, others are tied over the saddle."

Tyler thought about Bobby Basset and nodded. "Yes," he said, "some come tied over the saddle."

There was some coffee on the stove that wasn't too old, and Tyler offered his guest a mug. With the strong brew the two men sat outside. "I don't recognize your accent," the deputy said.

"It's New Orleans," Tom replied. "My folks live there. My father brings in men further south and I work to the north."

"So, it's a family business," Tyler replied. "What does your mother do?"

"When she's not taking care of my father," Tom replied, "she helps grandmother with spells and medicine."

"Spells?" the deputy asked.

"Voodoo and stuff like that," the man hunter replied.

"I have read about it," Tyler told him. "It can be bad for some folks."

"Or it can be good," Tom said. "They've healed a lot of folks."

"I should get some of that healing for the sheriff," the deputy laughed. "He's got a bad back and takes too much laudanum."

"That's bad," Tom replied. "A man can get stuck on that stuff."

After the horses were put up in the livery, the slim man came back to watch his prisoner. Tyler left at the end of the day and went to Mary's for supper. He promised to bring something back for Tom and the prisoner.

The town folk had seen Tom coming in with the prisoner and were all abuzz about it. At supper Tyler brought Mary and her parents up to date on what the mysterious man's business was. "I read that man hunters bring most of the men they catch tied over a saddle," she said.

"Mary!" her mother scolded her. "Where would you be reading that kind of stuff?"

"Maybe I overheard it one time," she replied.

"Mary is correct," Tyler told her. "If you have more than a day of travel, you have to watch the man you caught, night and day."

"Like Bobby," Mary said, trying to prove the point. Then she saw her fiancés face and wished that she had not brought the subject up.

Tyler forced the bad thought to the back of his mind and said, "Tom will be here for about a week, and I hope to bring him down to the marsh. He says New Orleans has lots of swamps."

That evening the two of them sat on the swing, enjoying the night air. They sat close and gently caressed each other. Mary was letting Tyler become bolder with his hands, but still had the control to say when.

Sitting still and allowing their passion to subside, the girl asked, "Where will you sleep if Tom has the cot?"

"The cabin is only a short walk," he said. "It will do me good to walk off some of the feeling I am having," he teased her.

She gave him a mock slap and then kissed him. "I best go in, or mama will come looking for me."

The walk to the cabin gave Tyler time to think. His resolve had weakened in the past year. He was thinking more and more of setting a date to get married. The work he was doing on the cabin coincided with marriage.

The back room was a big enough bedroom, but to have the front room serve as kitchen and sitting area just wouldn't do. His intention was to move the kitchen into the addition, providing a large eat-in room. The new stove would have its own chimney. The fire place would once again be functional and help warm the sitting room.

The covered porch would be the final part of the building. When it was done, he'd have a place to take his bride. Tyler knew that she wanted a house in town, and eventually he'd give her that, but they could start their family here on the marsh.

The next day, the deputy was pleased to see Sheriff Kent at the jail. He would manage to come in one or two days a week to allow Tyler to spend more time around town. On the weekends there was always the possibility that a drunk would be brought in to sober up, and when that happened someone would have to be at the jail most of the time.

Leaving the sheriff to watch the prisoner, the two men went to walk around the town. Emma was on her folks' porch with the kids when they went by. "There's a corn bread in the oven," she called to them. "Stop by on your way back and enjoy a warm piece."

"I do love corn bread," Tyler said back. "This here is Tom. He'll have some also."

The two continued up to the tavern. The young deputy was following up about a fight the night before. Lee Jackson was behind the bar. "If you are in here to eat, we got bear stew and some kind of berry pie."

"I appreciate the offer, but we have a promise of fresh corn bread," Tyler said. "I was wondering if you could fill me in on the fight last night. I heard one of the men ended up with some broken bones."

"It wasn't much of a fight," Lee told him. "One of the men in the ruckus tripped over a chair and broke an arm when he fell. That pretty much ended it."

"The fellow with the broken arm said it was two on one," the young deputy replied. "He said he was holding his own on one when the other cut him down with a chair."

"Is that what he said?" Jackson asked. "That must have happened when my back was turned. All I saw was a man tangled up in a chair."

"I imagine it was," Tyler agreed. "It appears that the two were good friends of yours and the poor bastard with the broken arm caught them cheating at cards. I'd hate to think your friends are running a crooked game. That would require me to close you down."

Getting a little heated at the threat, Lee replied, "Those that come in here to play cards are grown men and they should know that there will always be some that will take advantage of them. We serve good whiskey in here and they should stick to drinking if they can't afford to lose at cards."

Changing the subject, Tyler asked, "Have you heard from any of the men that went with Wil to California?"

"I heard that one was killed," Lee told him. "Other than that, nothing."

"Did you hear who?" the deputy asked with some concern.

"It wasn't Wil," Jackson replied.

As they walked out into the sunshine Tyler was forced to squint. "When you were talking to that Lee fellow, one of the hangers-on got up and was coming from your blind side. I stared him back."

"I heard him get up and hoped you would," the deputy said. "I appreciate it."

They were treated to warm cornbread and cool buttermilk served by Emma. She was as talkative as ever, asking Tom about where he was from. She had always found it easy to strike up a conversation with people and make them feel comfortable. Even when Tyler was just a boy, she had brought the best out of him.

"Has Tyler taken you down to the marsh yet?" she asked. "It is just heaven down there."

"He had spoken of going down there after rounds today," Tom told her.

Tyler didn't tell her that Lee had said about one of the Cedar Creek men having been killed in California. It hadn't been Wil and would only have made her worry about his safety.

That afternoon the two men got their horses from the livery and rode down to the cabin. A flock of passenger pigeons flew up, creating a cloud. "When I was young," Tyler told him, "I had this squirrel gun with shot loaded in it. I would fire up at the birds and three or four would come down for our supper."

Putting the skiff into the water, the two men went fishing. "We have swamps and bayous in Louisiana," Tom told him. "There's good fishing, but you have to watch out for snakes and gators."

"We got some snakes, but most aren't too bad," Tyler replied. "I have read about the alligators, but we don't have them. A gar is the closest thing, and they don't bother people except to get on your hook and maybe break a pole."

While the two men sat on the ends of the skiff fishing, Tom said, "I heard you asked about some men from your town that went to California."

"Yes," Tyler replied. "In fact, Emma's husband went in '49. He's been gone a long time and she hasn't heard from him."

"It doesn't surprise me," Tom replied. "I was there and most men work from dawn to dusk washing dirt to make enough to survive on. I was told that that was the place to look for my father, Rufus. It turned out that he was a mountain man with no interest in panning for gold."

"Is he the one that tracks men further south?" Tyler asked.

"He does," Tom told him. "He doesn't want to get too far from my mother. He left New Orleans before I was born and was gone for 20 some years before I found him and he came back with me."

"Did he know she was with child?" Tyler asked, thinking of Wil.

"He did not," the man hunter replied. "It was a great surprise for him."

Tyler caught a fish and dropped it into the bottom of the boat. Once he had the line back into the water he asked, "I hear there are thousands of miners in California. How can there be that many places to pan gold?"

Smiling, Tom replied, "It is not thousands, it is tens of thousands. Every river, stream, or ditch has someone digging for gold. Prices for everything are high. A head of beef can sell for $75 and a shovel for $20."

"Damn," Tyler said, shaking his head. "And I take it the gold isn't just lying on the stream beds to be picked up like pebbles."

Laughing, Tom replied, "No, it is not. I panned gold for six months and it was the most blistering, wet, and cold thing I had ever done."

By the time the two men got back to the dock they had eight decent-size fish. They planned to bring four to Mary's and four to Emma's. After looking over the cabin, the two men rode back to Cedar Creek. They stopped at Emma's first. She insisted that Tom come to supper that night. He accepted. Tyler offered to watch the prisoner until after they'd eaten. He then took the other four to Mary's.

The deputy dropped the fish off and went to relieve the sheriff. Kent thanked him for coming and slowly moved across the jail. "Your prisoner was complaining about having to go, but I couldn't take him."

Grabbing the keys off the hook, Tyler unlocked the cell. Keeping his distance from the man, Tyler followed him to the little house behind the jail. The prisoner was taking his time doing his business. The deputy knocked on the side of the building. "Let's hurry up in there."

"It's that damn food you serve," he heard the man complain. "It's got me some bound up."

Finally, Tyler heard the door start to open. Stepping around to the front of the little house, the deputy waited for the man to come out. A handful of something awful came flying towards him. Ducking to avoid the flying stuff, Tyler couldn't avoid the man as he bowled him over.

Falling backwards, Tyler landed onto his backside. Leaping back to his feet, he saw the man sprinting around the jail. At a full run, the deputy was after him. He figured that the prisoner's intention was to find any horse and hightail it out of town.

The deputy's long stride quickly overtook the man and Tyler caught up with him as he reached a horse. Grabbing the back of his shirt, Tyler pulled him away from the startled horse and threw the man to the ground. Drawing the Colt, he threatened, "Go for the horse and I'll put a hole that will solve your being bound."

Slowly getting up, the man put his hands up. "Put your hands behind your head, and if you touch me, I swear I will shoot you," the deputy threatened.

Marching the man back to the jail, Tyler locked him into the cell. "Ain't, you going to let me wash my hands," the prisoner asked.

"You got a bucket of drinking water in there," the deputy told him. "Wash up in that."

Going to the bench in front of the jail for fresh air, Tyler sat down, waiting for Tom to come and relieve him.

It was after seven when Tom came to the jail. "That Adam is quite the boy," he told Tyler.

"I agree," the deputy said, trying to be upbeat. "Your man in there gave me a little trouble when I took him to relieve himself."

"He can be creative," Tom said, smiling. "What did he do?"

"Go in and find out," Tyler suggested.

As Tom walked into the jail, he wrinkled his nose. "Sure does smell in here."

"I think your man needs a bath," the deputy told him. "I suggested he use his water bucket."

Mary had his supper waiting when he got to the house. There was fried fish with new potatoes and beans from the garden. Tyler had gone to the pump before coming in and made sure he had none of the stuff the prisoner had thrown on his clothing.

Tyler felt relief when the U.S. marshal rode in. He was accompanied by a horse drawn-wagon that resembled a cell on wheels. It would be the prisoner's home until he reached his final destination at the end of a rope. The man was cussing and shouting as Tom and the marshal dragged him over to the cage and tossed him in.

Before leaving, the marshal gave Tom the reward money. The two men watched the wagon rattling as it was drawn away by the team of horses. The marshal talked to Tom for a few minutes and gave him some posters.

The deputy watched as the man hunter put them into his possible bag. "Are they your next paycheck?" he asked.

"There's two men that killed a teller while robbing a bank," Tom told him. "Word is they are headed into Indian territory."

"You could be a while tracking them down," Tyler told him.

"They'll need places to spend the money," Tom said. "I'll be waiting for them to come to do it."

Emma invited Mary and Tyler to supper that night and Tom was also included. After she learned that Tom had been to California, she had loads of questions. Being aware that her husband had gone, the man hunter was careful of how he answered her questions.

The next morning, Tom resupplied at the trading post and then headed out of town. Tyler had found him refreshing and, in a way, envied all the places he'd been. Two things kept the deputy in Cedar Creek. He liked to think Mary was the first, and then there was the beauty of the marsh.

September, came and with it the ducks. Tyler could enjoy the sights and sounds of them coming in, splashing onto the marsh waters, but all his spare time was focused on the cabin. He put down a well in the kitchen for a pitcher pump on the counter. That would save him from having to haul water in the winter.

The kitchen stove made cooking much easier and the redhead even tried doing some baking. The results were less than great, but he now had biscuits whenever he wanted. He had a wide doorway going from the sitting room to the kitchen. He also built a doorway going into the bedroom

With the inside mostly finished, he began to build the porch. He ordered planks from the mill and he already had the base for the deck planks ready when they arrived. Emma and Mary often came to the cabin and were making curtains and other things that made the place look a little less like a bachelor's home. They both loved having the pump inside.

Tyler followed many of her suggestions during designing and building the addition, wanting to make it feel like it was hers too. She still talked of it being their first place before moving to town. Little Adam and baby Eve would wander from room to room, squealing and playing.

In October everything came to a halt when some cattle were stolen from a local farmer. Tyler was at the jail making his morning coffee when Ralph Johnson came in. "They stole my cows!" he blurted out.

"Mr. Johnson, please have a seat," the deputy replied. "What do you mean, they stole your cows?"

"I ain't got time to sit and neither do you," the man said. "I've had five cattle taken from my back pasture."

Realizing that the man was upset, Tyler took two mugs and began to pour coffee. "Have some coffee with me and tell me about the cows."

"While your drinking coffee the damn cattle are getting farther away," Johnson told him.

The deputy had just woken after being up late the night before with Mary, and really wanted his morning coffee. "The cattle don't move too fast, so a few minutes with coffee won't make much difference. Do you know who took them?" Tyler asked.

The anxious farmer finally sat and took the coffee offered by the deputy. "I don't know who took them, but when I went to bring hay to the young stock this morning, the damn cattle were gone. The back fence had been opened and they drove them right out of the pasture."

"You said 'they'," the deputy pointed out. "Was there more than one rustler?"

"I saw tracks of two horses," Mr. Johnson replied. "Two of the heifers are carrying calves and I am depending on them for milk this coming year."

The loss of the cattle would impact the farmer's income, and Tyler could understand his desire to have him hurry after the cows. With their coffee finished, the deputy told Ralph he'd meet him at the back pasture fence after he got a few items together and picked up the horse at the livery.

Thirty minutes later the deputy met Ralph. Tyler was carrying some supplies and a bedroll, anticipating a night or two retrieving the cows. The farmer pointed out the two horses' tracks and had already put the split rail fence back up.

Leaving the angry man, the deputy followed the rustlers. The stolen animals were being driven east. The last of the leaves were still on the trees, the nights had started to get cold, and a killing frost had finished off the gardens. He had a wool coat tied to the bedroll, just in case a north wind began to blow.

Tyler figured that they were heading for the slaughterhouses to the north. That would be a two to three-day drive, and then they'd have to find a place to hold the cattle while they made a deal to sell them.

As he'd expected, the trail turned to the north, and the deputy noted whiskey bottles discarded as the men rode. The picture began to emerge. The deputy guessed that the two rustlers had been drinking and decided to steal a couple of cows to get more money for more whiskey.

Then Tyler found a spot where they had stopped to rest. They had tied the cows to saplings to prevent them from wandering back to the farm. The deputy now figured that he would catch up to the rustlers before dark. He brought the bay to a trot for a while to close the distance.

About an hour before dark, Tyler caught the sounds of the two men pushing the cattle. Checking his Colt and Hawken, the deputy rode wide around the cattle. He then waited for them to come. The two hungover men and the cattle came into view. Tyler rode out to meet them.

"Your little caper is over," the deputy called to them. "Drop any weapons you've got and put your hands up."

The sleepy rustlers were instantly awake and spurred their horses in opposite directions. Tyler had his Colt drawn and could have easily put a bullet into the near rider, but he had recognized them as a couple of young men who hung around the tavern. They came from good homes, and he had no desire to kill either one.

The sounds of their running horses faded and Tyler was left with the five young stock. His only choice now was to drive the animals back to the farm and wait for the boys to show up in Cedar Creek. Turning the cattle, they seemed willing to head back for the pasture and the hay they were fed each day.

Tyler stopped at a pond with decent grazing nearby. It was dark and he needed to get some sleep. He had no way to corral the cattle, so he had to hope that they would graze and then rest to chew their cuds, or continue back towards the farm.

After making some coffee and frying up some side meat, the deputy put out his fire and led the horse closer to the cattle. Pulling off the saddle, he picketed the animal so it could graze. Wrapping his blanket around his shoulders, Tyler sat against a tree and dozed on and off. Each time he woke, he'd listen for the cattle, then he would again slip into blissful sleep.

Suddenly he was awake. The deputy wasn't sure what had woken him and he listened to the night sounds. He heard one of the cattle coughing, letting him know that at least one of the cows was still near the pond. The horse stood sleeping not far from him.

Then he heard it again! It was whispering. Hardly breathing, he strained his ears. "I think his horse is over there," someone whispered. Then there was the snap of a twig nearby and the sound of someone shushing the other.

Tyler pulled out the Colt. "Wally, Earl, I can hear you. You are in enough trouble already and unless you are planning to kill me, you best give up the cattle stealing business. If you're lucky, the farmer might decide not to press charges if you help me drive his cows back."

To punctuate his advice, the deputy cocked the Colt. Unaffected, one of the boys said, "We want you to drop your gun and let us take the cattle."

Tyler moved behind the tree and fired into the air, shattering the quiet of the night. "I warn you boys, I will shoot to kill. I let you go, Earl, when you ran earlier, but now you are close to feeling the sting of a bullet. Show your damn selves and do it without any weapons!"

He heard the boys walking towards him. "We don't have any guns, just knives," Wally called out.

"They are considered weapons, boys," Tyler said. "Drop them and show yourselves."

The sun came up with the deputy making breakfast for the two rustlers. The boys sat near the fire and looked scared. Hungover from drinking, they ate little.

"Are we going to prison?" Earl asked.

"In Texas they would hang you," the Tyler told him. "I will give you a chance to talk to Mr. Johnson. He works the farm with just his wife, and just maybe you two can come up with a deal that will keep you out of jail."

"We needed money," Earl told him. "We owe Lee, and he suggested we sell a few cows to pay the debt."

"Shut up, Earl!" Wally snapped. "You'll get us killed."

"Stealing cattle will sure as hell get you killed," the deputy told them. "What do you owe Lee?"

"We lost at cards and he gave us each $25 so we could try and win our money back," Earl said, getting a poke from Wally's elbow.

"Did you win your money back?" Tyler asked.

"No," both boys said.

Shaking his head, the deputy told them, "Clean up the dishes here. It looks like the cows are starting to wander."

Pushing the cattle back to the pasture went well, and soon Earl and Wally were putting the rails of the fence back. Mr. Johnson saw the cattle coming and came out to the pasture. The cows, seeing the man who fed them, walked over to him. The farmer looked them over before he came to the deputy.

"It doesn't look like any harm was done to the animals," he said. "The two that are bred will have calves in the spring."

"Earl and Wally here had a change of heart after taking them," the deputy said. "They hope there is some way they can make it up to you."

"Damn boys will make more work for me than they'd do," the farmer said. "Let the law deal with them."

"You are probably right," Tyler agreed. "But I did see you got posts and rails to fence in another pasture. We got another month before the ground freezes. If they did it, it would save you a lot of work come spring."

"You boys know how to set posts?" Mr. Johnson asked.

"We've done it before," Earl told him.

The farmer stood looking at the two disheveled boys. He seemed to be debating with himself. Then he looked at the deputy. "If they don't do the job, what happens?"

"They will spend some time in the county jail," Tyler told him. "As it is, with the deal, they will be on probation and have to check in with me every Sunday."

"Sounds like pretty easy punishment," Mr. Johnson snorted.

"The decision is yours," the deputy replied.

The two boys sat on their horses, their eyes large as their future was being discussed.

"If they do a good job, I agree to let them build the fence," the man said. "If not, I'll drag them down to the jail for you to deal with."

"Is tomorrow soon enough for the boys to start?" Tyler asked.

"It is," Mr. Johnson replied. "There won't be any meals included."

Thanking the man, the two boys followed the deputy to the jail. Tyler was exhausted by the long ride with little sleep. He motioned the boys to follow him into the building. "I thought we weren't going to jail," Wally said.

"You're not," the deputy replied. "Some rules are going to be set. You both better get your rest tonight, because starting tomorrow you must prove to Johnson that you are hard workers."

"We can do that," Earl said.

"For the next six months you'll be on probation," Tyler told them. "That means if I catch you around town drunk, with a firearm, or just plain making a nuisance of yourselves, you will end up in jail. Every Sunday you are to check in with me. You will find me at the church."

"Are you making us go to church?" Wally asked.

"I did not say that, but you will find me at the church, starting this Sunday," the deputy said. "You can stand out in the cold and wait for me to come out if you want, but you best be there every Sunday."

"What happens if we take just a couple drinks?" Wally asked.

"It will probably get you killed," Tyler told him. "I am going over to the tavern and fine Lee $50 for being an accessory to cattle rustling."

"What the hell!" Earl exclaimed.

The deputy watched the two boys walk away, arguing amongst themselves. Tyler was glad that Johnson was willing to let them build the fence. Otherwise, he would have had to turn them over to the county and that would have gotten them time in prison.

After catching a couple of hours sleep on the cot, Tyler cleaned up and made his rounds around the town. He did stop at Mary's and she warmed up some soup for him. He had one more thing to do, and he told her he'd be back later.

The Colt was loaded and he carried a Hawken in the crook of his arm. It was dusk and the lanterns were lit at the tavern. Being a week night, the crowd was light. Walking in, he saw Lee sitting towards the back of the room, having his supper.

Tyler walked across the tavern and stopped at the table. "We have some issues to discuss and we can do it here or come down to the jail," he told the man.

The owner waved a hand, inviting him to sit, while looking at the Hawken he was carrying. Jackson had just taken a big bite of a slice of bread and chewed as the deputy sat, waiting for him to swallow. Once he did, Lee asked, "You going to tell me what the problem is?"

"It appears you were an accessory to cattle rustling," the deputy told him.

"I don't know what the hell you are talking about!" the man said, pushing his bowl away.

"You put the idea into the heads of two of your customers to rustle cattle to pay a debt they have with you," Tyler told the man.

"You are talking crazy," Lee said with a sneer on his face.

"Earl and Wally owe you money and were told by you to rustle some cattle to pay it off," the deputy told him. "That makes you a partner in the crime."

"If they told you that, they are damn liars!" Jackson snapped.

"Well, we can have a hearing to sort all of this out, or you could just pay a fine," Tyler told him.

The deputy could see the veins pulsing on the man's temples. Lee was staring at the rifle that was tilted in his direction. "And, how much would this fine be?" the angry man asked.

"Now, you didn't tell them what cattle to rustle, did you?" Tyler asked.

"I didn't tell them nothing," Jackson snorted.

"I will take that as a no," the deputy said. "In that case we don't need to go to court and a $50 fine should settle things."

"You son-of-a-bitch," the owner growled. "You think your big stuff around here. One day you'll push me too far."

"And that push will put you into prison," Tyler threatened. "I got no problem with you doing business in Cedar Creek, but I know your games are crooked. You get the players drunk and then loan them more money to lose so you can control them."

The man just stared at the deputy with blood in his eyes. "By the way," Tyler added, "I got the boys working for me and will owe them right around $25 each, so I'd like to consider us all even. Does that work for you?"

"It doesn't work at all," Lee said. "It sounds like I am out $50."

"And out of jail," the deputy replied. "I apologize for disturbing your supper. Now I have to go to mine."

As he walked out, he turned back and said, "The boys are working for me, and I would be very disappointed to have anything happen to them."

"You just tell them they are banned from here forever!" Lee Jackson shouted, getting the last word in.

CHAPTER EIGHTEEN

There was wind and snow on many of the Sunday mornings, but the two boys showed up to report to Tyler. At first, they stood out front waiting for church to be over. As the temperatures dropped, they chose to come inside where it was warm, sat towards the back and then partook in the coffee and sweets that Bethel made.

They had done a fine job on Mr. Johnson's fence and on one Sunday morning Tyler had heard the man offer the boys some more paid work at his farm. The boys' card playing and drinking days at the tavern were over. The deputy had told them that their debt there had been settled.

Emma's children were growing fast and she continued to tell them that their father was in California finding gold for them, but Tyler knew that she had pretty much given up on ever seeing Wil again. She was working at the trading post while her mother watched the children.

Tyler had the cabin finished, and with Mary's help it was looking more like a home. They had finally set the date to get married. It would be the end of August. They would start their life together in the cabin and then see what happened from there. She had become quite attached to the place on the marsh.

There was talk of a couple from Momence building a café in Cedar Creek. They had staked out a location just north of the trading post. The winter snows had buried the stakes but not the hopes of the town to have a place to stop in and eat.

Lee Jackson's meal business was somewhat hit and miss. He tended to go through cooks and some he got were quite good, others were not. Once a week, Tyler would stop there and eat his midday meal. The deputy hoped that by giving the tavern some of his business, the owner would one day get over Tyler interfering with things.

The first signs of spring were coming when a man named Dutch came running to the jail looking for the deputy. "You got to come!" he shouted. "Warner Blake is going to kill his wife!"

Checking his Colt and grabbing a shotgun from the rack on the wall, the deputy followed the man. "Do you know why Warner wants to kill his wife?"

"He thinks she is seeing another man," Dutch replied.

"You work for him, don't you?" the deputy asked.

"Yes," the man replied.

The Blake home was off the trail that led to Tyler's on the marsh. Warner was a big man and raised chickens and supplied meat and eggs for most of the area around the town. Dutch was an employee. "Do you think she is?" Tyler asked. "I haven't heard anything about it."

Hurrying down the slush-covered trail, his boot laces flapping, the man said, "I don't . . . know." Then he added, "Warner has no reason to think so."

As they walked the deputy said, "Warner must have some reason to think she is cheating."

Tyler saw tears in the man's eyes. It could be the cold air, or maybe not. "How did you learn that he wanted to kill her?" Tyler asked.

"I heard him say it," Dutch replied.

"And where were you when you heard the threat?" the deputy asked.

They stopped near a large oak tree that was just short of the house. "I was feeding the chickens and I heard the yelling."

"Do you think he knows who it might be?" Tyler asked the man.

"Maybe," Dutch whispered.

"How long have you been seeing her?" the deputy asked, looking at the house rather than Dutch.

"A while," the man said, then realized what he'd done and swore. He then decided to come clean. "We were going to run away," Dutch told him. "Warner caught her packing."

"So, you weren't feeding the chickens," Tyler told him.

"I was in the house, and went out the bedroom window," Dutch replied. "He didn't see me."

"Had she started packing?" the deputy asked as he debated on how to approach the house.

The man hesitated, and then said, "She was going to."

The deputy knew that he had one angry man in that house. He had come from the mill early and had caught his employee in bed with his wife. Beside him was the lover without a coat, his boots untied, and without a hat. He had left the house in a damned hurry.

"You just stay out of the way," Tyler told him. "If Warner sees you, I am sure he'll shoot."

The deputy ran to the corner of the house. He could hear the woman crying. "Warner, it's me, Tyler."

"You got that damn Dutch with you?" the man yelled.

"Can I come in so we can talk" Tyler asked.

"You can if you want to see this cheating woman die," Warner said.

"Nobody needs to die," the deputy said. "You don't want to hurt her and ruin your life."

"My life is ruined already," the man said. "Folks around town will be laughing at me."

"Nobody is going to laugh at . . ." There was a shot!

Tyler went to the front door and kicked it open, ducking low as he went in, the shotgun leveled and ready to fire. "Warner!" he shouted.

The deputy prayed that he had fired out of frustration or even taken his own life. His wife might have cheated, but she did not deserve to die by his hand. There was no sound in the house, just the smell of spent powder.

"Warner," he said, "Mrs. Blake." There was no answer.

Tyler moved toward the bedroom, realizing that Warner might be loading the rifle. Looking around the edge of the door, he saw the man sitting on the edge of the bed. The rifle rested in his lap.

Steeling himself, the deputy moved into the room. He saw Warner's wife slumped over in the corner, covered with blood. "Why Warner?" Tyler asked. "Why?"

Walking to the bed, Tyler took the rifle and leaned it against the wall. "You'll have to come with me, Warner."

As they walked through the house, the man said, "We always wanted a child."

The deputy had no response to that. What would happen now was really quite simple. Nate would come and get the body. Warner would stand trial and be hanged. A jury might be sympathetic to the man whose wife had cheated, but not enough to let him live. Tyler pulled the broken door closed.

When they walked past Dutch, who was sitting and crying near the oak, the man did not even look at him. "Go and get Nate," the deputy told the weeping man. "Tell him to bring a wagon."

The word spread quickly in the small town. Various versions of what had happened were circulated. Tyler was tight-lipped about the incident. He would tell his story to the authorities that came to get Warner, and then at the trial if it went that far. He would not attend the hanging.

The big man sat in the cell, not talking and hardly eating. Tyler watched him and waited for the county men to come and get the prisoner. He had lots of time to second guess the moves he'd made. Tyler racked his brain, trying to figure out if there had been something else he could have done to save the woman. Maybe he could have gone around back and shot Warner through the window before he killed her.

Tyler slept on the cot in the jail, watching the prisoner. He had written about what had happened to give to the county men. Mary would bring him and Warner evening meals. Other meals would be bought from the tavern.

He and Mary would sit out in front of the jail and talk. The only thing that the girl said about the shooting was, "I would never do to you what she did to him."

Just over a week after the killing, a man rode up to the jail leading a horse. "I've come to get the prisoner."

Tyler was glad to get the reminder of the tragedy out of his jail. Nate had taken care of everything else. The woman had been buried with the mourners and curious attending. Tyler and Mary had been there, but those with questions for the deputy were disappointed and got no answers.

Someone saw Dutch watching the county man lead Warner Blake out of town. Two days later he was found dead by his own hand. He had a note that requested he be buried with the woman he had loved.

It was the final act that put a gloom over the town that even the fresh breezes of spring couldn't lift.

In May, everything changed. Wil came home! He rode into Cedar Creek on a tired horse after spending the winter at Fort Laramie and he was still wearing the $3 hat. The adventurer not only came back, but he had found gold. Not as much as some, he admitted, but he had a canvas sack with dust and nuggets.

It was a great time at the Wilson house. Emma had a welcome back party on the front yard and she invited the whole town. They purchased a hog from Burt Jakobs and roasted it. There was food, drink and music to rival the 4th of July celebration. Watching Wil play with his children made Tyler's heart swell with happiness.

Mary walked with him in the crowd. "You never thought he'd come back, did you?" she asked the deputy.

"I cannot lie, Mary," he admitted. "It's not that I thought he'd abandon his family, but there were so many things that could have prevented him from doing so. Most of them bad."

"Now he can be your best man at our wedding," she said, pressing against him.

"That is something I look forward to," he told her.

"Having him as best man, or our wedding?" she kidded him.

Tyler gave her a kiss on the cheek and replied, "Our wedding."

The celebration went well into the night. Slowly the crowd dissipated until it was just Mary, Emma, and Tyler. "Where did Wil go?" he asked Emma.

"He wanted to go to the tavern and buy a round or two," she said, forcing a smile.

Wil had heard at the tavern that there was a man in Lowell that was some kind of assayer. He did metal work and would buy gold and silver to melt down. Some said he was tied in with counterfeiters, but Wil assured Tyler that that was just a rumor.

The next day Tyler went with Wil to Lowell to change the gold. The man had a small place off the main street of Lowell. He had scales and a forge and by all appearances was an assayer. "Let me see what you gave in the sack," the man said.

The assayer poured the contents out of the canvas sack in a pan, bits falling onto his table, and prepared to weigh it. Poking around the contents looking for sand or pebbles, he commented, "I don't get much raw gold this far east. I mostly get old jewelry and things like that."

Laughing, Wil replied, "Out in California every one carries bags of gold, but everything cost more than it should."

The nuggets, flakes and dust were weighed on the dusty scale, and the man said, "Just under seven pounds." Then he asked, "You carried this all the way back from California?"

Proudly Tyler replied, "I did."

"You're smart," the man said. "You would have gotten cheated out there."

Wil received $1,600 in coins. The coins were put into another bag, which was lighter than the original. Tyler asked about the seven-pound bag they brought becoming four pounds of coins. The man explained that raw gold was about 18 karats. The coins were pure and closer to 24 karats. "And then," he said, "there is a charge to change one to the other."

The deputy had to believe what he said. Tyler had read some things about gold and gold mining, but had not gotten into raw gold verses pure gold. Wil was thrilled with the amount he received. The deputy shrugged and figured if his friend was happy, that was all that was important.

The two men left the assayers office and Wil insisted on buying them both a meal. The best place to go was a boarding house with a good kitchen. The two men took a seat at one of the long, family-style tables. They had it to themselves, seeing it was midafternoon. A woman came from the kitchen with a stained apron. Wil said, "Give us two of your best meals."

The place lived up to its reputation. They were served roast beef, mashed potatoes, a side of early peas and freshly baked bread. Tyler dipped the bread into the gravy covered potatoes. While they ate the deputy remembered the meal that he and grandpa had had at Momence. Wil talked on about how much stuff cost in California.

It was late afternoon when they got back to Cedar Creek. "You best find some place to hide the coins," Tyler suggested to his friend.

"Hide them, hell," Wil replied. "I am going to show them off to everyone."

"You do and someone will knock you over the head and steal the coins," Tyler warned him.

The deputy had to work every day but Sunday and he didn't see too much of his friend. Wil would sleep late when home with Emma, and by midafternoon he was at the tavern. The deputy had stopped and warned Lee about his dealers cheating his friend. Whether it would do any good or not, Tyler couldn't be sure.

One morning, while making rounds, he saw Wil sitting on the front porch. He went over and his friend offered him coffee. He called to Emma to bring out another cup.

She came out with a big smile for Tyler. "I am glad to see the two of you visiting," Emma told the deputy. "Things have been so busy since Wil got back."

"Tell me about California," Tyler said.

"There ain't much more to tell," his friend replied. "The trip to the gold fields was tough. We didn't take enough food, and after Fort Hall there wasn't any place to buy any until we got to Coloma. We had quite a shock at the prices there."

"All that must make Cedar Creek seem mighty small," the deputy said.

"It will be okay for now," Wil replied. "I have thought about going to the Minnesota territory."

"It could be wild country," Tyler told him. "You got the Ojibwe, Dakota, and Ho-Chunk that might take exception to you being there."

"Hell," said Wil, "I was in rougher areas on the trip to and from California."

"I hope you stick around for a while to be with Emma and your children," the deputy told him.

"If I did go," his friend said, "it would only be to look the area over, and if I found a good place for my family, we could move there."

They continued to talk while Tyler finished his coffee. His friend was a dreamer and had the itch to see new country. The deputy thought about where he had been putting his efforts to make a home for himself and Mary.

Before he left, Tyler suggested, "The Blake place is still vacant. You should consider spending some of the gold and buy that for Emma. It's got the coops, so she could even raise chickens if she wanted."

"Ain't that the place the man killed his wife?" Wil asked. "I don't think Emma would want to live there."

"I've been in the place since," the deputy told him. "Her family came in and cleaned everything up and I understand they plan to sell."

He got no reply from Wil and it was time to continue his rounds. His friend went back into the house. Mary was planting something in the garden and the deputy stopped to watch her. "Is visiting and watching others work the job of our town's deputy?" she asked kiddingly.

"No," Tyler replied. "I just like looking at you."

She stood up with her hands on her hips. "Tyler Tomas. Are you saying you like seeing me covered with dirt?"

Smiling, he replied, "That, and even when you are freshly scrubbed."

"I got tomatoes to set here," she said. "You best continue on your rounds before you talk me into sitting on the porch with you."

"You know the Blake place?" he asked.

Shaking her head, she said, "It was a shame what happened to them. Warner couldn't have been thinking straight when he done what he did."

"I told Wil he should buy it for Emma and the children," he told her. "He said Emma wouldn't live there."

"She helped them clean the place up," Mary replied. "I don't think she would mind that place or anyplace so she could get out of her folks' house."

Then she gestured him to go and turned to continue planting. Edmond was talking to the smithy and Tyler joined them. They were talking about some detectives from the east that were in Lowell, asking questions about a robbery. They wanted to know if Tyler had gotten anything on it.

"Things are nice and quiet here in Cedar Creek," the deputy replied. "If a robbery out east affects us, they will send flyers out."

Then he asked the smithy, "Could you reshod the bay later this week? It's been almost two months since that was done."

Arrangements were made and the deputy moved on. Not long after he'd gotten the job, Tyler had learned that a good part of the duties was to listen to any and all gossip that was being spread around the town. After a lifetime of isolated living and working in the marsh, he kind of liked knowing what was going on.

His next stop was at the tavern. It sported a newly painted sign: *Lee's Tavern*. They had even painted the weathered clapboards. The windows were still fly-specked and the floor covered with sawdust. The deputy walked into the dim and smoky place.

"I like your new sign," he told Jackson.

"I figured it would give the place more respectability," Lee told him.

Leaning onto the bar near the owner, Tyler said kiddingly, "It's the silk on this sows' ear."

Pretending to be offended, the man replied, "Ain't nothing makes you happy."

Then the owner said, "I got fresh bread and some aged cheese. Do you feel like a sandwich?"

While the deputy ate the food and drank a sarsaparilla, he and Lee talked. Unexpectedly the owner said, "Wil's gambling the gold away and buying everyone drinks."

"Is he being cheated?" the deputy asked, setting the sandwich down.

"No," Lee said. "At least not by my regulars. He is just a damn bad card player. He bets high on nothing and folk know this and call."

"You could bar him from the place," Tyler suggested.

"When you were hunting ducks on the marsh, would you ever shoot and then only pick up every other duck?" Jackson asked.

Taking a sip of the sweet drink, the deputy said, "It ain't the same."

"Will brings players in and players drink," the owner said. "It ain't my place to tell you, but he has even gone to the back with a woman or two."

You could have knocked Tyler over with a feather as shock from the revelation went through him. "Have you talked to the women about not doing that?"

"It's how they make their money and Wil is a big tipper," Lee said. "I just wanted you to know these things. I could have kept quiet and let him waste all his gold, but then when he was broke, you'd come in here and blame me."

The last of the sandwich was tasteless as the deputy finished his meal. Lee had gone to serve some other customers. Tyler was torn up inside. He knew that the gold was as good as gone. It was only a matter of time, but the information that Wil had gone back with the women in the tavern overwhelmed him. He knew it was information he'd have to take to his grave. He could never hurt Emma.

The deputy left Lee's Tavern with a heavy heart. It wasn't always so good to know all of the gossip. He began to think that it might be good if Wil went to the Minnesota Territory. Maybe some of the wildness would be gone when he came back and he could be a proper husband and father.

There was a little bit of a drag in the deputy's steps the rest of the day. He stopped in front of the new café and saw that they were finishing up the inside. A sign in the window said, "Opening in one week." Tyler had already had a preview of one of the things that the café would offer. She had been frying donuts, or what some called bear sign.

Tyler wished he'd have skipped stopping at the tavern. Most everything the deputy learned around town, he would share with Mary. What he had learned today could not be shared. He walked up to the trading post to visit with Jules.

To his surprise, Emma was working. "I thought this was your day off," he told her.

"I need the hours," she told him. "The young ones grow out of their clothes faster than Mrs. Price can make them."

"That shouldn't be a problem with the gold that Wil brought back," he told her. Inside he was screaming, *It would be better than losing it at poker and spending on those ladies!*

"That's his money," she said. "Wil made it clear that he worked hard for it and it should be his to spend."

The last shred of respect for Wil disappeared from Tyler's mind. Emma finished putting the cans of fruit onto the shelf and came over wiping her hands on her apron. "I took some coins from his bag one night when he got home drunk. It wasn't much, but it will give me a fund for a rainy day."

"Maybe I could talk to him," the deputy told her. "You had asked me a long time ago, and maybe it is time. I did mention he should buy you the Blake house."

"They are having a hard time selling it," Emma said. "I wouldn't be afraid to live in it."

"I imagine you wouldn't," Tyler replied. "You have always been a brave one."

Jules came from the back and the woman continued stocking shelves. "Did you hear the news?" the owner asked.

"Nothing that I liked," the deputy replied, offhandedly.

"We are opening a post office right here in the trading post," Jules said, as proud as a father with a new baby.

"That is great news," Tyler said, suddenly interested. "Now we won't have to wait for someone from Lowell to find time to bring it this way."

"It will still come from Lowell," the merchant said, "but they will bring it regular, three times a week."

As the deputy left the trading post to head for the jail, the cloud had lifted from his thoughts. The café was going to open soon, and Cedar Creek was going to get mail. The next thing he knew the stage would come through or hell . . . even a train.

Supper at Mary's was somewhat subdued that night. A man working at the mill had some logs roll onto him and right now it was touch or go whether he would survive. Tyler tried to cheer everyone up talking about mail coming in and the café opening.

Suddenly, out of the blue, Mary asked him, "Do you like fried green tomatoes?"

"I don't know," Tyler replied. "I don't believe I have ever eaten one."

"I was talking to Mrs. Johnson today when she walked by and she saw me planting the tomatoes. She asked me if I fried any of the green ones, and when I said no, she told me how to make them."

"I will look forward to fried green tomatoes," he told her.

"She also said that Wally and Earl are still working on their farm and they are a great help to her husband," Mary told him.

Smiling, Tyler replied, "That is the best news I have gotten all day."

"Even better than the mail coming?" Helen asked.

"Yes. Even better than that," he replied. Tyler felt that he was losing with Wil but knowing that two troubled boys had come around made him feel very good.

The next day was Sunday and Tyler came to church with the buckboard. Mary had told him she would like to go fishing. The two of them sat on the pew, just a little closer than her mother thought was proper. Mary whispered to her, "We could be holding hands, you know."

That set Helen's jaw and she looked straight ahead.

Mary no longer turned up her nose to riding in the buckboard. She had learned what a functional wagon it was and it had carried the beautiful stove to the cabin. Tyler had cleaned the skiff and put the seats in. He also had gotten some oars and fashioned some oar locks using pieces of wood.

The girl sat in the back of the boat, looking at him as he rowed to the fishing hole and dropped a hunk of metal on a rope to anchor the skiff in the current. "Do you think Wil and Emma will have another baby?" she asked.

Hoping the hell that they didn't, he said, "Time will tell. I'd like to think the first two should get a little older before they have another."

"Emma wants to get pregnant again," she said as she took the rod from Tyler. "She thinks that will keep him around. He is always talking about going to the Minnesota Territory to find them a place to live."

Then he muttered, "I just wish I could figure out a way to keep him away from the tavern."

"There's nothing wrong with a man going to a tavern to meet with friends," Mary said. "He comes home every night and they spend the mornings together when she isn't working. My papa stops for a drink on his way home from the mill some nights."

A drink is one thing, he thought. Tyler had so much more he could tell her, but he decided to change the subject. All he knew was that when the two of them got married, he would not be hanging around the tavern or doing what Wil was. Then there was a squeal. Mary had caught a fish.

Mary made him an early supper on the new stove. Then the two of them sat at the small table and enjoyed the tender meat and fresh vegetables from his garden. "Papa said that a guy he knows at the mill has a table that he wants to sell. It has four chairs. We could have Emma and Wil over to eat and the children could sit at this small table," she informed him.

Agreeing that it would work well for company, Tyler said, "We could keep the small table on the porch so we could eat on nice evenings and watch the ducks come in."

Priming the kitchen pump, the two of them cleaned the dishes, then Tyler went down to the dock and got the stringer of fish for Emma. The bay stayed at a trot pulling the buckboard back to Cedar Creek. Mary commented on every bump, but never told him to slow the horse.

Pulling up at the Wilsons' house, Tyler followed Mary in carrying the fish. "Emma," she called. "We got a surprise for you."

The young mother came to the door and it looked like she had been crying. "What's wrong?" Mary asked.

"Wil came by with a friend of his that had gone with him to California," she said. "The two of them were going hunting and he asked me to pack enough for them to last a week or two. I told him we had plans for the 4th of July. He got mad and told me to just do it. Then I saw him take the bag of coins. He reached in and tossed a handful onto the bed and told me I should buy food to replace what he took."

"Maybe he just wants to get away from things," Mary told her. "It is crowded in this house with the children and all. I bet he comes back in less than a week and is happy to be home."

The deputy stood wondering what they could be hunting this time of year. Anything big that they shot they would have to can or make into jerky. Out on the plains they wouldn't be able to can. Then it came to him. Wil was going with his friend to the Minnesota Territory to look things over. He was just forgetting about his responsibilities here in Cedar Creek and looking over the next horizon. At least he left her with some money. Why the hell hadn't he done the right thing and left her most of it to hold here?

CHAPTER NINETEEN

Things got back to normal in Cedar Creek. Soon it was like Wil had never come back. The 4th of July came and Tyler successfully defended his shooting championship. Roy told him that this would be the last year he would be making the circuit. He had met a woman and they were going to settle down. He had already found a place for his gun shop.

With the memories of the July celebration still fresh in the deputy's mind, he sat on the front porch of the jail. He had lit his grandpa's pipe and blew clouds of fragrant smoke to catch the breeze. The two weeks had come and gone without Wil showing. It did not surprise Tyler. A trip to the Minnesota territory and back, plus some looking around, would easily take a month or more.

Gripping the pipe stem in his teeth the deputy was looking at some flyers that had come in by mail that day. Having mail delivered to Cedar Creek had made communication with the outside world much more efficient.

There was the sound of a horse coming down the dusty main street. The deputy looked up and did not recognize the rider dressed in dark clothing. As he got closer Tyler said, "Well, I'll be damned." It was Tom Lefevre from New Orleans.

The man waved and rode the sorrel up to the jail. "I see you're not leading some bad man today," the deputy called to him.

"I am not," Tom replied, "but I am always hunting some."

"I just got some flyers in," Tyler told him. "Maybe it's one of these men."

Tom swung down and came over to look. "No, that's not them," he said, shaking his head.

"Hello stranger," they heard a woman call. It was Emma pushing the young girl in the carriage and with Adam tagging along behind her. "We were just heading for the café."

Smiling, Tom removed his hat and bowed, "Why hello, Mrs. Lane."

"What brings you to Cedar Creek?" she asked.

"Same old thing," he told her. "Still hunting those that don't want to be found."

Laughing, she said, "This is a small town. Give us the name and we can probably point out where they are."

"I haven't eaten yet," Tom said. "You say there is a café now. I will join you if you think it won't cause talking."

"Folks are tired of talking about me," she told him. "You are welcome to come along also, Tyler."

The three of them, along with the children, headed for the café. The deputy was anxious to sit down and visit with Tom to find out what was going on outside of Cedar Creek, but after they ate would be soon enough. It was mostly small talk about the children at the checkered table. Tom asked how the 4th was and whether she'd ever heard from her husband.

Emma frowned and then replied, "He came back for a while, but then got the itch to go hunting. He must be chasing something awful big, because he should be back by now."

She got Adam a donut and he managed to frost his whole face while eating it. Sandy, the owner of the café, brought over a cloth to wipe him up. With their meals finished, Tom insisted on paying for everyone. "Last time I was in town you folks pretty much kept me fed," he said. "I am happy to pay for this one."

The two men walked Emma to her folks' house before heading back to the jail. "I need to bring my horse to the livery," Tom said.

The deputy made his rounds of the town, and met Tom coming back from putting the horse up. The slim man said, "You have a nice town here."

"For most part it is quiet," Tyler told him.

Arriving back at the jail, the two went in and the deputy put a couple of sticks into the stove to warm the morning's coffee. Coming back to his desk, he sat and asked, "What brings you this way?"

"I got some posters on some men that robbed a gold shipment. The driver and two of the guards were killed," Tom told him. "Additional guards were trailing behind because of some trouble with some

Lakota. The robbers didn't get away with too much gold when the returning guards drove them off."

Trying not to show anything on his face, Tyler was getting a sick feeling in his stomach. "How is this related to Cedar Creek?" the deputy asked.

"The robbery was some time back," Tom explained. "The Wells Fargo detectives finally caught up with one of the robbers. After some interrogation and an offer that he could avoid being hung, he gave up the other names."

"Was the gold carried in seven-pound bags?" the deputy asked.

"It was," Tom told him. "Each bag was worth about $2,000. There were four men and they grabbed six bags. One of the bags was dropped and reclaimed about a half-mile from the robbery."

The first thought that went through Tyler's mind was the assayer in Lowell could have been crooked and might have known about the robbery. Then he said, "I can't believe Wells Fargo has come all the way from California to search for the men."

"The robbery was just north of Independence near the Missouri River," Tom told him. "The man they caught was hiding out in St. Louis. They had alerted all the assayers of the robbery and one of them let the detectives know when a man came in asking about converting dust and nuggets to coins or paper."

Now, Tyler knew that the Lowell assayer was crooked. He would have known about the robbery. Wil needed to change the gold into coins and the man had done it at a great discount. The assayer would melt it down so it couldn't be traced and make $400 for his efforts.

Spreading the posters out on the deputy's desk, the slim man said, "I think one of these men is Emma's husband."

One read, Wanted: William Lane for murder and robbery.

The deputy read no further. The other was for Pepe Laure, who was the man that was with Wil and supposedly going hunting.

"He was here until three weeks ago," Tyler told Tom. "He had gold with him. In fact, I went to a local assayer with him when he converted it to coins. Wil said he'd gotten the gold panning in California."

Tom looked down and said, "The detectives told me that Wil and his friends had left the gold fields just ahead of the law that was intent on hanging them. They had been robbing and even suspected of killing miners for their gold. They lived high until one of the miners didn't die and identified them."

Then he looked up at the deputy. "The detectives figured that it was just a coincidence that the wagon they went after was a gold shipment. It is believed that they thought it was a freight wagon and were after supplies or something they could sell. You can imagine their surprise when they pulled up the tarp and saw the gold."

"I can believe that," Tyler said. "My understanding was that all the gold went by ship from San Francisco to the Philadelphia Mint."

"Most of it does. This was a corporate shipment of gold," Tom said. "They hired Wells Fargo to haul it to St. Louis."

The coffee was steaming so the deputy went to get it. *That son of a bitch!* he screamed inside. He poured two cups with shaking hands, and then gave one to Tom.

"It's a damn mess," Tyler said, "and now Emma is drawn into it."

"How so?" Tom asked. "She had nothing to do with what her husband did."

"Wil spent a fair amount at Lee's Tavern, but before leaving he gave her about $100. That is stolen money," the deputy replied.

"Did he take the rest?" Tom asked.

"He did," Tyler told him. "As best I can figure, he took $1,000 with him."

"Do you know where he was heading?" the slim man asked.

Tyler could have just played dumb at this point and no one would be the wiser, but he had taken an oath to uphold the law. That oath was important to the deputy.

"My guess is he went to the Minnesota Territory," Tyler said. "He talked of it a lot while he was here."

Tom tasted the coffee and made a face and set it back down. "On the east side of the Big Horn mountains there's a valley that the Powder River comes from. Riding in you run into several canyons that someone that does not want to be found can hide," the slim man said. "The Cheyenne and other tribes will winter there."

"I don't know how Wil and Pepe would know about it," Tyler replied.

"They have been around bad company," Tom said. "It is a place where outlaws hang out when they are on the dodge. I'm guessing they've heard about it, and that is why he talked of it."

Then Tyler asked, "How do I tell Emma?"

"You don't have to tell her," Tom told him. "And as far as the money he gave her, she can keep it. It isn't my job to get the money back. I just need to bring the kill . . . the robbers in."

"She will still wonder why I went with you," the deputy said.

"You're not going," the slim man said, furling his brow. "These men killed people and there is a chance that Wil won't be taken alive."

"And if he is taken back alive?" Tyler asked.

"He will be hung," Tom replied.

"I have to go," the deputy emphasized. "If for no other reason, for Emma."

"What about your wedding?" the slim man asked. "Emma said that you were going to get married in August. I don't think you'd be back for your wedding."

"I'll talk to Mary," Tyler said, his voice sounding weak, "but I have got to go."

That night Tom was invited to sleep at the cabin. The deputy had to go and see Mary before leaving town. The shadows were getting long as Tyler walked towards her house. The plan was that he'd meet with the slim man back at the cabin.

Mary saw him coming and broke into a wide smile. "I can make you green fried tomatoes for your supper. They are big enough now."

"We got to talk," Tyler said.

She saw the look on his face and tears came to her eyes. "Something is wrong," she said. "Is it you and me or is it someone we know?"

"It affects you and me, but we are good," he said as her tears spilt down her cheeks. "It is Emma and Wil."

A look of terror came to her face. "Is Wil dead?"

Tyler was trying to find a way to break the bad news gently to her and he was doing a damn poor job of it. Seeing the myriad of emotions going through her, he took her arms and said, "Wil did some bad things and is wanted by the law."

This seemed to settle her, and she asked, "Will he go to jail?"

"He was involved in a robbery and some men were killed," Tyler said. "Tom is here and he will be going after him."

"Wil wouldn't kill anyone," Mary said. "He just couldn't."

Now the deputy's emotions were overtaking him and he was finding it hard to talk. "He didn't have to kill anyone. He was there and will . . ."

She went pale and her eyes grew large. "He will be hung. Emma's husband will die."

All Tyler could do was nod. His throat hurt too much to talk. She had said what he'd been thinking all along. Wil would die being caught or be brought back to hang. The only possible positive was that the hanging would be far from Cedar Creek.

The two of them sat on the swing, arms around one another, and giving each other comfort. Then in a small voice she asked, "You said it affects us. How?"

"I should go with Tom to find Wil," Tyler said. "I may not be back before our wedding."

He expected her to say something, but she did not. She just kept holding him. The deputy knew he had to leave to go and see Tom.

After what seemed like an eternity to the deputy, she asked, "Do you have to leave in the morning, or will it be a day or two?"

"I don't know," Tyler admitted. "It might be a day or two. It's not like we will be following a hot trail."

She sat back, staring straight ahead. "I want us to get married before you leave."

"What if something happens to me?" he asked. "I am not saying it will, but I will be going after men that have committed murder."

"Don't you talk like that Tyler Tomas!" she cried.

He pulled her back close to him and whispered, "I will be careful and come back to you."

"I want one night together with you as husband and wife," she said, her voice becoming less hysterical. "And then I will pray to God that I will get another night when you come back."

It was after three when the deputy rode up to the cabin. Tom was still sitting on the new porch listening to the sounds of the marsh. "I figured you'd be sleeping by now."

"I've been thinking about things," Tom replied. "You have a beautiful place here. It will be a great place to raise a family."

After putting the bay into the corral, Tyler came back to the cabin and heard the slim man at the stove. Hearing him coming, Tom called, "I got some coffee on. I thought you might want to talk."

"I talked to Mary," Tyler said. "She is not against me going with you."

Coming out with two mugs of coffee, Tom replied, "I find that hard to believe."

The two men sat on the edge of the porch, facing the marsh. "She wants to get married before I leave," the deputy told him.

"And your honeymoon would be you chasing Wil and her alone here in Cedar Creek?" Tom asked.

"We'd have the rest of our lives to make up for not having a honeymoon," Tyler told him. "But I would need a couple days before we left to arrange things."

"Hell, when I get married, I won't even get out of bed for the first week, and you are talking about one night together?" the slim man asked.

"If you leave tomorrow," the deputy replied, "I will have no nights and I am going with you."

"You are probably right about where they are going and another day or two won't make a difference," Tom conceded. "But it can't be more. We aren't the only ones that are hunting for them." Tyler knew that he was thinking of the reward.

The next morning Tyler and Mary went to see Emma. She had just gotten up with the children and was in her nightclothes and making them breakfast. "You two are here mighty early. I haven't even finished making coffee."

"You need to sit down," Mary told her friend. "We're here to talk about Wil."

Continuing at the stove, Emma replied, "It can't be that he's back and Mary's not crying, so it can't be that he'd dead."

"This is hard," Mary said, tearing up. "I need you to sit."

Emma turned, her night clothes hugging her shapely body. She picked up Eve and sat facing them with the girl on her lap. "You've come to talk about Wil," she said.

Realizing that Mary wouldn't be able to say much more, Tyler felt it was up to him. "Wil has gotten himself into some bad trouble. He was involved in a robbery where men were killed."

Expecting a reaction from Emma, the deputy was surprised when there was none. "Do you understand what I am telling you?" he asked.

"Yes," she said. "You're saying that Wil will be going to prison. I have expected this kind of news for some time now."

Mary managed to say, "It won't be prison. The men he was with killed guards of a gold shipment. Even if he didn't fire a shot, he'll be just as guilty."

The young mother's face grew pale and she appeared stunned. "Will they bring him back here?" she asked.

"It is unlikely," Tyler told her. "If he did come back, he'd be arrested and taken away by U.S. marshals.

There is a bounty on his head and there are men hunting him."

"Will you be going after him?" Emma asked Tyler.

"Tom and I will be leaving tomorrow," he told her.

"You got to find him, Tyler," she replied, her eyes becoming glassy. "I don't want a stranger to take him."

Then with the tears spilling on her cheeks, she said, "I got to get dressed and feed the children." Putting Eve down, the child ran for the bedroom.

Turning to Tyler, Mary said, "I want to stay for a bit. Emma can help me get ready for the wedding."

Then they saw the first emotion in the young mother. "Wedding?"

"We are getting married today," Mary told her.

Emma gave them both a hug and said, "I have waited so long for you two to get married. Who is going to stand up with you?"

"It will be you and Tom," the deputy told her. "The wedding will be this afternoon."

As Tyler left the house to visit those he needed to make arrangements with. He wasn't sure Emma realized that if not killed in capture, Wil would be hung. He had seen tears of joy flowing down Emma's face after learning they were getting married. He was happy for her, but couldn't be sure if they were a mixture of pain and joy from the things she'd heard.

The next couple of hours were a flurry of activity. Tyler stopped at the church and made arrangements with Pastor Woods. Mary's family was made aware that the wedding would happen that afternoon. The mayor was talked to and Sheriff Kent was told he'd have to cover while the deputy was gone.

When the deputy stopped into the trading post to let Jules and his wife know about the wedding, the subject of Wil came up. The merchant stood stone-faced as Tyler brought him up to date. The only comment he had about Wil was, "It is that damn Hugo's fault. He ruined the boy."

As for the wedding, Jules assured him that he and his wife would be at the church. "We have waited a long time for this. Mary will make you very happy."

Thanking Jules, Tyler headed for the cabin. He had to find Tom and change into proper clothes.

The wedding was well-attended considering that the announcement of it was by word of mouth. Tyler was dressed in his Sunday clothes and Mary had a white wedding gown that her mother had made her some time ago anticipating an eventual ceremony. She looked like an angel.

While the deputy had known that this day would be coming soon, he stood at the front of the church with shaking legs. After completing the vows, the two of them kissed. They turned to those attending the wedding and were presented as man and wife.

The gathering after the ceremony was in the front of the church. Everyone must have gone to making something right after they learned of the wedding, because a feast was spread out across the tables. After everyone ate their meals, picnic-style, the fiddler started to play and there was dancing.

It was all a blur to Tyler. For the moment the pain of knowing he would be hunting his best friend was pushed to the back of his mind. Mary was now his wife and the years of sitting on the porch swing and fighting the feeling inside would now be over.

Edmond had a carriage decorated to drive them to the cabin. The married couple sat in the back, holding hands and wondering about what was to come. They had been given a bottle of wine to enjoy at the cabin.

To Tyler's surprise they had had company at the cabin earlier. The place was decorated and the fire place was ready to light if they wished. A table cloth had been put on in the kitchen and a little something had been set out for them to eat. Still, undiscovered were the fresh linens that had been put onto the bed.

The night was warm, so they chose to leave the fireplace unlit. The wine tasted sweet as they toasted their marriage. Tyler wanted to grab the woman he loved, tear off her clothes, and rush to the bedroom, but he fought the urge one last time as they moved around the floor, holding each other with only the music in their hearts to guide them.

Mary went to the bedroom to put on a night gown her mother had made for her while Tyler undressed in the front room, leaving his summer underwear on. "You can come in now," she said softly to him.

The moonlight was shining in through the window, silhouetting her body under the thin gown. She whispered, "I won't need the gown." She slipped it off, exposing her firm, round breasts and satiny skin. Tyler stood entranced, by the beauty in front of him.

"Let me help you," she told him as she removed his underwear. With only the light of the moon they stood naked, looking at each other as she ran her fingers across his muscular chest. Tyler took her into his arms and lay her onto the bed, her warm softness making him almost dizzy with anticipation.

When the morning sun woke them, they lay together, refusing to face the day. It would be a day of sadness and right now they were enveloped in joy and did not want to break the spell. "I will be here in the cabin when you get back," she whispered.

"You might want to stay at your folks," he whispered to her. "I could be gone several weeks."

She pressed close to him. "The happiest memory of my life is right here in our cabin," Mary replied. "I will live with that until you return."

Then, overwhelmed by emotion they came together again, fighting to delay the reality that was just outside their door.

CHAPTER TWENTY

Tom was in front of the livery with a loaded pack horse when the deputy got back to Cedar Creek. Riding over on the bay, Tyler swung down. He was wearing a vest over is wool shirt, and the flat-brimmed hat tilted back on his head. Tyler had the Colt on his right hip, on the left he had the possible bag and Green River knife in its sheath. The Hawken was cleaned and ready in the saddle scabbard.

A blanket roll with a change of clothes, a coat, and a ground tarp was tied to the back of the saddle. His saddle bags contained extra powder and lead balls for both weapons, as well as enough food to start the trip. Tied to the saddle were the coffee pot and blackened frying pan.

Tom suggested that he transfer some of the heavier items to the packhorse. "I bought it from the livery, with the promise that he'd buy it back at a discounted price should I return it."

The slim man kept breaking into a grin every time he looked at the newly married man. At last, he said, "I'll take the lead so you can snooze on the bay."

"I will be just fine," Tyler said. "I got lots to think about."

"I bet you do," Tom replied as he climbed onto the sorrel.

The deputy knew that he could expect a good amount of ribbing for a day or two. He did not mind because it made their mission less real for the time being. Tom told him they would head west to Fort Des Moines, which would take most of two weeks, then they would travel another three weeks to Fort Laramie.

How far they went would depend on whether they found any sign that Wil and Pepe had traveled that way. Tom was depending on them having to travel to places where they could resupply, and with luck they would be noticed by the locals. They would be traveling through Indian territory, so the two men would have to be always on guard.

That morning, Tyler became aware of the enormity of the hunt they were taking on. His idea of a few weeks was in reality going to be a month and a half, one-way. Mary and Emma were prepared for a lengthy trip. Tyler had the winter's wood already made at the cabin, but despite this he still encouraged Mary to stay in town with her parents. It would be winter before they returned, and there was always the possibility that they'd have to winter someplace.

The first day, they had ridden nearly 40 miles. Tom pulled up at a small stream and the two of them watered the horses. "I'll get a fire going for our supper," Tom told Tyler. "You can pull the gear off the horses. The weather should be dry so we can roll our blankets out under some trees."

The deputy had not slept under the stars much. Ahead of him could be months of sleeping on the trail. They had a fly tarp to use in case wet weather was expected. He pulled the saddles and packs off the animals and placed them under some pines to keep the dew off.

"Have you had frying pan bread?" Tom asked.

"I've warmed biscuits over a fire or in a pan before," Tyler told him.

"My father showed me the best way to make it," the slim man said. "Rufus loved to cook over a campfire."

Tom made a meal of frying pan bread and side meat. They ate the fare off tin plates with hot coffee in their tin mugs. Everything tasted remarkably good. "Food is always better when eating in the outdoors," the deputy told Tom.

"It is even better when you eat it right out of the frying pan," the slim man replied. "Less dishes."

Tyler lay in his blankets under the pines. A breeze blew across his face bringing the fragrance of the trees around them. His mind was back in Cedar Creek. Twenty-four hours ago, he was lying with his bride for the first time. Already feeling the loneliness without her, he questioned his decision to go.

By the time they reached the abandoned Fort Des Moines, Tyler was low on supplies. The fort was located on the confluence of the Raccoon and Des Moines Rivers. It had been occupied by the army from

1843 until 1846. It had been built to control the Sauk and Meskwaki tribes.

When the army left, settlers occupied the fort and the area around it. It was much the same feel as Cedar Creek. It had a church, a courthouse, a mercantile, two taverns, a livery, and other dwellings of logs, lumber, or brick. There was still evidence of the flood on 1851, which had damaged or destroyed most of the original buildings.

The two men stopped at the first tavern they reached. The area around the town was prairie, with rolling hills. Within the town there were few trees to offer shade from the blazing August sun. The deputy carried his badge in a vest pocket. They would be asking about Wil and Pepe, who might have caused trouble in the town, so he could flash it if they had to prove they weren't friends of the two.

It was early afternoon, and the tavern was empty except for two men sitting at a back table and the bartender reading a newspaper. The place had a sour smell about it. "You want a shot or a bottle?" the man asked without looking up.

"Two whiskeys," Tom said.

Grunting due to the massive girth he carried, the bartender got a bottle and two cloudy glasses. Pouring the drinks, he said, "That will be four bits."

"That's kind of high," the slim man said as he doled out the coins.

"I didn't think you'd want the peppered-down stuff that's sold to the tribes," the bartender replied.

"You're right there," Tyler told him. "About a month ago two friends might have come through this way. We had to wait before we could leave. Wil and Pepe claimed this was the shortest route west."

"You men hunting them?" the savvy bartender asked. "You're carrying lots of hardware."

"Let say we got common interests as them," Tom replied.

"Lots of men come through, heading mostly for California," the man said. "I wouldn't know one from another."

Finished talking, he went back to his paper. After tossing down their drinks, Tyler and Tom left the vomit smelly tavern.

They had the same luck at the next tavern. The town had a jail and a newspaper. Tom headed for the newspaper office and Tyler to the local sheriffs. Neither had any luck, and they met at the mercantile to purchase supplies.

The owner wore a visor on his bald head. The two men bought supplies they'd need and asked about Wil and Pepe, describing them to the merchant. The man totaled up their items on a piece of packaging paper and shook his head.

"We got folks coming through regular," the merchant said. "I don't pay much mind to them. They come and pay with good money and they go."

Spending a moment putting the supplies into the packs and saddle bags, Tom said, "It sounds like the two of them are behaving."

"The two of them would have been only a week away from Cedar Creek," Tyler replied. "They may have still felt the shadow of the law over them."

Leading the horses, they walked through town. The deputy was thinking about going back to the last tavern and ordering some food. He had smelled something good cooking in the back. Tom agreed that a meal would be good right about now.

"Let's put the horses up at the livery and then we can go and get something to eat," the slim man suggested. "I know I could use another drink."

Two men were playing checkers just out of the sun at the livery. "One of you the hostler?" Tyler asked.

"I'll be right with you," a short player said. "I just about got Rob beat."

Two moves later the game was over and the short player got up. "Two bits for each horse with grain," he said. He then added, "You can call me Shorty."

"That should take care of our horses," Tom told him. "Now can you recommend a place for us to sleep?"

Accepting the money from the two men, Shorty replied, "Both taverns have rooms. I wouldn't stay in them. I could let you sleep in the loft if you don't mind my snoring. I sleep in the office and keep the door open."

"Would you recommend the food in the closer tavern?" Tyler asked.

"Joey makes a good stew," the hostler replied. "I usually get some and bring it back here to eat. I could get a bucket for the three of us."

Smiling at the little man, Tom asked, "What would that cost?"

"Two bits for the stew and another eight bits for the bottle I bring back," Shorty replied, smiling, and exposing his missing lower teeth.

It was a done deal. The gear was stripped off the horses and the two men led them to a stall. Then Tyler stopped suddenly. "Is that your horse in the last stall?"

"It is now," Shorty said. "A man brought it in lame and asked to rent one of mine while it healed. The bastard up and left town with my skewbald."

The deputy described Wil and the hostler replied, "That was him. He was friendly enough and dug the rent money out of a bag of coins. I didn't take him for a horse thief."

"We are after him and if we catch him, we'll bring your horse back," Tom replied.

Shorty smiled, "In that case, the stew is on me. You can still buy the bottle."

The hostler headed for the tavern to get the meal. Tom asked Tyler, "How did you know that was Wil's horse?"

"See the scars on its rump?" Tyler asked. "The horse was hit by a tree when it was a foal."

The two men brushed their horses while waiting for the hostler to come back with the bucket of stew. They then went through their packs and gear so they would be ready to leave early. The two now knew they were on the trail of Wil and Pepe and felt a renewed urgency.

The stew was a bit greasy but good eating. It included a loaf of bread that the men just tore chunks off. By the time they finished eating the sun was low in the west, casting a nice shadow in front of the livery.

The four of them sat outside and drank coffee laced with whiskey. Tyler pulled out his pipe and tobacco from his possible bag. Shorty got a burning stick to light it. The deputy was feeling mellow after the whiskey and with a full belly after eating quick meals on the trail.

Shorty stayed out after dark working on the bottle while Tyler and Tom climbed into the loft with their blankets. Sleep came quickly and neither one was disturbed by the hostler's snoring.

"I got porridge down here if you're hungry," came the call from below.

Tyler heard a rattling sound and looked over expecting to see Tom, but he and his blanket were already gone. "Damn," the deputy grumbled. "I must have overslept."

He noticed it was still dark when he climbed down. Shorty and Tom were drinking coffee near a lantern. It turned out that the rattling sound was rain on the roof. Tossing his blanket near his saddle, Tyler got a cup of coffee.

Shorty had remembered that Wil had asked about the trail to Fort Laramie. "He said it was his first time here in Fort Des Moines, but that he'd been to Laramie on his way to California."

"We don't figure he's going back to California," Tom told him. "There are folks there looking for him also."

"I don't know how a young man gets onto the wrong side of the law," Shorty said. "It is a damn shame. Now let's have some porridge."

Shortly after daylight the two men were back on the trail west, with their rain gear on. They now knew they were on the right trail following Wil. They felt confident that it would remain so until they reached Fort Laramie. From there they guessed their quarry would head to the Mormon ferry and then north.

While Tom had seen this all before, Tyler was fascinated by the rolling hills and the thousands of buffalo they passed. Back in Cedar Creek they had bison, but it was getting harder and harder to find them. He knew that hide hunters left the meat to rot on the prairie, and it was hard for Tyler to fathom the waste. Grandpa had always taught him that you eat or sell what you kill. Even the mergansers.

Once they reached the trail along the Platte River, they had plenty of company. They passed hundreds of wagons heading west. Most figured that the two men were also on their way to California, and they would just nod when asked.

The grass was sparse along the trail. It had been grazed off for miles on the south side of the trail. Tom and Tyler carried grain, which helped the horses some. When they reached Chimney Rock, the two of them set up camp at its base. The tall spire of rock was something for Tyler to see.

Using buffalo droppings for their fire, Tom sliced side meat into a frying pan and then made frying pan bread. Early on the trip he had shown Tyler how to do it, but the deputy figured Tom's tasted better.

The two men had been on the trail for over three weeks and had another couple of days before they reached Fort Laramie. Tom suggested that they rest the animals a few days at the fort, then try and confirm whether Wil and Pepe had come through.

It was late evening and the two ate while watching the wagons continue to roll west. Most were pulled by oxen that were showing the wear of the long haul. They just set the frying pan between them and speared the meat and bread with their knives. It was a lifestyle that Tyler had never experienced before.

Fort Laramie was an adobe fort that gleamed white in the afternoon sun. They crossed the Laramie River just upstream of some wagons and watched as the canvas tops rocked back and forth in the rutted and washed-out bottom. Less than one-third of the wagons had women or children walking beside them. The rest were all men on their way to riches.

Tom led the way to Louie's Livery, where he was met by a middle-aged man with one eye. "Kenny," the slim man said. "I want you to meet Tyler."

After introductions were made, the horses were taken care of. The hostler observed, "You have a different pack horse."

"I left the other in New Orleans," Tom replied.

"How is Rufus doing down there?" Kenny asked.

"He is as happy as can be," the slim man told him.

Once the horses were taken care of, the deputy figured that they'd go to the fort, but they did not. It was the Buffalo Hide Saloon that was their next stop.

Tom walked in and got a grand welcome from a grizzled man named Louie. Again, he was asked about Rufus.

The place was pretty fancy for out here in the west, and Tyler felt somewhat under-dressed. The whiskey and food were as good as the deputy had ever had. Louie's sister Lucy ran the dining area.

The next surprise was when they got a room in the boarding house next door. Tyler couldn't believe they'd be sleeping in real beds for a few nights. After stowing their few items, the two men went back to the saloon to ask about Wil.

Louie did not remember anyone like the man they described. "If he liked to gamble, your best bet would be the tavern at the fort," the grizzled owner told them.

Tom remembered the bartender, Hube. Tonight, both men were tired, and after a couple of drinks and some catching up with Louie, they intended to get some sleep. Lucy came by with cigars for the two men and Tyler caught the smell of her perfume. It reminded him of Mary.

For the first time since they'd started on the grueling trip, the deputy felt sad. His new wife was weeks away from him and it would be many more before he saw her again. While Tom talked with the owner, Tyler closed his eyes and thought about the last night he'd spent in Cedar Creek.

That night he laid in a comfortable bed, unable to sleep while his mind brought him back to Mary. He could hear Tom snoring nearby, yet he felt all alone. He decided that he'd take advantage of the mail that was now delivered to Cedar Creek. He would write a letter. It was something he'd never done before.

The next morning the two men went straight from the boarding house to the fort. Several teepees were erected at the front. Tom told Tyler about getting some buckskins from them. The fort had loose security at the front. There was a constant stream of gold seekers or those heading for Oregon coming and going from the fort, purchasing supplies.

The two men found a place to get some breakfast and watched the activity around Fort Laramie. "I can't believe folks are still going to California to pan gold," Tyler said. "By now most of it must be gone."

"What many of these folks have is almost a fever," Tom replied. "All they can think about is getting rich. I was there and it is damn hard work, and not everyone finds placer gold. Some just find dirt."

Tyler felt much more comfortable in the fort. The Buffalo Hide Saloon was impressive and had great food, but the potatoes and buffalo that they had for breakfast within the adobe walls, was just fine. The deputy began to feel that chances would be slim that Wil would have stood out in any way here at the fort.

After eating the two men went to check on prices of supplies. They found them to be high, as expected. Some things were in short supply. The tavern would open at noon, so with time to kill the two men went to check with the army.

An American flag flew in front of their headquarters, and Tom led the way into the office. A corporal sat at a desk to one side. He looked up when they entered and asked, "Can I help you?"

"We are looking for some men that robbed a Wells Fargo gold transport and killed two guards and the driver," Tom told him.

"That was east of here, about two or three months ago, wasn't it?" the corporal asked.

"It was," Tom replied. "I was wondering if you had posters on the gang that did it?"

The corporal dug around for a minute and came up with four posters. He showed them and told him that one of them had been caught. The other three described Wil and Pepe, along with a man named Rex.

"Rex?" Tyler asked. "He didn't go with Wil to California."

"They must have met up in the gold fields," Tom replied.

"It makes sense now," the deputy said. "Rex liked to think he was good with a gun and liked to wave it around. He could have been the one that got them into robbing and killing miners."

Then he told Tom, "There was another that went with Wil, but we heard he was killed."

Each of the posters was offering a $100 reward and ten percent reward for any gold returned. The reward on each man would be three months' pay for most laborers. It made Tyler wonder how much Wil had left of the coins. Based on the size of the reward and money for getting the gold back, they must have really angered someone.

The corporal put the posters away and said, "We are authorized to pay the reward if you find any of them."

"That's good to know," Tom replied.

When the men left the headquarters, they went to the tavern. Hube was getting ready to open and was about to tell whoever was coming in that it would be a while. Looking up, he saw Tom and said, "Welcome back. Did Rufus come with you?"

"No, he's busy in New Orleans," the slim man said. "We are looking for some men and wanted to find out if you've seen them."

"Have a seat and I'll be finished here soon and you can tell me about the men you're looking for," the bartender said, continuing to get things ready.

Sitting at the table in the corner, Tom told Tyler, "I found Rufus right at this table. He was passed out from too much enjoyment the night before."

"I am all done," they heard Hube say. "Can I get you something right now?"

"I would like coffee," the deputy replied. Tom agreed that coffee would be a good idea.

The bartender went into the back room and returned with a small tray holding three coffees. "Old Rufus would have started out with a whiskey."

Sipping the hot brew, Tyler described the three men they were looking for. Hube wrinkled his brow and thought. "You say one might have been a big spender?"

"Yes," Tyler replied. "And he liked to buy rounds of drinks."

"We have had a few men like you're describing come through in the last couple of months," the bartender told them. "One was a buffalo hunter and he smelled every bit like one, but nobody turned down the drinks he was buying."

"They weren't buffalo hunters," Tom said. "They came back from California and robbed a gold shipment east of here. They would have been coming back west and spending coins from the stolen gold."

"There was a young fella that didn't have much luck at the tables," Hube said. "I remember, because even though he lost he was buying drinks."

"Do you remember what he looked like?" Tyler asked.

"It was a busy night," the bartender said, "and he was wearing his hat. I can't say I would recognize him if he walked in right now."

It gave the two men some hope that it might have been Wil. Pepe was the quieter type and would not have stood out. The manhunters realized that it could be three. It was always possible that Pepe came into town to warn Wil, while Rex waited in hiding.

The two men thanked Hube and headed out of the fort. Then the deputy got an idea. "A skewbald would stand out, and that was what Wil was riding. We should have asked Kenny about that right off."

"Why don't you do that," Tom told him. "I am going to see if I can get some moccasins from one of the women in the teepees."

Tyler headed for the livery. He now felt confident that Wil had come this far, and if Kenny remembered the skewbald that would confirm it. The bay doors were opened to let whatever breeze there was to blow through. Flies buzzed around the sunny front of the building as the deputy walked in.

"Kenny," Tyler called out. "I need to ask you about a horse."

The one-eyed hostler came from the back carrying a pitchfork. "I just watered and gave your horses some hay."

"About a month or so ago," the deputy asked, "did you have someone board a skewbald here?"

"There's a fellow north of here that rides a piebald and he keeps it here when to visits the fort," Kenny told him. "Last spring there was a skewbald tied up at the saloon. I remember it because it was a fine-looking chestnut and white horse."

"That would have been too long ago," Tyler said. "It would have been less than two months."

"Did you check down around the teepees?" Kenny asked. "They notice horse flesh, and one of the braves might have seen it."

Realizing that his inquiry wasn't going anywhere, the deputy thanked the hostler and headed back to meet up with Tom. He decided to cut around the back of the fort to find his partner near the teepees. He also guessed that there would be another stable in the fort. Wil might have left the horse there. He would suggest that they go there next when he found Tom.

Fort Laramie was built on a bluff overlooking the river with the same name, and the deputy got a fine view of the water and beyond. In front of him were the teepees with the women cooking over fires. Many of the braves appeared to be gone, probably scouting out areas to hunt buffalo. After the hunt, they would move their teepees to a protected valley to spend the winter.

Something tugged Tyler's shirt and stung his back and there was the sound of a shot! "What the hell!" he exclaimed, turning.

There, above him, stood Rex less than 50 feet away, with smoke drifting from his Colt. He had an evil smile and snarled, "Surprised!" as he fired again at the deputy. Where his second shot went, Tyler did not know, but Tyler drew his revolver and fired back.

The killer's eyes got big, his third shot going wild as he turned from the impact of the deputy's Colt. One of Rex's legs went weak, failing to support him and the man went to the ground and slid down a few feet. Tyler kept his revolver aimed at the struggling man. If Rex's Colt came up again, the deputy was ready to put another ball into him.

Walking up to the downed man, the deputy noticed that the gun had slipped from his hand. Rex lay curled up, holding his midsection. Fighting to calm his nerves, Tyler growled, "Where are your friends? You can't be here alone."

"They're running north," Rex sneered, taking ragged breath's. "Wil and the others were stupid and started spending the gold. I told them to wait until things cooled down."

The smell of whiskey was strong on Rex, and his being drunk and shooting downhill, had probably saved Tyler's life. That and his false sense of being in control of the fight.

The man had always liked to brag, so Tyler would give him a last opportunity. "So, you stayed here at the fort."

Coughing, Rex replied, "I got me a sweet Cheyenne woman that I plan to winter with. Next year I will go east and live like a king."

The deputy could plainly see that the man would not be wintering with anyone. He was gut shot.

There was information that the deputy needed and he asked, "Were you the brains of the outfit? How did you meet up with the others?"

"I found them starving in California," Rex said. "They were finding odd jobs to get by. I was making good money and showed them how to do it."

"By killing and stealing from those that did the work?" the deputy asked.

Again, Rex coughed, flecks of blood on his lips. "Most miners dressed in rags and hid what little gold they found in their shacks. I did them a favor and put them out of their misery."

"That is until you got run out of California," Tyler replied.

The deputy felt that his visit was about to end and he could now see the sweat on the bastard's face. "Where is your gold?" he asked.

"Hidden," the man said, then his eyes got a scared look.

"Where did you hide it?' Tyler asked, but Rex was gone to face whatever his maker had in store for him.

The deputy realized that he was still holding his Colt. He put it back into his holster as he stared at the dead man, feeling little regret for killing the man who ruined so many other lives.

"Tyler! Tyler! Are you hit?" It was Tom running towards him.

"I don't think so," the deputy replied. "He come from nowhere and began shooting."

"I heard the shots," Tom said. "I started running towards you and saw him going down."

Feeling something stinging on his back, Tyler slipped off his shirt. Tom pointed out a burn behind his shoulder. "He came damn close."

"That was his first shot to get my attention. His might have thought he hit me better and kept shooting to make sure," the deputy replied.

"Who the hell was he?" the slim man asked.

"His name was Rex," Tyler told him. "He was the brains of the gang and the man that is responsible for the others facing the gallows."

"Then he's worth $100," Tom replied. "I wonder where his gold is?"

Still shook from almost being killed, not to mention that he had killed another man, Tyler said, "It might be in the teepee of the woman he was staying with. All he said was that the gold was hidden."

Slipping his shirt back on, they saw men running from the fort. One of them stopped at the body. "Damn," he said. "You got him plum center. We were up on the wall working and saw you two go at it."

"Can you men help us carry this bastard to the army headquarters?" Tom asked. "There is some whiskey in it for you."

They heard the man commenting on Rex being hit dead center as they carried the body. The deputy figured he must have hit something that caused Rex to bleed out. He was damn lucky the man was a poor shot and only grazed him with two tries.

The first question asked by the army was, "Did he have the gold with him?"

Once it was established that Rex did not have it, the $100 reward was paid and the army took over the body. Word would get out quickly that there were thousands of dollars in gold hidden someplace around the fort. Soon there would be men searching everywhere.

As they left the headquarters, Tom said, "The reward is yours. You got the man."

"We are on a joint mission here," Tyler replied. "We take out expenses and then split what's left."

Tom and Tyler went to see the woman Rex was staying with. She knew nothing of the gold. For her loss, the slim man gave her ribbon, hawk bells, beads, a mirror, and then to her father a knife.

The next morning, Tyler and Tom rode away from the fort after a hearty breakfast made by Lucy. The deputy was glad to leave. He had taken another life at this fort and wanted it behind him. The only thing about this one was Rex had had a loaded revolver and was intent on emptying it at Tyler.

The two men were now heading towards the Mormon Crossing. They should reach it in four days. Once across the North Platte River, they would continue north to a small trading post near the Powder River, which should take another two to three days.

Tyler was glad to be back on the trail. Every day behind them brought him a day closer to getting back to Mary. It was now the end of August and soon the weather would start to cool. As they rode west, they were climbing in elevation, and the cooler air made sleeping better.

A day out from the crossing they camped off the trail. It looked like rain and Tom had suggested putting up a fly tarp. A meal of side meat and frying pan bread was eaten and then they sat back with coffee. It was near sunset and there were still some on the trail, anxious to get in line at the ferry.

An old man leading a mule came by the camp and hailed them. "Come on in," Tom said, his hand on his Colt. Tyler was busy arranging the gear under the fly tarp and he sat in the dusk, ready if there was trouble.

"I smelled your coffee about a mile back," the old codger said.

The old man was carrying a knife and short axe in his belt and his rifle was tied to the pack on his mule. He appeared to be harmless. "Grab your cup and have a seat," Tom invited him.

The deputy moved under the tarp and the man jumped. "I was just here putting things away," he said to calm the man down.

"Don't like folks to come without warning," the old man said. "I see you clear now. Damn, I spilt some of my coffee."

While the two men were unsure in the beginning, the old man soon turned out to be a wealth of knowledge. He had trekked across almost every foot of the Big Horn Mountains. When they mentioned where they were headed the man nodded and said, "Been there."

Then he began to talk, "Right now, you are about three days from the Middle Fork of the Powder River. That will take you into the red cliffs. Good grazing and water for your stock. Just a mile up from your camp there is a decent crossing of the Platte, and that will save you time and the price of the ferry. Nice boys at the ferry. They have most anything you need and one of them is a fair doctor."

He looked into his cup and held it out for a refill. Tom poured what little remained in the pot. Then the man continued. "Once you get to the Middle Fork, a half-day walk east, you'll find what's left of a stockade and some buildings that was called the Portuguese Houses. It was built by Antonio Montero, and he sold to trappers and the Crow until Bridger and his crew came up and all but put him out of business by undercutting his prices. Antonio is gone, but folks still got stuff to sell."

The old man continued to talk about the area, describing the red cliff valley and the many splits it made with the north and south forks, then to the north the Tongue River. He warned them that they might find some tribes camped in the valley this time of year. Most were friendly, but not all, he told them.

Tyler asked, "If some men went there to hide out for a year, maybe two, is there such a place?"

"Why hell, yes," the man said, slapping his knee. "I once spent almost that just trying to find my way out."

The deputy lit his pipe using a brand from the fire. The old codger breathed deeply and said, "That is mighty fine-smelling tobacco you're smoking." He dug out his clay pipe from his possible bag and tapped out the ash. "Mind filling this one?"

CHAPTER TWENTY-ONE

It was a good thing that the old man only spent one night. He was tough on supplies and the only thing the made it worthwhile was his knowledge. When the two men led the pack horse across the North Platte River, they realized that they were just two days from the Middle Fork. Knowing that there was a source of supplies there had eliminated the need to go to the Mormon Crossing.

There would have been one advantage of going to the Mormon Crossing. They could have made inquiries about the men and their stock, but the odds were that the men at the crossing would not have remembered them.

They had foothills and mountains with their bluish-purple lines in the distance on both sides. They cut through winding valleys and over rises. Both men rode with jaws set, knowing the danger that lay ahead. One morning the two riders had Indians on an eastern ridge watching them. The fact that they boldly showed themselves gave the riders some confidence that they wouldn't be attacked.

They camped the second night at the Powder River, sheltered by cottonwood trees. Tom figured that the Portuguese Houses were a few miles downstream to the east. The Big Horn Mountains were to the west and the men could see the cut in the mountain chain where the river came from.

Hungry for a change in diet, the two men rigged fishing poles and sat on the river bank watching their cork bobbers. The river originated in the mountain watershed, and was clear and fast-flowing. The two men hooked strong fighting browns and rainbow trout.

That night they sat under a spreading tree and anticipated the snapping trout in their frying pan. "When we go for supplies in the morning," Tom said, "we can ask if anyone with a skewbald stopped there."

"I think they came this way. There was nothing to the west that should have drawn the two men in that direction," Tyler said. "Wil had no desire to farm, so Oregon is out, and they couldn't go back to California because they're wanted there."

"It makes sense for them to come this way," Tom agreed. "There is always the chance that they continued north to Canada."

"If they were seen at the Portuguese Houses but we don't find them in the area," the deputy asked, "will you continue north to find them?"

"I think this will be the end of the chase for me," Tom told him. "If they were caught in Canada, it would be difficult to collect any reward without bringing them all the way back to Fort Laramie."

Tyler had a vision of bringing the body slung over a saddle all the way back. Winter would stop the smell, but loading and unloading the body every night would be required, which the deputy was all too familiar with as he recalled bringing Bobby back to Cedar Creek.

The night was clear and cold. In the arid area, they slept under the stars. Tyler watched them slowly move across the sky for a long time before he finally slipped into restless sleep. He had dreams of Mary and she was angry. He was walking through the town with a body over a horse, and she was yelling for him to take it away.

He woke suddenly to the sounds of Tom lighting the fire. "Did you have a bad night?" the slim man asked.

"It wasn't one of my best," Tyler replied.

"You were talking and it sounded like you were arguing with someone," Tom said. "Move the horses to fresh grass while I make us some breakfast."

The deputy shook off the feelings he'd had in the dream. Somebody had told him that dreams had meaning and could foretell the future. He was a skeptic. Once, when he was young, he had dreamt that he'd fallen from the loft and didn't reach bottom. That never happened.

Coming back from tending to the horses, Tom looked up from the fire. "I can feel their presence," he said.

"Is that because of the voodoo you have?" Tyler asked.

"My grandmother gave me an amulet to keep me safe," he said. "It has been lying heavy onto my chest. It is a warning."

"Maybe you just slept on your back," the deputy replied.

Tom laughed and told him, "I do not believe it will be long before you see your old friend again."

The words "old friend" rang in Tyler's head. For years Wil had been his oldest and best friend. Now he wasn't sure. Thinking back, the deputy wondered, *Had he ever been a good friend?*

With their breakfast meat having a hint of fish taste from the frying pan, the two men finished their meal and packed up to leave. Tom hoped that he could leave the packhorse where they planned to purchase supplies. It would he an hinderance hunting for the men in the valleys and canyons upstream.

An hour after leaving their camp, they came to what was left of the Portuguese Houses. The stockade had all but fallen away. Several buildings were in disrepair. A couple had been burnt. There amongst the ruins stood the small trading post and two homes that had been maintained.

Going in, the two men would have hardly called it a trading post. The low building had poorly stocked shelves and junk of one kind or another stacked in the corners. An old woman with a corncob pipe sat on a rocker in the middle of the building, watching them as they walked in.

"If you see something you need," she said, "let me know. My son is out after mule deer and if he comes back with one, I can sell you a haunch."

"We are looking for a man that rides a skewbald," Tom told her. "He may have been here in the last couple of months."

"Was here a week ago," she said. "Had his Cheyenne wife with him. He seemed like a good man. Bought things for his wife and paid with gold coins."

Both were shocked by the wife thing, but Tom was able to ask, "Was he traveling with another man?"

"First time I saw him he was," she replied. "I believe they left him on the North Fork."

Now that was more information than the two had expected to get. "I would like to leave a packhorse here for a few days," Tom told her.

"Grain will cost you," she said, "but I got hay. How does $2 sound?" Seeing no reaction to the price she added, "And $1 for grain. You are talking of three days, right?"

Sounds like robbery, Tom thought, but he said, "Sounds fine. It shouldn't be more than three days. Where do you want me to take the horse?"

"Just leave it outside," she said. "My boy will bring it to the lean-to when he gets back from hunting."

They found some beans and coffee, as well as jerky. She had no flour or side meat. Again, the prices were high. Both men left thinking that they should have stopped at the Mormon Crossing for supplies. Going through the packs, they put things they'd need on their horses and then looked doubtfully at what they were leaving.

"She'll have our stuff on the shelves for sale before we get out of sight," Tom said.

Tyler was chewing some of the jerky as they rode away. "It is good jerky," he commented.

"It should be, at the price we paid," the slim man said, glancing back at the pack animal. "I hope to see you again, old horse."

Acting somewhat indifferent, Tyler said, "I think you will be losing the money Edmond promised you on bringing that pack horse back."

All he got was some kind of growl from his companion.

* * *

The river wound through the valley leading into the mountains. The cliffs on both sides were a rich, red color with eroded rubble at the base. They rode wide of a cluster of teepees. The sound of dogs barking alerted the residents, but none came out to look.

"You can be sure they see us," Tom said. "If they take offense to our presence, it will be away from their wives and children."

As they rode, Tyler caught movement at the top of one of the cliffs. "I saw a lookout," he told Tom. "I imagine we can expect that throughout these valleys."

"That's what makes this the perfect place to hide," Tom replied. "You can see anyone coming before they can see you."

The riders passed a place where the river split around a small island. On the grass-covered island there were two spreading cottonwoods. Tyler's thoughts went to Mary. She would love picnicking in a spot like that. Then they reached a place where the Middle Fork split to the north.

Stopping, the two men looked around, scanning the cliffs. "This would be the North Fork," Tom said. "I wish Rufus was here now. He would know every bend in this river."

"How far do you think the North Fork goes?" Tyler asked

"We will probably run out of trail before we run out of river," the slim man replied.

The valley walls on each side were steep, and covered with pine and fir trees. Above on the updrafts, hawks glided, looking for prey. Along the main river valley were countless canyons. Any one of them could hide the men they were looking for. Tracks of horses were spotted often enough to let them know that those they were looking for, or braves from a tribe, had passed through.

The sun was low over the mountains when Tom pulled up. "Do you smell that?"

"Smoke," Tyler replied. "The breeze is coming from ahead of us."

"It could be another tribe's village," the slim man said.

They continued slowly, catching the smell ever so often. Their eyes were scanning from the valley floor to the top of the steep walls of the valley. A small stream came from one of the canyons, flowing into the North Fork. In a sandy area they saw several tracks leading toward it.

Sitting on their horses, the two men strained their ears for any sound. Other than some birds flitting from branch to branch and the screech of the hawks above, there was nothing. Then a crash in the pines had them both pulling their Colts!

A startled mule deer bound out and disappeared into the canyon. The two men's hearts had just about settled down when there was a shot! Off the horses they went and into the pines. With their Colts drawn, the two men looked and listened. They heard voices, but could only make out, "I got it."

Someone must have shot the mule deer that they had pushed into the canyon. The realization that they were not far from a camp sent the two men back to get their horses out of sight. Whether it was the one that Wil and Pepe were at was unknown. The fact that they spoke English confirmed that it wasn't an Indian camp.

While all this was happening, darkness was quickly coming to the valley. "We best find someplace to camp," Tom whispered.

Leading the horses away from the canyon mouth, they found an open spot in the pines that they could make camp. Both knew it would be a cold camp due to them being so close to whomever was in the canyon.

Tom got out his moccasins. "I'm going to check out the canyon," he said.

"I should go with you," Tyler said in a hushed voice.

"You stay here with the horses," the slim man replied. "Once I get the layout of the camp, I'll come back. It may not be the one we're looking for so don't get your hopes up."

Tyler sat with the horses and wondered what Tom would find. Even if it wasn't Wil, it could still be some men who didn't want to be found. They could be as dangerous. A sliver of the moon came up while he waited. It offered feeble light. The horses cropped on the sparse grass.

Sitting nervously, the deputy couldn't stay still, so he got a curry comb and began to groom the horses. They were at 5,000 feet and the night air was cool. He thought about getting his coat from the blanket roll and then he heard a slight sound.

Dropping to a crouch near the horses, Tyler drew the Colt. He heard some muttering. Then he saw a shadowy figure appear and heard a whisper, "Tyler."

Standing up with the Colt hanging by his side, the deputy answered, "Over here."

The camp was less than a quarter-mile into the canyon. A water fall came over the canyon wall and splashed into a pond. It then fed the small stream. The water hitting the pond would be an advantage. It would mask the sound of their approach.

"I counted three men sitting around the fire," Tom said, "and they were broiling some of the mule deer."

"Did you see anyone that fit Wil's description?" Tyler asked.

"I couldn't get close enough to recognize anyone," the slim man said. "Even if I could have, it is unlikely that I would have recognized him. I did notice they were passing a bottle while waiting for the venison to cook."

"They are living a hell of a lot better than we are," Tyler told him. "I can't even light my pipe for fear they'd smell the sweet smoke."

"That makes the argument for learning to chew," Tom replied.

Though he was exhausted, Tyler again slept little. Come morning, he might be facing Wil with the Colt and he wondered if he'd be able to pull the trigger. It was one thing to have to tell Emma that he took him in to be hung. It was another to tell her he'd killed her husband.

Both men were up before daylight and made a breakfast of jerky and water. It made little sense to bring the horses into the canyon. They would just be taking a chance of them being hit should there be gunfire.

As they started into the canyon, there was the smell of smoldering ashes. They could hear one of the men snoring over the sound of the falls. Both had loaded their Colts with five chambers. They carried their Hawken's, giving them each six shots. That should be more than enough against three men.

Tom was wearing his moccasins and moved soundlessly. Tyler felt clumsy in his low-heeled boots. Once he almost tripped due to staring at the sleeping camp rather than where he stepped. There was just enough light to make out the three men.

Just beyond the camp were their horses, and hanging in a poplar was what remained of the mule deer. One of the men sat up and the two men froze, caught in the open. They were still 100 paces away, well within range of the rifles. Both knew that any movement would give them away.

"Parker, get up," the man said, rubbing his bearded face. Then his eyes grew large. "What the hell!"

He looked at the two men with the morning sun shining onto them. Reaching under his saddle, the startled man brought up a revolver. Tom had his rifle to his shoulder and fired, knocking the man back down.

Parker came up with a gun and fired twice while running stocking-footed for cover. Tyler fired his Hawken and brought him down just shy of some boulders. The remaining man, still in his blankets, had his hands up and was screaming, "Don't shoot!" It was Pepe.

A quick check confirmed that both shots with the Hawken's had been killing shots. Parker and a man whose named Hamlin were dead. After taking Pepe's rifle and tying his hands, Tom said, "Why don't you go and get our horses, Tyler."

The deputy's hands were shaking and he felt kind of sick. "I will do that," he said, walking away from the death they just caused. Tyler didn't understand how Tom could be so calm. They had just rousted a sleeping camp and killed two men. The slim man had had his rifle to his shoulder before the deputy could even react.

As he saddled the two horses, Tyler realized that they did have Pepe and that should lead to finding Wil. He now feared Wil would suffer the same fate as Parker and Hamlin. If he drew on them, Tom would surely kill him.

When the deputy got back with their horses, Tom had the fire going and was cutting up some of the mule deer to roast. Both of the dead men still lay where they fell. Pepe sat near the fire, his head hanging.

"He wanted to talk," Tom said, "but I told him to wait until you got back."

With the smell of venison roasting, Tom told Pepe to go ahead. The man that Tyler only knew by sight began. "It was Rex that got us into stealing gold. We weren't doing very well in California and had just started working for some big outfit for food and a place to sleep. Rex showed us how to get money robbing miners. He did any killing, we just backed him up. We got run out of the gold fields and we were coming back to Cedar Creek when we saw the wagon. Rex told us it might have some food and other things that we could sell. There were only three men with it. We come up on it quick and started shooting. I don't know if they even got a shot off."

Then Pepe stopped as though he was reliving the incident. "When we opened the tarp, we saw bags of gold. Then there was shooting behind us. More of their men were coming. Rex told us to grab what we could and then we were out of there. They didn't follow us. I guess they had to stay with the rest of the gold. I had two bags, but one slipped when we were running. I didn't dare to go back for it."

"Wil and I stayed with Rex," Pepe continued. "Rudy, he left us and then we heard he was caught and had given us up. Rex told me to go and get Wil, and then we'd all meet at Fort Laramie. Rex said if we laid low for a year, maybe two, we could live like kings some place far from Cedar Creek. When we got back, we found Rex living with the Cheyenne at the fort. He had hidden his gold someplace and told us we should do the same. He didn't know Wil had already changed his to coins and got mad when he found out. Wil didn't want to stay with Rex. He said he knew of a place to hide. He bought himself a wife before leaving the fort and we come here."

Much of what he'd told them Tyler and Tom had already surmised. The deputy then asked, "Where is Wil now?"

The meat was done, and Tom set the pan near Tyler so he could spear a piece. They'd feed Pepe before leaving. The deputy had no desire to eat. Again, he asked, "Where is Wil?"

"His wife, the Cheyenne one, wanted to go to some tower to send prayers," Pepe told them. "It is less than a week north of here. He then talked of continuing to Canada. I got family in the Carolinas and told him I wanted to go there."

Without thinking, Tyler had speared a piece of the venison and started to chew it. He now knew where Wil was and hunger had overtaken his revulsion of the scene around him. Leaving their prisoner at the fire, the two men wrapped the bodies in their blankets and put them onto their horses. They then saddled Pepe's.

After Pepe ate, they took what they could use from the camp, including two bottles of whiskey, and were ready to go. Tom pulled Pepe to his feet. "Before we go, I would like you to tell me where your gold is."

The prisoner then made his last pitch. "If you let me go, I'll tell you and you can have it. I won't tell anyone that I gave it to you."

"The gold isn't yours to give," Tom replied. "We got a long ride back, and I can make it very uncomfortable for you before you are hung, or you can tell us and I promise your trip to Fort Laramie will be the best days you have left."

"No deal, no gold," Pepe said.

"Okay," Tom replied as he got a rope from his horse and looped it around Pepe's neck. "I guess you walk back to the fort."

Tyler stood watching, not believing that Tom would do this. He found himself leading three horses while the slim man led Pepe. "Stop!" the prisoner shouted. "I could trip and be dragged."

"Yes, you could," Tom said. "And once you are dead, I will tie you over your saddle. You are worth just as much to me dead or alive."

The deputy wanted to intervene and stop this but he was almost sure that Tom wouldn't drag Pepe. They hadn't reached the mouth of the canyon when Pepe said, "I will tell you."

"It's back there near the camp," he said. "Wil and I got here first and I hid mine. The two you killed came later. I think that's why Wil left. He'd been sticking around so I wouldn't be alone."

The gold was hidden a short distance from the camp. Tyler had an opportunity to ask Tom if he would have dragged the man. "No, I wouldn't," the slim man replied, "but he didn't know that."

An hour later, with the gold and Pepe on his horse, the group left the canyon and headed for the Portuguese Houses. Tom had recognized the two men they'd shot as wanted men. The rewards for them would be small, and it wouldn't be worth hauling their bodies around for the two to three weeks before they got back to Fort Laramie. And then the fort might not have paper on them and wouldn't pay the reward.

They camped near the cottonwood again and left Pepe tied to one of the trees while the gold was again hidden. When they came back from the tower with Wil, they would retrieve it. A stop to see the old lady gained them knowledge of where the tower was.

She told them that it was called various names by different tribes, but they all had "bear" in common. The old lady called it "Home of the Bear." She told them that it was on the Belle Fourche River, which flowed into the Cheyenne River.

The old lady told them a story she had heard from the tribes. "Once, some young girls were playing and were chased by some large bears. The girls prayed to the great spirit to save them. The great spirit heard their prayer and made the tower rise, putting them out of reach of the bear. The columns that make up the sides of the tower were made by the claws of the giant bears as they tried to get to the girls."

All the tribes in the Minnesota Territory believed that the tower had divine power and came here to pray and bring gifts. Wil's Cheyenne wife was no exception. After some additional directions, the two men were sure they could find it.

They offered to give the dead men's horses to her if the old woman promised that her son would bury the two bodies. Tom told her that they would be back to put markers on the graves, hoping that that would assure that the men got buried.

With their prisoner and the packhorse in tow, the two men headed north to find the tower. Pepe spoke little and refused to eat for a couple of days. Again, Tom explained, "If you starve yourself, it will make carrying you back to Fort Laramie all the easier. We'll leave you alongside the trail until we get Wil, and then on the way back we will pick up what's left and bring it to the fort."

Whether it was the threat, or if Pepe just got hungry enough, he did begin to eat like there was no tomorrow. For him there wouldn't be that many of them left.

The 876-foot-high tower came into sight while the men were still twelve miles away. The two men had their Colts and Hawken's ready as they got closer. Stopping a mile from the base, Tom got out a spyglass and looked around the area.

There were many camps with Lakota, Crow, Kiowa, and Cheyanne near the tower. Their medicine men or women would come to gain strength and wisdom from the tower. Seeing no sign of Wil they continued around, skirting the base of the towering butte.

All of a sudden, Tom hissed, "The horse!"

Tyler saw the skewbald tied to a poplar near a makeshift camp. Swinging off the bay, he drew his Colt. After warning Pepe that he best not call out to warn Wil, Tom cautiously approached the camp. There were smoldering coals in the fire, indicating that the occupants had left recently.

The site was near the river below the butte. Tyler and Tom were surrounded by several other camps and they quickly became aware that several braves were watching the gun-toting men. Finding there was no danger in the empty camp, they put their Colts away.

"Wil and his Cheyenne wife must be at the tower," Tom said.

The deputy looked up at the butte. It was just across the river, above the slope with scattered pine trees. Once across the river they could work their way up to the tower through the trees. To the west the land fell off into a valley. To the east there were red rock ledges below the base that would be difficult to climb.

The south base was littered with scree made up of the igneous rock columns that had broken off and crumbled into jagged boulders and stones. Several of them were large enough to give them cover.

Their first thought was to wait for Wil and his Cheyenne wife to come back to camp. Deciding to do so, Tom added bark and sticks to the smoldering coals and got a fire going. Tyler watched for Wil's return. After tying Pepe's feet together, they untied his hands so he could partake in a mid-day meal.

Getting restless, the deputy said, "We should be going up after them."

"All their supplies and the horses are here," Tom replied. "It would be better to catch them coming back rather than try and flush him out of all the rubble near the base."

While he ate, the deputy saw Lakota, Cheyenne, and others from various camps go to and from the tower. Several carried items to tie onto the tree branches as presents to the gods. Tyler kept fidgeting, anxious to get any confrontation that was coming over with.

After waiting and watching for about an hour Tom said, "Someone is climbing up the butte." He went over to the sorrel and got a spyglass. "It doesn't look like an Indian," he said.

Handing the glass to Tyler, he told him, "Take a look."

The deputy looked and exclaimed, "I think that's Will!"

Tom quickly tied Pepe's hands behind his back and freed his feet. Pulling him up, the slim man said, "You lead the way. If your partner starts shooting, you will be between us and him."

Wading across the river, they started up the slope armed with rifles and their Colts, the two men watched the slow progress of the climber. Pepe required constant prodding with the Hawken barrel as he stumbled along. The climber was already over 50 feet up the side. Unsure if his Cheyenne wife would defend him, they searched the base, trying to spot a lone woman.

The two men with their prisoner stopped in the trees about 200 paces from the base. Tyler again looked with the spyglass. "It's Wil. The son-of-a-bitch has the bag of coins hanging on his side."

They watched as he got between two columns and, bracing his back against one and his feet on the other, he pushed himself up, finally stopping to rest almost 70 feet up. He then waved at them. "Did you come here to pray, Tyler?" he shouted down.

Then they saw a woman they guessed was his Cheyenne wife kneeling below and praying. Tyler walked toward the base and looked up, ready to duck and run if the man threw something at them. "What the hell are you doing?" he called.

"Friends of my wife came and told us two white men were at our camp. I guessed it would be you and I decided that I would not let you take me," Wil called down. "I have nothing to shoot with, so if you shoot, I am unarmed."

"It does not matter," Tom called up. "You are fleeing and wanted. We can shoot if we want."

"Tyler won't let you," Wil replied. "He and I are best friends."

The two of them moved back from the base. If Wil should fall, it made no sense being so close and possibly hit. "How do we get him down?" the deputy asked.

"We don't," Tom replied. "We just wait until he decides to come down."

Rather than come down, Wil continued to climb and reached a 20-foot-wide ledge left after the column had broken away. Gaining the ledge, he sat with his legs hanging over the edge. He was now over a hundred feet above the base.

Around them, they could see items that had been tied to the trees. "Maybe he intended to give the coins to the gods," the deputy said.

"It is unlikely, but if he had tied the bag of coins to a tree, it would have been difficult to convince those praying around the butte to let us take them," Tom admitted.

For an hour the two men tried to convince Wil to come down. At one point he removed his hat and flung it spinning through the air. He called down, "You can have the hat. You bought it."

Tyler watched as the aged, worn $3 hat bounced, deflecting off the curved base. He knew that was exactly what Wil would do if he fell. Walking closer, the deputy took the hat. "I've got it, now climb down here."

"So you can take me back to hang?" Wil taunted. "Be a friend and ride away, then I will climb down. You will never see me again."

"How about Emma and your children?" Tyler asked.

"I got a new wife," Wil replied. "We can make more children. You've always wanted Emma anyway. She was the only thing I beat you at."

"Don't keep talking to him," Tom said. "He's trying to make what happens your fault. He is just trying to hurt you now."

The deputy felt the pain of Wil's words. His friend had become mean, like the father he'd hated. Tyler wanted to throw that fact back at the man high in the rocks, but Tom was right. Nothing could be gained by more conversation.

"We should fire a couple shots with the Hawken's near to let him know how easily we could shoot him," Tom suggested.

"If we hit close and he slipped," the deputy said, "then his death would be on my hands."

Walking back Tyler looked at Pepe. "You might want to say something to him."

The prisoner looked up at Wil. "I'd jump if I was you. It would be better than the gallows."

Then he did! With his arms spread wide, and a smile on his face, Wil came down. Tyler looked away, but he heard the sound of the body hitting. It sounded like Bobby had when he'd gone down.

There was a scream. It was his Cheyenne wife as she ran to his limp body. The bag of coins had broken open and they cascaded down the base. Those praying did not move. They just looked up for a moment and then went back to their prayers.

The two men were unsure whether Pepe was crying or cheering. He began to babble and make some very unearthly noises. Tom turned to him. "Your partner is dead. Pray for him if you want, but shut the hell up." It did no good.

Oddly, Tyler felt relief with Wil jumping. Maybe his friend had truly been a friend and at the last minute he took his own life, preventing the deputy from having to be a part of his dying, be it from gun shots or a rope.

The coins were collected up and Pepe continued to blubber. It appeared that seeing Wil jump had snapped something inside the man. The Cheyenne woman finished her prayer and wrapped her husband in a buffalo robe. The difficult part came when she wanted to give his body to the gods and Tom had to explain that they had to take him back to Fort Laramie.

They spent the night in the camp and looked at the tower rise towards the heavens in the star-studded sky. Tom said that he could feel the power of the place. Tyler was just in awe of how large it was. They opened one of the bottles and drank to forget the day and help them sleep.

The trip back to the fort provided no surprises. The old lady showed them the graves. Tom had no markers for them. Again, her son was gone and the two men began to wonder if there was even a son. The gold was dug up and packed onto the horse with Wil's body. Pepe was in his own world, talking gibberish and drooling.

The Cheyenne woman did guide them on a more direct route back to the fort, saving a couple of days. She rode ahead, leading the skewbald with Wil, winding through valleys that brought them to the North Platte River. Only a few hours away stood the fort.

Tyler let Tom take care of business with the army. He would take care of the woman. Most of the Cheyenne were out on the plains hunting. Those left promised to take care of the woman until her father returned. Tyler gave her Wil's hat and what was left in the packs, which included a knife, some powder and lead. The Colt and the saddle he kept for Emma and he'd get the skewbald back in Des Moines.

Pepe would go to the gallows with a broken mind. Once Wil's body was released by the army, there was a small gravesite service attended by Tyler, Tom, the Cheyenne wife, and an army chaplain. As it turned out the army was looking for the two men they'd shot, and after they both signed an affidavit that they'd been captured and killed and providing the location they'd been buried, whatever reward coming would be sent to Tom at the Cedar Creek post office.

After some good meals and a couple night's rest at Louie's boarding house, the two men rode east, each leading a horse. It would be mid-October before they reached Des Moines, and then they'd have another 10 or 12 days to Cedar Creek. There could be snow when they got home.

CHAPTER TWENTY-TWO

Cedar Creek was quiet in the late afternoon when the two men rode into town. It was the end of October and snow could be expected anytime. They were carrying difficult news and had learned some things that could never be told. They rode straight to the jail carrying the reports given by the army at Fort Laramie. The door was locked and Tyler found the key in his possible bag. It did not appear that Sheriff Kent had been there recently.

Leaving the reports on the desk, they stepped out to find Emma hurrying across the street, a wrap around her shoulders. "Did you find Wil?" she was calling.

Tyler and Tom took her into the jail. They told her as much as they could without causing her more pain. She sank into the chair near the desk and wept, covering her face with her hands. Tyler wished that he had something, anything, to tell her that would help. They had money for her and a horse, but neither of those would replace a husband.

Her eyes red from crying, she looked up. "I am glad you didn't have to shoot him and that he didn't have to stand on the gallows," Emma told them, tears continuing to run down her cheeks.

The door opened and it was her mother. Seeing her daughter in tears, Ruth knew that Wil had to be dead. "I'll take care of her," she said. Urging her daughter to come with her, the two of them walked slowly back toward their house.

The two men had received $300 in rewards and $250 for the return of the gold and coins. At some time, another $50 would come for the two men they'd shot. On the way back, Tyler and Tom had decided that they'd give Emma $200 and split the rest.

Tyler was physically and emotionally drained. Now he only wanted to see Mary and prayed that he could be good company for her. He invited Tom to use the cabin while he was in town. Tyler figured to stay with Mary at her folks' house. It would be okay now that they were married.

Tom offered to bring Wil's horse to Emma's before going to the cabin. Tyler took up the reins of the bay and walked towards Mary's. He had imagined her opening the door to him over and over in his mind in the past several days. He looked forward to seeing her eyes light up.

There was the ringing of metal being shaped as he passed the blacksmith, and he heard a piano playing in the tavern. Other than that, the streets were empty on the late fall afternoon. Reaching the house, he tied the horse to the post and went onto the porch. He knocked softly and waited.

The door opened and he was looking at Helen. "Tyler!" she said. "You're back!"

Forcing a smile, he replied, "I have come for Mary."

Frowning, Mrs. Price said, "She isn't here."

"Where is . . ." he started to say when she cut him off.

"Mary has been staying at the cabin," Helen told him. "I tried to get her to stay here, but she told me that the cabin was her home now."

The woman had barely gotten the last words out when Tyler was climbing onto the bay. Waving, he left the yard at a trot and headed for home. Clouds of steam were coming from the horse as he pulled up in front of the cabin. Dropping the reins, he bounded onto the porch and threw open the door.

Mary's eyes grew large with surprise as she knelt at the fireplace. Then she recognized her husband. Her eyes lit up and she ran into his arms. She covered his whiskered face with kisses as tears of joy ran down her cheeks. "Welcome home, my Kankakee Kid."

Pulling back to get a good look at his wife, Tyler asked, "Why is everyone crying when they see me?"

She continued to hold him tightly for several minutes, letting the tears soak into his shirt. Finally releasing him, she looked out the open door and saw the bay. "Did you run our horse from town?"

"Well, I did ride kind of fast," he admitted.

"You best walk it and cool it down," she told him. "I was just making supper in the fireplace. I will put out another plate for you."

With a sheepish grin, Tyler told her, "You better put out three. I invited Tom to the cabin."

Shutting the door on his way out, the deputy led the bay around the yard as he reveled in being back home and thinking, *She said our horse.* He was thrilled that Mary had decided that she'd stay at the cabin. He looked at all the familiar buildings. Tyler saw that she had harvested the garden and it appeared ready for spring planting.

With the bay in the stall watered and fed, the deputy headed back to the cabin. He hesitated at the pump shed and then shook his head. It would be useless to try and clean up in the cold shed. Walking back into the cabin, he was taken aback.

When Tyler had first been in the cabin, Mary had looked inviting and beautiful, but in the few minutes he'd been gone to put up the horse, his wife had transformed into an angelic beauty. What she had done, he did not know, but he was almost afraid to take her into his arms again out of fear of spoiling something.

She had supper on the table, and apologized that it was just stew. "Had I known you were coming home tonight, I would have made something special."

"Being home with you is all the special I need," Tyler told her.

Then she said, "We should eat. I'll keep the stew warm for Tom."

The deputy was starving and began to shovel large spoonsful of stew into his mouth. Then she put her hand on his to stop him. "There is one more thing you should know," Mary said, giving him a glowing smile. "We are going to be parents. I am pregnant."

Tyler was stunned. "You're kidding me. We just spent one night together."

"The memories of that night, and the letter you wrote, were what made your absence bearable," Mary told him.

Coming home suddenly had a whole new meaning. The deputy had come home to a family. In the glow of the news, he sat, covered in dust, sorely in need of a shave and haircut, as the two of them ate their meal.

"When we finish here, you'll have to clean up," she told him.

"I rode for days to get to you," he complained.

Smiling sweetly, she said, "I will make it worth your while. Now hurry and finish your meal."

That night Tyler experienced many things he had wished for since he'd been orphaned so many years ago. He came back to a home, being welcomed by someone who loved him. He was pampered and taken care of with gentle hands that could only be found in a loving mother or wife.

Just coming out of the winter weather to a warm home filled with smells of something cooking had been only a dim memory of his youth. The cabin had been given the woman's touch from one end to the other, with crisp curtains, things hanging on the wall, a table cloth and every nook and cranny free of wood chips or dust.

Most of all it had the warmth and friendship of the woman he loved, someone to share with and give oneself to, and in turn receive love back tenfold. With the meal finished, and after he was scrubbed from head to toe, the two of them retired to the bedroom to receive the pleasures only found between two people deeply in love.

Tom did not show up that night. He spent the evening visiting the Wilsons. Then, with only a little encouragement from Emma, he spent the night on a straw tic put down in the parlor. It was made very clear to the slim man that with Mary staying at the cabin he would only be in the way.

After a couple of days of enjoying being home, Tyler drove the buckboard to take Mary to town. The deputy had much to do getting caught up in the jail. His wife wanted to visit Emma. Tyler had told her as much as he could about the capture of Wil. She asked why the body wasn't brought back to Cedar Creek, and he simply said that the body was in control of the army and buried there.

Collecting up the papers brought back from the fort, the deputy went to visit the mayor. Over coffee Mayor Weems read the reports. "I guess these take care of everything," the man said. "I'll send them on to the county court."

Tyler figured that the meeting was over, and was about to get up and leave when the mayor said, "While you were gone, Sheriff Kent had to retire. Some of the town council wanted me to hold a special election to vote in a new sheriff. I talked them into waiting until you got back and that you could do the job until the next election."

"I appreciate that," the deputy replied. "Was there someone in particular that they wanted to run for the office?"

"I didn't let it get that far," the mayor boasted. "As sheriff you will make $70 a month. When you get to it, you can look for a deputy."

He left the mayor's wearing the sheriff's badge on his shirt. During the long ride back from Fort Laramie, Tyler had been seriously thinking about getting out of the law business and going back to harvesting ducks and trapping muskrat. Being the sheriff changed everything.

Jules was on the porch of the trading post and called him over. "I heard you'd come back. I imagine that wasn't good news for Emma."

"Wil fell to his death while being pursued," Tyler told him. "He had a Christian burial at Fort Laramie."

"It was too bad that it came to that," the merchant said. "My wife always liked the boy and she feared the news wouldn't be good."

Tyler was anxious to put the death of Wil behind and was finally able to leave the trading post. He went back to the jail and got a fire going in the potbelly stove. Tom came in shortly after. "Sorry I didn't come to the cabin," he said. "It was decided that I would stay at the Wilsons'."

Grinning, Tyler replied, "You were not missed."

"I mentioned to Emma that she'd have some money coming," Tom told Tyler.

"Did you tell her how much?" the new sheriff asked.

"I figured that should be up to you," the slim man replied. "She did ask why she should be getting any money and said what Wil had had been stolen."

Frowning, Tyler said, "I hadn't thought about needing a reason. I sure as hell can't say it was part of the reward for hunting Wil down and bringing him in."

"I am glad it isn't my worry to find a reason," Tom told him. "I have been invited to spend a couple days at the Wilsons' to rest up before heading back to New Orleans for the rest of the winter."

Wearing the new sheriff's badge, he and Tom left the jail and made rounds. The sky was overcast and the temperature barely over freezing. The slim man stayed at the livery to spend time grooming the sorrel as Tyler continued the rounds.

The tavern was quiet this time of day. Lee was sitting towards the back and waved Tyler over. As he sat, the new sheriff noticed that the man's eyes were fixed on the badge. "It felt good to be back in Cedar Creek," he told the owner.

"I see you got Kent's badge," Lee said.

"I do," Tyler replied. "That is until the next election."

"You going to run again?" the owner asked.

"I haven't given it any thought," the new sheriff replied, "but I don't see any reason not to."

Sitting back in his chair, Lee told him, "You're fair. I think you should."

While Tyler didn't show it, he felt some relief from the offhand endorsement. As a deputy he had been kind of tough on Jackson a few times. After a cup of coffee, he continued making rounds. By the time he reached the jail he had no more idea of what he was going to tell Emma concerning the money.

Mary and Emma decided to have a welcome home meal for Tyler and Tom. It would include her and the children, along with their folks. It was put together quickly before Tom headed south. Early November weather cooperated and the snow held off. Some ice was beginning to form around the shores of the marsh.

On the day of the meal, Tom and Tyler went out to bring in some extra wood while Mary and Emma worked in the kitchen. "Did you think of what to say to Emma?" the slim man asked.

"I figured we should just give it to her," Tyler said. "Maybe she won't ask about where the money came from."

"I did some checking and the Blake house is still vacant," Tom told him. "I guess folks are squeamish about the wife being killed in it."

"What do you mean, checking?" Tyler asked.

"We could buy that for her. I think it could be bought for $200 or less. That would include the coops and other out buildings." Tom said.

"It has 40 acres with it," the redhead told him.

"Land is cheap around here," Tom pointed out. "I am sure the 40 acres would be included."

Suddenly Tyler felt excited inside. A gift of the Blake place to Emma wouldn't be money. It would be offering her a home for her family. The place had been vacant for a while and would require some work.

Walking into the cabin with arm loads of wood, the smells of good things hit the two men. Dumping the wood into the box, Tyler brushed the bark pieces off his sleeve. "Don't be making a mess over there," Mary warned him. "We need to raise hogs next year."

The two sentences made no sense to Tyler. Emma quickly cleared things up. "Mary and I have been talking about what she spent on the ham in the oven. If you two raised hogs, you'd have all the ham and side meat that you wanted for very little."

"I will get two feeder pigs from Burt in the spring," Tyler promised.

The rest of the guests arrived just before the two ladies finish making the meal. Young Adam begged to go out and play near the marsh. Eve wanted to help her mama cook. Emma asked her father, Hank to keep the children out of the kitchen.

With the help of Tyler and Tom, the two children were corralled and kept entertained. Promises were made about going down to the marsh after the meal. The meal was a success, with a juicy ham, yams, potatoes, a vegetable, pickles, and freshly baked bread. Apple pie was the dessert.

Tyler couldn't have been prouder of his wife. She was at home in the kitchen and a great homemaker. With the meal finished the two children were bundled up and taken to play near the marsh. Emma joined the two men.

While the little ones played, Tyler took the opportunity to talk to Emma. "Tom and I would like to do something for you and the young'uns," he said.

Smiling at the redhead, she said, "You have already done plenty over the years. Seeing you and Mary together is all the gift I need."

"What Tyler's doing a poor job of saying is that he and I would like to purchase the Blake place for you and the kids," Tom said.

With concern on her face, the young mother said, "No. You can't do that." Then her eyes grew large. "Do you think I blame Wil's death on the two of you?"

"Wil has nothing to do with it," Tyler said lamely. "Both of us want to do this for you. Tom has money from California and grandpa left me some. You need a home of your own and we want to do this for you and your children."

Her eyes filled with tears and she ran towards the cabin, disappearing inside. "Well, that didn't go very well," Tom said.

"I wonder if she thinks we want to pay for the place with blood money," Tyler replied.

"Blood money?" Tom asked, sounding upset. "Rewards are paid to bring men to justice. It is not a price on their head to go out and kill them."

"You're right," Tyler said, feeling bad about what he said.

In silence the two men watched the carefree children play only cautioning them when they got too close to the water. The two of them had tried to do something good and it had not worked. Tyler noticed the cabin door open and Mary came out with a wrap over her shoulders. He could not tell whether she was coming to scold them or not.

She stopped short of them and said, "Tom, would you watch Adam and Eve while Tyler and I have a talk?"

Unsure of how much trouble he was in, the redhead followed his wife towards the barn. *At least she didn't stop at the woodshed,* he thought.

"Was it yours or Tom's idea to make the offer to Emma?" she asked.

Unable to read anything in her voice, he said, "Sort of both of us." He was not going to leave his friend to take the blame.

He saw Mary's eyes become misty and she said, "The offer overwhelmed her. She said she had been praying that somehow, she could make a home for the children with Wil. Everything he did made it seem more and more impossible. With him gone she had lost hope. Then you two come up with . . ." Her tears began to flow.

Unsure of what she was saying, he asked, "Are we in trouble?"

Throwing her arms around him she said, "You two are the most generous men I know."

"You got to stop crying," Tyler begged. "Tom is going to be wondering what's going on."

Fighting her emotions, Mary said, as she wiped her eyes on the wrap, "It will have to be on her terms. She wants to be able to pay you two back. She will raise chickens and sell eggs and meat to earn money so she can."

"Will it be okay if we buy things for the house?" he asked. "Sort of like gifts?"

By the time everyone was ready to leave, a deal was made between Emma and the two men. She didn't have to pay anything back until she was making money with the chickens. There would be no interest and no time limit on the loan. Tom told her he'd be coming up a few times a year and she could give him any money earned towards the loan at those times.

Two weeks later Emma owned the Blake house. It had cost $175 and included the acreage. Everyone pitched in and help make the house livable. Tom ordered a kitchen stove as a house warming gift and Emma graciously accepted it.

Jules promised to purchase 100 chicks come spring to help stock her coops. Emma's folks provided things the house needed and labor to make it comfortable. Tyler was able to give her another $50 for stuff she would need to set up housekeeping. The redhead hardly recognized the bedroom where the man had shot his wife. Furnished differently, and with new wall paper, it had a different look.

Tom spent time in the room saying some kind of chant. After a time, he emerged smiling. Emma motioned him to a chair. 'What? What happened?" she asked.

"Mrs. Blake and Dutch are together on the other side," he said, looking earnestly into her eyes. "She likes what you did with the room."

No one laughed at what he said. Something had happened when Tom was in the room alone, and they were all sure that he had spoken with Mrs. Blake. Before leaving the house, Tom put the amulet from his neck around Emma's. "This will let me know you are safe and happy in your home. Hold it tight to your breast and I will feel you near."

Emma shed tears when Tom rode out of Cedar Creek. Adam and Eve waved wildly to him, shouting goodbyes. Tyler missed Tom's exit from town. He was busy interviewing his new deputy, Earl. The sheriff had high hopes for the young man.

Being married to Mary brought a series of surprises for the redhead. He found that she made clothes and earned money doing so. When Tyler came home a few days before Christmas he found the cabin decorated for the holiday and the glow of the fireplace softly lighting the room. The two sat together in their new cloth-covered sofa, Mary leaning close to Tyler. He had his hand on her growing stomach as they watched the fire.

"You have made me so happy, my sweet Kankakee Kid," she whispered.

www.ingramcontent.com/pod-product-compliance
Lightning Source LLC
Chambersburg PA
CBHW051438260626
47162CB00001B/143